Book One of the Death Marked Quartet

THE ROYAL TOURNAMENT

G. E. McConaghy

✳✳✳

To Liza—

For starting this journey and letting me continue it.

✳✳✳

THE ROYAL TOURNAMENT

G. E. McConaghy

PROLOGUE

AURORA

When she was younger, Aurora had adored sneaking out of the Palace. Under the cover of darkness, she would drag her sister and brother along to drink up the sprawling city of Cerenia. Nothing else had mattered to her then, only craving a temporary escape into anonymity. So much had changed since those lost nights three decades ago.

Now, just days away from the New Year, Aurora set out to a place she despised. Dressed in roughspun garments alongside Sir Josiah Renner—better known as the Captain of the Queensguard—he led her through dank alleyways. The Agonia Pits weren't far from the Palace; it was quite absurd how direct their route could have been. Instead, Renner twisted them through so many maze-like streets that Aurora considered it excessive.

The city centre of Cerenia was a disorganised tangle of narrow streets and skinny buildings. With the Palace at its heart, the populace had scrambled to be as close as possible to the royalty. Further out, there was decidedly more order to the city, but Aurora rarely sighted it, only driving through in horse-drawn carriages with closed curtains.

These thoughts accompanied her until, soon enough, she and Renner reached the iron-wrought gates of the catacombs. It was deserted save for two guards, who watched the pair approach. Renner threw a pouch of coins, and a guard caught it with ease, spilling its contents into his open palm. Silver glinted in the torchlight, and with a grunt, he allowed them to pass.

The catacombs were an endless network of tombs and bones that housed the ancient dead of the Kingdom of Darcan. A few generations before, parts of it were hollowed out to create an underground sewer system for the city. In this era, the greed of man also decided to carve out fighting dens within the earth of the kingdom. Aurora wasn't sure if the Agonia Pits were the first of its kind, but she knew they were the most famous.

Their journey through the catacombs was silent. Torches lit the way through the twisting hallways with smog turning the curving walls black. Aurora let out a breath; no matter the nighttime getaways of her youth, she had never dreamed of entering a place like this. It was an illegal cesspool dressed up in dust and iron. She was supposed to end it, but the nobility always got in the way, throwing other problems in her face to distract her.

Now, as she entered the jeering crowds of the Pits, she could see why the nobles never wanted her to touch it.

It was a coliseum, the grandstand spiralling up in a curve while theatre boxes protruded over the rabble. Sitting comfortably in one of the boxes was Demetria Winterbride, the Duchess of Canwal. Aurora scowled before her gaze wandered over the rest of the boxes. She recognised no one else but didn't doubt that her other nobles frequented these halls.

Renner came into sight, and she let her rage dissipate. He led her into the spectator stands, avoiding the men and women screaming at the centre of the coliseum. Aurora spared a glance as they manoeuvred the cramped quarters. Bleached sand flooded the lowest level of the coliseum, the true *pit* of the whole place. She knew there were other arenas in the underground network, but this was the main stage. The best and bloodiest fights resided here, and, in disguise, the Queen of Darcan had come to watch.

As they sat down, the current fight came to a close. Two bruisers, thick with muscle and domineering height, had been locked in a hand-to-hand brawl. It was only until one of the brutes swung a kick that concluded the match. All it took was the dislodging of teeth, blood, and flesh. Aurora's stomach churned, but she could not look away from the pile resembling pearls smeared in oil.

"Esteemed guests!" A man strode into the arena, arms aloft. "We have a winner! Meet our newest Champion of the Agonia Pits, Nelson Bovris!"

Nelson was all smiles, whooping and shaking his bloodstained fists. Aurora frowned and looked to Renner for further explanation.

"'The Champion of the Pits' is a title won by the best fighter of the entire place," he answered. "However, there's a new Champion every night. 'They don't make them like they used to,' many would say."

"And what were they like?" Aurora asked. "Those old Champions?"

Renner looked down at the fighting pit. "Only two really left any impact, though that was almost a decade ago now. The First Champion won dozens, maybe even *hundreds* of matches, until the Undefeated Champion took her down. Since then, no one has been able to maintain a true winning streak. If we stay long enough, we may very well watch the rise of a new Champion."

Aurora nodded, turning her eyes back to the assembling of the next match. The fighting dens predated her reign, and despite the violence, there was no death in the Pits.

Aurora only knew this because the nobles would never let her forget it.

It can't be that bad if there are no fatalities. Look at this instead! The Kherian King is always up to no good! Have you sorted out trade routes with him yet? You managed that with that magic man from Jaranna in Pedreikrari!

She hated discussing the Pits with the nobles because they hated hearing her mention it. So it had surprised them all when one noble suggested she try her own version.

"Hold it at the Palace," they had said at the council meeting. "In one of the courtyards, or maybe *all* the courtyards if you want the numbers. Show us how you can make these fighting pits better, legal even. Either the undergrounders will switch to adhere to your style or completely disappear if you provide enough competition. I'll help fund it myself, and I wouldn't be surprised if my fellow nobles would provide, too."

Aurora had been too shocked at the proposal to answer. The rest of the nobility had pressed the advantage, calling desperately for a legalised version of the underground fighting pits. All the pieces started moving too quickly, and Aurora could not stop it. Her nobles would make it happen whether she stood at the helm of it or not, so she agreed to consider it.

After the meeting, she had singled out Renner. He'd watched the proceedings at her side, and she knew he would guess her intent. "I want to go to Agonia," she'd whispered beneath her breath. "Tonight, we shall see the chaos my nobility wants to flood my home with, and we will hone it *my* way."

Renner had made plans immediately, but they didn't occur that evening or the next. Her constantly full schedule gave her no choice but to watch the days drain past while

Renner set everything into motion.

The council meeting was two weeks ago, and the nobles nervously awaited Aurora's announcement of the Palace Pits. She hated that name, preferring her *Royal Tournament* title instead, but the gossip festered amongst the courtiers like a rotting log. Aurora hadn't said anything on the matter, keeping silent until she made her decision. She was the Queen; after all, she could still refuse if she wanted to.

But you won't, a nagging voice reminded her. Aurora lifted her chin, closing her mind off endless politics to watch the new fight.

Nelson remained in the pit, the injuries he'd sustained in the previous match now wiped away by magic healers. Aurora already knew she'd provide her own cohort of healers at the Royal Tournament, but she was surprised to find that the Agonia Pits did the same.

A newcomer entered the stage, and Aurora already felt sympathetic. They were small and wiry, shoulders hunched as if panicked. Empty sheaths lay at their hips, and they kept clasping and unclasping their hands.

"We're leaving after this match," Aurora said, her eyes never leaving the newcomer. "We won't be seeing a new Champion rise."

"Of course, Your Majesty," Renner murmured.

"Esteemed guests!" the same announcer from before called. "Let me introduce you to Ratty Jo! They may not look it, but they've got a few tricks up their sleeves! No weapons, of course! Unless you're planning on a disqualification there, Jo."

Ratty Jo didn't reply; their eyes were already focused on Nelson. The announcer exited the pit, and when the gate clanged shut, the fight began.

Nelson was slow to start, no doubt still drunk on his victory. He ambled forward, giant fists seeking a target. Jo moved like water, deceptively staying out of reach as Nelson's hands came up empty. Anger rolled through his features, and his pace quickened, pawing for purchase on his opponent once again. Jo dodged it, diving between Nelson's legs. One foot connected with Nelson's ankle, dropping him down. A jab to the other thigh brought him to his knees.

Jo rose, now able to stand over Nelson and wrap an arm around his throat. Nelson clawed at the arm, but Jo did not relent, tensing harder until his face shaded purple. Jo let go, kicking Nelson in the spine and sending him sprawling. He shifted onto his back just as Jo leapt on top, thumbs aloft. Landing on the Champion's chest, Jo gouged their thumbs into Nelson's eyes. A howl shattered through the bellowing arena as Aurora covered her open mouth.

Nelson struggled on the ground, stirring sand into the air and obscuring the actual violence. A moment passed before the pounding of Nelson's fist against the floor stopped everything. Surrender for the fallen Champion.

The announcer was back at once, whisking Jo to their feet and raising their arm in the air. "Esteemed guests! Meet our new Champion, Ratty Jo!"

The cheering crowd exploded as Aurora rose from her seat, but Renner pulled at her sleeve. "This isn't all the Pits are, I know what I said about the changes, but it's usually not this frequent. Stay, we've been waiting two weeks for this."

Aurora arched a brow. "I didn't realise you cared this much." She sat back down.

He looked away. "It's an unorthodox practice, but if honed correctly, as you want to do, something like this could bring more soldiers into our armies."

"Or it could secure the endless cycle of violence Darcan is trapped in."

Renner gave a shaky laugh. "You are right with that, Your Majesty, but I would rather trust a mess like this in your hands. You'd be better than Winterbride over there, or any of the nobles for that matter."

Aurora's gaze drifted to the theatre box. "You spotted her too? I shouldn't have been surprised one of them would be here, really."

The next match began, Ratty Jo against another bruiser type. Aurora had lost interest in the fight, eyes flitting across the spectator stands. She knew Renner was watching her, but he stayed silent. A cheer went through the crowd, but Aurora was staring at Winterbride again.

"The Tournament will go on," she said. "It'll be announced tomorrow."

***

Dawn broke through the stained windows of the advisory hall, setting the papers Aurora held alight in the fresh sun. Her fingers brushed against the pages, the whispering noise filling the otherwise dead silence. Shouting that had reminded her of the Agonia Pits had overwhelmed this hall only an hour before. A dull ache blossomed in her skull, and she sighed, dropping the papers.

They were the declaration of the Royal Tournament, every aspect of its proceedings penned perfectly. Every sheaf had her signature completing it, the wax seal of her family crest adorning the final one. Her eyes danced over the words, the churning in her stomach making her worry she'd made the wrong choice.

A knock at the door jolted Aurora from her thoughts.

"Come in," she said.

The door opened to reveal Ferrand, one of the newest members of the Queensguard. He looked nervous as he entered, barely stepping over the threshold as he bowed. "Your Majesty, the fliers have been completed, and distribution will begin at once! Captain Renner has asked me to apologise for not giving you the news himself and has suggested you make an announcement in the banquet hall this evening to your guests!"

Aurora nodded. "That would be wise. Please find Master Orlo and tell him of this; he will have some suggestions, too, so make sure those get back to me."

Ferrand looked up from his bow. "Of course, Your Majesty! Right away, Your Majesty!" He disappeared without another word.

The door snapped shut, and Aurora's eyes drifted to the wall beside it. Ten banners covered the stone, each one as garish as the last. They were the noble houses, each one presiding over a province. At its centre was her own banner: Winthorpe of Wychar. Aurora detested the sight of the rest of them, how they surrounded her lineage like a trapped animal.

"You will not ruin my kingdom," she murmured. "None of you will; I won't ever allow it. Any foul play, and I will burn you all to the ground."

The Queen of Darcan rose from her chair, knowing very well that her threat did not go unheard.

1

LYRA

The pearlescent spires of the Palace of Darcan climbed higher than any other building in Cerenia. Lyra swept back her hood, eyes squinting to examine the creamy white towers set against the blue skies. It had been an age since she'd last seen the Palace up close, with its many guards standing outside the iron-wrought gates. She never grew bored of the sight; the Palace grounds were one of the few places in the city that Lyra had never entered—until today.

The Royal Tournament was estimated to last up to four days, shorter if the Queen had overestimated numbers. Lyra hoped not, or she would lose the much-needed time for sleuthing.

Anyone who had heard of the upcoming Tournament knew it bore similarities to the Agonia Pits. *The Queen supposedly despised the underground fighting arenas, so what had changed her mind?* Lyra had barely been able to focus when Astrid told her the news, handing over a flyer announcing the Royal Tournament. The words had bled into blurred forms, rage colouring Lyra's senses as five words thundered through her skull: *I have to stop it.*

At first, it was a deluded desire. How was Lyra meant to defy a queen? Then, a theory started to form in her mind, and soon enough, so did a plan. She might not know how to defy a Queen, but she knew how to fight a noble. Lyra was aware of the nobility's love of the fighting pits; it was difficult to ignore their jeering cries amongst the dozens of voices that crowded the amphitheatres. If her theory was correct, she could trick the nobles who'd manipulated the Queen and stop the whole thing herself. First, Lyra would have to find the bastards.

She'd considered sneaking in as a spectator, just another face in the crowd, until Twylla suggested another route; hiding would get her nowhere close to the nobility, so why not parade right in front of them? The nobles were known to sponsor skilled fighters in the pits, betting and winning, all in the name of victory and greed. The acquired fighters would wear an armband denoting their allegiance to a noble house and, in exchange, reap benefits from their sponsor. For the right price, a conversation would be all Lyra needed. It wouldn't be difficult for her to achieve it; all she had to do was embrace an old name.

Outside the Palace gates, tables had been set up with advisors dashing back and forth behind them. They sifted through the mountains of paper piled up on the desks, no doubt detailing the hundreds of applicants waiting to prove their worth before the Queen. Several lines had already formed, so Lyra joined the queues, which fluctuated as applicants entered the Palace gates. The wait was thankfully short, allowing her time to plaster an impassive smile on her face as she strode up to the nearest advisor. "Surname?" he asked.

"Avenyard."

He rose from his chair, heading to the other piles of applications. A moment later, the advisor returned with several forms in hand. He spread them out before her; drawing closer, she recognised the careful curvings of her handwriting.

"Lyra Avenyard," he said, reading the sheet. "Twenty-five years of age, female, and from the province of Wychar. Yes?"

Most of her answers were false: pretending to be younger was a good way to be underestimated, and her true birthplace wasn't anyone's concern. Still, she nodded as he scanned through the information. The application form required an occupation. Lyra would have preferred to be known as something else, but only one title would matter to the Tournament.

"The Undefeated Champion of the Agonia Pits…" he choked out. His face turned white before adding meekly, "Yes?"

Lyra cocked her head to the side. "Who else?"

She hated the smile she plastered on her face. Lyra had left Agonia for a reason, earning a title she damn well didn't want. *Undefeated* only because she ran away before anyone could overthrow her. It was an insult gilded in praise, and even after nine years, her name haunted every fighting pit. The Royal Tournament would be swarming with those who remembered the legend.

The advisor's reaction secured that, and it felt like a thorn in her back. Lyra had never been this powerful Undefeated Champion; it was all a part of the drama, but the stories and the rumours had provided all kinds of characters. There was the cold, cunning one who manipulated everyone with a cruel smile; the haughty, cocky woman who glutted herself on glory and bloodshed; or the girl who'd stolen the First Champion in a vain attempt to hide her own flaws. The list went on, and Lyra despised every single one.

But to succeed, she would fake loving it and this façade of arrogance and brutality. Lyra had to make everyone think she wanted a new title and that she wasn't entering the Tournament for other troubles.

The advisor scrabbled through the papers, not daring another look at her. She crossed her arms, chin raised. He held out a card with the Darcan royal crest stamped in its centre with a shaking hand. Below it was her name inscribed in silver script. Lyra smiled, examining the jittery handwriting and blots of ink that scattered the crisp card.

"Thank you," she said sweetly, tucking the card into her trouser pocket. "Shall I head to the gates?"

"Yes… just show the guards the approval card. The Tournament will begin once everyone is accounted for."

Without bothering to reply, she walked through the Palace gates, where Lyra's features shifted into a feline smile.

The charade was practised for this moment, just another strand in her complex web of lies. She elbowed past anyone who dared hinder her path. The crowd of hardened fighters swarmed around her, and her gaze cut across all the weapons and armour they wore. Even if they'd tried to conceal the blades or shields, Lyra could see the brutality lying underneath.

In the bitter cold of the new winter, Lyra was glad for the insulated layers of her armour. Twylla had suggested she wear something flashy for the Tournament: a plate armour embossed entirely in gold, but Lyra knew it would only weigh her down. The Tournament would not involve any fatal battles, so she would not need to dress for one.

Still, beneath her long-sleeved tunic, she wore a padded gambeson covering her from the neck to past her hips. Upon it, a layer of mail matched it, ready to deflect any blade strike. Her leather armour was sporadic but placed over the mail shirt for maximum protection. Her legs were the least defended, for the constriction of movement would worsen her chances of evading unexpected attacks. The risk was one she took in kind, favouring her own abilities rather than the stiffness of the leather.

It was an arrangement she was used to, though the lack of a shield and mail coif left her feeling exposed. She needed her face visible to keep the Undefeated Champion recognisable, and hiding behind a shield would only suggest she was afraid of the battles to come. So, she relied instead on her weapons. Six knives were sheathed to her body—two on her forearms, two on her thighs, and the last two in her boots. But the longsword strapped to Lyra's back beneath her cloak was the true sign of her motives.

Her platinum blonde hair was plaited away carefully, framing her tanned skin and sharp features. She felt eyes of all kinds following her, and she kept her head high, forcing a smirk at the reactions that rippled behind her. It was working, but Lyra almost wished it wouldn't. All her life, she had depended on her ability to lie and act, but was the

Undefeated Champion more than that? Would she like to become this name truly? Could she keep those two parts of herself separate?

Or were they already intertwined? After so many years, had the legend and reality become the same? She ignored her thoughts as best as possible, distracting herself with the present. Her walk through the Palace grounds was lined by guards, keeping her and the other participants under watch so they did not stray from their path. Lyra knew vaguely of the Palace's design and that they were heading through the Queen's Promenade into a courtyard where courtiers spent their empty days wandering the pretty parts of the grounds.

Instead, over two hundred people filled the transformed arena. The courtyard had been divided into three subsections: the fighting area, the participants' seats, and the spectators' stands.

The grandstands were separated into two themselves. Tight, narrow lines of wooden benches tiered upwards and jutting out at intervals were private boxes dressed in velvet and torchlight. Commoners gathered in the cramped quarters of the stands while the nobles perched comfortably in their plush seats.

The fighting area was lined with more benches for the participants, but at its centre were twenty chalk circles drawn onto the stones. The immaculate circles were large enough for two fighters to manoeuvre and battle easily.

Lyra sighed in relief; it barely resembled Agonia or any other fighting den she had seen. The Queen hadn't announced a proper justification for why she was conducting the Tournament, but from this first look, it wasn't to truly replicate the Pits as Lyra had feared.

Lyra straightened, the smile on her face dissolving as she took a seat on one of the benches. Now, all she needed to do was wait.

Midday dragged past, and soon enough, the courtyard became a faceless swarm. More than just Cerenia residents lurked in the square; hundreds from every province in Darcan were present. It almost made Lyra wish the rest of her clan had come along as well. Despite the huge crowd, she was alone.

Her thoughts were suddenly disrupted as a chorus of shouting filled the courtyard. The chatter directed all attention to a small group of six participants circling a sole warrior. The lone fighter wore a long black cloak, with its high collar and hood raised to conceal their features. As the six participants continued to shout and leer at the figure, one suddenly wrenched the hood back.

Even from the distance, Lyra's gut twisted at the sight of the loner's face. Ice-cold blue eyes widened at the exposure, searching and devoid of warmth. Their olive skin was criss-crossed with scars, a history of violence written out in the dizzying white strikes. Their hair was an unruly mess of ash black, tied back into a knot. Loose strands escaped the string, framing their face in tangles that they scraped back with a hand.

But it was the scowl that sent horror and disgust through the crowd. Despite being healed, two jagged scars distorted the skin on each side of their lips. As if blades had been wrenched out of their mouth, ripping them into a grizzled permanent smile.

Lyra couldn't tell whether or not the warrior was a male or female, instead supposing they were genderless.

A growl filled the space suddenly, sending the leering participants skittering back several paces. The warrior was now baring their teeth, sharp incisors elongating. Lyra recognised it then; they weren't just any ordinary fighter but a werewolf warrior about to tear these people to shreds. Lyra's body moved before her mind as she tried to force her way through the crowd, but it was like walking through mud. Any success of movement resulted in a shove back further than before. It was hopeless; she could not reach them.

Despite the bow and quiver of arrows tied to their back, the warrior stepped toward their targets. As they did, dirt-flecked claws began to extend from their nail beds, each sharp and deadly—their only necessary weapon.

Lyra cursed as the six drew their swords. It was ridiculous to her that no one was stopping this madness. She whipped her head around and realised there were no guards around. Not only that, but the fighters beside her didn't want the brawl to break out.

They all wanted to see the werewolf dead.

Discrimination of non-human species had always been a curse across the continents, particularly in their neighbouring country, Kheria, and within the Kingdom of Darcan. Lyra had had that belief drilled into her when she was a child, but she had since decided that monsters lurked everywhere, regardless of whether they were human. It didn't matter what she thought; blood was about to spill before the Tournament even had a chance to begin.

Trying again, Lyra elbowed past a cluster of fighters watching the ongoings. They jeered instead of letting her pass, grabbing her arm to drag her back.

"Hey! What are you doing? Trying to ruin the show?" one asked her.

"You can't possibly think it's a good idea to let this happen!" she yelled back, pulling her arm to free it from his grasp. "If we don't do anything, someone will *die.*"

The man held firm, a grin twisting his features as he refused to let her move. "Ain't that the point?"

Already a dozen ideas flowed to Lyra's mind, stabbing this man being her first idea and then escaping in a way only she knew how to, but before she could do so, the shouts and leers of the crowd suddenly silenced.

A man broke through the tight-knit formation of fighters, his broad shoulders propelling him past everyone. He towered over both the werewolf and their assailants. The six flinched; something was strange about this newcomer as he approached the warrior. They exchanged looks, an ominous silence filling the courtyard as everyone waited for the two to speak.

The werewolf spoke first, their words sounding more like a reply than an opening: "Why not? These humans are asking to die. Why shouldn't I provide what they so desperately want?"

The man did not respond, but the werewolf's features

twisted, worsening their scars' appearance. Lyra couldn't breathe with the tension in the air thick and heavy. Even so, the werewolf's claws suddenly retracted as they dropped the battle stance.

They looked the six in the eye, undoubtedly marking the faces of the mortals who'd threatened their life before making a promise. "We will meet in the fighting rings," the werewolf warrior said, voice husky. "Where I will make you all plead for your death."

They stalked out of the circle, the crowd parting around them as if diseased. The warrior swooped up their hood as they left, hiding their scarred face once more. Lyra loosed a breath, attention turning to the man who had stopped the brawl from breaking out.

He had hair as black as night and dark brown skin. He wore shining armour forged in darkness, the steel a shade of onyx black. In one arm, he cradled a glorious helmet of the same design. Concealing most of his face was a grey scarf, allowing only his eyes to be visible. He gave a stern nod to the six, whose faces went slack. In his silence, he, too, headed into the thick of the crowd, but his tall stature made it easy for Lyra to track his movements.

Though she didn't care to do so. Pulling out of the grasp of her own assailants, who'd gone silent now that their fun had ended, she turned her attention back to the benches. She stalked away, no longer desiring to stand amongst those who wanted to watch another die.

2

AVERY

Morning light broke through the heavy shelter of leaves, making the dewdrops soaking the grass glitter like diamonds. Pine needles crunched quietly underneath Avery's feet as she strode on, swiftly avoiding the low-hanging branches. The earthy smells of overturned soil and rotting wood had always comforted her, filling her body with calm and belonging.

But every step took her further and further away from that feeling.

She was no longer surrounded by the comforting touch of ash trees nor the rippling laughter of her sisters. Instead, the trees of thick pine curled and twisted around her, with some reaching to trip her purposefully. The Forest of the Dryads may have been her home, but to the land that she stood in, Avery was a stranger.

The dryads were concealed from sight, but Avery knew their many eyes followed her. They listened and watched, waiting with morbid curiosity for someone brave to strike. Avery could only anticipate it, though that did little to comfort her.

"Why do you walk this way, naiad?"

She froze, her blades clattering and waterskin sloshing noisily at her waist. Turning slowly, Avery faced a long-limbed woman whose hazel eyes met her gaze. The newcomer's dark skin shone in the Forest's light, every inch of her body unblemished and beautiful. Her black hair was tucked away, revealing the pointed tips of her ears. Immortality, as it always was, had been kind.

"I'm sure you've heard, but I have a job to complete, *dryad*," Avery drawled, mockery rich in her voice. "I can't possibly be late now, can I?"

The dryad laughed, the low sound dancing across Avery's bones. "You'll be dead before you are even able to speak. None of our kind can survive outside of these trees."

It should have been true. The Forest of the Dryads was home to thousands of nymphs, though dryads vastly dominated its population. It was their home, but in another sense, it was their prison.

Avery was a naiad, a nymph of freshwater. She was supposedly an anomaly inside the Forest but could not be easily eliminated. Her life as a nature spirit began when her lake formed almost three centuries ago, her life force and physical being tied to that body of water. Escaping the boundaries of the Forest was an impossible feat for the dryads—a fact all of them knew too well.

"Will you try to stop me?" Avery asked in their shared language. "Curl your roots around my limbs and hold me for your enjoyment?"

The dryad pondered that thought before replying, "I haven't encountered a naiad in a long while. I've missed gazing into those blue eyes and being held by such pale skin; Mother Famara truly gifted you."

The goddess of love, light, and peace was the mother of all nature spirits who all lived across the globe, but very few differing nymphs interacted with one another. They were kept in their respective homes, protected and safe. Mother Famara was not just a goddess; she was their very existence, the divine being all nature spirits would follow without question.

"In more ways than one," Avery replied, her voice dull.

"Shame there's no water for you, though. That little flask won't do anything against me," the dryad simpered. She lifted a hand, and immediately, dark roots began to warp the earth beneath them.

Avery staggered back, losing her balance momentarily. Even the dewdrops on the leaves were nothing against the vast rising pine wood curling slowly towards Avery. But she smiled, for there was more to her than just an affinity to water; she wasn't *just* a naiad.

Avery's eyes of blue swarmed into a storm of darkest greys.

The dryad gaped in shock as the roots at her feet retreated inwardly. The cunning smile on Avery's face deepened, honeyed words leaving her mouth: "Take a walk, little dryad. Find the copse of ash trees and tell my naiad sisters what you had planned for me. If you survive that, then you may come home."

"*Siren,*" was all the dryad could gasp before the commands took effect.

Her movements were rigid as she tried to fight back, but the pine roots had already slithered away, leaving the dryad no choice but to walk. Every step was laboured and disjointed, so unlike the immortal grace Mother Famara had gifted her with. But the dryad continued walking back to the copse of trees where Avery's lake resided, where the spirits of the ash trees danced, and her sisters laughed. Oh, how they would enjoy her little present.

No one else was foolish enough to interrupt the rest of Avery's walk now that the stench of fear tainted the air. She was no longer a stranger in another's home but now an enemy too strong to defeat. She no longer needed to avoid the hanging branches as each shivered out of sight, making her path impossibly clear.

When her journey ended, the trees creaked as she stepped out of the Forest and into the mortal lands. The Forest of the Dryads was its own realm—confined to the Kingdom of Darcan—but the magic concealed its immense size from plain sight. Avery's lake could have been hundreds of miles from Cerenia, but her journey had been less than a half-hour walk.

With one last turn, Avery bowed to the invisible spirits of her home, a smile blooming on her face that made even the grass beneath her feet recede.

"Performing a show, are we?" The rolling Darcanian tongue sent shivers down Avery's spine.

She spun on her heel and met Torr's soulless eyes. Avery scowled but ruffled a hand through her hair, rearranging the strands to ensure her pointed ears were concealed. In the land of mortals, Avery always did her best to hide her immortality. "It's best to keep my audience enthralled, don't you think?" she replied, switching to the same language.

Behind him, the entrance to the city was just metres away, the spires of the Palace of Darcan visible to the eye as the sun burned against the frozen sky. Torr ruined the picturesque landscape. If she hadn't already learned, Avery would consider him just another mortal. Short-tempered, unassuming, and arrogant. She knew better now, but it still didn't change how smoothly he fit the description.

His skin was an unhealthy pallor, worsening the appearance of the dark veins snaking up his arms and the purple circles beneath his eyes. There was a permanent downturn to his sandy brows and a scowl etched into his face that made him even less appealing than when he opened his mouth. Torr's dirty blond hair shone greasily in the light and lay limply on his head. His eyes glittered with unchanged rage, poison green and swimming in death.

"Not when it makes us late," he snapped. "Come on, naiad, we have a Tournament to win."

Just entering the city's outskirts was a struggle as mortals surrounded Avery in a throng of bodies. Participants and spectators were heading to the Palace of Darcan, making the capital's hubbub of activity inescapable. Avery spied the fliers for the Royal Tournament at uneven intervals, some now speckled with age as they flapped in the breeze.

It had been almost a decade since Avery had been to Cerenia. It was so long since she'd been near so many with such short lifespans. It made her nose wrinkle and eyes glower with distaste. There was an ugliness to mortality of how insignificantly pointless these lives were in the face of immortality.

Torr had a tight grip on Avery's forearm as he led her into the city's centre. It was a maddening crowd, one she was immediately crushed within. Her short stature made it impossible for her to move without the harsh pull from Torr.

Despite their time together, Torr had yet to speak more than his client required. Avery despised the logistics of her employment as she didn't even know who Torr's client—her sponsor—was. No matter how often she asked, he would ignore her, worsening their already tense partnership.

Torr was only to act as a chaperone for a little while longer, but he would keep watch of every step she took after they separated. She wasn't sure what he was, only that he was immortal and older than her. Avery's theory leaned closest to being a Thoughtsinger witch, but even then, it held no weight. Because despite her powers of compulsion, it had failed to work on Torr. Neither could either of her sisters' honeyed words subdue him. Their god-given gifts were supposed to protect the three, and yet Avery was defeated by a man who wore false mortal skin.

As they walked, the waterskin on Avery's hip sloshed ferociously, yearning to escape and return home. It was her loophole to escape the Forest's confinements. Even then, it kept her trapped within the Kingdom of Darcan. Avery had heard stories of courageously foolish nymphs who'd tried a trip to Kheria or the uninhabited Eternal Mountains— neither had ended well.

Finally arriving at the Palace gates, untrampled and in one piece, Torr let go of Avery's arm. He stared down at her with those haunted eyes and gritted out his farewell. "Don't lose, naiad, if you want your sisters to keep their heads."

Avery's nostrils flared, but before she could say anything, he vanished, disappearing into the crowd.

Her sisters would have preferred death instead of parading around for a mortal competition. At first, Avery didn't have much desire to participate either. Only the money she would earn appeased her, but it did little to silence Torr's endless threats to her sisters' lives. It was all talk, though, as both Bellama and Caliadne remained unharmed. And so long as Avery complied, it would stay so.

Joining the queue of applicants, Avery was overwhelmed by the smell of leather and metal coating the mortals in front of her. Even so, hidden within, she could sense those of ancient blood. She was not the only immortal taking a bite at the Tournament.

Nymphs never wore mortal clothing, let alone armour, but Avery was always willing to be an exception. Though it was rare, she didn't mind needing to wear the tight-fitting black trousers and knee-high leather boots she'd purchased decades before. The armour she wore was a quilted vest paired with a leather breastplate and various armguards she could not name, but she carefully tended to everything in case of their need.

But Avery's most precious possession she had procured from the mortal world was her weapons. Sheathed to her waist were two large daggers, identical in appearance; their sharpness was second to none. No carvings decorated the blades, for Avery saw it as an unnecessary expense for such tools of destruction. Along with the daggers, several knives were tucked away beneath the folds of her clothing.

Soon enough, she passed through the Palace gates with her approval card held between her fingers. Inscribed on the front was her name, even if it was false, *Avery Nash.* Nymphs did not have surnames, and her true forename was Averaline, but whenever mortals demanded names, she would only provide lies.

She had chosen the surname to refer to the ash tree copse that surrounded their lakes; however, 'Avery' was a nickname chosen by a mortal village when she attended its school. Bellama and Caliadne had also received shortened 'Darcanian' names, but after all these centuries, only Avery continued to use the name chosen by mortals.

The false name was also to conceal her identity as an immortal. All kinds of treacherous people would be heading for the Tournament, all kinds of evil wrapped in leather and steel. Immortal species could go for a high price, especially one as old and powerful as she. And as she already had one kind of evil following her, Avery knew she didn't need any more.

Three days earlier, Torr had ventured into the Forest to hunt Avery and her sisters down for one reason: their powers. Avery had mastered manipulating water before she was barely a decade old. When her sisters' lakes formed, she had been quick to teach them how to control all the water that swirled around them. But the power of the Siren had truly set the three apart from all.

No longer was it just their appearances that lulled mortals into a trance, but the ability to control minds had everyone who came near the sisters wrapped around their fingers. No longer were they just lake naiads, but now Freshwater Sirens. And that was how Avery's sponsor intended her to win, not through brute force but mental scheming of the dangerous kind.

It was arguably cheating, but immortals always had that advantage.

***

Within the Palace grounds, Avery was lost to the encroaching crowd. Despite the courtyard's large size, Avery could barely move as the pack of fighters thickened. Her breathing quickened as seeing anything beyond the tops of heads became impossible. On the tips of her toes, she spied the stacks of benches along each side of the courtyard; if only she could get up there…

Her eyes met a mortal of impressive height barrelling through the crowd with brutal efficiency. A smirk graced the woman's face as she saw Avery struggle amongst the horde. Avery's eyes darkened, a soulless storm conjuring deep within her irises as the compulsion formed.

Mortals had always been easier to control, their mental shields thinner than a blade of grass. Unlike the dryad Avery encountered, the woman did not know to fight as her mind was ensnared, and that damned smirk wiped from her face.

"Take me to the benches," Avery demanded.

The trance had the woman at her feet in a second, mindlessly ambling forward to guide her through the crowds with an outstretched hand. No one took any notice of the pair when they climbed up the benches together. Avery settled down, checking her knives for a second while the woman stood idly beside her. Exhaling a breath, Avery watched as the glaze of compulsion dissolved from the woman's eyes, bringing her back to her own mind.

"What the bloody hells?" she cried, blinking down at Avery.

"Go back to whatever you were doing," Avery replied in a bored tone. "Oh, and forget we ever had this encounter."

The woman nodded, another command taking effect as she sauntered down the steps, her arrogance returning. Avery sighed exasperatedly; some things never changed about mortals. Finally, she could view the courtyard from a better angle. There were thousands of people milling about above and below her, the chatter deafening in such close quarters.

Looking upwards again, Avery spied one of the private boxes beginning to fill with guards. She recognised their armour, the Queensguard emblem of green and silver stamped upon their breast.

A fanfare trumpet drew the courtyard's attention to the box, with many spectators rising from their seats to get a better look. Striding past the guards was Queen Aurora. Her raven hair was swept back for her silver crown to glint proudly in the winter light. A pleased smile lifted her cheeks as she surveyed the crowd of participants and spectators alike, so many of them Avery couldn't begin to count.

"Greetings, my citizens," the Queen called out. "Thank you all for your attendance at my Palace. I would like to thank my council of nobles for assisting in curating this exciting event for us all, and I hope you enjoy the following proceedings. Your task is simple: defeat all your opponents until no one can stand to face you."

She held a silver goblet encrusted in emeralds up in the air. It was the Winthorpe Chalice, the symbol of the kingdom and the Queen's dynasty. "Good luck, my citizens," Aurora toasted the crowds. "Let the Royal Tournament begin!"

3

NOX

Even as a cheer reverberated through the courtyard, the air rife with excitement, Nox wanted nothing more than to slaughter anyone who dared come close. The desire to unsheathe their claws once more and sink them deep into the flesh of one of those six humans was almost unbearable. None of the mortals before them deserved to participate in the Royal Tournament, let alone win it.

And Nox was more than ready to reveal that to anyone who could bear to watch.

As a child, they had been forced to believe that werewolves were a plague to the world. Nox's parents needed them to be cured and miraculously transformed back into a human, into something 'right.' Ever since they'd been bitten, Nox was nothing to be respected or helped. They were only a beast in borrowed skin.

But they knew they could prove themselves as the Champion. Nox had travelled from Feynos, almost halfway across the Kingdom of Darcan, for the Tournament to prove to the ignorant how wrong they were. This victory would be won by the hands of a werewolf. It was a blissful thought to behold in Nox's mind. Now, all they needed to do was make it into a reality.

It wouldn't be difficult. Nox was already venerated as *the Unhallowed One* in the fighting halls known as Ironhavell.

Nox was unbeatable in every way, and even if no one recognised them, they would be sure to reveal it to the world in no time.

Queen Aurora had settled back into her seat, the Winthorpe Chalice already taken back to whatever ancient vault it lived in, and in her place was an advisor and a guardsman. The former unfurled a scroll, which he began to read aloud:

"You may still be curious about what the Royal Tournament and your success in these battles will entail. Simply, you shall all be duelling until only one still stands. The sole fighter will be our winner and earn a monetary prize funded by the Queen and her nobility.

"The Tournament shall take place over the course of the next few days. On any given day, each fighter will have the opportunity to fight at least once and at most twice. The Tournament's proceedings for the day will conclude once two rounds are completed."

The advisor continued through his scroll, his words becoming a droning garble to Nox.

"With that cleared up, the first matches shall begin. Here's who is duelling first; if you are called, head to an empty ring," the advisor said, beginning to list the names from his scroll.

Even at the crowd's edge, Nox could feel the sudden movements of the fighters in the courtyard. Shouts and shoves rippled like raindrops in a puddle as those named forced their way into the centre, either to their victory or their doom.

"Nox Parker."

Nox couldn't help but grin, pushing off the wall to head into the horrendous cram of people. But as they came close, a sudden contraction in the crowd had Nox standing untouched, giving a wide berth between them and the rest. Tension drenched in bigotry, the taste sour on Nox's tongue, but fear lingered in the eyes of everyone they swept past. Just for the hell of it, Nox bared their teeth, causing a tremor to ripple through the faceless crowd. Sometimes being the scum of the earth had its perks.

Nox eventually stood in one of the chalk rings, the white lines freshly applied to the stone grounds. Nox couldn't help but wonder how much blood would soon soak each cobble, how many times these lines would need to be sponged off and reapplied to hide it all. The scarred smile remained, knowing that the blood of ignorant humans was about to soak their claws, too.

Once one fighter stood in each circle, the advisor drilled out twenty more names. The opponents made their way to the rings, all in random order. Nox drew back their hood before shrugging the black cloak off completely, their bow and quiver of arrows also clattering to the floor. Long-ranged weapons were useless in a duel like this; claws would be more than enough.

Nox felt a shiver through the crowd as they met the eyes of the onlookers. Cocking their head to the side, Nox almost felt inclined to bow. After all these years, receiving the constant stares should have been tedious, but they took the attention with an emboldened smirk.

Even without their scarred mouth and werewolf blood, Nox would always be followed by these stares. Nox's neck was dominated by ink—black columns beginning at the base of their jaw that shot down their throat and flared across their chest and shoulders. Those designs were hidden by their shirt, but even in the cold, Nox enjoyed exposing a tattooed throat to the world.

A titanium stud was pierced through the skin below Nox's lower lip. There used to be more piercings, but eventually, many got snagged during duels. The one pierced through their eyebrow had been torn clean off, shearing the hair into a diagonal scar.

Nox's olive skin made every scar on their throat, chest, and face stand out, reminding them of happier times but also worse times. To distract themself, Nox started adjusting their clothing. They wore a loose black shirt, long-sleeved with leather straps at the wrist securing the cuffs in place.

A belt was at their waist, cinching the loose shirt and trousers. Beneath the black trousers were impeccably crafted leather boots, currently caked in mud from the days Nox spent constantly traversing the wilderness. If it were not for their high quality, Nox would have had to replace the boots several times.

The loose clothing was as much for comfort as it was concealment. Their belt was free of weaponry as Nox liked to keep opponents surprised at how many blades they had on them. Beneath the shirt were half a dozen sheaths, though some empty in case any knives needed a new home.

They tucked errant strands of ash-black hair behind their ears before tugging at the string, tying back their hair to ensure the knot stayed in place for the battle.

"Haynes Smithe."

A large man strode into Nox's ring. Haynes seemed to be in his mid-thirties, skin tanned dark from long days in the sun and muscular arms to show for it. He wore basic brown trousers and a sturdy leather breastplate, and strapped to his waist was a shortsword. Nox nodded in greeting, though they kept their face clear of expression. He grunted in reply, eyes scanning them with near disappointment as if Haynes expected something more from the werewolf who sent everyone skittering back in fear.

I'll impress you, Nox thought darkly, *then you'll be sorry.*

"Before the first matches shall begin," the advisor droned, "we must go through the rules of the Tournament. Captain Renner shall explain."

Nox looked up to the guard who had stood silent in the spectator stand since the Queen's departure. He flashed a grin at the advisor, snatching up the scroll for himself before addressing everyone in the courtyard.

"There are several rules of the Royal Tournament, and if any of them are seen to be broken, you shall be instantly disqualified, and if necessary, harsher punishments shall follow," Renner began, a slight chuckle in his voice. "As the aim of the matches is to incapacitate your opponent or have them surrender, killing is prohibited."

Protests erupted amongst the warriors; even Nox growled in distaste. Renner took the dissent in stride, a damning smile on his face.

"Anyone found to commit this crime will be prosecuted by Darcan law for either murder or manslaughter. Betting and bribery between *opponents* is also off the table; any money exchanged shall be confiscated by the Crown with all involved participants disqualified."

There were lesser arguments at that rule, though Nox couldn't help but listen to the clinking of coins being hastily returned to their owners before anyone noticed. But Nox could still see the glint in the eyes of those who pointedly ignored the rule, risking everything the Tournament had to offer for coppers; it was pathetic.

"Any fighting outside of the rings or before the matches have begun will not be tolerated, and you will be detained as a result."

Nox's eyes flashed, hands clenching into fists. Before Renner or the Queen entered the courtyard, they had almost unknowingly broken that rule. Their chances of winning the Tournament were nearly ruined by the goading of those six humans, which made Nox's skin crawl. Weakness, that's what it was; it was what so easily tricked them into taking that fall. Only the mental whispers of that nameless man stopped it all.

Nox could tell from the second he came near that he was immortal. His ancient blood was overpowering amongst the turmoil of mortal waste. Their conversation was brief but haunting—a telepathic mindspeaker strode through the crowds of mortals, and everyone was none the wiser.

Wait until the Tournament begins, he had said into their mind in a low voice; then you can dash their brains on these stones. But do not touch them, not now, not yet. You'll only regret it.

The mindspeaker's demands hadn't made much sense to Nox at the time; only rage and bloodlust had roared through their mind. But the immortal had known that, for he knew how to clamp it down into a quiet drone.

Fight only in the matches. We must all pick our battles; you must save your strength for the wars that will undoubtedly come.

It had been unnerving to meet the mindspeaker's gaze of hardened intensity. A scarf had covered half of his face, so Nox could only see his russet brown eyes and unruly black curls. Not that it mattered; the mindspeaker's words had distracted them long enough for their rage to dissipate slowly.

Thinking about that memory made Nox unconsciously growl, detesting how the telepath had more or less controlled them into submission, knowing they couldn't stop themself. Haynes, who had been watching them, grinned as if he was the reason for their annoyance. The two met eye-to-eye, neither saying anything as Nox stared at Haynes' missing teeth.

"As you can all see," Renner continued, breaking the silence. "The matches are all decided at random. The first round will continue until everyone has fought. You will all be required to stay and watch, even if you have lost. The benches are divided by the winners and the losers; if you even try to say you won and sit there, you will be detained.

"As the matches are randomised, both fighters can decide on whether the duel is hand-to-hand or with weapons. If the latter is chosen and unauthorised weaponry is found, you will be disqualified. And unless specified before matches, fighters with powers will be allowed to use them as they wish, and you will not be forced to reveal those powers."

"Weapons only, wolf," Haynes spat. "No parlour tricks, you hear me?"

Nox raised a hand. "My claws are weapons," they proclaimed. "That is no parlour trick, you hear me?"

He didn't reply, only cursing under his breath. The continuation of the rules drowned out his voice, much to Nox's delight. The man could have probably contested Nox's words, but he didn't even *try*.

"Cheating in any way, such as receiving outside help or sabotaging your opponent, will result in disqualification. If you leave the ring during the fight, this will be seen as surrender, and you shall lose the match immediately. Finally, in the event of a tie, both fighters will be deemed successful in the match and will, therefore, continue onto the next round." Renner cleared his throat. "And that concludes the rules. Good luck, warriors, we'll be watching."

Suddenly, stomping filled the otherwise hushed courtyard; within seconds, dozens of guards swarmed the arena. One headed to each chalk circle, the referee of every match. Those that remained lined the walls of the courtyard, dark eyes scanning the vicinity. Agitation seeped into the crowd of fighters, the gleaming weapons of the guardsmen suffocating any idea of dissent that dared to spark.

The display was humorous to Nox, even a little bleak, given the salted sweat that now lined the faces of those guards. The fear that leached through the courtyard was almost palpable on both sides: the fighters who still risked punishment and the guards who knew they could never detain these fierce warriors.

Pathetic, as many humans were. Nox was glad they no longer stood among that species who allowed fear to suffocate their entire being. Nox had been taught long ago that fear deserved nothing from them, even in the face of death.

With the guards in place, the advisor began to speak for a final time, letting Renner return to the background. He discarded the scroll to announce what everyone was waiting for.

"Referees, begin the matches!"

***

"Here are the match's rules: weapons are allowed, powers are not. Do you both understand?" the guard shouted over the din of the beginning matches.

Nox nodded, a dark grin on their face as Haynes unsheathed his shortsword, waving it above himself. Nox crouched to the floor, claws beginning to lengthen and curl into weapons sharper than any blade.

"With that settled, start!"

Nox exploded into action, leaping from the ground with such force the stones beneath them cracked. Their quick movements had them on Haynes in a heartbeat, slashing the man with their right hand in a ferocious strike. He barked a curse, blood already staining the ground as Nox skittered back to where they started the match. A chorus of yelling thundered from the spectator stands; Nox had drawn first blood.

Nox remained smiling, deepening the scars upon their face as they dashed again, keenly avoiding Haynes' attempt to swipe at them with his sword. They dragged a claw down his face, four lines of hot blood seeping down his tanned skin. A moment later, Nox kicked him between the legs. The large man dropped like a stone with an ugly groan.

Nox was on him in a second, claws at his throat. Nox's scarred smile deepened, sharp incisors barely inches from Haynes' quivering flesh.

"Are you impressed now?" they crooned, claws lazily dragging across his jugular.

Nox needed no battle strategy, not against fools such as Haynes. Even before unsheathing his blade, Nox could see he was as skilled in combat as an infant. Growing up in the wild, Nox could do better and was taught to do better. Werewolves only had one way to survive: through the bloodshed of their enemies. Nox learnt the hard way, as they all had to. Even the most innocent werewolves knew what it was like to sink their claws into greying flesh and stain the world in red.

"I surrender!" he yelled, violently shaking as anger coloured his face. "Get this wolf *bitch* off me!"

Nox's eyes of ice hardened as their lip curled into a snarl. With one last strike, they raked their claws across his face deep enough for it to scar. Haynes began to scream, disgust and horror in his voice as Nox drew themself up, flicking the ribbons of flesh off their claws. Blood covered the man's face, the hot liquid sticking to his eyes and mouth as he spat and cried.

"I claim this victory," Nox said darkly to the referee whose face had gone white before turning to the watching spectators, eyes roving over the six mortals they had marked before the Queen arrived. "Human filth, you will regret the day you ever crossed me." They held up a hand, blood dripping down their fingers. "Death would be a mercy that you shall never have, not from these claws."

With a shaky voice, the referee declared Nox the winner. They ignored the jeers of the onlookers and the sobs of Haynes as they sauntered towards the winners' bench, becoming its sole occupant. All of the matches continued to rage on, leaving Nox alone to watch the symphony of battle.

They sat down as if on a throne, blood still dripping from their claws as they retracted back into their nail beds. Nox didn't need to keep smiling, for their scars painted the picture well enough: they were a beast in borrowed skin, a warrior of swift brutality, walking amongst fickle humans.

4

ELIAS

Trapped in the mass of untried participants, Elias couldn't help but watch the continuous dripping of blood that began to stain the wood of the bench black. The monotonous rhythm made it impossible to look away from the werewolf who only wanted to drench the world in blood.

He was surprised he'd managed to stop that from happening, though only just.

Two hundred and nine years of life had shown Elias the horrors of mortals and immortals alike. And yet, it had taken him years to learn how to fight back against those cruel intentions and not to sit by and watch while misery transpired. The first time had rewarded him with love and power greater than he deserved, but then only tragedy had taken its place. Even so, it was an instinct to come to the werewolf's side and convince them against making the wrong choice.

He didn't even need to read their mind to know how badly they wanted to win. But he did it anyway; the telepathic temptation of Nox Parker's thoughts was fuelled with such agony that it was impossible to ignore. Despite his actions, Elias was glad to see the young warrior sit alone, claiming victory with fiery desperation.

It was also the most exciting match so far. No one else stood out to Elias, but he did enjoy the display of powers the lesser magic users had. Although rare, some mortal families possessed such abilities from elemental manipulation to skin healing. But the practice became taboo once the nobility of Darcan—most definitely the more corrupt side of the kingdom—swore against such power. As a result, there was a weakening in those bloodlines of magic, meaning they were nothing like the fiery blaze buried beneath Elias' skin.

He had lied on his application form to hide it, but it didn't mean he wasn't prepared to cast his duels ablaze with the power of broiling fire that all phoenix-bloods such as himself could wield. They were once a remarkable race with hidden tricks unknown to many mortals. But his people no longer dwelled in the Kingdom of Darcan. Their strength was nothing less but a whisper in the wind, gone but never forgotten by him.

It always made Elias feel like he didn't fit in with the rest of the kingdom. There was only one person in the world he felt he belonged with, but just like the phoenix-bloods, she had gone missing centuries ago. Unlike the phoenix-bloods, however, Kalla Thoughtsinger's disappearance had only Elias to blame. And it was his own guilt and cowardice that kept him from searching for her.

Elias adjusted the grey scarf that covered his face. In the past fifty years, he had become attached to the anonymity the cloth provided him and how it made conversation with strangers somewhat easier.

Elias had been born mute, and it was through mindspeaking that he communicated. Speaking without a natural voice had always scared newcomers of his powers. The scarf kept that fear at bay, though it only succeeded in shifting it into confusion. By now, Elias was used to the reactions and tended to give a sparse explanation of his ability. He had done so with Nox Parker, and the werewolf was kind enough not to judge him too harshly.

There was another reason he wore the scarf to conceal his features: to avoid questions about his jewellery. Pierced through the middle of his lower lip was a golden ring. It had no adornings, unlike the original piercing that had once been there. He kept this one plain, a mournful reminder but an insistent one. No one he met in the past fifty years understood the piercing's meaning. It wasn't a custom of the mortals but the phoenix-bloods, and Elias craved that one day someone would recognise its symbolism.

Participating in the Tournament only intensified his feeling of displacement. Elias wasn't here to win, didn't need the money, and couldn't care less for the glory. No, he was hunting for a particular assassin and his procured fighter.

Elias only knew of the assassin's name in passing, *The Haunted Shadow.* He was an immortal being who took jobs from whoever paid the most, mainly the wretched nobles. This Shadow had been lurking in Elias' home province, Vespis, causing enough of a stir for the Western Arrows to take notice.

The Western Arrows were a rebel group that fought against the leadership of Gideon Eastbow, the current Duke of Vespis. The group was led by a woman named Bea; Elias assisted mainly with weaponry but occasionally provided a deeper look into an enemy's psyche if needed. Bea wanted information from the Shadow, so Elias headed after the assassin.

But whatever the Haunted Shadow had planned with Eastbow, Elias couldn't read the assassin's mind to see it.

His telepathy had failed, impossibly so. Only those with mental barriers could do such a thing, yet Elias couldn't detect *anything* from the Shadow. It was like he *lacked* a mind. The sensation didn't sit well with Elias, so he'd broken into Eastbow's manor and taken as much information about the Shadow from the duke's head.

It wasn't much; Eastbow was just a messenger. The Shadow had only dropped by to discuss the upcoming Royal Tournament and the potential sponsorships the other nobles were considering. The assassin kept his actual client's identity anonymous, so Eastbow only knew the Shadow's job was to find a fighter and deliver them to Cerenia.

Elias immediately left for the Tournament at that revelation, signing up to learn more. Entering as a spectator wouldn't allow him to get close to the Shadow or his fighter, but Elias was confident enough in his ability to battle and remain in the first few matches as he rooted out the pair. It was vague work, and Bea hadn't understood his sudden desire to leave Vespis.

She had only wanted information from the Shadow, but when Elias couldn't get it, it was all that consumed him. He needed to understand the blankness of the assassin's mind, how it had been achieved, and if it could be replicated.

So Elias would find the Shadow and his fighter to shake the truth out of them both. Something darker was coming, Elias could sense, and the Tournament was only the beginning. He hoped he could squash it before it became too great to beat.

Elias' eyes returned to Nox Parker and their bloodied claws. Could they be a friend or foe in what was to come? Or could they not care less? He shook his head at the thought, remembering Bea's words. *You just can't help yourself when it comes to strays, can you?*

She'd meant it as a joke. Throughout Elias' time with the Western Arrows, he had made a point to help all the lost souls they came across. He thought it was a common courtesy, the least these people who had suffered so much deserved. However, it appeared his intensity on the fact was now considered a trait of his, which he decided to take as a compliment.

Even so, he made a promise to himself. *No strays this time. I have to stop the Shadow. That's all that matters.*

***

Elias tried to keep a close watch on every set of matches, but they all swept past in a blur. It would take over two hours for all the fights to be completed, and they were still less than halfway through. The advisor began calling names once everyone was ready for match thirteen.

Elias didn't pay much attention to the names called, finding it almost unending as the fighters rushed forward to begin their first battles. But within the deluge of people, he noted a change within the mortal mass that splintered off—ancient blood was entering the rings.

"Avery Nash."

With skin so pale it was near translucent, a young woman began her descent from the benches. Every precise movement allowed Elias to see those ageless eyes and ethereal looks that no mortal could ever possess. Her face was stern as dark waves of brown hair trailed down her back, ringlets bouncing evenly around her shoulders at every stride. She stood a foot or so below the rest of the fighters heading to the rings, but Elias knew better than everyone else that swarming through her veins would be an unstoppable force—he was just clueless about what it may be.

With no rules to go through and all names called, the matches started with thunderous applause. Elias would usually watch every fight at least a bit, but for this round, his eyes only rested on the sole immortal standing in its rings.

Avery's opponent was a bulky man with thick arms and

black eyes. From where he was sitting, Elias could only assume the rules decided for the match: weapons and powers were allowed. Avery loosed two daggers from her belt; the blades' points came to her elbow, glinting in the winter light. But her opponent only flexed his arms, cracking his knuckles in deafening succession.

"Referees, begin the matches!"

Unsurprisingly, the bulky man attacked first, his large hands outstretched to choke the small woman. Despite the sudden speed, Avery sidestepped with graceful ease, her toes skipping across the stones as if in a dance. The man towered over her as he drew close, still using his tactic to grab at her. However, Avery remained untouched as she dodged once more and dealt a blow with the slash of her dagger.

Blood as bright as rubies erupted from the man's forearm, droplets staining Avery's shirt. Elias couldn't help but smile while she skittered back, wiping his blood off the dagger. But her opponent barely reacted, only giving her a dark grin as his wound continued to decorate the courtyard in red. Avery clenched the hilt of her daggers so tightly that her knuckles turned bone-white.

He attacked again, hands raised above his head to smash her to dust. Her eyes widened. Too slow to escape his attack, she was only able to twist up her dagger to stab at his palms. The blade tore through flesh with brutal efficiency; the squelch of metal colliding with meat was audible even to the stands. Elias winced as the man howled in uncontrollable agony, the long dagger wedged through his open hand.

Avery scrambled back, knees bent as she raked curls out of her eyes but didn't tuck the strands behind her ears. Elias found it strange that she'd entered the Tournament with her hair unbound and could now see the problems it would cause her for the rest of the match.

Not only that, but she had no choice but to abandon the dagger still shoved in her opponent's skin, leaving her with just one. She rose unsteadily, her depthless blue eyes watching warily for his next move.

The man panted heavily, sweat pouring from his forehead in waves as he stared at the dagger. Despite his trembling muscles, he grabbed the hilt and, in one sickening slide, pulled the blade out from his hand. The metal shone a gruesome red slopped with loosed flesh and skin. A fountain of blood gushed from his palm, mixing with the dust on the stones in a swirling spool. With his uninjured hand, he brandished the dagger, the fine-handled weapon dwarfed by his massive fist. Avery's eyebrows knitted together, distaste apparent on her delicate features.

A knife cut through the air, whistling quickly from Avery's fingers and into her opponent's left shoulder. Seconds later, another hit him in his abdomen, which caused him to collapse. Avery dashed forward, kicking him where the knife stuck out of his stomach and reaching out to steal her dagger from his grasp.

But before she could claim the blade again, he used her closeness to his advantage. Grabbing her leg, the man smacked her to the ground with a mighty crash. Avery's face collided with the stones, where a resounding cracking of bones filled the courtyard. Her hair covered her face, but Elias could smell the blood.

Her opponent lifted her off the ground, revealing a broken nose and bloodied mouth. Even so, she spat at him just before he curled his fist around her throat. Avery began to choke, her saliva bubbling and turning pink as she thrashed, fingers grappling for her dagger.

She stabbed unthinkingly, causing him to drop her like a

sack of stones. A groan escaped her mouth as she crawled to her feet, one dagger still in hand.

"Let's end this," Avery spoke, her voice surprisingly clear despite the bruises that decorated her throat like a necklace of dark jewels, "with your defeat." The man staggered to his feet, fists still clenched and a devilish grin on his face. But when their eyes met, everything changed.

"Stop."

His entire body went slack, losing a breath at the sensation. Confusion swept through the audience as his shoulders drooped. Avery strode towards him carefully, finally reclaiming her fallen dagger and raising it to his eye level. The errant strands of Avery's brown hair could not hide her eyes, which resembled a stormy sea, no longer a clear blue but ancient darkness roiling beneath.

Elias leaned forward, his brows knitting together as he watched the deep concentration that swarmed in her eyes. He jerked suddenly, an electrifying jolt running through his veins as he realised what was happening.

Too far away to read her thoughts, he watched in roaring silence as Avery controlled her opponent into submission.

All it had taken was one word, but it was more than apparent to him. Elias had met mental manipulators in his life, and if it were not for his own abilities, he would have fallen under their commands, too. However, in the full view of the gathering of mortals, no one else understood.

With the man frozen in place, Avery's dagger caught the light as she sent it flying towards his bare neck.

"Halt!" the referee yelled, his face red. "Avery Nash wins the match!"

The blade remained inches away from his throat, and it was with painful slowness that Avery sheathed the dagger.

The spectators watching the match were silent, with no jeers or cheers joining the chorus of shouts that thundered through the courtyard. Avery turned to the referee, her eyes suddenly clearing into bright blue.

"Thank you for the match," she said, wiping blood from her chin. "I request a healer for myself."

Before the guardsman could reply, the man she had been controlling only moments before howled. All attention turned to him as he barreled towards Avery, believing the match was ongoing and that he hadn't been forced to lose. The referee unsheathed his blade, the screeching noise causing Elias to wince at its poor craftsmanship, and held it in front of the man, protecting Avery.

"Connor Balt, you have lost the match. Desist now or face punishment," he spat, the sword's point grazing the man's nose.

"LOST?" Connor screamed. "She didn't touch me! This conniving witch has you fooled! I demand a rematch!"

"You will have no such thing," Avery replied, her face a blank wall as she sidestepped the referee to approach Connor. "You dropped your guard, and therefore, I won. But you're right; I didn't touch you. And that's the only reason why you're still alive."

The spectators sitting beside Elias scoffed at that, the cockiness of her statement drilling into their skulls.

Elias could imagine her commanding a fleet of men or standing before the Haunted Shadow, unarmed save for those sea-storm eyes.

He blinked, piecing together his own thoughts. Would she be *able* to stand against the Shadow? A man without a mind? Elias watched Avery again, now sitting on the winners' bench with a healer at her side.

She was undefeatable, pure and simple. The perfect fighter for the Tournament, precisely what the Shadow would want. His stomach churned; it was only a hunch, but Elias knew at that moment he needed to do anything possible to get close enough to this woman of ageless cruelty and ensnare her mind.

5

AVERY

The thunderous jeering of the spectators who watched the matches did nothing for Avery's relentless headache. Nausea ricocheted through her small frame, the sun bearing down on her sweat-slicked body. Blood—both her own and not—still stained her shirt. Even with only one more match ahead of her, Avery wished it would end.

One of the servants of the Palace had taken to braiding her hair away as the match had left it a tangled mess. Avery combed a finger through the end, trying to find comfort in the repetitive movement. When the servant had offered, Avery had clasped the sides of her head, ensuring the newly arranged hair lay flat against her ears. She couldn't afford to be blinded by her hair, but also couldn't allow her nymph features to be so visible.

"Water, ma'am?" a voice asked.

Avery looked up slowly. Her eyes had been glued to the wood of the bench, not daring the sudden movement. Still, nausea roiled through her head, her vision blurring for a second as she met the eyes of another servant.

The woman held a wicker basket of clean towels, and balanced upon it was a tray of glasses that sloshed with water. Avery's heartbeat tripled, her hands moving before either could react as she claimed two.

She finished each one in a single gulp, the liquid

revitalising her in a way she hadn't imagined. It had been an age since Avery exerted so much energy on an outing to the mortal kingdom, and despite the waterskin on her hip, its water content didn't seem to be enough.

Avery returned the empty glasses before grabbing two more, not caring for the judgement. Once left alone, she took more cautious sips from her glass as her headache began to ebb away. All other pain in her body was now gone, her injuries and broken nose no more than a memory, thanks to a magic healer.

Avery had been alive for almost three centuries, and yet such use of power was rare to see from mortals in the kingdom. The Queen's reign was starting to squash the taboo of magic, even if only her Palace comfortably reaped the benefits.

"All matches are complete! Round sixteen shall begin momentarily."

Avery blinked back into reality. She'd barely been focusing on the previous matches, an error on her part, as the winners' bench slowly accumulated everyone she would need to defeat. If she wanted to keep Torr happy, Avery knew she needed to keep an eye on those who won, but she was already behind. So she started focusing that round, making bets with herself on every fighter that was called.

It wasn't difficult to discern the bruisers to the bladed foes or the magic users and their tricks. But Avery liked to focus on those who blurred between the lines—the fighters who could hold their own with a gleaming weapon but also trip someone up with a power that lurked beneath. It was them who Avery placed her imaginary bids on because the man who could control ice and nothing more would be useless against the woman of fire, but in turn, that fiery woman would be squashed by the user of water. Possessing the talents of many would be their only way of victory: brute strength and steel in exchange for bloodborne power.

It was why Avery had entered these halls armed; relying on her abilities alone would have her crushed instantly. Weakness was an inescapable burden that would always hold her in its claws. She just needed to ensure its grip on her wasn't as tight.

"Elias Hearth."

It wasn't so much the name that made Avery look up, but when she beheld the man entering the rings, it made her subconsciously clench her teeth. A sense of recognition sparked in her chest, barely an ebbing ember in the fire of her ancient memory. She didn't know the man on sight, but something about him reminded her of when she was a young girl who slipped on dew-soaked grass and cut her palms beneath the stray stones surrounding her home.

Ignoring him was impossible, not when Avery could sense the immortality thrumming beneath his skin. His blood boiled with unparalleled flame, swarming her senses in dark smoke. None of these mortals would realise, but Avery recognised from the hidden heat rippling from his form that Elias Hearth was a phoenix-blood. A powerful one at that, and maybe more ancient than she.

Avery's gut twisted; she thought they had all but disappeared after their dreadful civil war against the Darcanian mortals, which ended in suffering on all sides. She had once been obsessed with finding evidence of their existence, if only to stamp it out for herself. The Phoenix Wars had started before she was born, and it carved out a hole in Avery's younger years, decaying from her memory but lingering still.

She shook the thought from her mind; despite her ancient grudge, the Phoenix Wars were long gone, so surely this immortal knew nothing of that tragedy.

She shook her head. None of this mattered; she would have to treat him like everyone else here—by defeating him in the Tournament.

Avery sized him up. Elias' hair was a short crop of perfect curls, shining like black gems against the sunlight. Taller than everyone around him, his staggering height and muscular frame were unignorable. His skin was a warm brown, palms lighter by a few shades. A scarf covered the lower half of his face, hiding any emotion that might have swelled there. At this distance, Avery could not completely gauge what resided in his eyes, only that his gaze was alert and searching.

Instead, she noticed the black steel of his armour that covered his entire body, save his hands, and the helmet held in the crook of his arm, suggesting he was much more than the blazes he could conjure from his fingertips. Attempting to drown him with her own powers could still end in her defeat. Avery could only hope she wouldn't have to battle him, but she knew not to expect he would lose this fight. No, it was evident that he planned to win with every suffocating breath.

The woman who entered his ring was skittish at best. Keera Eden's lithe frame was similar to Avery's despite the slumped shoulders and unconscious tremors that racked through her. No pity swept through Avery; the Tournament hadn't hidden its intent, so to sign up and not understand the risks of failure was to enter the Palace already defeated.

"What'll be the match rules, then?" the referee barked, sending Keera into a frenzy of panic.

Elias didn't reply, letting his opponent teeter with deciding. The referee's patience began to thin in those moments as unintelligible words spilt from Keera's trembling lips. It made Avery question Elias' lack of response and why he didn't bother to save the fearful woman from herself.

But in turn, she realised he *had* been talking, just not aloud, nor to anyone but the referee who watched the match. The man paled considerably, a whole conversation flitting through his mind while the crowds watched dumbfounded. Avery recognised the work of a mindspeaker, thanks to tales told by the eldest dryads of the Forest. The reaction of those first spoken to in that way was always the main clue of this power.

"I'm sorry, sir," the referee said, eyes downcast. "I didn't know of your ailment."

Since he'd entered her eyesight, Elias' emotions had been nonexistent, hidden behind the scarf he wore. But the way he flinched then, though unnoticeable to the mortal eye, spoke a thousand words to Avery. No creature was without weakness, and though his inability to speak didn't hinder Elias physically, it still forced him into a space of pity that destroyed him from the inside.

Keera had gone quiet, eyes scanning Elias as if to seek out what the referee had described. But he ignored her, most likely continuing to explain his choice for the match rules to the referee. Avery's chest tightened, unable to tear her gaze away from the guttered flame of Elias' confidence.

The referee turned to Keera. "Do you accept both weapons and powers be allowed in this match?"

She yelped in reply, furiously nodding as if she'd be scolded for disagreeing. She drew her weapon, a longsword flecked with years of battle and carelessness. Elias fitted his helmet onto his head, and his face was lost to the shadows of the crown of onyx black. Then, he unbuckled his weapon from his back. The greatsword's blade soundlessly slid into view. It was meticulous and bold; carvings of crackling fire shone upon the metal. He held it in both hands, his brown fingers clenched upon the supple leather hilt.

"Alright, on my count. Start!"

It was no surprise to her as Elias set his greatsword alight in a thick swarm of reds and oranges. She wished she could see his reaction. Would there be humour in his eyes or grim determination?

Keera fell back in fear, a stray hand skirting the edge of the ring. Avery snorted at that. The match had only begun seconds ago, yet it seemed she would surrender already.

But that lingering hand turned to a clenched fist, one that pushed Keera up to her feet with swift ease. The fear in her eyes scattered beneath the spitting stare of Elias' blazing sword as the will to fight and win finally reached her, much to Avery's amusement.

Keera began to prowl the ring, her battered longsword now gripped tightly in her hand. It was nothing like Avery's own blades, which she had cared for over the decades. No, this was poor craftsmanship, and she hoped Elias would realise that, too.

A moment later, he gave a mighty swing on his sword, slamming it down to strike her. But the large weapon became Keera's advantage as the blow fell too slowly, leaving her unharmed. So the greatsword hit the ground, cracking the stones and charring the dust into blackened ash.

Keera retaliated, raising her longsword in a swooping arc. Even so, Elias caught the blow as he raised his own sword. Their blades sang against one another, the impact reverberating through the courtyard to the extent that Avery could feel the jarring in her bones.

Elias tensed, his hands clenching the hilt tightly as he

drove the sword down upon Keera's, refusing to lose the battle. Sweat shone on her face, the flames upon his sword licking close as her knees buckled.

She could not manoeuvre away from their clash of swords before a new swarm of fire flooded the blade. Elias' veins began to colour with the flame as it flowed from him, turning the once red-hot blaze into a searing white.

The metal of his sword remained intact despite all logic demanding it to melt at his feet, but the same couldn't be said for Keera's. Hers dissolved into globs of molten metal, causing her to scream. The longsword turned to a ruined stump, the hot flow trailing towards her vulnerable skin. The metal swarmed her fingers. Avery's stomach lurched at the sight as her screams turned into howls, her hands no longer visible beneath the molten steel.

Avery could sense Elias' panic, even if the mortals sitting beside her could not see through the thick spirals of smoke that buffeted from the flaming sword. He dropped the blade, the fire winking out in a flash as he dashed towards the grey-faced referee.

Elias' words suddenly flung across the courtyard, his fear soaking through the mindspeaking so that everyone in the vicinity heard his demands. *We need a healer!*

"PLEASE!" Keera cried. "I SURRENDER!"

At that, the referee reacted, unfreezing to throw a hand in the air and shout, "Elias Hearth wins the match! Bring a healer to the rings!"

His demand was answered as someone leapt from the winners' benches and into the fray. Avery recognised the healer; the magic in their veins had fixed her broken nose. The healer descended upon the shaking Keera, their calloused fingers delving towards the molten metal without care for themself.

But Elias knocked their hands out of the way, shucking off his helmet to reveal a pleading visible in his eyes. If the mindspeaker spoke, it was closed off from the audience, but Avery could see the healer had frozen. It gave Elias a chance to intervene, where he began to pry the metal—now reformed into crude shapes—off Keera's burned fingers despite the heat.

Tears stained Keera's cheeks as she spoke to him; her voice was raw from screaming. "It's okay. I understand you wanted to win, as did I. You deserve this victory. I forgive you."

Avery's nose scrunched in disgust. She'd forgotten how easily mortals could forgive; even the more stubborn ones would relent eventually.

Whatever Elias replied with went only to her, his mindspeaking still closed off. It didn't take long until her hands were cleared of the metal, revealing a charred mess that once was skin. Blood and burns in a myriad of reds and blacks covered Keera's hands, and she moaned as the cold wind buffeted against the mangled flesh.

Elias' fingers remained unharmed, a useful trait all phoenix-bloods possessed. The healer had retrieved bowls of water and cloths and set to work at healing Keera, shooing Elias away with the flick of their hand.

He obliged, staggering away from the rings. Now officially the victor of the match, he strode towards the winners' bench, eyes scanning the vicinity with dull exasperation. The expression changed when Elias stopped to stare at her. Avery pursed her lips, meeting his gaze. His eyes settled on her as if she were an old friend; she raised a brow, realising he may have recognised her, too.

He headed towards Avery, their eyes never leaving one another until he sat beside her, the tension in Elias' body evaporating.

"Congratulations on your victory," she said softly. "You've been watching me, haven't you?"

His eyes still roamed across her, no doubt cataloguing every inch of her. Avery had never been a stranger to a man's gaze. Once, she had a mortal entranced by her for days, no compulsion needed, refusing to leave her side until Caliadne cut his throat out.

However, she returned Elias' gesture, taking her own time to look upon him up close. Long eyelashes fanned his cheeks, and hiding underneath was the russet-brown of his irises. His eyebrows were suspiciously manicured and were just as dark as the rest of his hair. His clothes covered all of his body, save his hands, so she could not tell what else he had hidden. That scarf unnerved her the most. What would she find there if she were to pull it away? Or if she made him do it for her instead?

Yes, I have, he returned calmly. *I've also taken note of your powers.*

An alarm flared in her chest momentarily, but she shoved it away, responding nonchalantly. "I suppose I did make it a bit obvious," she admitted. "But that's not against the rules, is it?"

Not at all, Elias replied, humour edging the words.

Avery smiled, turning to meet his eyes once more. "Good. I intend to use it every match. You've probably also noticed that I'm not exactly the strongest of fighters."

He shrugged. *Some battles must be won with our minds and others with our bodies.*

She huffed a breath. "Are you suggesting these fools throw themselves into the fray without a single thought to guide them?"

Elias didn't respond immediately, his eyes moving far away from her. *Yes, sometimes you need that mindlessness to win the battle.*

Avery shook her head. "I pity the mindless."

You've met them before, though, haven't you? The mindless?

She let out a false laugh. "What's that supposed to mean?" she asked, waving a hand. "Another metaphor?"

Have you heard of the assassin known as the Haunted Shadow?

Avery blinked. In fact, she had not. The name meant nothing to her, but the intensity of his words made her gut churn. She looked at Elias, truly meeting his eyes in an attempt to seek out the truth. "Why have you come to the Tournament?" she asked.

I'm looking for him, isn't that obvious?

The attempted casualness of his tone did not fool Avery. "Why?" she pressed.

He works for the nobility and is dangerous. He is the kind of man you cannot afford to leave alive.

"So why are you here?"

In order to find him, I had to find someone else first.

A shiver went through Avery's spine, and a part of her already knew the answer to her question even before she asked it. "And who is that then?"

You.

6

ELIAS

Even though she was immortal, Avery's mind was unbarred and free to roam. He only prodded her with questions to keep her unaware. It also wasn't part of the plan to talk to her *first,* but the irresistible tug of her eyes had drawn him in.

But Elias had been right. *She* was the Haunted Shadow's fighter, even if she didn't know him as that. Frankly, Avery knew nothing of the assassin's past, only his name, Torr, and the job he'd forced her into. In spite of her casualness, she despised him more than anything. Her malicious thoughts concluded one thing: she wanted to see the assassin dead. Elias hadn't thought too far about how to deal with Torr, but now, he couldn't see an outcome without Avery's wish being granted.

"So you found me," Avery said. "Now what?"

Elias barely heard her. He was too busy cutting through her mind like a blade through paper. He hadn't figured out *what* she was, but the dreamy display of the Forest of the Dryads filled his mental trespassings. Averaline was the true name for this naiad, and she was most definitely a powerful one. She was the eldest of the Three Freshwater Sirens—a term Elias had actually heard before but thought it to be a legend.

Different retellings said there was only one and that she separated her stories into three to confuse those who tried to find her. Singing her victims into submission, it wasn't Avery who was at the seat of that legend. He searched further and found the right sister: Bellama, the middle of the three.

Was she who Torr was hunting for originally? If so, why did he end up with this one?

"Are you even listening?"

Elias blinked, pulling out of Avery's mind. Her beautiful face was formed into a scowl, but he couldn't help glancing at where her pointed ears were hidden. During her match, he should have spotted them, and maybe then he could have recognised her as the nature spirit she was.

Avery's arms were crossed, and new thoughts of violence rushed through her head. Did Torr select her for this ferocity? Elias hoped it wouldn't make her a difficult person to convince.

Yes, sorry, he replied. *I was just thinking.*

"You're the one who's thinking after you drop that threat on me?" she accused with a finger.

It wasn't a threat, he replied with a frown. *I'm just surprised you haven't attacked me or called for backup yet.*

She tilted her head to the side, eyes narrowed. "I don't need backup, just answers. So we can do this amicably, or I can force them out of you."

Even though you couldn't force answers out of Torr?

Avery blanched. Her mind raced with dozens of questions, but she only voiced one. "How did you know?"

Because I cannot read him either, but I don't think that makes him a witch.

It was almost amusing to see how her eyes widened, the

ocean of blue irises something any mortal would willingly drown in. "How? You—" Avery's words caught in her throat. "You're a telepath."

Elias nodded. Telepathy and mindspeaking did not always work in tandem, so it wasn't surprising that Avery had not expected it. Not just that, but she knew that neither ability was a phoenix-blood trait to begin with, but he wasn't going to explain how he had gained them. It was a story Elias had never repeated to anyone because it ended in tragedy for the woman who had given him the powers.

And your mind has been ever so useful, he said, ignoring the past. *I think we can help each other kill Torr.*

"*Help* each other?" she hissed. "You just admitted to reading my mind, you filthy bas—"

We have a common enemy, Avery, he interrupted hastily. *Neither of us understands what Torr is, but we both know he is dangerous. In order to protect your sisters, you may very well need my help.*

"No. You need *my* help. I've organised a deal with Torr; he won't touch my sisters if I win this Tournament. And *no one* here can stop me from doing that."

Elias' mind whirred. How could he get her on his side? If they did not ally, this conversation would leave him vulnerable. He had no plans of stooping to blackmail, but Avery's stubbornness refused to see beyond her agreement with Torr. She continued to rant at him, but her words were a deluge of meaningless anger. Her hidden desire to kill Torr was just out of reach. There was something else that urged her to work alongside the assassin. Why did she want this so badly?

Slipping into Avery's mind was like Elias dipping his hand into a rushing river. Thoughts and memories bubbled and frothed against his palm, the life of a naiad who had lived for almost three hundred years collecting in his own mind. If he hadn't been used to the rush, it would have overwhelmed him entirely. Instead, Elias met each memory in kind, skimming through them until he found the correct one.

If we work together against the Shadow, I will buy you that cottage.

Avery's mouth hung open, her silence a resounding victory to Elias. Hidden deep within her mind was that true desire—escape.

I've lived in this kingdom for centuries and have more than enough money to fund it. Even if we find a way for you to win the Tournament, I'll still do it. Because you're right, only I need help, and for that, I'll compensate you.

In the past decades, Avery's mind always wandered back to a sleepy village in the province of Hyvera. It was seated indirectly beside a weak spot between the mortal realm and the Forest of the Dryads. There was one patch that all the mortals steered away from, not realising it was just metres from the borderline of Avery's birthplace. She wanted it so badly; it made her heart ache whenever she thought of it. In a home of her own, away from the constant gossiping of her species, she'd be content and alone.

She could have manipulated the village to construct this cottage for her, but there was pride in knowing that *she* truly brought this dream into existence. Buried at the bottom of her lake was a chest of *feram,* waiting to be spent on this home. Elias didn't know much about real estate, but if Avery thought the Tournament winnings would be enough to build this, he surely had that amount, too.

What do you say? I already know you want him dead, so together, we can make that a reality.

She blinked tears from her eyes. Elias only knew they

were tears from her thoughts; otherwise, he would have thought he was imagining it.

"On some conditions," she said, her voice stronger than Elias anticipated. "For starters, stay *out* of my mind. I don't want you infiltrating my head whenever you want things your way. Next, I want to know *what* Torr is before we kill him. Witch or not, he's something I've never seen before. And the killing blow is mine. His skull will make a perfect ornament."

A housewarming gift.

A small smile greeted her face, but she twisted it away. "Lastly, I want half the money now. I don't trust you, Elias Hearth, but your coin will soothe it."

He shook his head. *That amount of money is back in Vespis. I can give you what I currently have with me, but it'll be more like a tenth of it.*

"That won't do, but it shouldn't be a problem. We can take a trip through the Forest."

I'm not sure being torn apart by nymphs should be included in this plan.

"You'll be with me. No one will touch you."

Despite her first condition, he couldn't resist finding all the stories that confirmed this. Finally, Elias nodded, and Avery's face brightened. A cheer went up through the stands, and they both turned their attention back to the rings. Their discussion had distracted Elias from the matches, leaving him disorientated on how many were left.

Avery knocked her arm into his. "Look, up there. He's watching us."

Elias didn't bother raising his gaze to the spectator stands. The crowd was too numerous to hunt out Torr, so he looked through Avery's eyes in her mind. Sure enough, Torr was scowling at the nymph, but his stare sometimes cut towards Elias. Elias hadn't seen Torr's face clearly before, as a hood always shadowed it, but he couldn't say he was very impressed by the assassin. He looked startlingly mortal.

I can move if you want to avoid suspicion.

Avery lifted her chin. "No. Let him stare. Our deal was to win the Tournament. It didn't say anything about not making friends."

I thought you didn't trust me?

She rolled her eyes. "Whatever. I take it you don't make friends very easily."

I could say the same for you.

"I have my sisters," she said sharply. "What about you?"

Elias looked to his feet. *My family is all gone. My village was destroyed, and we were separated. I haven't seen them in centuries.*

He didn't like talking about his past, but the memories swept into his mind all too easily. Avery didn't ask for further details; instead, she turned her attention back to the matches to allow Elias to stew in his own thoughts.

For a time, his family had only been blacksmiths, working to make ends meet and teach the trade. Elias had been smithing since he was a young boy, melting ores into a molten flow of metal before hammering and warping it into something more. His first attempts had always been crude and brittle, but the joy of picking up a sword *he* had made, still hot from the fires snapping at him, was worth every moment.

But the trade had stopped being for money or his enjoyment. No longer did he make countless horseshoes for the people of his village nor fix doorknobs long rusted to disuse. Rebellions and war required weapons and armour, so he had no choice but to provide while his family plunged into destruction.

It had been for a good cause, Elias had thought. Like so many non-humans, his people had suffered under the oppression of humans who believed the world owed them everything. The phoenix-bloods had fought back, taking control of their lives to free themselves from the slave-like world, bringing the Phoenix Wars to life. But as they took power into their own hand, corruption began.

Human villages burned to ash at Elias' feet, his brothers-in-arms whooping and cheering at the screams of innocents. His lovingly crafted swords were drenched in blood as they tore through the flesh of any mortal who stood in the way.

War was an old friend of his, creeping in the shadows to remind Elias of the horrors he had witnessed, hissing at him every time he forgot about it. Everyone was gone when the Phoenix Wars ended; sometimes, he wished he'd gone with them, too. Other times, he thought he deserved to be left behind; he betrayed his people halfway through the war, after all. Who would want to keep a traitor and a coward?

Elias looked up, eyes barely making out the blurred shapes of fighters in the rings. He was doing better now, wasn't he? Ending a threat by running towards danger instead of away. Bea thought so, but she didn't know half of his life; sometimes, he wasn't even sure she knew what a phoenix-blood was, let alone that he was one of them.

The matches came to an end, and from the corner of his eye, he saw Avery politely clapping. Catching his gaze, she raised a brow. "Wanna make a bet?"

On what?

"The next rounds. We're going to be here for who

knows how long. We won't get anywhere near Torr just yet, so let's have some fun."

He gave a nod, and Avery's eyes sparkled. Elias thought back to Bea and her obsession with his strays. But today, it felt like *he* was the stray, following around this ancient nymph. Even so, he let his eyes drift to a particular winner, still picking dried blood off their claws.

I'll keep an eye on them, Elias told himself as he watched Nox. *Just to make sure they don't do anything stupid.*

The names of the next match began to be called.

7

LYRA

"**L**yra Avenyard."

It took twenty-two sets of matches until she heard those words. Lyra's mouth twisted into a wry smile as she headed down the steps of the benches. She started cracking her knuckles in quick succession while hunting for an empty ring.

A moment later, she stood with her hands on her hips, waiting for an opponent. Her blood thrummed. Was it excitement? Nerves? Whatever the case, it jittered through Lyra's body like a swarm of bees desperate to escape. After watching the horde of fighters, she wanted something *more*. It was like everyone at the Tournament was purposely floundering at every obstacle. Now, Lyra could show everyone what a real fight looked like.

The calling of names came quickly, and within the second group of twenty, Lyra saw a man forcing his way through. Murmurings filled the courtyard as everyone watched the sole competitor dash into her ring. His green eyes met her own, crude excitement lighting them up.

"Undefeated Champion," he rasped, chest heaving in exertion as he bowed mockingly. "It's a *pleasure* to meet you. My name is Harry Martyn."

Lyra's hands fell from her hips. Wasn't this what she wanted? To be recognised? Even without the Pits title, she was a common name in Cerenia's underworld, yet this pronouncement sent shivers across her skin.

She didn't let it rattle her. "I'm glad to hear Agonia is still active," Lyra said smoothly. "I really thought for a moment that all the rats would have jumped ship by now." She canted her head. "Hello, little rat."

Harry didn't wane; rather, his excitement seemed to heighten. "Not just active, but *alive*. You are a legend, cursed by the Pits and spat upon, all so you could take its rusted crown. I never saw you fight, but now I get to, at first-hand. I hope you impress me, Lyra Avenyard."

Her face twitched in distaste. The poetry of Harry's words set her at unease, which he noted with a feverish grin. Just how many of them were waiting to see her fall? Lyra had come here to act as if she wanted to claim a new title, but it seemed they were waiting to prove she didn't deserve what she already had.

"I don't need to prove anything to you," she huffed. "Nor the Pits, I already did that."

Rules in the Pits were scarce, far less than in the Tournament, but one similarity they had was no fighting outside the rings, even in the case of self-defence. Lyra only found out about it after another spectator attacked her; his intentions cruel and unforgiving. She killed him, manslaughter of the highest order, not that it was his death that mattered. Lyra had fought him, so she deserved a punishment fit for those who fought when they shouldn't: fight in the central pit every day until you defeat three opponents in a row.

At first, the task had seemed simple; Lyra had been training to fight since she was fourteen, so three opponents would be easy. That was until Astrid Shernev took it upon herself to beat Lyra every single day. The First Champion of Agonia forced her through a cycle of losing for six months.

Despite the humiliating defeats, Lyra had held respect for her. Astrid was untouchable, but the title was still a fragile post; one false movement would have had her tipping into oblivion. Worse than any punishment, she'd walked into the trap and had to fight anything that moved to stay alive.

So when the winning blow was finally in Lyra's palms— the new Champion of the Agonia Pits—she had fled. Her time at the Pits was over, and her escape defined that all too well.

Harry straightened, the wry smile on his face dissolving. But he took it in stride, bouncing on his toes and clenching his hands into fists in an almost childlike way. "You'll still need to beat me, right?" he asked. "Here are my rules: no weapons and no powers. Just good old roughhousing, like the Pits, eh?"

"I would prefer a weapons match," she replied. Lyra unbuckled the longsword strapped to her back and revealed the naked blade. "It'd be such a waste not to use this."

Harry paled, his dark curls unable to hide the alarm in his eyes.

Lyra could now see just how young her opponent was; despite the age limit on the Tournament, a teenager had managed to slip through. She sighed; she'd go easy on him, even if his idea of the Champion would have not.

"Fine, weapons free."

A crooked smile lifted his cheeks, the colour returning to his face. Harry began dancing on his toes again, his fists lazily swinging up. Lyra rolled her eyes as she returned her blade to its sheath—another time.

Hoots and jeers littered the crowd while she shrugged off her cloak. Ignoring them, Lyra folded the cloak, laying it on the stones and her sword upon it. Next, she removed her gauntlets. Even though that extra layer of leather would be an advantage, she did not want people to think she *needed* it in a fistfight.

She continued disarming herself, pulling every knife off her person. The satisfying sound of steel against steel drowned out the blood roaring in her ears. This was finally it; even without her blades, Lyra knew she'd win. One way or another, victory would be hers. Maybe it wasn't just nerves or excitement; it was *both*. She *did* want to win, Champion or not, façade or genuine, it didn't matter to her.

And that was truly terrifying.

"Match rules:" the referee cut in, disturbing her thoughts. "No weapons, no powers, only yourselves. Got it?"

"Yes!" they shouted in unison, a smile creasing Harry's features.

Slow. The world began to slow as she loosed a final breath. Lyra could already feel her nails breaking the skin of her palms as she clenched them tight. She put her panic aside for now, refusing to let it distract her in this fatal moment. She only saw rather than heard the referee begin the match, the exertion on his face bright as he yelled that single word.

Go.

Within a second, her right fist connected with Harry's jaw. Blood spurted from his mouth as he bit his tongue. Lyra managed to dodge the spray of red so that it stained the stones beneath her. A howling cry escaped him, anguish roiling through him as he bent down to the ground. The referee winced watching, his arm raising to call the match over. But Lyra instead watched the teen crawling on the floor.

The way his knees buckled had been practised, this was a trap.

Harry was up in a moment, fists flying towards her. Only one punch made contact as his knuckles grazed across Lyra's cheek. She hissed through her teeth, retreating from his reach before he could hit again. The stinging was bearable for the moment as the pain rippled across her skin.

"That was impressive," he breathed, massaging his jaw. "I thought I had you in my grasp."

"I've seen that move a thousand times; those tactics won't work."

"So, what will?"

"Skill."

The battlefield was like a dance to Lyra. One wrong move would cause everything to come crashing down. You could practise over and over that single piece, but the only thing that mattered was when the world stopped to watch. She had had those eyes glued to her for six months, every faltered step, every bruising defeat. It was a dance she had yet to learn, to hold in her grasp, and refuse to let go. But now, the battlefield was hers, so she let it play.

Two steps had Lyra back within range of Harry's clenched fists. She ducked low, avoiding the pummelling as she swiped at his legs. A pointed punch in the stomach had him crumpled on the floor, the air exiting his lungs in an instant. She reeled back just as Harry clawed upwards, his nails barely scraping her shirt. Her long legs brought him to a halt, kicking him squarely in the face.

He barked a curse, blood pouring from his nose. Lyra crouched down, extending her hand towards him.

"Do you surrender?" she asked. "End this suffering now."

Those were borrowed words. Astrid had said them a dozen times to Lyra in the Pits. But the First Champion was not being kind; she had wanted to finish the fight. A foolish girl trapped in punishment was no match for Astrid, and those words were a blessing to Lyra when she first fought. It meant she would no longer have to worry about swollen skin and bruised bones for one more day.

But three months of failure had changed that.

It was no surprise to Lyra to hear those words she used to scream come rasping from Harry's bloodied mouth.

"Like *hells* will I surrender."

She smiled like a fool in love, so similar to Astrid's all those years ago. The jeering and yelling were no longer directed at her; *she* was the Undefeated Champion; *she* held the match in the palm of her hand. And so the dance continued, every rhythmic movement fuelling the delight in her eyes even as blood began to stain her knuckles, the skin split beneath the force. Every spinning dodge, every missed hit, it was a symphony in her bones that she never wanted to end.

But that's what made Lyra realise she needed to stop.

There was one move Astrid would always use when she had grown tired of the match between the two of them, when Lyra's sluggish movements were too painful to witness, and when the crowd jeered for more excitement. It was a blow that not only hindered the fight but also wounded her pride. A downed dog, unable to breathe as Astrid paraded the sandy pits, bellowing in her victory.

It was a surprise to everyone when the two women left Agonia together, a friendship forged in humiliation. Astrid hadn't doled out punishment for callous enjoyment. She had wanted to make a final ally within the sea of monsters. The First Champion knew she would fall one day, so she chose Lyra to be her unexpected successor. Because every defeat was a lesson, every wrong move brought Lyra one step closer to the right one. That final blow was now the easiest to counter.

But the same couldn't be said for Harry Martyn, whose pummelling fists began to feel like pebbles thrown by a child. There was no chance he could escape this defeat, not now, not ever. Lyra unclenched her fists; her thumbs slightly jutted out as she approached him. She met Harry's eyes for one moment, the apple green startlingly bright against his bloodied face. But that wasn't her target as she raised her hands as if to strangle him. Then, she shoved her hand into his neck with lightning speed. The strike was debilitating, knocking him off his feet.

Lyra could remember that choking feeling as Harry's face turned purple, clawing at his face as he tried to force air into his lungs. It had left her unable to speak on several occasions, the attempt to do so leaving her insides on fire. She pitied Harry, for she knew the pain well and what it was like to watch helplessly as someone destroyed you.

The next move was simple: stomping on his abdomen until he wheezed, hacking up globs of blood and spit. There was no coming back from this.

Lyra had won.

***

She sat cross-legged on the winners' benches, longsword balanced on her lap. The steel glinted in the sun, glowing as if bathed in starlight. She grinned, tracing a finger over the intricate carvings etched into the blade.

Roses and thorns, long overgrown, curled towards the hilt in slinking slowness. Wrapped amongst the thorns were three words, each carefully inscribed by her hand: *Forever in blood.* It was a mantra to Lyra, words to remind her of the world she lived in and the ones she had managed to escape. She sighed quietly, her gloved hands slithering across each letter.

It was one of the few items she had taken to the Pits and the only one that remained in her possession. Staying in the streets of Cerenia would have got her killed, but in the cavernous halls of Agonia, if you ever loosened your grip on what you held dear, it was as good as gone.

At the time, the Pits was a perfect hiding place for a girl like her. Anyone who had been—or wanted to be—forgotten by society could find a place in Agonia, sometimes without the choice.

She had only spent nine months there, far less than the average member, but as Harry Martyn said, Lyra had taken its rusted crown. The fight she had just won confirmed that she wouldn't let it fall from her grasp. Was that a part of the ruse? Or was that her true desire?

Among the turmoil of Cerenia's underworld were dozens of gangs and clans. Turf wars were more frequent than not, and the internal battle continued right under the Queen's nose. But it was the only way for many to survive, for those who slipped behind unnoticed by the general population and whose lives had turned to blood money.

Lyra and her clanswomen were just a part of that, fighting for control and establishing the all-female warriors called the Incarnatus. Lyra had named the clan after the mythic handmaidens of the goddess of death, Lady Rasthena. The real incarnatus were immortal beings who dictated where each soul went after death.

The clan's inception occurred when she was eighteen years old. She settled into the role of the leader with her closest companions, Astrid Shernev and Twylla Cometborn, at her side.

She took a piece of paper and a pencil from her trouser pocket. Quickly, she scribed a message: *Just won my first match, now everyone knows the Undefeated Champion is here. Yet it still feels like I should not have come alone.*

Once Lyra finished the note, she snapped her fingers, conjuring a spark of flame. If anyone else had seen it, they might have guessed it was the trick of the light, but no one would have suspected it to be a paper blaze. It cindered to ash, where the paper would arrive in Twylla's hands. It was their way of communicating. The paper was inlaid with Twylla's magic that was undetectable once alight. It helped to have a Cometborn witch as a friend.

Minutes later, a returning paper blaze formed in Lyra's palms. She unfolded it, the crisp paper cool to the touch despite being ashes only seconds before. She recognised Twylla's graceful scrawl that swooped and swirled through the ink: *I had no doubts about your victory, but you can still walk away if you desire. We can find another way to disrupt the Tournament, though this will be the most successful option. Astrid and I must remain here for the clan's sake because it isn't the Incarnatus the world wants to see; it's you. We would only get in the way.*

Lyra crumpled the note in her hand. All her Incarnatus would have been capable of entering the Tournament, but Lyra hated to admit that Twylla was right. To keep her ulterior motives hidden, the Incarnatus could not follow. Rival gangs might not notice Lyra absent from their missions, but if half of the nineteen clanswomen suddenly appeared at the Tournament as spectators or cooped up in a city inn together, suspicions would arise.

A cheer went through the courtyard, and Lyra looked up, past the fighting rings and the commoner stands, to the theatre boxes. Aristocrats huddled together in their plush confines, opera glasses allowing them clear sight of the matches. She scowled at them. *That* was why she was here, not to relive the past but to end its cycle. Her eyes drifted over every box, putting names to faces of all the nobles. Every single one was in attendance: the Ambroses, the Branigans, the Eastbows, the Glasswoods, the Greenfords, the Harrigots, the Holloways, the Whitehallows, and the Winterbrides. All ten province leaders were accounted for, with Queen Aurora Winthorpe finishing the list.

And one was looking right at her. The Duke of Clarmere, Castor Glasswood, met her scowl with the rise of his glass. Lyra's expression didn't change, but she lifted her chin, raising a challenge. *Spill your secrets, Castor. I know you have them.*

By the start of the next round, she had a messenger holding out a purple and blue armband and asking exactly what she wanted to hear.

"His Grace the Duke of Clarmere formally asks to sponsor you in the Tournament. Do you accept?"

8

NOX

"And that concludes the first set of matches, fighters!" Renner exclaimed, clapping his hands together. "You all fought well with no disqualifications necessary. Those who have lost will need to leave, and the second set of matches shall begin soon."

Nox couldn't stop the slight smirk from appearing on their face as they watched the losers of the first matches trudge out of the courtyard. One thousand fighters had entered, and now only five hundred remained. Nox could already imagine the bags of coins they would win.

Even so, hundreds still had to leave, and the smaller the number, the more complicated the decision would be. It already gave Nox a headache. They needed to focus on defeating their opponents, but boredom pressed into their skull like a knife. Even the shock of the Undefeated Champion of Agonia's attendance had worn thin.

Nox had never been to Agonia, but even in the underground dwellings of Ironhavell, Feynos' own fighting arenas, everyone knew who Lyra Avenyard was. That name was synonymous with victory, glory, and violence. Her match in the first round proved so, but Nox could already imagine all the ways they could beat her. Victory was the only reason they were here, but destroying an icon's title sounded like a nice touch.

With an exasperated sigh, Nox leaned back on the bench,

waiting for the drone of names to come. If they weren't fighting this round, they sure weren't planning to sit around.

Forty new fighters stood in the rings, none of them being Nox. They scowled, lurching upwards from where they sat to leave. Surprisingly, no one paid any mind to the werewolf who stalked past the benches and further into the courtyard.

They stole an apple from one of the servants and began to shave away its skin with a knife. The peel pirouetted to their feet, the perfect slices satisfying to watch fall. Nox finished the apple in three bites, the bitter aftertaste sharp on their tongue.

Tossing the core over their shoulder, Nox headed past small groups of men and women who lined the walls, murmuring amongst one another. Nox noticed an empty spot on the wall, perfect for them to lean against and complain more. But a moment later, two men claimed it, their shoulders hunched towards one another as they talked in hasty whispers.

Nox watched quietly, huffing to themself while the men's discussion turned almost feverish. They stalked towards the two, intrigued by the sudden change of tone. But before Nox reached the duo, the men had hurried off, disappearing through what seemed to be a crack in the wall.

It was barely noticeable from any angle. Only those who knew about it could detect the jagged scores in the stone wall. Yet, the markings were old, carved out by generations past. Whatever lay behind the wall intrigued Nox very much.

It took three steps for them to reach the gap, squeezing through its tight quarters so that its man-made carvings scraped against the length of their bow. Snaking across the floor were strings of paper that twisted and curled through the crack in the wall and back out into the courtyard. Nox ignored the strings and headed inside until they reached the end of the carved-out wall.

In the centre were six men, each crouched around a pile of what appeared to be firewood. The small space was exposed to the air, sunlight shining down, with the only entrances being three similar cracks in the wall. The shadows of the walkway provided a blanket of protection for Nox, allowing their eyes to adjust to the dim light as they watched the six.

However, the words they spoke were unknown to Nox, a foreign spill of lilting tones and short sentences. After spending all their years in impoverished hovels, Nox had never received the luxury of learning the tongues of the continents' nations and had barely been taught their own. An ugly feeling began to develop in their throat, a question entering their mind they wished not to be answered. What were these men doing here?

Nox's eyes widened, staggering back in revulsion as they finally realised. Scanning the six crouched men, it wasn't difficult to note the pale, gaunt faces and sunken-in eyes that all Kherian men and women possessed.

Nothing good could come from hiding within the courtyards' walls and speaking in hushed voices. Were these men soldiers, spies, or maybe just mercenaries paid off generously by the Kherian king? To do what? Nox scanned the rest of the vicinity, their heart hammering as they inspected the closed quarters.

It was the paper strings they paid the closest attention to, crouching to pick one up and sniff its contents.

Gunpowder.

Nox dropped it in surprise, finding what it was connected to. The pile of wood at the Kherian's feet was actually barrels, filled to the brim with even more of the explosive powder, the grey dust coating the men's fingers. It was a bomb plot. The entire ruling class was here, alongside their Queen, to watch the fearsome warriors of Darcan do battle. Destruction lay at the Kherians' feet; their foreign words no doubt those of malicious intent.

In the roaring silence of Nox's mind, they unsheathed their claws—still flaked with old blood—once more. It was like the beginning of the Tournament all over again, although this time, these men *needed* to die unless Nox wanted to be complicit in the death of thousands.

But as they leapt forward, already imagining a fresh coat of death to soak their claws, they were suddenly yanked backwards.

What are you doing? a familiar voice ripped into their head. Nox turned to find the mindspeaker—whose name they learnt to be Elias Hearth—glowering at them, his fist clenching the back of their shirt. How he'd managed to fit into the crack in the wall without them noticing, Nox was clueless. Instead, they scrabbled fitfully, trying to get out of his grasp and finish their plan.

Stop, he growled, holding their shirt collar tighter. *You were going to kill these men! What did I tell you!?*

"They're Kherians!" they hissed loudly enough for all to hear. Whatever discussion the Kherian spies were having halted, replaced with skittish whispers in the gunpowder-choked air. Nox's heart stopped. The element of surprise was lost.

"Shit," they cursed, meeting Elias' eyes and glaring at him. "Help me kill these men or watch this whole place burn."

Before he could make that choice, one of the Kherian spies appeared before them, eyes wide at the two of them. Nox bared their canines at him, growling but out of reach to kill him as Elias still held them aloft.

The spy yelled, his words a command that was quickly followed as the six men dispersed like rats fleeing a sinking ship. Elias dropped Nox, who tried to run forward and tear the barrels apart but found one of the men had remained. A flickering match in his hand.

"Corrupted One says you shall be first to burn," he spat in broken Darcanian before throwing the flame upon the gunpowder, where all hells broke loose.

The barrels combusted at first light, splinters of wood scattering across the Kherian as bellowing plumes of yellows and reds consumed him. The fuses upon the floor devoured the flames, sending more explosive matter down every entryway the Kherians had come through.

Nox fell back, landing hard on the stone floors as thick heat met them, only thinking of the many deaths that would come, including their own.

But the initial blaze erupting from the barrels met resistance. Elias stood in front of Nox, his hands open wide. As the gunpowder exploded, the wave of fire abruptly halted before Elias. He twisted his arms, and the blaze was sent spiralling into the sky. The perfect blue above them quickly turned to black, smoke framing their world into an unseeable haze.

Even as the flames flew upwards, the curling edges of the blaze slithered past Elias' control of the fire. The stench of burnt flesh erupted in Nox's nose before the pain did, and a sea of reds and oranges began to run across their skin. Already on the ground, they started to tense, eyes snapping shut as all their muscles went taut, every nerve in their body blazing in agony. Their claws extended, ripping through their flesh to distract themself from the pain.

With a snarl, Nox forced their eyes open, sitting up awkwardly. A sentence engraved in their mind flashed into focus, as did the destroyed world before them. *Pain is an illusion of death—to let it consume you is to be already dead.* It was a sentiment they could never forget. For a time, it was the only thing that kept them alive. Although it was the only feeling in their body, Nox was damned if they would let the pain destroy them, not now, not yet.

But the ground shook beneath their feet, and a crescendo of cracking filled their ears. Nox's eyes drifted to the skies, where the belching smoke dissipated for only a moment. It was at that moment that Nox realised they had not avoided death. No, because high in the sky, where the pearlescent spires had sparkled in absolute glory, chunks of marble and stone began to fall.

The symphony of screams that erupted throughout the Palace grounds fell on deaf ears as Nox was consumed by dust and debris.

9

AVERY

Avery hadn't understood Elias' insistence to leave, even as her name was called for the first match. She couldn't watch him go as she descended the stairs of the benches, flitting towards the fighting rings. After bringing Elias out of his gloom, they spent the rest of the first round quietly betting on the rest of the fights. Elias' judgement was impeccable, as he correctly predicted who would win every match. It was strange, to say the least.

She guessed it was because of his telepathy, something that concerned Avery more than she liked. Every time he glanced in her direction, she couldn't help but fear the invasion of her mind. Controlling him to stop his intrusions would only work in bursts, and every time her compulsion would fade, he could find her memories of controlling him. In order for this alliance to work, Avery doubted he would appreciate being puppeteered at every given moment.

And yet, it still felt unnatural for a phoenix-blood to possess telepathy. She'd never heard of it before. The only species Avery was aware of having such flawless mind powers were the witches. They resided in the Klyvning Swamps, where seven queendoms separated the witches by power. Avery couldn't remember all the names, but the Thoughtsingers stuck out best to her.

Depending on the witch, they could perform an array of mind powers: telepathy, telekinesis, mind control, and mindspeaking, to name a few. Elias possessed two of those, but male-born witches were rare, and he was most definitely a phoenix-blood, so how could any of this align?

Her previous assumptions that he wasn't from Darcan had been wrong, which also concerned her. He had lived in this kingdom for centuries and possessed a perfect Darcanian accent, so had he also lived through the Phoenix Wars? Was she colluding with the enemy who had destroyed her second home? She didn't believe so, not after he said his own village had been burned to the ground—making him not an enemy but a fellow victim of that hateful war.

Avery flexed her fingers, stealing one last look around the courtyard to find him, but the crowd had gobbled him up. She swallowed unevenly, her tongue like a lead weight in her mouth as dehydration began to sink in once more. She wished she'd had the chance to take another drink and save herself from the dread that spooled in her stomach. But it was too late now; winning this match was her only priority.

Her name was one of the last to be called, so she chose a ring occupied by a woman. Avery recognised the platinum braid that snaked down her back and those hard green eyes. But the woman's name and her previous match were less than a whisper in Avery's mind.

It appeared to be the same for the woman as she asked, "Your name?"

Avery scanned her with narrowed eyes before answering, "Avery Nash, and yours?"

"Lyra Avenyard."

It clicked, then. This was the woman who had fought with only her fists, becoming victorious with barely a blow upon her pretty face. Elias had decided from the moment she'd shown off her sword she would win.

And, of course, he had been right as she left her opponent a slobbering mess. Throughout the match, Elias swore she was *enjoying* destroying the boy. Her eyes had been aglow, with a determined grin lifting her cheeks. She was an obvious threat, which only meant Avery did not have the slightest chance of beating Lyra Avenyard in a fair fight. Even if Avery were armed to the teeth and her opponent empty-handed, it would not be the mortal who would fall.

"What rules do you propose?" Avery asked, flexing her fingers again.

Lyra's eyes fell upon Avery's daggers and smiled. "Blades allowed, powers not."

Avery's stomach twinged; she couldn't possibly disagree with the rules, for otherwise, everyone would look for the powers she possessed. Hopefully, neither this mortal woman nor the referees of the match would notice her mental manipulation; or else, the Tournament was as good as over. She and Elias still hadn't devised a plan, only that they both needed to complete today's matches successfully to keep Torr off her back. Avery regarded the woman, and she forced herself not to scowl. Why did she have to walk into *this* ring?

"I agree to those terms," she replied finally, unsheathing a dagger.

Those green eyes sparkled with delight. "Good luck, Avery Nash."

A sentiment I can't return, she thought bitterly.

Their referee stepped out of the ring. "Weapons are allowed in this match while powers are not. Let the match begin!"

Lyra prowled forward, the cloak no longer on her shoulders and the longsword gripped between her fingers.

The mortal slashed quickly, the blade inches away from Avery's face as she managed to fall backwards. With her dagger, their weapons clashed in a spray of sparks that set Lyra's eyes alight once more.

But she fell back, avoiding Avery's low swipe to the legs. Lyra moved like quicksilver, dodging every stab and slice. Laughter hummed from her, an infuriating smile playing on her lips. Sweat began to glisten on Avery's forehead after every laboured attempt to hit her. Barely a minute had passed, and both remained unharmed.

"You possess a power, don't you?" Lyra asked suddenly as the two stood at opposite sides of the ring. "It's why you grimaced at my rules, and yet you agreed to the terms."

"I need to give you a fighting chance, don't I?" Avery panted, not entirely understanding the woman's words. "And besides, one day, those powers may be stripped away from me when I need them most. To be unprepared for that moment is a sure way to die."

Immediately, Torr came to mind. He deflected her powers, but with Elias' help, her blades would sink deep into the assassin's flesh. But no one could help Avery right now. Torr would only die so long as she took down this mortal first.

"I like you," was the response, a new smile upon Lyra's face. "We both want to win, and we both could. But it seems you'll be disqualified before that happens."

It was Avery's turn to laugh. "Do you think I would try to use my powers? Win the match through cheating?"

Lyra dashed forward then, throwing a knife at impossible speeds. Avery dodged the flying blade, only to have its owner smash the hilt of her sword into her skull. Darkness swarmed Avery's vision as she dropped like a stone, barely able to use her blade as a block from Lyra's sword.

Inches away from her face, the mortal woman's words only fell upon her ears, "I know you would. Because you already have."

Avery's eyes darkened, the gathering storm within the watery blue of her irises drawing her powers into full clarity. But Lyra did not baulk at the sight; instead, she drove her sword further onto Avery's dagger that it began to dig into flesh, a dark smile ringing her smooth face.

"As I said, I knew it," she murmured as blood began to soak Avery's shirt, pain shooting through every nerve. "Manipulate me; I dare you."

But those words, laden with the inescapable grip of the Siren, were never spoken. The ground beneath them started to shudder violently, toppling Lyra off Avery in a second.

Avery stayed crouched on the ground, eyes scanning the vicinity for the cause of the noise. Whispers and questions fluttered through the courtyard while the spectator stands fluctuated with agitated movement.

The moment of quietness was destroyed by the explosive blow of something igniting. A sudden belch of thick smoke ripped through the air, flames of devastating beauty setting the world before them alight as debris began to rain down on the courtyard. Avery shuddered on the ground, the explosion sending jitters through her body. She looked up at the stands and couldn't believe her eyes.

The courtyard walls caved in and shattered into oblivion at the stress of the explosions, pitching the stands to the ground in a plume of dust and debris. Unadulterated screams joined the cacophony of deafening noise as solid chunks of marble and stone descended from the spiralling towers of the Palace.

Spectators crawling out of the ruined stands were the

first crushed by the first impact of debris, staining the world in red while shattered pieces flew through the air, finding new targets to destroy.

Avery staggered to her knees despite her body's protests. Buckling behind the two women within the haze of grey smoke was an entire tower. Its spire fell in horrifying silence, so close that Avery could see the pearly etchings upon its surface.

There was no escape.

Even if she ran to avoid the initial blow, the after-effects of its impact would still be impossible to escape. She already imagined the dust consuming her, filling her lungs as the debris crushed her bones.

Avery collapsed to the floor, eyes wide. Her powers were useless, her immortal grace a waste. Today, she would die.

Darkness filled her vision, but not from the spire's shadows. Violet stars decorated the sudden infinite black that swarmed her. Lyra knelt before Avery, the mortal's hands grabbing her arms in such a deathly tight grip she flinched. Purple light edged around Lyra's frame as her brows creased with concern, causing a glittering darkness of fantastical beauty to curl around Avery.

"Trust me," Lyra whispered as the two shattered into nothing but stars.

10

ELIAS

Elias had always hoped for a painless death, one so swift there could never have been a way to stop it. The falling debris above him didn't seem like one of those. It was certainly unavoidable in every way but not painless. Especially as an immortal, his suffering would be outstretched far longer than everyone else before death truly claimed him.

And yet, it *was* painless.

Because Elias realised he wasn't dying.

He sucked in a breath, fresh and clear despite the thick plumes of ash and dust that surrounded him. Marble cracked above him, making him flinch at the harsh sound. Looking up, Elias saw the crumbling white stone landing on an invisible ceiling he was standing underneath.

Through the sound of debris cracking, Elias heard the incessant cursing of a particular werewolf. Turning, he found Nox kneeling on the ground with one arm in the air and their fist clenched so tightly that blood trailed down their palm. More stone collapsed upon the ceiling that they had conjured. Elias couldn't help but smile, amazement thrumming through his body.

I didn't know you could manipulate air, he said to Nox.

Sweat broke out on the werewolf's face as they growled, "You don't know *anything* about me."

It was true, and yet Elias wondered if that would soon change.

The hardened air above them flickered, and Nox paled considerably as ash filtered through the cracks in the ceiling. They shook uncontrollably, claws outstretched as their fist unclenched.

We need to go, Elias demanded. *You're going to pass out soon.*

"Fuck off."

It was at that moment that Nox fell over, eyes rolling to the back of their head as unconsciousness took over. It was Elias' turn to curse as the ceiling of hardened air truly dissipated, leaving the two exposed to the dregs of falling debris. He ran towards the fallen werewolf to protect their vulnerable frame just as the ground started to vibrate.

Elias had no time to think as he grabbed Nox's unconscious body and carried them out of the hulled-out space. Only a moment after clearing the exit, the walls finally collapsed, sending up another cloud of thick dust into the smoky air.

As his vision cleared and the courtyard returned into view, Elias realised they were not alone.

Men dressed in black leather started to leap over the fallen walls. Elias recognised the clothing as the same as the men who had set the Palace to blow. Nox had said they were Kherians, but what were mortals from Darcan's neighbouring kingdom doing here? Elias had only ever seen the relationship between the nations as neither positive nor negative, just a simple stalemate of ignoring one another.

This seemingly infinite sea of heavily armed soldiers suggested otherwise.

Until one of them spoke, in clear, unbroken Darcanian, *"For the nobles of Darcan!"*

Elias frowned, looking up at the theatre boxes that held the nobles. Despite the destruction, they stood mainly unharmed. Not only that, but they were empty. The Queen's royal box also stood unafflicted by the chaos, but gripping its railing was Captain of the Queensguard. Just what was going on?

Renner jumped out of the theatre box, his sword swinging through the air. "You've attacked my Queen and her people," he yelled at the attackers. "I do not care for your motives, not when you are about to die. Queensguard! With me!"

Elias couldn't think about it anymore as the cries that filled the courtyard became punctuated by the slashing of steel. The surviving guardsmen followed after their captain, two forces of silver and black colliding in battle.

Panic filled Elias. Even if he didn't truly understand who the enemy was, he knew he had to save these people. With Nox still in his arms, he had no choice but to drop them to the ground. The werewolf slumped against a broken slab of stone, still breathing unevenly.

Elias gave Nox one last look before unsheathing his greatsword in one gliding movement, setting it to flame like a beacon. Unlike his earlier opponent, he was more than ready to burn these men to ash.

A single slash had three torn in half, flesh sizzling in Elias' wake. The 'noble sympathisers' had no chance to parry the blazing sword as their own weapons melted beneath it at first touch, allowing Elias to cut the men to pieces. Before long, the surviving soldiers had skittered away, disappearing in search of easier targets. The guardsmen followed, jeering and bellowing until silence descended once more. Elias slumped inwardly, eyes now scanning the ruined courtyard.

The twenty rings were indiscernible by the blood and shattered stone that littered the open space. Bodies scattered the cobblestones, each too bludgeoned to recognise who they once were. A pounding filled Elias' head as he remembered Avery. She had entered the rings for her fight when he left.

And now she was gone.

He wanted to shut down, the ruin before him turning him hollow. Everything was gone; everyone was gone. All because he'd stopped Nox from saving them all.

Elias fell to his knees, unsure what to think, until a new voice thundered in his mind.

Gods above, save me! Help me, please! I don't want to die!

A cry for help from someone unable to speak aloud but still screamed inwardly nonetheless. Elias staggered forward like a drunkard, searching for the one who cried amongst the misery.

A young woman lay half-crushed beneath a rock, her free hand trembling in anguish. Elias recognised her as one of the magic healers; she could save every injured being here, but not herself.

The gods were cruel, cutting down those who could bring prosperity into the world. The cycle of corruption was palpable at the helm of Lady Attalin, undeserving of such a divine title and the misery she brings. The Kingdom of Darcan believed in the Order of the Seven Deities, but sometimes it felt like they could never return that sentiment.

He didn't hesitate as he grabbed the corner of the rock and heaved it upward. The healer shook violently, blood escaping the gaping wound on her chest. But she was free, which was enough for him as he bent down and uncorked a bottle.

Centuries ago, when his life was at its best, Elias learnt more of the unending magic of this world. Kalla Thoughtsinger was a witch who had given him so many gifts, one of which was the magic of witch blood. Depending on the potion or recipe, witch blood could create all types of power for good or bad.

Everywhere he went, he brought the tincture of healing solution. It worked only in small bursts, one bottle a full dosage. He'd made it with his own hands, his own blood. It wasn't something of the phoenix-bloods, but now it was something of Elias.' His telepathy and mindspeaking might have been more obvious, but Elias always treasured the witch blood that now ran through his veins.

The solution was precious; its power was deadly if administered to the wrong person. Only the creators of this potion should take it, but the healer's refusal to accept her fate told him she could survive and *thrive* in this. Gods and witches be damned.

He tipped the blood-red liquid into her open mouth. A few seconds was all it took for the healer's wounds to disappear, the blood upon her skin no longer flowing as her crushed bones began to reform. She rose with a steady grace Elias hadn't imagined and started to run. Her movements were precise despite the littered courtyard as she began searching through the unmoving bodies as if she could sense those still living.

The healer collapsed to the ground in front of a heaping of smashed rock. "Help me," her voice barely a whisper from her screams. "I can save him. His heart still beats."

Elias' strength was not wasted as he pulled the rock from

the crushed frame of one of the fighters. Blood splattered his shirt and armour, painting a grim picture. And yet, the unsteady rise and fall of his chest was all the healer needed as she planted her red-stained palms onto his skin. Her body shook with the effort, her power flowing through the man's veins as every wound he possessed slowly sealed.

He sat up with a hacking cough, splattering blood onto the healer's apron. She didn't seem to care as she clasped his face.

"You will *not* die today," she rasped, a smile blooming on her features. She turned to Elias then, her face hardening. "There are still more alive."

He nodded. *Let's save everyone we can.*

The two worked in quick succession. The healer—whose name he learned to be Erinna—closed every blood wound and fixed every broken bone she could while Elias pulled the survivors to safety. With her magic soon spent, she cried with joy as they found her sister, Sowenna, another healer of the Palace whose heart was still beating. After embracing, she took over the healing, allowing Erinna to rest and comfort those she had saved.

Once they had recovered the rest of the living, Sowenna swept away all the burns on Nox's body before finally bringing them back to consciousness. But the werewolf had a dagger at her throat and a snarl on their lips before they opened their eyes.

Sowenna swallowed back a scream, skittering away from them as Elias smacked the dagger out of their hand. *She's a healer!* he barked at them. *The sympathisers are gone—for now.*

"Sympathisers?" Nox echoed, reclaiming their dagger. "What the hells are you talking about?"

Elias did his best to explain, but the werewolf wanted nothing of it. Shaking their head, Nox grabbed their fallen bow and arrows.

"I know a Kherian when I see one," they spat. "Could you understand what they were saying? Why would Kherians root for Darcan's nobility? But not the Queen? Don't the Kherians have nobles of their own?"

Sowenna, who'd been listening, mumbled, "King Theron killed them all a decade or so ago, keeping the children captive in his court."

Nox pointed at her. "See! Even more reason for them to root for their own! These aren't sympathisers; they're Kherians playing you all for fools. I'm not depending on you lot to ensure that I won't die. Everyone here is a liability. I'm going."

Where? Elias asked.

"Where do you think? I'm going to find those rats and *kill them all.*"

There are probably hundreds.

They scoffed at that. "Like that would stop me."

Nox began to skulk out of the destroyed courtyard; eyes focused only on what was ahead. Elias sighed heavily, slumping to the ground as the werewolf hopped over the fallen debris with ease, notching an arrow in the process. He knew it best to stay in the courtyard if the sympathisers attacked again, so all he could do was hope that Nox would remain safe.

Erinna began calling for Elias and Sowenna; she'd found another survivor hidden amongst the rubble. He rose unsteadily, eyes dark as he pulled more men and women into safety. The healers' touch was a blessing as their wounds were sewn shut. Every time he saw one of those faces, Elias couldn't help but check to see if it was Avery, who still breathed beneath the dust, fighting for life like so many. But it never was. As the number of trapped survivors dwindled, he stared into the empty eyes of the corpses, none resembling those blue irises trapped in a storm.

It was as if she had disappeared from the courtyard completely—escaping the destruction unscathed. Or so he hoped.

The healers beside Elias panted heavily, every drop of power spent on the thirty-two that now stood above him. Thousands had entered the Tournament's halls, whether for entertainment or participation. Yet, the grip of death had its way, a single flame crippling the heart of the kingdom into destruction—a masterful plan, one that continued.

Elias opened his mindspeaking to everyone around him. *We need to head somewhere safe. Save whom we can and find out who these attackers are.*

Confusion filled the group, and he found more than one estranged look directed his way. Through his telepathy, Elias read the thoughts of the men and women who had already suffered enough. *No. I can't. I won't. I want to go home and never come back. We can't do this.*

But they weren't given a choice.

Explosions ripped through the air, scattering the courtyard with a fresh layer of dust. Sowenna screamed, grabbing her sister's hand as the two dashed out of the open space. Panic drove everyone towards the two, running to where they hoped it was safe. Elias' palms warmed, fire flickering through his veins as he waited for the attack. It was too precise of a blow to be anything but a way to draw them out. It was clever and cunning but also fuelled by arrogance, which Elias was more than ready to sputter out.

Steel shrieked against sheaths as the soldiers dressed in black met the thirty-five of them. Greedy grins flecked with spilt blood met the haggard survivors' faces of terror. Elias' hands erupted into pure flame, sending a wave towards the so-called sympathisers.

We have to fight! He roared, meeting his people's eyes. *Together.*

11

LYRA

Lyra always thought the void should be cold, cutting through your skin like a vice and stealing the air in your lungs. But it was nothingness; it was pure oblivion.

And they were falling through it.

Avery clung to Lyra fiercely; her head ducked down. The pair careened through the darkness haphazardly. There was nothing to hold onto in their maddened descent through the void. Violet stars rushed past in the darkness, showering Lyra and Avery in a galaxy of empty space. Swarming together through the black, purple doorways appeared before dissipating a moment later.

Lyra's fists were clenched, bunching up the fabric of Avery's bloodied shirt as she pulled all her concentration into their escape. Entering the void was much easier than leaving it, especially when accompanied. She already had an idea of where she wanted to go, the thought having bloomed in her mind before she had let the void consume them. But in past excursions, she had found herself in very different places.

Lyra's brows scrunched together as a doorway surged towards them, the purple light curling to claim their bodies. Avery tensed further—the edge of her daggers digging into Lyra's back—as they smashed out of the void and into brightness once more.

They landed ungracefully with a clatter of weapons. Lyra laid on her back with Avery still holding onto her chest, their limbs tangled together. Lyra huffed a sigh of relief, recognising the Palace gates. The iron-wrought entryway was wide open, and the vicinity was deserted. The tables the advisors had been sitting behind earlier were turned over and smouldering. Not a single guard was in sight, leaving the Palace totally defenceless.

Avery peeled herself away from Lyra and stood up. Her limbs shook so much that it looked like she would drop her daggers. Lyra also rose to her feet, and when their eyes met, she gave Avery a mischievous grin. Despite the landing, it was quite a successful trip to the void and back, lifting her spirits in a way she'd not experienced in a while.

She walked toward the Palace gates, grabbing the hulking metal and pulling them to a close. Without any guards standing watch, she didn't like the idea of leaving the front door unlocked. Satisfied, she turned back to Avery, who now had her daggers raised at Lyra.

"What," she began, her lip curling into a snarl, "in Famara's name *was that*!?"

The spark in Lyra's eyes died as she averted her gaze. "The void," she said. "It's not something I can explain. Nor do we particularly have the time for me to do so. All I can ask of you is to keep quiet about it."

"What sort of *mortal* has a power such as that?"

Lyra huffed a laugh, forcing herself to meet Avery's eyes once more. "Guess I was correct. You *are* immortal." She spied the waterskin tied to the woman's waist. "A naiad?"

"If you dare tell anyone that, I will—"

"You don't need to make threats," Lyra interjected. "You have my secret, and I have yours. For either of us to spill them would lead to our untimely deaths. Are we in agreement?"

Avery straightened, all emotions disappearing from her face as she lowered her blades. "Fine," she huffed. "We are in agreement. But what did you mean by us not having the time?"

"The explosion," Lyra replied, eyes dragging towards the smoke that stained the sky. "I took us here to avoid our deaths, but if there's a chance we could help—"

"*I'm* not going back in there," Avery snapped. "It's a death trap."

"Don't you care? People are dying; we can save them!"

"I don't need to care; mortals come and go."

"Oh yeah?" Lyra arched a brow. "What about the mortal who just *saved* your life?" She shook her head. "During our match, I said I liked you; you're a keen fighter with more intellect than half the people here. Out of hundreds, I chose to save you; don't make me regret it."

The naiad opened her mouth—no doubt to retort—but before she could reply, a chorus of steel and heavy-pounding boots filled the air. Suddenly, men dressed in black leathers appeared from the opposite side of the otherwise deserted Palace gates.

Lyra knew the uniform of every Guard of Darcan. The Common Guard wore sturdy brown leather armour, the nobles liked their Noblesguard dressed in the garish colours of their banners, and the Queensguard always wore hulking steel. Whoever these black-leathered men were, they did not come from any Darcanian garrison.

Lyra's heartbeat leapt up as she counted at least a dozen mercenaries. Helmets shielded their faces, and their swords were already unsheathed. They had not come to help the wounded from the blast. They were here for death.

The mercenaries halted at the sight of Lyra and Avery, who stood in their way.

"Move!" one of the mercenaries boomed. "This is for the nobles of Darcan! Get out of the way before we end you!"

His Darcanian was flawless, but Lyra recognised the accent. The Kherians had a delicate lilt to their tongue, but surely that was only a coincidence. And yet, Lyra knew the nobles would never hire a Kherian native.

Lyra's fingers itched for her longsword. From the Kherian's words, the nobility had orchestrated the blast that destroyed half the spectator stands and ruptured a tower. Now, the foreign mercenaries were here to finish off the slaughter. The battle had only begun, but Lyra was ready to see it through.

The odds weren't perfect, but with an immortal at her side, Lyra could see them making easy work of the dozen before them. Her optimistic trail of thought tapered when she saw Avery sheathe her daggers.

"What are you doing?" Lyra hissed as the men regarded the pair. Thankfully, she hadn't yet grabbed her sword, but the soldiers would attack any minute now.

"Take us away from here. Void us." Avery crossed her arms.

"And leave the Palace defenceless?! You're as stupid as you are old."

Lyra didn't give Avery any time to answer before she attacked, death singing in her bones. Her longsword cut through the first three like wheat in a field. The element of surprise kept her unscathed, but her instincts and skill brought the world to her feet. Lyra's braid whipped around as she dodged every hardened blow, their steel meeting only air while hers met flesh and bone.

"You don't even know who these people are, and yet you attack so blindly!?" Avery's voice was only just audible within the roaring of blood in Lyra's ears.

It was true. The soldiers claimed to be for the nobles, but what sort of motive was that? Who would willingly fight *for* the nobility and not the Queen? Lyra had had her fair share of aristocrats and knew they deserved much less than even the air to breathe. And the purposeful omission of Queen Aurora's name must only mean that these mercenaries were not to be trusted.

The Tournament had taken a darker turn. Didn't the nobles *want* the rabble to fight for their entertainment? Why slaughter them all now? Lyra's thoughts moved too fast to think of answers, and all it did was slow her attacks down.

The Palace gates were shut, but in the corner of her eye, Lyra saw mercenaries peel away from the group to wrench them open. Not only that, but her count of twelve men had accelerated to an innumerable blur. The twelve were just the first wave, and the rest were coming to take their claim in the bloodshed.

Countering a sword strike, she was glad to see that Avery had finally joined the fray, though hardly. Her twin daggers slashed the shins of only those who moved close to her. Lyra cursed. The odds were tipping against them.

She skittered away from the men, allowing the glittering dark of the void to consume her. Quick flitterings into the void were easier to control as she slipped from one pocket of reality to another. She had barely disappeared for a second before landing on the shoulders of a soldier, slitting his throat with a knife. Lyra voided away once more, standing back to back with Avery, who was murmuring words beneath her breath.

"Fight for me," the naiad commanded.

The soldier whose sword had intended to chop her in half halted, suddenly swinging the blade to meet with one of his comrades.

"Glad to see you've decided to help me," Lyra huffed. "And I *was* right; you can control the mind."

"I can't exactly leave without *your* powers," Avery gritted out, sweat framing her forehead. "Come on, let's *go.*"

"No can do."

Lyra disappeared in a flurry of purple light before she could hear Avery's protests. Reappearing before the gates, she cut out the throat of a man trying to open the way into the Palace. As she flitted back, Lyra kept an eye on the naiad. Avery manipulated another soldier to support them, her honeyed words inaudible within the clash of swords.

Lyra almost took a blade to the throat when she saw Avery sheathe her daggers. The naiad stood between her manipulated soldiers, hands hanging to her sides. A second later, her fingers flexed, and a manhole a few feet away began to rattle. Lyra took out the man closest to her and backed up a pace. The manhole's contents shuddered with tremendous effort as the woman who controlled the sewer water clenched her fist.

The swarm flooded the vicinity immediately, dragging the men at the gates down the streets in an inescapable pull. Lyra couldn't help but stop, admiring the display for half a second, enjoying the realisation that the naiad she stood with had so much more power than anyone could ever imagine.

Lyra continued to slash soldiers down with brutal efficiency, a tally of the dead on her lips as she avoided the manipulated ones who defended Avery. The streets became slick with water, thankfully clearing away the gore of the battle in a stream of pink and brown. She continued voiding to meet the soldiers, the violet stars creating a kaleidoscope of colour in her vision.

Avery cried out, her voice cutting across the clash of steel so that Lyra could only watch as she crashed to the ground, blood pouring from the arm she cradled. Immediately, six soldiers descended on the fallen immortal, and her manipulated men were unable to hold back the bringers of death. She sent a wave of sewer water to her aid, forcing back three of the men. But it only slowed down the inevitable as a sword became drenched in shimmering immortality.

Death no longer sang in Lyra's bones. It was now survival. She couldn't leave this world, not yet, not ever. And neither could the naiad whose life she had just saved.

Lyra cut two more soldiers into ruin and ran towards Avery, whose body had been overwhelmed by the mass of corpses. The soldier who stabbed Avery bellowed in victory, his sword swinging in the air. Lyra's own blade came to meet him, to fight him, to *destroy* him.

But her target became no more.

An arrow of silent brutality ripped through the air. The shining arrowhead embedded itself into the soldier with such force that the cobblestones beneath him shattered. Lyra didn't care for the archer, didn't care that the man's blood soaked the ruptured arrow and its splintered pieces. She pulled through the heaving mass of bodies, fingers searching for the naiad whose heart *had* to continue beating.

But her actions were for nought as a dagger ripped its way through Lyra's left thigh. Pain shot up every nerve in her body, the blood hot against her sweating skin as she fell into the heaving mass. She hadn't worn much armour on her legs, prioritising easy movement over complete protection. The Royal Tournament had never hinted at this level of danger, and now it was going to get her killed. Another blade swiped at her throat, grazing the gambeson she wore beneath her breastplate as she shunted to the left, her movements clumsy and sluggish.

Her assailant was suddenly knocked out of the way, the fear in his eyes almost palpable as he disappeared from view. Instead, all Lyra saw was a lean figure drop to the ground. They had been perched on the Palace gates, but now they had come to join the rabble.

More arrows flew through the air, taking out mercenaries faster than Lyra could track. She struggled to her feet, every limb shaking as she applied pressure to the wound on her leg. Looking around, she saw Avery cleave through the mass of corpses, sitting up only to cough up a mouthful of blood. The fresh wound on her stomach bled profusely, exposing only the slightest of skin amongst the mass of red.

Her voice was hoarse as blood choked the strength usually found in her words. "I need my waterskin."

Lyra didn't ask any questions, though many were buried on her tongue as she grasped the bloodied waterskin from Avery's hip. Lyra knew of its contents. It was from the body of water the naiad had been formed by. Lyra unscrewed the lid, handing the waterskin back to Avery.

With shaking hands, Avery splashed the liquid onto her stomach, hissing in pain as it made contact. But through the heavy blood flow, Lyra watched as the stab wound began to shrink, clearing away the worst of it in an instant.

"This is only temporary," Avery said. "I need a healer."

Even without a full explanation, Lyra understood the water's power. "We'll go to the Palace," she said. "There must be healers there. Stay here; I'll finish this."

Lyra picked up her sword, barely able to stand as blood ran down her leg, and turned to face the men she would need to end. But instead, she found the archer doing what she had intended to.

Ice-blue eyes met hers, their canines shining as they gave her an unnerving grin. With a jolt, she recognised the werewolf—the one from before the Tournament—now shooting the soldiers into pieces, three arrows at a time, every bolt hitting its mark.

She stumbled into the fray, avoiding the silent arrows that flew through the air. Her sword clashed with any who dared come near, blood and gore decorating her skin while the werewolf remained untouched, no soldier surviving long enough to reach them.

Their numbers dwindled completely so that the archer with the scarred smile loosed their last bolt and left the remaining survivor for her. Lyra obliged, driving her sword through flesh and bone in a sluggishly downward swipe that the blade slammed into the cobblestones.

"Thank the gods," she breathed, death no longer curling at her heels.

"Don't thank *them*, thank *me*. I saved your sorry asses," the werewolf snarled.

"No, I think I will thank the gods that you weren't shooting at *us*," Avery muttered, her voice carrying across the desolate streets.

Lyra clumsily sheathed her sword, silencing the growls that guttered from the werewolf. Aches reverberated through her body at the movement, but she ignored it and surveyed the carnage.

Her boots were stained black, gore clotting the ground as blood dripped down her shirt. Lyra's eyes wandered across the bodies before them; she had become accustomed to the stench of killing and its aftermath, even in such vast quantities. But only three people had caused this destruction, the deaths of almost four dozen soldiers.

It brought a devilish grin onto Lyra's face.

"Stop smiling like an idiot; we need to go," Avery grounded out, staggering to her feet despite her wounds.

Lyra opened her mouth to answer, but the werewolf butted in first, "As a matter of fact, *I* shall be taking my leave. I'd rather not have to save you again."

They had finished retrieving all their salvageable arrows, hands now bloodied. Lyra couldn't help but notice they'd taken a helping of the dead soldiers' daggers, now tucked away in the werewolf's sheaths. They stalked away, heading towards the Palace, where they scampered up the gates without hesitation. Lyra's gut twisted—for the werewolf to return to the Palace grounds would mean more trespassers were inside.

Still, Lyra grinned. "Charming, huh?"

"Like you care," Avery replied. "Now, to the Palace."

She pouted. "Only if we bring your lackeys with us."

Sure enough, Avery's manipulated soldiers remained standing. Their task to fight for the naiad had been fulfilled for now. She was about to reply when twin arrows shot through the air, cleaving through the throats of the men. The soldiers crumpled completely, their frames turning limp as blood splattered onto Lyra's face.

There was only a moment of silence before she burst out

laughing, her voice echoing across the desolate street. Avery's body slumped in defeat, pressing her palms into her eyes. Lyra clutched her stomach, ignoring the pain running rife beneath her skin as she continued to grin.

"Guess we can't bring them, huh?"

"You're insufferable," Avery groaned, tipping her head back. "I leave the Forest for one day, and everything goes to hell."

"Thank the gods I was here to watch."

"Shut it, mortal. We almost died five minutes ago, and you're laughing!" Avery cried.

"Well, let's go do that again, *naiad*. Maybe the werewolf will show up again to save our sorry *asses*. Now, to the Palace!" Lyra began rubbing her bloodstained hands together, conjuring darkness between her fingertips.

Within an instant, the two women disappeared, leaving only the void curling at the cracked cobblestones and bloodied corpses.

12

NOX

Blood was everywhere—in these two women's hair, on their clothes, and all over their skin. It distorted anything about their appearance that could be recognisable, and so Nox decided not to care.

All that snagged Nox's attention was how little the bloodshed had seemed to faze the women. It explained enough to Nox that this hadn't been the first time either of them had felt the life of another drain through their fingers like sand. Nox grinned, hiding the churning feeling in their stomach at the memory of when they had first spilt blood.

It, too, had been everywhere, matted in their hair, drying beneath their claws, and dripping slowly down the walls. They hadn't realised just how much blood two bodies could contain, how much could spray out with one small blow from a child who had already seen too much.

Nox returned to reality, still walking through the Palace gates, before noticing the two silent men who stood beside the women as they talked quietly. With a huff, Nox drew their bow again with two arrows slotted onto its string before marking their targets.

The Kherians fell like a dead weight, just as they deserved. No matter what Elias said, these men *were* Kherian; every single one of them just *had* to be. Why else would their eyes haunt Nox in the dark of night?

Blood spurted from the soldiers, noticeably showering the taller woman with even more gore. Nox couldn't help but grin, imagining her getting angered by their actions.

Instead, she laughed.

Nox stopped walking, feet halting as her voice skittered across their bones. A strange woman, indeed. The two continued to converse, though too low for even Nox's heightened senses to hear well. Snatches of words flittered by, *insufferable, mortal, Palace*, giving them little to care about. But then, despite their grumblings to one another, they clasped forearms and disappeared into nothingness.

Nox's jaw went slack. Only a fizzing of purple remained in the air, glittering darkness dissipating in their wake.

They had seen all kinds of magic, all kinds of power in mortals and immortals alike, and yet Nox had never seen *anything* like that; it left a sour taste in their mouth. Shaking off the shock, they continued, forcing themself to forget the curlings of power still lingering there.

Nox counted their weapons: sixteen arrows in their quiver, seven daggers lifted from the Kherian corpses, and their own assortment of blades. Their knives clacked against one another, a satisfying sound to behold in the desolate open space of the Palace grounds. They hadn't walked this way to the courtyards, which were little more than mounds of rubble, but they now headed to what they guessed would be the entrance into the Queen's home. The blast's effect was less seen here, with only dashings of ash upon the manicured bushes lining the cobbled promenade. It was wide enough to fit two carriages beside one another, no doubt what its actual use was, not for lone archers itching for blood.

Stables and servant halls stood behind the bushes as if in an attempt to hide the lower orders who resided in the enormous Palace. But with the hundreds who did live there, Nox couldn't help but wonder where they had gone.

Maybe they were all dead.

They halted as another sound rang in the silence. It was not the satisfying clack of *their* blades; it was of scraping steel against the cobblestones. Slow and careless, almost as if the owner of the blade was enjoying the stretched-out movements and the fear it could create as a sword dragged its way towards death.

A moment later, the stench of fresh blood bloomed. The unwavering coppery scent made Nox's vision turn red. They headed towards it, guided only by their nose before laughter curled through their ears. Sick enjoyment edged those voices, fuelled the slow scrapings of the sword, and conjured the muffled cries that slipped through the cracks, barely audible.

Nox's pace quickened, holding their bow in hand once more as they surveyed the area. They'd stepped off the promenade, away from the Palace and deeper into the endless rows of servant halls, each identical in size and appearance. With every step, those sounds of misery heightened, with no end for the tormented.

Nox wasn't a stranger to death; they did not fear ending the lives of countless faces nor the chance of their own demise. But the enjoyment of that continual torment was a savagery they could not bear but still knew like an old friend.

They snarled at the sight of seven Kherian men. Crumpled beneath the soldiers' leering stares were nine women, all gagged and bloodied. Maids of the Palace, no doubt, fleeing from the chaos, only to meet it at knifepoint.

One moment, the Kherians were enjoying themselves, snickering at one another. The next, they met the eyes of Nox. Those last moments alive were stolen away before any blade could be drawn, silent arrows hitting their mark. Seven men lay dead before Nox's feet, blood staining the cobblestones. The maids screamed beneath their gags louder than before. It was at the sight of Nox, scarred and bloodied that they feared—the one who had saved them. Nox's blood turned cold.

They pulled a knife out, its blade winking in the sunlight. It skittered across the stones, meeting the quivering maids' feet.

"If you don't want my help, then you won't get it," they barked, pulling out several of their arrows from the Kherian corpses before stalking away.

The sound of ripping fabric filled Nox's ears, the sharp blade no doubt making easy work of the bindings upon the women's wrists and ankles. The nine talked erratically to one another, their words still loud enough for Nox to hear despite the distance between them.

"We need to go to the Palace! This is Protocol Black!"

"How will we get there without running into those bastards again?!"

"We're not alone! That archer was here, so there must be others!"

"That scarred son of a bitch is probably *with* the sympathisers. What sort of sadist looks like that?!"

"SILENCE! They can hear you."

Nox had halted moments ago but could feel the eyes of all the maids upon their back. It took more effort than they liked to turn around and meet those stares. Anger, fear, and disdain covered the features of the women. Yet, out of the nine, only two didn't flinch, holding the werewolf's gaze.

One of them stood, her fingers clenching her skirts as

she spoke, "Thank you for saving us. *You* helped us, whether some of us appreciated it or not."

Nox cocked their head to the side. "Do I look like a sadist? A Kherian bastard?"

"Kherian?" another asked, looking at the corpses. "Why would they... We were told it was noble sympathisers."

The second maid, still kneeling on the floor, spat, "Kherian, nobles, it doesn't matter. Look at you; you're covered in soot and ash! *You* caused this!"

Fear danced in the eyes of the first maid. Nox wanted to snarl, wanted to drag the maid through the hells they'd been through and see the world through their eyes.

Instead, they forced a laugh. "At least one of you has a spine. You may survive this shitty world, after all. I won't hurt you; I'm not the enemy. A little tip: sometimes the worst beings in this world are the ones who look most human."

The first maid's fear faded. "Then help us again. We need to go to the Palace, as all servants must. During Protocol Black, the Queen is taken to a safe place. Only those who are fast enough can join her. Even so, the Palace will be the most secure place to go!"

"That's where you're wrong. It's going to be *overrun* with Kherians. The explosion was to kill the participants and spectators of the Tournament. If they're truly noble sympathisers, I wouldn't look for help from her lackeys. You're just collateral damage."

"How could you say that about the Queen!? And how do you know so much about what they will or won't do!?" The second maid butted in once more, eyes aflame. "You *did* cause this. You lying bast—"

"Layla!"

"It doesn't matter!" Nox growled, baring their canines without thinking.

Only a moment of silence passed before the screaming started, the maids who had sat quietly flinched back as they fell onto one another, fear clutching their every nerve. Layla's eyes, which had been burning only with rage, guttered like a light, softening into something else—understanding. She clenched her skirts tightly, meeting Nox's eyes while the maids continued to scream.

"You're a werewolf," Layla whispered so that only Nox could hear it.

They could only nod.

"Is it really an attack from Kheria?" she asked.

"I'd recognise those bastards anywhere. It's them."

Layla threw her hands up, eyes hardening once more as she silenced her companions, turning to the one who also stood.

"I believe them, Naia," she mustered. "The Palace is unsafe for us."

"And you believe them *now*?" Fear still graced Naia's eyes, and despite her thanks to Nox, she could only see a killer.

"Werewolves aren't welcome in Kheria; you know this. They are *slaughtered* the second they enter its borders. You know *why* we know this."

"*Cederic*," Naia breathed, her voice catching.

Layla nodded, swallowing unevenly. "We cannot go to the Palace."

For once, the maids were in agreement. Nox sighed inwardly, no longer needing to yell at the skittish women who still gave them unwary stares. They pulled out another knife, one they had stolen, and held it out to Layla, whose eyes were brimming with tears.

She took it, a tremor wracking through her arm. "Go to the Palace," she said. "We'll stay far, far away."

Nox grunted in approval. "Try not to die."

***

The calm dribbling of fountain water was ruined by the crimson flow it had become. The clash of steel and flesh hid the imposing dark wood of the Palace's doors, Kherians against Darcanians in a battle so tight Nox couldn't tell who was winning.

Bodies littered the Palace entrance, the circular driveway drowning in the mass of death so that the gravel was stained black. Nox recognised the shining armour of the Queensguard; the fighters had all been handpicked to protect Darcan's ruler.

It could only mean the Queen was closer to the chaos than she should have been if this was a noble sympathiser attack. Death was not a faraway idea for the upper class, but now it was curling around their ankles.

Nox notched two arrows, raising their bow with careful ease as they made out their targets. Kherians slashed down more of the guards than Nox liked. Maybe the battle wasn't as close as they thought; maybe they really were losing.

Nox marked each fighter, over forty enemy soldiers dressed in black leathers against a dwindling number of guards in bloodstained armour. And yet, amongst the madness, stood one, unlike the rest, not a man, and not dressed in either kingdom's uniform. Only when she disappeared into a violet light did Nox realise who it was.

And who was coming to kill them.

The woman from the Palace gates appeared from behind, the kiss of cold steel meeting Nox's neck. They bucked unconsciously, narrowly avoiding a slit throat. Nox kicked her in the shin, moving both arms to grab the blade.

Instead, the woman disappeared first, leaving Nox's grasp empty. They collapsed to the ground, gravel cutting into their palms.

"It's *me*, you idiot," they seethed at the empty air. "I saved your sorry ass; you can't repay that by *killing* me."

But their words were left unheard as the woman appeared once more, jumping onto the fallen Nox and aiming for their throat once more. They grabbed her by the shoulders, claws sharpening as they threw her to the gravel and rolled atop her. Their eyes met, and only then did she halt.

"Bastard," she breathed. All the tension seeped out of her body as she lay flat on the gravel.

Unlike at the Palace gates, she was no longer drenched in blood. Nox could see the harsh green light of her eyes and the thick plait of platinum blonde. Recognition bolted through them like a shock to the heart. Was this the Undefeated Champion?

"I'm the bastard?" Nox demanded instead, unmoving from their position on top of her. "You tried to kill me!"

She grinned. "It's a *pleasure* to see you again."

It had to be. Nox had unknowingly fought alongside the Undefeated Champion of Agonia and now was threatening to kill her. Nox's shoulders sagged, their claws sliding into their nail beds.

"You're Lyra Avenyard."

She sighed. "Of course." An insufferable smile lifted her

cheeks. "Does that scare you?"

The question snapped the awe out of Nox. "One day, I think I will kill you," they muttered.

"Now, where would be the fun in that?" she asked.

Before Nox could answer, she winked and disappeared into infinite darkness. Nox fell to the ground, meeting the gravel face-down at her abrupt departure. They heaved themself up, shock reverberating through their spine.

Grabbing their fallen bow, Nox could see that the supposed Undefeated Champion had returned to the Palace doors, slashing down her enemies. Cursing under their breath, Nox held the bow aloft, a tremor running through their arms as they finished the task she had interrupted.

Arrows began to rain upon the battle as Nox aimed to find the Kherians. Lyra zipped through the madness, blades shining. Could she *really* be her? Where was the arrogance? And since when did she have *powers?* Nox shouldn't have been surprised the legends were wrong. They were just shocked to meet her.

Nox changed their focus, loosing arrow after arrow until fourteen dwindled to only one. Their claws appeared, ripping through the air as they passed the blood-filled fountain and toward devastation.

13

AVERY

The symphony of battle was still audible to Avery's immortal ears despite the thickness of the walls. Her heartbeat stuttered against the sound of steel clashing and grunts of pain. She shivered, eyes wandering across the pearly walls, imagining them to be made of bone. Despite the sunlight shining through the large windows at even intervals, setting the emerald and silver adornments of the Palace's antechamber alight, Avery could only see it as a tomb, too suffocating for the immortal who belonged to the clean air of the Forest.

Silence dragged across Avery's soul as the din of battle outside suddenly ceased. A moment later, the dark oak doors slammed open. The mortals that sat around flinched, the sound cracking open a fissure of fear in the hall. Avery straightened, her hands reaching for her daggers as she waited for enemies to flood into the tomb of bone.

But it was only the jostling of steel armour and men with the Queen's emblem who entered, old blood wrinkling Avery's nose as they did so. Her eyes scanned the men, searching for Lyra's bright smile that always seemed to remain on her face. Instead, she met the dark grin of scars.

Her eyebrows twisted in distaste, recognising the werewolf who prowled into the halls, blood streaking their claws and cloak. The two met gazes, but no emotion glimmered in their irises of ice. Avery looked away first, not caring for the werewolf who had begrudgingly saved her life. A moment later, she saw Lyra appearing through the dwindling number of men, where she clapped the werewolf on the shoulders, grinning like the fool she was before heading over to Avery.

"I see you've been healed up," she began, eyes skimming the naiad dryly.

"And you still managed to remain uninjured," Avery replied.

"I wouldn't say that."

Just then, a healer appeared at her side, and Lyra collapsed to the floor and began removing her armour. The leather breastplate was torn and bloodied, revealing the sheen of a metal shirt beneath. Avery wasn't well versed on the differing names of the armoured pieces Lyra wore, but she watched in silence as the mortal shucked it all off. Once left in just her tunic and trousers, Avery's eyes widened at the blood, and fresh bruises the armour had kept contained.

Lyra's long-sleeved shirt was practically in shreds, cuts and slashes joining the already numerous scars on her arms as the healer sealed the wounds into lines of white. Avery realised then just how exhausted the warrior was, with sweat making Lyra's hair stick to the nape of her neck as each breath came out laboured. The euphoria of battle was fading, leaving only the realities of what dancing with death brought.

Lyra managed a grin. "Enjoying the show?"

"Shut it, mortal."

"I thought that you would have worked it out by now how I can't *possibly* do that."

Avery rolled her eyes. The healer finished then, leaving the pair alone so he could tend to the other injured fighters in the hall.

"How'd you find the werewolf again?" Avery asked. "Did they have to save you?"

Lyra snorted. "No, of course not. I actually tried to kill them. And they never introduced themself. How rude. But anyway, where's the Queen? Shouldn't she be here?"

A shrug was all Avery responded with. She hadn't cared about Aurora, only herself. To think of others is to lead yourself to death. And Avery had courted the goddess of death's inky caress too many times for one day.

"Brilliant!" Lyra exclaimed. "Not as if she's our ruler, and you didn't think to worry about her whereabouts."

"She's no ruler of mine," Avery retorted, crossing her arms. "I follow my mind, not any mortal."

Lyra's eyes flashed, fists clenching at sides as if she was going to strike her. Avery held back a flinch, mirroring the anger that graced the woman's face. Her interactions with mortals were always one-sided, Avery holding the advantage through her Siren tongue and immortal grace. And yet, the darkness that coiled in Lyra's emerald eyes told her she'd regret uttering the words that thundered through her heart.

"Go find your Queen. She'll probably be hiding in the Palace."

"And where will you go?" Lyra asked, her voice softening.

"Home."

"Okay, at least let me take you. The Palace is secure, but the grounds are no doubt still in mayhem."

"No."

Avery needed to get out of this place and *fast*. Now that the chaos of the attack had ceased, Torr would seek her out.

She wanted nothing more of today's horrors and instead wanted the comfort of the Forest and her lake. Even searching for Elias was something she could hardly consider. She truly hoped he'd survived, but it wasn't a problem she wanted to deal with right now.

Avery stormed out of the Palace hall, knowing Lyra would follow her. With so many eyes inside, she lacked the privacy to manipulate the mortal into submission. Once they were alone, Avery would force her away.

Gore and corpses painted the carriageway, the fountain still bubbling away in its red waves. It should have been empty of life, with everyone tucked inside the Palace or dead on the ground. But of course, there would always be the one who stood out when he should not have.

"There you are, naiad," Torr sneered. "And here I thought you were dead." His clothes were lashed with blood and dust, and his hands were jammed into his pockets.

Avery managed to keep the shock off her face. "Thought or hoped?" she asked.

He gave her a flat stare. "Come on. We're leaving. *Now.*"

Before she could make a move, Lyra grabbed her arm. "Who is that?" the mortal hissed.

"No one of your concern." Avery tried to pull out of her grasp, but Lyra held firm.

"Seriously?" Lyra demanded. "I just saved your life more times than I can count, and now you're going to walk off with a man who looks ready to kill us both?"

"It's complicated," Avery said through gritted teeth. "And it has nothing to do with you."

"What if I wanted to change that?"

Before Avery could reply, Torr's voice broke through.

"Who's the mortal, naiad?" he drawled. "Drop her before I do."

"Fine," Avery snapped at the assassin. "I'm coming." She turned to Lyra, compulsion thick in her following words. "Let go of me and *stay*."

The mortal froze. Lyra's fingers released Avery's wrist, allowing her to turn to Torr. His eyes flicked between her and Lyra, making Avery's gut twist. A moment of silence dragged on before Torr grunted, walking away from the Palace. Avery was quick to follow, refusing to give Lyra's immobile frame another glance.

"So that's how you survived," Torr said as they walked down the desolate carriageway. "I can practically *taste* the void coating your skin."

"You know what that is?" she asked. "And you can… sense it?" Goosebumps wrapped Avery's flesh.

Torr looked straight ahead. "It's rare. Strong, too, if nurtured correctly. Pathetic if not."

A lump formed in Avery's throat. Was he suggesting Lyra's control of the void was *pathetic*? That? Avery hugged her arms, training her eyes on the endless cobbles beneath her. She wasn't entirely sure where Torr was leading them, but she knew asking if she could just go home was pointless. Her bones were heavy with exhaustion, and her whole *being* felt like it was about to shut off and collapse.

"We have company." Torr's voice was hoarse with anger. "If they get in our way, deal with them like the void girl."

Avery looked up, her body tensing. They'd stopped walking as she heard the sound of dozens of feet running towards them. Avery spared a glance to Torr, whose jaw was clenched.

A line of shimmering steel filled her eyesight, but instead

of black leathers, as she expected, a mismatch of survivors stood. Avery's shoulders drooped; maybe she wouldn't need to control anyone after all.

Over four dozen people stood before her, grim faces and soaked in blood. Torr started walking again, and Avery followed, passing the group with her head down.

Until their leader spoke up.

Avery, you're alive.

She froze and looked up, meeting eyes with Elias, who seemed to be grinning at her. His scarf still covered his mouth and nose, but his eyes were crinkled with joy. The rest of the ragtag group passed them, cutting through the pair that stood still.

Shock ricocheted through Avery, her mouth hanging wide open. Elias' armour was slick with blood, creating an oily sheen upon the black steel, warping her reflection into something much more gruesome.

"I—"

"Just how many friends did you make today, naiad?"

Avery tore her eyes away from Elias to look at Torr. The assassin had stopped walking too, and he stared down at her, a fresh gleam of rage in his eyes. She'd been so surprised to see Elias she half forgot Torr was with her and what was about to come crashing down between them.

It's him.

Avery ignored the telepath's words. "Was there a rule against that?" she asked Torr. "I was sponsored to win the Tournament, that was all."

The assassin scowled. "Let's go." He turned without a backward glance and continued walking.

She grabbed Elias' arm and looked him in the eye. *Listen to my thoughts carefully,* she demanded mentally. *I have no choice but to follow him, but we need to meet tomorrow. I'm getting that money, and we're finding out what Torr is.*

There was more she should have told him, but she didn't know how to verbalise it. There was Lyra to account for, the attack on the Palace, and all the other clueless theories that grew in her mind.

Okay, Elias said. *I'll meet you at the Forest tomorrow.*

She nodded and released his arm. He walked away from Avery, heading towards the Palace. Turning on her heel, she dashed after Torr, who had already left her in the dust, clueless to the silent conversation she had just shared with the mindspeaker.

As soon as she and Torr were alone, he began to speak.

"The Tournament will be recommencing," he said. "It's not been decided *when,* but regardless, your sponsor will expect your attendance."

Avery's skin crawled. Why had this been decided so quickly? Would there be no moment of reprieve from the attack? She hadn't doubted a recommencement, but for Torr to already know the information meant it would be soon.

They reached the Palace gates, and immediately, Avery's senses were overwhelmed by the stench of bloodied corpses. The Palace had been shuddered into silence, slumbering into a pavilion of grief and death. But the city was unlike that. There were civilians, eyes as wide as pools, staring at the massacre that Avery had helped bring about. Her heart hammered in her chest, and her gut churned with nausea as she willed herself not to heave. She was used to mortal death, but such quantity of gratuitous violence made her head ache.

Torr's face betrayed no emotion. His eyes flitted across the mess, nostrils flaring to take in the scents before moving on. He grabbed Avery's arm and dragged her through the deep crowds of civilians. They moved at a sluggish pace before finally reaching the city limits. As soon as they were free, Torr let her go, pushing her out into the dirt road.

"In two days, there is going to be an interview process at the Palace to weed out any traitors," he said as if their walk through death had never occurred. "It will all be a waste of time, but I have to take you there and back in order to secure your position as a fighter. We will meet at the Forest boundaries at noon. Do not be late."

"That's it?" she asked. "You drag me out of the city to tell me this? Why not tell me at the Palace?"

Torr scowled. "Go back to the Forest, naiad; it's where your kind belongs. Don't do anything stupid, and do not disobey me."

Avery's hands clenched into fists as the desire to refuse screamed through her head. If he hadn't appeared, she wouldn't have controlled Lyra and could have talked with Elias. Instead, she was treated like a prisoner, with every ounce of her autonomy stolen.

She opened her mouth to argue when the smells of rotting wood and loamy soil suddenly filled her senses. The Forest of the Dryads materialised all around her, trapping her deep inside its magic confines.

Torr was gone, and there was no way she could reach him.

***

The walk through the towering trees was filled with murmurs, each one flittering past like ghouls on an ancient wind—voices of immortals filled with scorn mingled within

125

the moaning of the lost souls trapped by them. Mortals who tread too far from the path would enter the Forest with dreams of dancing in paradise and falling in love with the ethereal nymphs. But the only guarantee those nature spirits could ever provide was death, however slow and undeserving.

Avery herself typically kept her mortals alive for only a couple of days, growing bored of their continual moaning and insatiable desire to meet her lips. But the same couldn't be said for the dryads, who left only ruins of men croaking out for a swift end, which was rarely given.

Leaves shivered past, allowing the gasps of curious nymphs to lull her into an arrogant step.

She entered the mortal lands and returned without a scratch.

Drenched in blood, though.

It may not be hers; I can smell human waste upon her. The Siren is a fool. I'm surprised she didn't die.

Avery whirled around, those last words tinging her vision red once more. "If you want to insult me, come eye to eye with me. Then we'll see who the fool is."

When no reply met her ears, she smirked with pleasure. Even soaked in her own sweat and blood, Avery made sure to crush the idea that she was lesser than any of the hidden nymphs. She was the naiad with the honeyed words and the ability to escape the Forest. Although weakness was her friend, she ensured none of these immortals knew it.

"A-vera-line! Is that you finally home?"

"Of course it is. Can't you *smell* the blood?"

Besides two specific naiads, that was.

She rolled her eyes as she slid into the copse of ash trees

so that three freshwater lakes came into view, each glistening bright despite the cover of leaves high in the sky and nestled close to one another so that only a lone ash tree stood between the three lakes. Two women sat together by the centre lake, one of them waving madly at Avery, an impish grin on her pale face.

"Averaline!" the naiad chimed again, standing so quickly water splashed around her.

"Hello, Bellama," Avery replied softly, her world fitting into place once more.

Her younger sister's smile broadened for a moment, her teeth shining so bright they reminded Avery of the pearl walls of the Palace. Bellama dashed forward, her light brown hair bouncing around her shoulders and revealing her tapered ears. The naiad faltered her step, eyes of ice blue settling onto her elder sister.

"What happened to you?" she asked, her voice a dangerous quiet. "Were you… attacked? Is *he* with you?"

Avery shook her head. "Torr is gone for now, but there is much to the story to tell. Where is Nemesia?"

The copse of ash trees that encircled the three lakes held nine sisters—dryads of grey hair and green eyes. They were the closest thing to mothers for Avery and her sisters, and Nemesia was the best of them all. Avery wanted her mother's presence, but she would never specifically voice that aloud.

Bellama shrugged. "Asleep, I suppose. Your tale will eventually find her."

The dwellers of the Forest already knew the terms of Avery's agreement with Torr and knew just about everything he had done to get her to follow him into the Tournament. There wasn't much point in trying to hide the rest of the excitement from her best listeners.

"Let me wash up first," Avery said. "Then I'll explain all."

Bellama's nose wrinkled. "Oh good, you do smell quite bad."

Before Avery could reply, she watched cold water hit her sister in the back of the head, drenching the naiad so that her fine features disappeared under its touch. Avery stepped back, mirth pulling up the corners of her lips as Bellama whined.

"Caliadne! I thought you said you'd stop doing *that*!"

A dark laugh followed. "I never did, nor should you ever believe such a statement."

Their youngest sister approached them, arms crossed against her slim frame. Her dark blonde hair was swept away from her face so that the sharpness of her ears and cheekbones were in full view. Caliadne's grey eyes swept over Avery in a singular moment, an unamused smile on her face as her nose wrinkled.

"Did you lose, then? You're covered in too much blood to ever call yourself a victor."

Avery rolled her eyes. "I did not lose. But as I said to Bellama—"

"'I'll explain all,' yes. You're awfully dramatic."

"Says the one who throws mortal blood at us whenever she has the opportunity," Bellama moaned as she wrung water from her soaked dress.

"You're insufferable," Caliadne huffed.

"And yet I suffer most!" she cried, dancing around her sisters, her bare feet hardly making an impression on the emerald grass.

Avery watched quietly, her lips pursing. She could still

see the falling tower flash in her mind, its inescapable weight threatening to crush her. Smoke had perfumed the air, turning the Palace into a hells-storm. Death licked at her heels, teasing her, testing her, threatening her.

One day, the tricks would end, and Lady Rasthena would come to claim what is hers.

14

ELIAS

The Palace was much more grandiose than Elias had expected, even with the lashings of blood and gore decorating its front door. Amidst the carriageway were the bodies of the dead, but as Elias' group of survivors filtered into the building, he headed towards the immobile woman standing alone.

He recognised her from the matches, with her platinum blonde hair and a shining sword. Her eyes were vacant of life, but when Elias clicked his fingers, the compulsion broke.

"Huh, what?" she mumbled, blinking rapidly. "Where's Av—?" She stopped, realisation dawning on her face. "I'm going to kill her."

How about you don't *do that?*

The woman blinked again, only just realising Elias was there. "Who are you?"

A friend of Avery. She told me to find you. Lyra, right? Let's go inside; we have much to discuss.

He didn't wait for her to follow and headed towards the front doors. He didn't know what to expect of the atrium, but inside, he found a hubbub of madness. The front of the Palace had avoided the entirety of the blast, leaving it unmarred from the fires, but the noble sympathisers had done more than enough to shake up the Queen's residence; even in death, their actions lingered in the hall.

Survivors were crouched upon plush green carpets stained with crimson. Healers hurried back and forth, reforming broken bones and sealing wounds shut. Chatter littered the cavernous entrance, the sound bouncing off the pearlescent walls in ghoulish tones. It was mostly Queensguard who filled the space, taking up the left side in their bloodied armour and hulking forms. Elias was glad to see his own group of survivors together, all still standing despite the sympathisers they had fought.

Even in the chaos of the room, Elias' eyes latched upon one person in particular.

Nox Parker was half-hidden in an alcove, their long legs jutting out. Instinctually, Elias headed towards them. The werewolf's arms were crossed, and they were staring intently at the floor. Their shirt was slashed to ribbons, but no injuries decorated their skin, much to Elias' relief.

Nox, he started.

The werewolf didn't look up at Elias, focusing on one of the brown stains on the carpet. "Seems you didn't die either. And I suppose it was you who brought the ragtag team of lowlifes."

"So you two *do* know each other?"

Elias turned around, glad to see that Lyra had followed after all. Her eyebrows were twisted together, eyes flicking between him and Nox. Whatever she meant by that question, Elias was clueless.

It was easy enough to slip into her mind. The physicality of the mind was a tricky one to decipher. Sometimes, thoughts flew past in a rush; all he'd need to do was dip into that stream of endless consciousness to know every thought.

But other times, a physical place could materialise. Elias' own thoughts were arranged like a library; each thought was carefully catalogued in ancient tomes cracked at the spine. He had entered many halls locked behind the eye, but they had only been fellow telepaths, namely ones who had slipped into his mind first.

So when he stood at the doorway of a manor, the oaken door encompassed by carved stone walls, he thought twice about entering the threshold.

But when a laugh curled at his ears, the door disappeared, forcing him into the lobby of her mental home. The entire room was shrouded in darkness, leaving only one corner visible at the behest of a fireplace, the flames bringing a lone armchair into view.

Sitting there was Lyra. Her legs were crossed at the knee, and with a hand resting on her chin, she gazed upon Elias. Her hair was unbound, a shower of platinum framing the damned smile on her face, like a queen upon her throne, watching the fall of a traitor.

Her smirk told him everything. *Get out, telepath.*

The real Lyra reappeared as Elias ducked out of her mind. Her eyes were wide, but the shock faded quickly. "And you're not just a mindspeaker, then," she confirmed.

"Okay, let's cut this out; what the hells is going on?" Nox had risen from the alcove and now stood between Lyra and Elias. "You two are disturbing my peace, so unless someone wants to explain why you're here, can you both piss off?"

Despite their crude words, Elias could hear the curiosity in Nox's thoughts. He sifted through Nox's mind to find the correlation they had with Lyra, his surprise growing further at the revelation that she was the Undefeated Champion of the Agonia Pits. Aside from that, Nox wanted to know how she and Elias linked to one another. At the moment, Nox was an outsider to the conversation, which, to them, was a problem.

"Yes, I agree someone needs to do some explaining." Lyra rounded on Elias. "How do you know Avery? Why did she control me, and who was that freak she was with?"

Nox scoffed. "None of that has anything to do with me."

Lyra didn't miss a beat, whirling on Nox instead. "Fine, I'll bring you into the conversation." She prodded them in the chest. "Who are you? You never told me your name."

The werewolf frowned, hesitating in their reply for a moment before relenting. "Nox Parker."

"Okay, Nox," Lyra replied. "It's nice to meet you." She pointed at Elias. "Is he your keeper or something?"

Nox's features turned feral. "I'm going to throw you across the room."

"We both know you wouldn't be able to catch me."

If Elias hadn't still been shocked by Lyra's resistance to his telepathy, he might have searched through Nox's to figure out what the pair were talking about. *Let's get back on track*, he said to her. *Your mental barriers are impressive; can you also read minds?*

She cocked her head to the side, meeting Elias' gaze. "Nope, but I've just been taught a couple of tricks," Lyra replied with a wink. "They're fun to play with."

It cleared up nothing, and for once, he could not root out the truth. The feeling left Elias uneasy, and he hated himself for it. His usage of telepathy should have always been for curiosity and investigation for good, but now, the desire to read Lyra's mind was purely selfish.

"Are you two flirting?" Nox interrupted his thoughts. "I'm only hearing half of this, but it sounds like flirting." They rolled their eyes.

We're not flirting, Elias snapped.

"What's your name again?" Lyra asked him, flashing Nox a grin.

Elias. Who taught you?

"It doesn't matter," she replied. "I want to know what's going on with you and Avery."

"That's irrelevant to me," Nox cut in. "How's this: where's the Queen? Shouldn't she be here by now?"

The Queen should be safe. Her seating, along with all the nobles, were unaffected by the blast.

Lyra frowned. "Noble sympathisers." Her voice drawled as if the word 'noble' tasted bitter on her tongue. "The Queensguard says all the nobles had disappeared from the seats before the blast. Apparently, the Queen was just about to follow after them before everything happened."

"Kherians," Nox seethed.

Elias ignored the werewolf. *The explosion was meant to detonate later than it did, most likely when the Queen was clear of the blast.*

"And how the hells do you know that?" she demanded.

Nox snorted before asking sarcastically, "Yeah, how do you know that? You sound like a real traitor, you know."

Elias felt his cheeks begin burning up, his head growing uncomfortably itchy as blood rushed to his brain. He knew that Nox wasn't serious, considering they were the one who had found the men who lit the fuses, but Lyra looked more than ready to spill his blood fresh onto the carpet. Sizing her up wouldn't be too difficult, given their stature differences and his powers. But there was a dark inkling wrapped around this woman, dressed up in flesh and steel to hide the onyx black inside. Elias looked away from her hardened stare.

I didn't mean that, and you know it, Nox, he replied, gritting his teeth although no one could see it through his scarf. The werewolf could only shrug, a hidden smile lurking beneath their nonchalance. *We found the sympathisers setting up the gunpowder during Avery's fight. Nox and I interrupted the plans.*

"Yes, if it wasn't for this trumping oaf, the blast wouldn't have happened!" Nox laughed, grinning widely.

Elias flinched so violently that both Nox and Lyra blanched. He recovered quickly enough, averting his gaze as he stepped back from the two.

Before anyone could speak, he left, shoving his hands into his pockets to hide how much they shook. Elias could hear Lyra's careful murmurs and the concern in her voice that quietened at every step he took out of the Palace. Fresh air; he needed fresh air, away from the death and misery that oppressed the pearlescent halls.

Instead, he found much worse.

The central fountain of the gravel driveway continued to burble liquid as bright as rubies as the overflow of corpses in its bowl poured the red water onto the ground. Bodies remained scattered across the threshold, flies already buzzing at the cold forms as birds screeched overhead, vying for their next meal of greying flesh. Bile rose to Elias' throat, the stench of the dead shoving itself into his nose. He adjusted his scarf, tightening the fabric around his face in an attempt to cover the violation of his senses.

The door behind him opened, and Elias turned to find Lyra standing there. Her hands were clenched in front of her as her eyes scanned the bodies.

"We'll bury them," she murmured before meeting Elias's eyes.

Or burn them.

She nodded grimly. "That too. But first, we should know their names, these people who fought for our kingdom. Ward off the flies and the crows, and give them the peace we all deserve."

And the Kherians? Nox's influence rooted the word into his mind.

"They don't even deserve to lay on our grounds."

Elias' palms warmed as the fire began to swarm his veins. *Then, let them become nothing but ash.*

The smell of burning flesh was not any better than that of decaying flesh, but it was satisfying to watch the black leathers of their enemies curl to dust at the roar of flames that blazed from Elias' skin. Lyra watched beside him, a single brow rising as his promise of ash became a reality within minutes.

"This wasn't your fault," she said finally. "Nox told me how you 'interrupted.' Mistakes happen, but if it wasn't for you, all of us would be dead."

Hundreds are dead because I stopped Nox from killing those men, he replied, the taste in his mouth suddenly turning sour. *I got in the way.*

"But what if you hadn't been there? What if Nox had failed to kill them? The blast would have happened all the same, and we would be dead. I would have died. Nox saved my ass and Avery's."

Nox saved Avery?

Lyra shrugged. "I was her opponent in the second round when the gunpowder went off. We were able to get away but were ambushed at the Palace gates. Nox turned the tide for us. And *they* only survived the blast because you were there."

Elias frowned. *How did you get to the Palace gates?*

"You ask an awful lot of questions." Lyra planted her hands on her hips. "I'm trying to be supportive right now, but all you're doing is interrogating me."

Usually, I don't need to ask, do I? he replied, a hidden grin cursing his face.

"Poor little telepath who's unable to infiltrate my mind."

It was Elias' turn to shrug as he said, *It does make the conversation much easier.*

"Well, you're going to have to get used to it," she said, nudging his arm with her elbow. "I have a feeling Avery needs our help, so you won't be getting rid of me just yet."

He smiled. *If you say so.*

"We should go back inside. I don't know how long Nox is going to hang around now that we're both absent." She surveyed the carriageway one last time, her face turning impassive. "We'll deal with the dead later; focusing on the living is a tedious task but a necessary one."

No lies there.

Without another word, the two went back inside, Elias holding the door open for her to slip inside first. The hush of the hall was no more as feverish chatter echoed pleasantly throughout. Standing at the centre of the room was Queen Aurora, the skirts of her sapphire blue dress billowing out as she kneeled beside two young children. Her crown was gone, revealing the unruly raven hair that had once been combed back so beautifully.

No injuries marred her skin, though Elias noticed a scattering of white dust on the bright fabric of her dress. He also realised the two children were Aurora's own, the heirs of Darcan looking up at their mother with no fear in their eyes. It was almost fortunate that they hadn't realised the kind of danger they had been in.

Elias watched the two siblings, neither blood-related to one another or their mother. After being declared heir following the death of her brother, Aurora had had no interest in finding a husband, nor time, as she argued. Despite her younger sister's family of many children, she decided to continue her own line as she adopted two children. Named Cressida and Nathaniel, both had been infants at their separate arrivals into the Palace and thus the Winthorpe dynasty.

Lyra halted at the sight of the royals before bowing her head in deference. Elias followed suit, but as he raised his head, he couldn't help but notice how her eyes lingered on the family, brows twisting in longing. It cleared within a second, making Elias wonder if he'd imagined it.

Aurora rose from the ground, the creases in her gown falling out like waves against the shore. Her children stood with her, their fingers clenched in her hands. Elias couldn't remember how old they were, but he could guess they couldn't be older than thirteen, maybe even less than that. Nathaniel, the youngest, now trembled under the infinite stares of the adults stained in blood.

But Aurora met her subjects' eyes one by one, her brows creasing together as if she could see the terrors they had faced. Her nobles were nowhere to be seen, no doubt all too spineless to look into the eyes of the survivors of their mess. Aurora's grip on Cressida and Nathaniel's hands tightened, her knuckles turning white with effort. When she met Elias' eyes, he could only feel sympathy for her; the weight of the Crown and everything it brought crushed her from the inside out.

But he knew she was strong enough to withstand it all.

"Due to the forthcoming circumstances, I feel that there is much to explain. The attack was *not* executed by the Darcanian nobility." Already, protests clustered in the air. Aurora allowed them to stifle the hall for only a moment longer. "My Liemaster has cleared the peerage of this accusation, and we found the true threat."

Nox had joined Elias and Lyra soon after the Queen arrived, and standing beside them, Elias heard the werewolf speak the same word as Aurora: *Kheria.*

Panic shifted the world off-kilter. Elias shouldn't have been surprised, not after Nox's relentlessness. But the rest of the survivors could not handle the news, and even Lyra's face paled. Had a fun game at the Palace really turned into the inciting of a war? For all their sakes, Elias hoped not.

"We do not know *why* they attacked under these false pretences, but it cannot be ignored. The Palace is no longer safe, and I cannot allow my citizens to remain in harm's way.

"Because of this, the Royal Tournament will be postponed so that the security of its proceedings can be strengthened and protected. You are all welcome to re-enter or leave, but I implore that you seek assistance from the healers, the Crown shall compensate you all. Please stay safe, my people. And thank you for all your efforts in saving one another. I hope to see many of you again."

Aurora waited only a moment before retiring, loosening her grip on her children to walk alone, back straight and head held high. The Queen of Darcan would not crumble, and as long as she ruled, neither would her kingdom.

15

LYRA

After the Queen left, Captain Renner took over, making announcements. "In order to re-enter the Royal Tournament, all participants must complete an interview at the Palace in two days' time. Please write out your name on this sheet if you wish to proceed."

Nox immediately joined the queue, jumping from toe to toe, while Lyra stayed frozen. For the most part, she didn't even *want* to sign up again. The Kherian attack had blown everything out of proportion. Could she possibly do any good within the Tournament now? A part of her had hoped the Tournament would end here, the gunpowder plot ceasing any more activities like this for decades to come. Then, she could return home and sweep this under the mat. Instead, the Tournament was continuing as if nothing had happened, as if hundreds weren't rotting in the courtyards.

Then, there was the matter of Avery and her mystery companion.

Lyra didn't understand why she was drawn towards helping Avery, especially after the naiad had mind-controlled her. But there was something tense between her and that man who had led her away from the Palace, something that required the involvement of a telepathic mindspeaker to solve.

Elias stood beside her still, and she looked up to meet his eye. Lyra was still unsure of what to make of the telepath.

He obviously cared a lot about helping Avery and Nox, but Lyra wished to understand his motive. Not only that, but, well, she knew *nothing* about him, and she cursed herself for not remembering his fight during the matches. She had so many questions, but she had a feeling she wouldn't get the answers unless she divulged many truths about herself first.

When neither of them moved to join the queue, Lyra broke the silence. "Reconsidering, too?" she asked.

He nodded. *My business here was never about the Tournament.*

Goosebumps rose on Lyra's skin. "It has something to do with Avery, doesn't it?"

There's more to it than that, but I'll only share if you do, too. Avery wants your help, and Nox thinks you're someone important; aren't you, Undefeated Champion?

She huffed a breath. "I should teach the werewolf how to create mental barriers. You have too much fun invading their mind, I think."

You're avoiding the question.

"You avoided mine."

We won't get anywhere if we cannot trust each other.

"True, but it sounds like you need my help more than I need yours. If I have to work with you to help Avery, then you will need to explain what's going on."

Elias shook his head, indecision clear on his face. Finally, he sighed. *Fine. Do you know who the Haunted Shadow is?*

"Yes," she answered. "He's an assassin who kills for the nobles. What part does he play in this?"

He's the one who dragged Avery away.

"So you want to kill him. Why? Can't Avery just force him to do it himself?"

That's where things get complicated.

Lyra opened her mouth to ask more questions when an all too familiar voice met her ears. "Ms Avenyard, finally, we meet."

She whirled around to find Castor Glasswood standing before her. He was still dressed in all his finery, not a single speck of dust upon his clothes nor a strand of hair out of place. Lyra wanted to scowl; everything that lurked beneath the folds of silk and skin was rotten to the core.

In the corner of her eye, she saw Elias peel away to join the queues. Her eyes drifted further away from Castor, and she saw several other aristocrats milling about the antechamber. Now that they had been cleared of all crimes and the Tournament fighters were distracted, they could more freely mingle. Lyra had forgotten entirely about her acceptance of Castor's sponsorship, but from his leering smile, he certainly had not.

"Your Grace," she spoke through gritted teeth. "I am surprised to see you here but glad to see you well."

"Yes, yes, of course I am well; it was you I was worried about. But I see that unnecessary now; you are unharmed, and your beauty does so wondrously owe to the rumours."

Lyra froze but pulled a fake smile. "Which ones?"

Castor mirrored her expression. "'Lovely Lyra' is the long-lost daughter of one of my fellow noble houses. With your platinum blonde hair and green eyes… yes, it is almost uncanny."

A favourite rumour of Agonia—she was a Winterbride bastard. Lyra wasn't the only human in the entire nation to have a similar appearance to a noble family, but she was a spectacle at the Pits, so, of course, a story had to be made up. The Duchess of Canwal was well known for her attendance at the Pits, further strengthening the rumours, but the Winterbrides never cared for Lyra, and, in turn, she never cared for them.

She cleared her throat. "Well, as you said, it is all rumours. Where would be the fun in telling the truth?"

"No fun at all," he chuckled lightly. "Though I am willing to be an exception to the rule…"

As if she would tell him any of her secrets. "It is a miracle that we are all safe and well, don't you think?" she asked, switching topics.

Castor nodded furiously. "Yes, yes! It was a miracle from the gods that allowed us to survive. Another miracle is that Her Majesty is continuing the Tournament."

"It was going to be cancelled?"

He waved his hand. "It was hardly considered, but yes, we convinced her well enough."

So Lyra's suspicion that the nobles concocted the Royal Tournament had been correct. Relief flooded through her, glad to find that the Queen was still against the formation of illegal fighting rings.

Castor continued. "I must say I'm surprised that *you* entered this little competition, given your history."

Lyra crossed her arms, reasserting herself. He wanted the Champion, so he would get her. "Isn't it that *history* that made you want to sponsor me?" she drawled. "When there's money to be made and glory to claim, I wouldn't be the one to sit idle."

Castor practically clapped. "Excellent, just excellent. I had just wanted to be sure." He cleared his throat. "Now that this mess is all cleared up…" he began, "as your sponsor for the Tournament, I have an invitation for you, one I hope you do not decline."

Lyra's skin crawled at his tone. His searching eyes ravaged her face as if snuffing out any attempt to defy him, forcing her to obey.

"And what is that?" she asked as calmly as her dry throat could manage.

Castor's face brightened. "A ball. Tonight."

Lyra blinked. The idea of the nobles throwing a ball after the Tournament's first day wasn't a complete surprise. Lyra had packed gowns in anticipation of infiltrating a formal gathering. What she didn't expect was for one to continue as planned right after the disaster, which they had all scarcely survived. Lyra had hoped she could spend this evening winding down, a moment of reprieve after all of the chaos. From Castor's stare, she let that wish die.

"A ball?" she echoed, forcing giddiness into her voice. "How exciting! Is it for all the sponsors to attend?"

Castor's smile turned sly. "Well, actually, no. It is a masquerade, and you are to be my secret guest."

She let out a laugh. "My, my, what a spectacle. How could I ever decline?"

Not that he would have given her any other choice, Lyra suspected. Immediately, he gushed on the details, and with a snap of his fingers, a servant of Castor appeared with a crisp card in hand. The servant gave it to Lyra, and she gave the invitation a quick scan.

"A masquerade every night?" she wondered aloud. "I'm afraid I don't think I'll be able to attend all of them, not if I'm to keep in peak condition for the Tournament."

It was the best excuse Lyra could think of on the spot. The opportunity to attend on any given night was a blessing, but it would be impossible to be there every time. The information she would need to gather could be acquired more concisely, and there would be less chance of her slipping up in front of any nobles.

Castor gawped. "How could I possibly forget? No, no, that is all fine, my dear. Though, of course, you can't miss tonight."

She mustered a smile. "No, of course not."

Lyra tucked the invitation away, making her distracted enough she couldn't stop Castor from reaching out to grab her hand. She froze, her body turning rigid. Unbothered, Castor bowed and kissed the back of her hand. It was a gesture no commoner deserved from a noble, and she should have fallen to her knees in deference. Instead, Lyra couldn't move.

Her heart pounded, her façade threatening to fracture. It was happening all over again. Was the bastard just as aware of it as she was? Another cruel joke to harm her? *Men like you are the reason why I'll never marry. You ruined that for me long ago.*

Dark memories swirled through her thoughts, cursed by even darker intentions.

Lyra?

Elias' mental voice broke her focus, forcing her back into the real world. Castor immediately let go at the interruption, and they both turned to find the telepath waiting for her. His brows were creased together in confusion, probably because she was amicably chatting with a loitering noble. Nox, on the other hand, was nowhere to be seen. Lyra blinked, shoving her hands into her pockets.

"I was just talking to His Grace," Lyra said shakily to Elias.

Castor nodded. "And now, my dear, I must take my leave. You may talk to my men about any needed arrangements for tonight."

He didn't wait for a reply and swept away, returning to the gathered group of nobles and their guards. Lyra didn't care to watch, gladder still that she didn't have to curtsy for him.

What was that all about? Elias' voice greeted her mind.

Lyra didn't reply immediately. Instead, she ventured further down the antechamber, as far as she dared to get away from Castor. Elias followed after her, much to her relief.

When she found an alcove, she answered his question. "I have a sponsorship in the shape of an ugly duke." She cleared her throat, wanting to forget that entire interaction. "What were you saying about the Haunted Shadow being complicated?"

I can go into further detail tomorrow. You probably already have much to focus on with your duke.

Lyra's face warmed. She didn't dare look around, fearful of locking eyes with Castor once more. She could get through a noble ball tonight, but right now, she only wanted to get out of this place. Her emotions were out of check, and her energy had been completely sapped from battle. Her stamina had always kept her breathing for longer than she deserved, but the after-effects felt like another form of death. It settled in her joints, rendering them almost useless even as she forced movement from her fingers.

After leaving the atrium, Lyra would void to the Palace gates to avoid the mess outside. It was a lazy use of her powers, but her senses couldn't bear the assault of corpses and ash.

"I'll be on my way out soon," she said. "So, what do you propose?"

Meet me at the Broken Shield Inn at noon tomorrow, Elias answered. *Then, we can reconvene with Avery. To do that, we'll have to go to the Forest.*

"The Forest?" Lyra echoed. "As in the Forest of the Dryads? *That* deathtrap?" She'd never entered its domain, but she knew enough myths and legends about the residents of the Forest and how many of the stories ended in mortal torment and death. She shuddered. "Are you sure? Can't she meet us in the city?"

Avery isn't very well-versed in specific locations in Cerenia. I thought the Forest would be easier, and she didn't protest.

"Of course, she wouldn't protest; she's not the one who might be slaughtered by a nymph." Lyra sighed. "Let's just hope our wayward naiad is okay with guests."

Friends, Elias amended. *At least, I hope.*

From the crinkling around his eyes, Lyra realised he must have been smiling. She returned the gesture, wondering if the sentiment was meant for anyone else.

"What of Nox?" Lyra found herself asking. "Have you been keeping an eye on them to get their help, too?"

Elias' mirth faded. *No… I don't think so.* He hesitated. *Even before the Tournament began, my intuition told me to make sure they were safe. Twice now, that gut feeling has paid off. Whether they will want to help kill the Haunted Shadow or not, I don't know, but I won't leave Nox behind.*

Lyra nodded. "Fair enough. I'd like to keep in touch with them, too." She stood up and sighed. "Can you make sure I'm signed up? I've got a manservant to talk to."

Elias raised a brow but didn't comment on her last words. *Your name is already at the top of the list. I can hear Nox complaining about it.*

Her skin crawled. "Thanks for checking," she said, biting back a shiver. She raised her hand in farewell. "Until tomorrow."

16

NOX

Nox tried to follow after Lyra, also desiring to get the hells out of there. They had missed most of the spectacle between the Champion and the telepath, meaning that any semblance of entertainment was gone. Not only that, but Nox found watching drama a lot more interesting than being involved in it, and they had the suspicion that sticking around Elias would hand them more of the latter.

It seemed like the telepath wasn't done. *Wait,* he beckoned. *Come with me.*

"Huh?" they barked, turning on their heel to stare into Elias' eyes. It was quite disconcerting how tall he was, towering over everyone in the room with shoulders broader than even Nox's.

Do you have anywhere to stay tonight? he asked.

Nox scowled. "Don't ask questions you know the answers to, telepath."

I was trying to be polite, he conceded.

"Well, it didn't work, did it? Why do you care where I go? You're not my *keeper*," they said, repeating the phrase Lyra had used. They'd first considered it a joke, but now the mindspeaker was slowly forging it into reality.

It's no longer safe to roam the streets. If any Kherians escaped the battle, who's to say they won't recognise you?

Dying before the Tournament begins again isn't a part of your plans, is it? Elias asked, raising an eyebrow.

Nox waited for a moment before replying, weighing his words slowly and questioning their worth. They didn't want to rely on this overbearing immortal, but there was truth in his argument. Thanks to their scars and canines, Nox was an easily recognisable character; more than once, it had impacted their stealthiness.

"Fine," they spat out. "Don't expect me to pay for anything. You're the one who wanted this."

Elias spread his hands out. *Of course, I don't think you'd be able to afford it anyway.*

Nox and Elias walked through the quiet grounds of the Palace. The entrance was still a mess of bodies, but Nox couldn't help but notice not a single Kherian soldier remained, only the scent of burnt flesh and leather.

"Did you have anything to do with this?" they asked, gesturing to the ashes scattered across the cobblestones.

Lyra and I decided it was best to leave nothing of them to bury. It was an easy enough task.

Nox arched a brow. "Ah, so that's what you two were doing." Their mind wandered to their previous assumptions.

You seriously thought we were flirting back there? he asked, eyes widening. *I feel like I should be honoured you presume such things.*

They shrugged. "It's more so on her part than yours. By responding, you fell into the category—she did all the work."

Elias grunted. *Fair enough.*

"So, where exactly are we going?" Nox asked as they passed the fountain and continued down the driveway. "You don't seem to be from the city."

There are several boarding houses, so I took it upon myself to rent a room. They only had rooms for two left, so I cut my losses and paid for it. Maybe it's fate.

Nox rolled their eyes. "Please, the gods don't intervene when someone decides on a boarding house. It's just a coincidence."

Whatever Elias thought on the matter, he left unsaid. Nox followed after the immortal as they eventually reached the Palace gates. The smell hit them before the recollection of what lay ahead did. Slowly, Nox remembered what their actions had brought upon the outskirts of the Palace halls.

Dozens of mangled bodies, many soaked in sewer water, lined the area. Nox surveyed the destruction without a change in expression.

Then, they noted the twin arrows sticking from the throats of those last Kherians they downed; the arrows seemed salvageable enough. Ignoring Elias' frozen state, Nox wrenched the arrows free, wiping the arrowheads on their trousers before refilling their quiver.

Did you *have anything to do with this?*

Nox turned to see Elias at their side now, a blank gaze in his eyes as he marvelled at the massacre. "I had some help," they admitted.

Recognition blazed in his eyes, no doubt taking Lyra's face from their mind. *It seems more than a coincidence that we've met the same women today.*

They cocked their head to the side. "So, who actually *is* the other one, then?"

Avery Nash. We became acquainted after my first match; her second match with Lyra had just started when I found you with the gunpowder.

Nox's skin crawled. As much as they hated to admit it, maybe Elias was right about the fates twisting the four of them together. From the look in his eye, they guessed he was thinking the same; no telepathy was needed on Nox's part.

I should teach you how to build mental barriers; it's actually quite concerning how much I can hear. You're practically shouting your thoughts at me.

Nox readjusted their quiver, looking away from him. "Let's just go. Lead the way."

***

Nox made them take a detour first to retrieve a sack of their belongings hidden in the city. The contents of their sack were practical and basic, consisting of an extra set of clothes, bowstrings, and some food.

When they arrived at the Broken Shield Inn, Nox realised it wasn't as bad as they had anticipated. It was modest in its niceties, rough around the edges and cramped to all extremes, but overall, it was warm, dry and wasn't threatening to collapse in on itself. Nox gave Elias a second look as the barkeep retrieved the keys; it wouldn't have been cheap to afford this sort of place. Were all immortals rich? It hardly seemed fair; a longer life did give more time to make money.

If the Tournament went Nox's way, they could lap up that same luxury without wasting away centuries. Even if not, everything necessary for survival could be stolen or scavenged. Nox had survived worse conditions to not rely on monetary success.

"What sort of job you got then?" Nox asked as they ascended the rickety stairs.

I'm a blacksmith, he said. *Have been for centuries.*

"Makes sense, with the whole 'immunity to fire' thing. Can't say I've heard of any immortals who can do that… or mortals, for that matter. How do you have it?"

I thought you would have known, he replied, a twinge of sadness in his mental voice. *I'm a phoenix-blood.*

"Huh." The phrase meant nothing to Nox, so they guessed they were a species not native to Tenneria.

Elias huffed. *The Falbikuth phoenix-bloods came to Darcan over eight-hundred years ago. I am as native as you. However, two hundred and fifty years ago, the Falbikuth disappeared. From what I can tell, I'm the last one here.*

Nox stopped walking, turning the number in their head. "If the last time anyone saw them was that long ago, you must be ancient, so how old are you then?" they asked.

Old enough. Elias reached a door, jamming the key in the lock before giving the door a shove with his shoulder. It wrenched open at his brute force, the hinges screeching in protest as he held the door open for Nox to go first.

The inn had been crammed along a row of dozens of other skinny buildings, each rising three or more stories above ground. Their room was on the second floor, and there was barely any room for the two of them to stand comfortably. Two single beds were pushed to opposite walls, one scattered with assorted weapons and clothing. Elias cleared it off for Nox, who dropped their sack on the floor and collapsed onto the bed, springs creaking beneath their weight.

"This is probably one of the finest rooms I've stayed at in a while," they admitted, raising their hands in mock celebration of such a feat. "You've done well, telepath."

He snorted. *Glad I could impress.*

They were both still covered in blood, so Elias made a

move to go to the bathing room, indicating where it was for Nox to use afterwards. They didn't care too much. As a teen, living in their own grime and gore had become a common practice. Not purposely, but there wasn't much else of a choice in desperate times. Now wasn't a desperate time, however, and Elias mentioned he would try not to use up all the hot water—a luxury rarely given to Nox in the first place.

Nox had never been to Cerenia before; instead, they remained close to the southwest of the country in Feynos, which sat beside the Kherian border. Despite the distance between the provinces, both offered similar underground activities of pit fighting. It was never as legendary as the Agonia Pits, but the brutes and thugs that battled for dominance in Feynos' pits, known as Ironhavell in the town of Avalward, were laughable at best. Nox had become a sensation overnight, claiming the name of *the Unhallowed One* for all the blood they brought.

Despite being the best fighter, their lodgings in Ironhavell were still pathetic. Better than their time in a wolf pack, but still pretty awful. Even living in a barn was better, and Nox had the experience to know it.

Word of the Royal Tournament had reached Feynos late, giving Nox no time to prepare and reach the capital city. They'd left everything behind: money, clothing, weapons. All they had managed to scrounge up was in the sack at their feet. Nox had arrived in Cerenia only yesterday, sunset casting its glow across the city. Using their keen eyesight, they'd found a place to camp down for the night, the towers of the Palace shining in the moonlight.

Nox was restringing their bow when Elias returned, washed and in a new change of clothes. He had also removed his scarf, revealing a clean-shaven face. Not only that, but he had a piercing on his lip. Despite their own piercings, Nox had not expected Elias also to wear facial jewellery. Then again, they barely knew one another; perhaps he had a hidden set of tattoos somewhere, too.

Evening was slowly descending, and exhaustion seeped into Nox's bones. Dropping the bow, they found the bathing room and scrubbed away every speck of dried blood upon their body.

Nox could hear the scraping of the whetstone before they walked back into the cramped room. Elias was sitting on his bed, a greatsword balanced on his lap as he sharpened its blade. Nox flopped onto their bed, closing their eyes and letting the noise wash over them; the monotony of it almost comforting. Thoughts of their room in Ironhavell came back to mind—it was a size similar to the one they were in now, scattered messily with Nox's belongings.

Didn't think the Tournament through all that much, huh? How badly do you need this money? Elias asked, cutting through their thoughts.

A growl reverberated past their lips as they opened an eye. "Stay out of my head, telepath."

Only if you agree to learn mental barriers with me.

"I don't *need* your help," they spat.

You may never say it aloud, but I hear it anyway. There's nothing wrong with accepting help.

"I wouldn't need your *help* if you had left me alone. Do you read everyone's minds as thoroughly as you've invaded mine?" Nox barked.

No, Elias conceded. *They tend to resist more than you. We can start lessons tomorrow after I meet with Lyra. Sound good?*

"You're meeting Lyra tomorrow?" Nox asked, suddenly

reminded of the drama they missed out on. "Whatever for?"

You can come and join us if you want. We're heading to the Forest of the Dryads.

"That exists? I thought it was just a myth."

You literally met *a nymph today. Avery Nash, remember?*

Nox frowned. They supposed it made sense that the woman at the gates wasn't mortal, but what was Elias' obsession with her? She was far from impressive. Standing before the Palace gates, she'd barely held her own against the Kherians; her display of spewing sewer water at them and convincing two to fight at her side had been all that was interesting.

She didn't just convince them; she manipulated them.

Nox almost flinched. "Do you ever stop reading minds?"

Elias ignored the question. *Avery is a naiad, a* Siren *at that. She can force just about anyone to do anything she pleases.*

The phrase rang a bell, making Nox's jaw clench. They hadn't considered *how* the immortal had gotten the two Kherians to do her bidding—mainly because they didn't really care. Immortals always had an advantage; why would seducing the enemy be any different?

"Wait..." Nox started, "'just about anyone'? Who's the exception?" They almost rolled their eyes before drawling, "Immortals?"

Elias took a moment to reply. *No. She can control us, too.*

"Is it like mental barriers then? If I'd known they could be *that* useful, then maybe I will try it—"

It's nothing like that, Elias interrupted. *I've only met one person she can't control, which links to the fact that I can't read his thoughts either.*

The story intrigued Nox, but they forced themself to pause. "Why are you telling me this?"

Elias shrugged. *You can learn the full story if you come with Lyra and me to the Forest. I won't force you to go nor expect you to help, but if you do, maybe the four of us could do some good. Together.*

Nox stayed quiet. Their curiosity had grown tenfold, but the idea that someone wanted their help solving a problem made Nox hesitant. They'd spent so many years alone, fending for only themself, that it felt strange to give out and receive this sort of thing. And not just that, but being given the *choice* to assist another felt odd. Usually, it was a matter of life or death. There wasn't much of Nox's life that hadn't inherently revolved around survival.

They decided not to answer, instead they turned onto their side to face the wall. It didn't matter what Nox's response was—the telepath would already know it. They had endured all kinds of powers and spells during their life, but those were always *physical.* It could be defeated with a show of Nox's own skills and defended from with a show of strength. But they had never contended with a power of the mind, at least, not knowingly.

Nox disliked the idea of mental powers. They were easier to hide and had harsher consequences. And as much as they despised Elias crawling through their mind, at least he offered ways to fight against it—a lesson Nox had never known they needed.

The mystery of the man who could naturally withstand it came back to their thoughts. Perhaps Nox could forgo the mental barriers lesson and learn how this person could avoid the mental manipulations of both a Siren and a telepath. It would make life a lot easier, though absently they wondered if this man could not understand mindspeaking and if that meant Nox would never hear Elias speak again.

They pushed the theories away. Tomorrow, they would make a decision; today had already been too hectic. Nox had just survived a terror attack at the Palace of their kingdom, but already they were being dropped into a new problem? Enough was enough; they needed to rest.

Goodnight, the phoenix-blood said after half an hour had passed. Nox didn't return the expression, only closing their eyes as Elias blew out the candles, sending the room into midnight darkness.

17

ELIAS

As much as he didn't want to admit it, Elias hated being locked out of someone's mind and all its thoughts. It would become an intrinsic challenge, teasing the edges of someone's barriers against his telepathy. Sure, he wanted to teach Nox and, if he could manage it, Avery the art of mental barriers, but he still knew they would slip. Everyone who played at shielding their mind did—only Torr was the true exception.

Not that it was due to mental barriers, but something about his brain *lacked* what it took to invade it. On the other hand, Lyra should have been someone he could infiltrate. She was only mortal, after all.

Elias wanted to trust Lyra, but without having an understanding of her mind, he wasn't sure where to begin. She had gained the attention of both Avery and Nox, and now she had his. Lies and mysteries lingered beneath the surface, and Elias decided that in order to continue an alliance with Lyra, he needed to know she was someone he could rely on.

But her thoughts had been locked tight ever since he first tried prying. Even when exhaustion had slumped her shoulders, Lyra kept her barriers sharp.

Not that it mattered. Elias hadn't relented in his attempts at slipping into her mind. He had to be careful to avoid her realising what he was doing. After his first attempt, Lyra's mental image of a house had always been locked, so he never dared go over the threshold. But it was during her conversation with Castor Glasswood that it suddenly broke open.

Men like you are the reason why I'll never marry. You ruined that for me long ago.

Her mental voice had been drenched in rage, and Elias had found himself dragged into memories long buried deep in her mind. Anger swarmed his senses as she imagined killing Castor right where he stood. Elias had batted past it, not hesitating in his prying, digging further to find out just what that meant. A chest locked in iron shoved into the darkest recesses in her mind, and as Lyra's resolve had slipped, so had the chest's chains.

She wasn't just the Undefeated Champion of the Agonia Pits; that story began when she was eighteen. Her first life had been decorated in lace and lies as the betrothed bride to the very man she had stood before in the Palace.

Elias had ducked out of Lyra's mind at the revelation, not wanting her to grow wise of the mental barrier slip. Since that moment, he had wanted nothing more than to find out just *what* all of it meant, even if he knew better than lurking in her mind. Lyra's emotions had overwhelmed her in that single moment, and it seemed unlikely to happen again.

So what was he doing here?

It was late morning, but the streets of Cerenia were desolate. Fortunately, the few people up knew their way around the city, so Elias used his telepathy and their minds to find the Archives Hall of Wychar. Every province city had one, and Elias was already familiar with the one in Vespis. They were administrative buildings stacked floor-to-ceiling with tomes and maps. It reminded him of a public library, though its content was far from fiction.

When he entered, only the sole worker in the Hall noticed his presence. Elias nodded at her in greeting, but she didn't return the gesture. Instead, she returned to the map of the Xiatror Empire, which she had spread out before her.

His plan also needed a map, as he suspected he could find information on the noble houses that ruled the ten provinces of Darcan. If it weren't for the Western Arrows, Elias would never have known about the duke who ruled over Vespis—it was not called that when he first lived there with his family. Darcan had not yet created provinces—or a monarchy, for that matter—when the Phoenix Wars raged on; instead, he waited for his people to disappear before giving structure to a world of anarchy.

Continuing on, he found that the province maps specified only noble surnames. Sifting through the nine of them, Elias finally found the noble house he was looking for: Glasswood of Clarmere. It was one of the larger provinces and one of the two to border Kheria. Putting the maps back, Elias went in search of the noble family records.

All the family trees were extensive in length, branching off to cousins in case of a need for a new heir. But Castor Glasswood's immediate family was unnervingly small. He had no siblings, and both his parents were dead. No wife was tied to his name, but an empty space lay beside him as if one *had* been there. Elias smoothed a finger over the blank spot, finding it to be raised slightly above the page. Someone had stickered over a face, and he was pretty sure he knew who lay underneath it.

With the slightest hit of flame, Elias spread warmth across his fingertip to melt the glue and lift the amendment free. It came away cleanly, the small square of paper flittering to ash once he pulled it away. His eyes devoured the hidden content, expecting to be flooded with the exhilaration of being right.

Only to find the wrong name and age, and a shifted face.

Celeste Adelina Whitehallow was drawn as a child with pale skin and chubby cheeks. White-blonde curls framed her infectious grin, adolescence dripping from the paint. Her date of birth made her twenty-seven, but Nox's thoughts had confirmed the Undefeated Champion of Agnoia was twenty-five. Did Elias read Lyra's thoughts wrong? Was *this* meant to be her?

Suddenly, he remembered the maps and all their noble families. Whitehallow was one of them, wasn't it? Elias abandoned the book and hunted the shelves for that confirmation. The records were alphabetically ordered, so he dragged his search down to the lowest shelf and found it second to last.

At the forefront of the page was the Duke of Neulith, Sirius Whitehallow, still alive, having two separate marriages. His first wife was Larissa Winterbride, and her portrait was closer to what Elias had been expecting. If Lyra had lived a plush life of hiding indoors, then Elias suspected she could have been mistaken for Larissa's twin. They had that same platinum blonde hair, piercing eyes and enigmatic smile. However, Larissa had died in childbirth, the infant surviving as a girl named Celeste.

Eight years after Larissa's passing, Sirius remarried Rosalind Phrasavath, a noblewoman from the aristocracy of Hyranda, who gave the duke a new son and daughter.

Elias looked back at Celeste's markings, and his blood turned cold. At first, he hadn't noticed it, but an addition was beside her birthdate. Not one for any pre-emptive marriage, but death. At seventeen years old, Celeste had died, simple as that.

A blank spot rested beside her, too, but Elias didn't

bother removing it, knowing that Castor's face would reside there. Instead, he grabbed the Glasswood book again, holding one in each arm to consider all their details.

It was an engagement that had been cut short by a young woman's sudden death. The Glasswood records showed they were supposed to wed when Celeste turned eighteen, just months away. There was no further information about what happened to her, but Elias could see it for what it was.

Celeste Whitehallow's death was needed to run away from a forced marriage. In exchange, a false identity had to be made: Lyra Avenyard. Even in death and supposedly two years younger, she had to hide where no one would think to find a duke's daughter—in the Pits. But it was that decision that had made him become her sponsor while he was none the wiser. It was a cruel twist of fate and one that had allowed Elias to slip through her mind to find it.

But why do you care? he asked himself, shoving the records back into their places. It had nothing to do with Torr or Avery. Was he really just sating curiosity? Worse matters were at stake; he needed *her* help, not the other way around. Lyra could hold her own against the duke she'd already fled from. What was even there to help her *with?* She obviously knew what she was doing, whether her original goal for entering the Tournament rested upon manipulating Castor. She didn't need Elias getting in her way. So why was there a tug in his gut to help?

"You just can't help yourself when it comes to strays, can you?"

Bea's voice followed him as he walked out of the Archives Hall. Cold air greeted him, but he was surprised to find Nox leaning against the wall and chewing on a bread roll. The werewolf waved at him, kicking off the wall as Elias approached them.

Nox was wearing what Elias recalled to be their only extra set of clothes—brown trousers and a loose grey shirt—reminding him he should probably buy something for the werewolf to wear. Nox wore no armour, and their bow and quiver were absent, but knives gleamed all along their arms and hips. Their hair was tied back, though errant strands of ash-black danced in the breeze.

"I saw you leave and wanted to see where you were going," they said, answering Elias' unspoken question in a way of greeting. "Thought you were going to ditch the inn's rent on me, so I had to make sure you weren't going anywhere. I would have joined you, but the lady kicked me out for trying to bring food in."

Well, we had better head back to the Inn. Lyra should be waiting for us.

***

Sitting alone at the Broken Shield Inn table, Lyra inhaled a hot drink from a mug. Elias could see dark circles beneath her eyes and pallid skin as they approached. She blinked sleepily at them as he and Nox sat down.

"Afternoon," she murmured.

Elias wasn't the only one to notice her fatigued state. "Rough night, eh?" Nox asked, their fingers tapping against the table.

"I have a change of plans," Lyra said. "Tell Avery that I still want to help her, possibly once the Tournament has reached its end. However, I have more pressing matters to attend to."

Which are?

She shot him a dark look. "The fact that half the Palace blew up yesterday and none of the nobility gives a damn. I was at their masquerade ball last night and everyone in attendance called the attack a spectacle and are brushing off the fact they were the original scapegoats."

Nox scoffed. "You attended a duke's ball? Just like that?"

It explained the lack of sleep apparent on Lyra's face. However, Elias found it perplexing, too. She obviously had ulterior motives from the moment she entered the Tournament, but the complex web was something even he couldn't fathom.

Lyra sighed. "My sponsor insisted. Of course, he didn't realise it was something I had hoped would happen even before the attack." She shrugged. "It's nothing. I'm accustomed to courting dukes."

Elias forced himself not to frown. The so-called dead Celeste Whitehallow breezed her way into the arms of her once-betrothed, and he never noticed. Hells, she probably even spoke to her own family, too. Her nonchalance about it all could possibly be a ruse, but Elias would never know with her mental barriers firmly in place.

"Back to what I was saying," Lyra continued. "None of the peerage know the true cause of the attack, but they sure as hells are trying to cover it up. From the way I see it, the plot was to assassinate the Queen and blame the nobility. Whatever the cause, it should have started a civil war, one perpetuated by the Kherians. The question I'm asking is: *why?*"

Nox perked up. "You're going to look into the Kherians?"

She nodded. "As best as I can. There's not much information, though. All the soldiers were either killed, captured or escaped. It'll be almost impossible to find anyone to interrogate."

Before Lyra had begun talking, Nox had shown little interest in being present for this conversation. But the more she spoke, specifically about rooting out the Kherians, Elias watched them brightening more and more to Lyra's plan.

"Before the Kherians set everything alight," the werewolf said. "The last one said, this is paraphrased, 'The Corrupted One says you will be the first to burn.'"

Elias recalled the words, too, though he hadn't thought much about it at the time. Yet the phrase reverberated in the silence of their group as everyone fell into their own thoughts.

Eventually, Lyra spoke, "Invoking the goddess of bloodshed, corruption, and deceit just before committing mass murder… it makes sense to a degree."

"It's a connection, at least," Nox replied, nodding along. "Something worthy of looking into."

Elias then realised exactly what was happening. The pair were separating from his original plan. He let out a breath of frustration, yet he couldn't blame them for changing their minds. It wasn't like he could force them to come to the Forest with him, but he would have appreciated their companionship as it could have forged a bond with Avery, too.

As if sensing his realisation, Lyra turned to face Elias. "See to Avery and your bargain with her. We'll be in the city if you need us." She gave Nox a sly look. "You're coming with me, right?"

The werewolf returned a fierce grin. "Most definitely."

I'll see you both later, then, Elias said begrudgingly. *I hope you find what you're looking for.*

Lyra and Nox waved their farewells and let him walk away.

***

The Forest of the Dryads was almost as old as the gods, as were a few of its residents. It predated any concept of Darcanian civilisation and was just as conscious as those who dwelled there.

Elias knew the stories and legends of mortals losing themselves in the Forest, only to be butchered by the nymphs. Some humans went purposely, desiring the perfection of immortal flesh; others were just poor luck. It didn't matter the cause, just that their chances of survival were nought.

The Forest of the Dryads knew of its reputation—at least, that was how books described it. It was an invisible force with a conscience that was trapped within the borders of Darcan—invisibly in plain sight and constantly moving. When someone it deemed unwelcome tried to enter, the Forest refused. Only the nymphs could readily come and go; even though many were physically unable to leave, the Forest would always appear for them.

So what made Elias think it would appear for *him*?

City streets turned to dirt roads beneath the rented horse's hooves. Although the horse vendor hadn't directly told him, Elias knew his horse was called Pietro. But as he couldn't understand animal thoughts, the journey was silent.

Instead, Elias' mind was open to the thoughts around him, hoping to snatch up the gossipy chatter of nymphs through his telepathy. It was from Avery's memories that Elias thought this plan would work. Whispers and taunts filled the Forest like a relentless flood—surely, the nymphs' minds worked similarly.

Even though there was a language barrier, he would still be able to hear it. He considered that a positive, as it meant he wouldn't accidentally follow after some farmers discussing rumours in Darcanian instead. And he was right:

flickering thoughts encroached on his mind, mortal troubles seeping into the air.

But then, he hesitated, pulling the reins to slow Pietro. Tangles of thoughts reached his mind, and no matter how much he concentrated, none of it sounded interpretable; he was sure of it. Elias slowly veered towards the quietest of those warblings, allowing it to become louder.

Abandoning the dirt road, he traipsed into a harvested field. Pietro trampled the empty land as Elias urged the horse into a canter.

There. He pursued the voices of the nymphs, their inner thoughts creating a path through the field and out towards a row of bushes. Immediately, it rippled and warped, reshaping itself into the gnarls and roots of an ancient treeland.

He dismounted from Pietro, approaching the Forest border hesitantly. It was suicide to enter its grounds, so there had to be other ways to reach Avery. News travelled fast amongst the nymphs; maybe they could lead her to him?

Just then, the Forest's fronds stretched open, forming an entryway. He froze, watching the trees form an endless tunnel deep into the ancient woodland. Was it the Forest teasing him into entering? He wouldn't play into that hand, not without Avery at his side. Exhaling a breath, he began to call out to the immortal occupants.

Avery Nash, I've come to honour our debt.

18

AVERY

very paced back and forth in the ash tree copse, her bare feet leaving an imprint on the grass she had flattened in the past hour. The black silk of her skirts floated around her ankles, the slithering sound reminding Avery of a snake. The silks and skirts were her much-preferred appearance in the deep of the Forest. Nature spirits rarely wore clothing, but Avery and her sisters had lived with mortals when they were younger long enough to enjoy the silken fabrics.

Bellama was sitting by her lake, twisting endless plaits through her hair. Her own attire was similar—she wore a cyan-blue dress of chiffon and silver thread. Caliadne was absent from the copse, but Avery hardly found that surprising. There was a tense rivalry between the eldest and youngest that none of the sisters ever commented on.

The ash tree dryads were hidden within their trees. It was a normal occurrence for the dryads to remain concealed—sometimes for decades at a time. Avery had spoken to Nemesia briefly last night, only to confirm that the dryad knew how she fared in the Tournament.

Bellama let out a sigh, giving up on her braiding. "Will you stop?" she asked. "Your pacing is loud, and it makes me nervous."

Avery halted, scowling at her sister. It was true that her pacing held no purpose, but her anxiousness made it impossible for her to sit still. Avery couldn't remember if Elias specified a time to meet her, and because she knew nothing about his lodgings in Cerenia, she couldn't risk leaving for the city. Even so, she wanted to do *something*. Waiting around all day was going to make her go insane.

Bellama patted the grass beside her. "Stop being noisy and sit with me." Avery found it pointless to argue and settled beside her sister, arms crossed. Bellama sighed again. "You shouldn't be so bothered about this Tournament."

"What are you talking about.?" Avery hissed. "This isn't something I can just *brush* off. I need to win the Tournament regardless of Torr or Elias."

Bellama straightened. "You actually want to do this?"

She looked away. "Mostly. If Torr wasn't in the picture, then I would gladly do so. I want things on my terms, not his or that noble's."

"But it's a mortal competition; why would you stoop yourself to their level? It's basically engaging in their *wars*, and gods know why that is a horrible decision."

Avery's skin crawled. Bellama was obviously talking about the Phoenix Wars. They had both been barely decades old, but now the memories were coming back, memories Avery had forced down for a reason. The sisters suffered in the war, most of all Bellama. It had led to a travesty of their own, and Avery shivered as she looked into Bellama's lake.

"There's no point trying to stop her," Caliadne's voice cut in coldly to the left of them. She strode out of the clutches of branches and towards her older sisters. "Besides, there's someone here looking for her."

Avery stood up. "Who?"

Caliadne scowled. "A phoenix-blood."

Silence descended between the sisters. When Avery first mentioned Elias to them, she tried to avoid explaining that he was a phoenix-blood. However, it had eventually come out, and from both of their faces, Avery knew her sisters still had reservations about her acquaintance with someone like Elias.

"Is he trying to get in?" she finally asked.

"How should I know?" Caliadne retorted, rolling her eyes. "I heard some dryads whispering about you and the filth you've brought to their home. Whether that means *he's* entered, I wouldn't know."

Avery threw her hands up in the air, cursing her sisters as she dashed past the opening of trees Caliadne had walked through. Sure enough, voices enveloped her, growing louder as they recognised who she was.

"Where is he?" she demanded. "I'll make sure he stays out if I'm led the way."

Roots and branches peeled back in her wake, forming a clear path to her right. Avery followed the opening, muttering under her breath and hoping it wasn't a trick being played at her expense.

Without her waterskin, she already felt a tug in her gut as she neared the edges of the Forest. Avery could travel its lands freely without harm, but the second she tried to leave would be the second she died.

Through the tunnel, Avery could see the light of the outside world. A figure was silhouetted in the sunlight, and she hurried her footsteps to reach him. Elias was standing as close as he dared to the borders of the Forest, his eyes closed and brows bunched in concentration. His eyes flew open at the rustling of the branches that Avery dashed past.

You came, he said in greeting, an almost breathless

quality to his mindspoken voice. *I was worried that it wouldn't work.*

Avery dipped her head. "Well, it did. I realise in hindsight this wasn't… the best meeting place for us." She looked around, noting the distance she had to keep from Elias to stay within the Forest. "You're lucky no one came crawling out to mess with you."

We can meet in Cerenia from now on, he agreed. *And don't be surprised if Lyra and Nox are present, too.*

"Nox?" she asked. "Who's that?"

Avery couldn't see why she would be meeting Lyra again, not after leaving the mortal frozen on the spot, and the name Nox meant *nothing* to her. Her face warmed at the outburst of her own ignorance. However, when talking to someone like Elias, trying to conceal her ineptitude was quite useless.

He sighed at the question. *I suppose it's not important right now. Just know that Lyra still wants to help you be free of Torr.*

Elias' words were meant to reassure her, yet Avery just wanted to walk away. She had managed to twist her alliance into Elias depending on *her,* but in the end, without his help, Avery would never resolve this alone. Having a *mortal* also say she would help made Avery feel more and more useless.

Accepting help is what will have us win. Torr is alone, and we are not. It takes time, but you will come to find comfort in companionship.

Avery watched Elias absentmindedly tug at the scarf covering the lower half of his face. Slipping it down to his throat, she froze at this new sight of him.

Clean-shaven, with a strong jaw and full lips. As an immortal, he would obviously be gifted with good looks, but it wasn't what she was focused on. It was his lip piercing.

"You're married!?"

The question was out of her mouth before she could stop it. Elias gaped, and immediately, his hand came up to his mouth, his fingers tracing the piercing on his lower lip. The first time Avery had seen a phoenix-blood with such jewellery, she did not understand its meaning, but now she couldn't stop staring.

H-how did you know? he asked, mental voice shaking. *No one has recognised it in centuries.*

Memories swept her back not just to the past but to her ancient rage she had squashed years ago. Avery had despised the phoenix-bloods, every single one of them. The Phoenix Wars had destroyed so much of her younger years that she hadn't been able to let it go, even after the phoenix-bloods had disappeared. Her rage had turned to obsession, and she had forced surviving mortals to tell her everything they knew of the phoenix-bloods. Even their mundane customs, like marriage. It had annoyed her at the time to learn how normal the phoenix-bloods could be and how their war suggested nothing of it.

I knew you had some reservations about me being a phoenix- blood, Elias said. His words were slow, as if unsure how to navigate her mind. *I never realised the cause.*

"Were you there?" she asked. "During the Phoenix Wars?"

Elias looked away. *From the beginning.*

Avery almost wished she hadn't asked. He was her enemy. His hands of smoke and flame had produced the deaths of so many innocents.

I never killed an innocent. I took no part in the village burnings, not willingly.

"So you watched?" Her voice was quiet, broken. "You watched my home burn?"

The war was with the mortals, not the nymphs. What did my people do to you?

She closed her eyes, wishing the memories wouldn't return. It was a history she kept buried, a tale she had never voiced since the day. Bellama and Caliadne were the same. A hidden secret they all pretended didn't exist because to vocalise it would only make it more real.

And yet.

"My sisters and I were educated in a village, Kavumir. It was my second home, where we learnt Darcanian and the customs of humans. Our classmates even gave us nicknames... Avery, Bella, and Callie."

In her mind's eye, three young girls stood together, ethereal even at that young age, interacting with a classroom full of mortals. These versions of the naiads were nothing like the present forms—their future as close companions with mortals tarnished by a different immortal threat.

"I had grown out of schooling when the attack came," Avery continued. "Phoenix-blood soldiers were burning down every building by the time I arrived to pick Bellama and Caliadne up from school. I rescued them and their classmates from the burning building, but even then, I did not save everyone. There wasn't enough water to stop the fire, but that didn't stop Bellama from trying.

"She overextended herself, dried up her water and *destroyed* her powers. Bellama was only seventeen... she's lived over two-hundred years without her god-given gift. Instead, she has a corrupted hold of ice and snow."

There was more to the story than that, but that was a tale she didn't wish to say. Still, flashes of it resurfaced in her mind. A frozen lake, an endless song, and drowned men.

"The village wasn't rebuilt until the new era. Kavumir's burnt remains stood as a reminder of the death and tragedy that the Phoenix Wars perpetuated for a hundred years." Her storytelling came to a close as she met Elias' eye. "You experienced it, too, didn't you? Not Kavumir, but another village burning."

Elias closed his eyes. *I saw too many villages burn. At the hand of humans, my own home. The rest was at the hands of my own people.* He opened his eyes and kept his gaze on Avery. *When the death toll grew too great, I regretted ever fighting. I was a coward and a fool who stayed as a soldier for forty years.*

Avery inhaled sharply. Despite her silence, her mind raced, piecing together the time frames. The Phoenix Wars continued for over fifty years, which did not match if Elias had been a soldier since the war began.

It was only through the courage of another that I escaped. Again, his fingers found his lip piercing. *Kallísta Thoughtsinger, the witch who went on to become my wife.*

She realised a moment too late that there in Elias' eyes were tears—unshed and defiant but blossoming with sorrow.

I don't know if she's dead or alive, he continued. *And I am too scared to search for Kalla in case all I find are her bones.*

19

NOX

The Archives Hall was just as gloomy as the first time Nox had been there. Granted, that was less than an hour ago, but they wouldn't have minded a change.

A different worker stood vigil over the entrance, though Nox was glad to see that. The previous one had practically banned them from ever entering, so a new face meant a new opportunity to receive the same threat. They didn't have any food on them for once, so that at least meant something.

"Where do you want to start?" Lyra asked after they had passed by the front desk. "Gods or Kherians?"

Nox shivered. Neither option was a comfort. Sure, they had enemies from all sides, but to suggest some might be *gods…*

"Let's start with the pantheon," Nox declared with as much false bravado as they could muster.

There were dozens of religions and myths across the world, but the Kingdom of Darcan believed in one set: the Order of the Seven Deities. They were a family stemming from the original creator of the world, Maragos. All the gods had titles and names. When speaking a deity's true name was still superstition, an epithet could take its place. In the recent century, Darcanians felt more secure in speaking any one of the seven's names, but Nox always felt a chill when they heard Attalin's.

Attalin was the youngest of the seven deities and the only child of Serian and Heresa. She was chaos-incarnate and arguably more destructive than her cousin, Diaron, the god of war.

Nox sometimes found keeping the Order of the Seven Deities straight difficult. Remembering each one's name was simple enough, but as each god claimed three traits, they struggled to keep track.

Nox understood the gods of their mother's homeland, the Xiatror Empire, better thanks to their lesser number. Not that Nox believed in Lord Fu Shenwei or Lady Jing Zhidao; they were just bedtime stories told by Nox's aunt. Only the Divine Emperor was real, but whether the Su Dynasty's emperors were actually mortal gods was another fairytale.

Lyra led them through the building. No torches burned along the stone walls; instead, there were only fireplaces. It left the place pleasantly warm, but the lack of lighting was unappreciated. Even if they knew it was to stop potentially setting the whole building ablaze, Nox wondered why they couldn't just fix it magically. Of all the Archives Halls in the kingdom, Cerenia would be the most likely to include such feats, but it seemed the Queen's influence hadn't yet reached this far outside the Palace.

There weren't any labels to distinguish the bookshelves, but Lyra seemed to cope just fine. Nox followed her as she went down a particular corridor of books, the wooden shelves towering far above. There wasn't much space either, and Nox started to wonder how Elias had managed to fit inside one of these narrow passages, conjuring a smile at the thought.

They only came back to the present when Lyra handed them a book. Then another and another, and then Nox realised she was using them as a portable bookshelf. They scowled but kept their protests quiet as she continued to stack books into their waiting arms. Nox was carrying about eight books before Lyra started holding her own, giving them fifteen in total before she was satisfied.

"That should be enough for now," she declared, sidestepping Nox and leaving the narrow shelves behind.

They rolled their eyes. "Oh, really? Thought there would be *more* Attalin books than this."

Lyra's voice carried through the Archives Hall as they walked on. "They're not all about Attalin specifically. Most of them are just general texts about the Seven Deities. I thought it would be best to cover all our bases."

"And *then* read about the Kherians?" Nox's eyes went skyward. "Maybe I shouldn't have suggested this."

"Oh, come on," Lyra teased. "It'll be fun."

They stopped at one of the many reading desks in the building. An unlit candle sat in the middle of the table, but there were no means to light it. Nox plonked the tower of books onto the desk, jostling the candle from its saucer.

Lyra followed suit, though more delicately than them, before settling into a chair. Nox took the opposite, and the pair of them beheld the texts.

There was a moment of silence before Nox asked, "Fun, huh?" Lyra rolled her eyes and opened a book. "Shut up."

Strangely enough, Nox did, saving their retort to grab one of the books from the pile. Soon enough, they fell into an easy silence as they pored over the endless texts. The first one Nox picked was a children's fairytale novel—how that had ended up in their stack, they were clueless. Ditching it, they grabbed a new one, but before they could open it, Lyra broke the silence.

"Here," she said just before starting to recite from the book she held: "Lady Attalin, the Corrupted One, is the bane of order. Her existence has only one end: destruction. She and Lord Diaron, the Warmonger, move in tandem, assisting one another to send many lives to Lady Rasthena, the Queen of the Underworld, early."

Nox waved a hand. "I know that bit. Is there anything specific about Kheria?"

She frowned. "King Theron III banished the worship of the Seven Deities years ago, so don't be surprised if I don't find anything," Lyra said, flipping through the pages. "Nothing. But I've found the cult section."

That was a start, at least, Nox thought. Granted, their book still wasn't even open yet. It was crimson-red, embossed in gold ink that had to be fake. Even so, Nox still considered scratching the detailing off, just in case.

"The cults of Lady Attalin desire her favour." Lyra's voice brought them back to the task at hand. "Their worship is typically fervent and used to involve human sacrifice. The practice has since been banned in Darcan, and the formation of such cults is now taboo. Even so, it is theorised these cults continue sacrificial worship and cause low-level disturbances to mimic Lady Attalin's need for corruption, deceit and bloodshed."

Quite disturbing, but wasn't that something Nox caused, too? Bloodshed undoubtedly, and when needed, deceit. Maybe not so much corruption, but if it presented its advantages, would Nox say no? They decided not to answer that. Despite their own immorality, Nox definitely knew they still wouldn't commit mass *terrorism* in the name of Attalin and her traits.

"Does it mention Kherian cults?" they asked, moving away from the dangerous topic in their mind.

There was a pause before Lyra answered. "No." Another pause as her finger traced the text. "These books will only really discuss Darcanian history in relation to the gods. If we wanted one to do with Kheria, we'd have to—"

"We're *not* going to Kheria."

"I wasn't going to say that. We'd have to *read* Kherian textbooks, and the Archives Halls already have some."

"Yeah, written in *Kherian*."

"Which isn't a problem to me." She snapped her book shut. "Stay here; I'll see what I can find. Maybe actually read something while I'm gone."

They wanted to protest, but it was lost on their tongue as Lyra sauntered off. It was true, mostly; Nox had opened one of the textbooks but had done little to read it. With Lyra gone, they scanned the contents page, searching for the section of Attalin and all her dread.

What Nox found wasn't about her mortal followers, however, but her immortal ones.

"Demons," they murmured, a chill running up their spine as they read the section's title. "Lady Attalin, the mother of demons."

The passage had nothing to do with the Kherians or the cults, but Nox couldn't stop reading. It was a myth about the creation of demons, the damned creatures of the Underworld. Nox knew stories of demons, but they had all been tall tales to frighten misbehaving children. They had never known there was an explanation for where these creatures came from.

Over a millennium ago, there was an era where only demons reigned. Attalin had caused so much chaos in the Overworld that she had been punished and sent to the Underworld. There, her bloodshed was kept at bay, locked inside the Queen's Court until she could be trusted to cause less damage. The deities knew Attalin could not stop what was in her nature, but they hoped the time spent with Rasthena would cool her temper. Instead, it did the opposite.

Attalin did not spend her time in the Queen's Court but in the Halls of the Damned. The souls of the damned are subjected to a torturous existence so that they may repent and enter the Halls of the Blessed. The worse the sinner, the furthest hall they must dwell in, clawing through all three Halls of the Damned before reaching the solitary Hall of Limbo. Centuries of endless nothingness must pass in Limbo before reaching the first Hall of the Blessed, where true paradise can begin.

The Corrupted One met with the damned souls and started to cultivate physical bodies for these tortured beings. Akin to godly forms, these new bodies for the dead were to be invincible, allowing them to wreak as much havoc as they pleased. Attalin created these empty shells that the damned soon took hold of, and with an escape route carved out long ago by Diaron, Attalin released her demons.

The era of demons lasted half a century, decimating the population of the world. Everyone from the undeveloped settlements to the established societies living in the sands, forests, and swamps was sought out by the demons.

During the reign, the Order of the Seven Deities was locked in a war against the demons. However, it was an endless battle as the demons could rematerialise their corporeal forms. The Order's power could not permanently destroy them without knowing who the true culprit of this creation was. Attalin was still locked up in the Underworld, now sequestered in the Queen's Court, and no other god would admit blame. This allowed the destruction to continue until Heresa caused an end to it all.

Before the fall of civilisation, she was worshipped most of all by the continent of Tenneria. The people of our homeland continued to call for her help in the demonic times, and so she grew sick of the lack of justice. Even if no one knew the culprit, Heresa did suspect her daughter most of all. As Attalin's mother, the goddess of loyalty, celebration, and hospitality, Heresa decided to be the vanquisher of demons.

She corralled all the demons into entering the Darcanian land by imitating Attalin. When all the demons were inside Darcan's borders, Heresa unleashed true godly power, creating a mass exorcism. All demons in the realm were destroyed, their bodies fading from existence and their damned souls returning to the Underworld. As thanks for using Darcan as her baiting ground, Heresa established an invisible border known as Heresa's Barrier to keep demons from ever entering Darcan.

There was more, but Nox could not finish it, thanks to the slamming of new books on the table. They jumped, snapping out of the myth. Looking up, they watched as Lyra settled back into her seat, a puzzled look on her face.

"Find something?" she asked.

Nox shook their head. "Nothing important; you?"

"Well, my Kherian is a little rusty, and my lack of sleep last night is not helping." She sighed. "This may not be as successful as I had hoped."

Nox had already forgotten about the demon myth. "Since when did you know Kherian?" they asked. "And how *was* that ball last night? I'm a pit champion, too, you know, where's my invite?" It was a jest, of course; Nox would never wish to attend a party full of upper-class fools.

Lyra huffed a laugh. Then her eyes turned downcast, something draining from her face. "I'm not a pit champion anymore," she murmured. "That life was meant to remain in the past, but I never let it go."

Nox recalled everything they knew about the famed Undefeated Champion of the Agonia Pits. She only spent six months in the rings, losing night after night against the First Champion. Nox didn't remember where she came from and why she went through the nightly defeats. It hadn't mattered much to the spectacle of the Champions—their job was to entertain.

"So you didn't join the Tournament to claim a new title?" Nox asked. "You... never wanted to be the Undefeated Champion?"

"I don't think I ever told you why I joined the Tournament..."

"To win!" they declared with the raise of their arms. When Lyra did not react, their hands dropped back onto the table. "Right? No? Isn't that the whole point of attending a Tournament?" Nox scoffed. "Unless you're a self-righteous phoenix-blood or a duke's favourite, I guess..."

She kicked them under the table, and Nox barked a laugh. In the quiet of the Archives Hall, their voice echoed. Disapproving glares came from the few people in the building, and Nox only rolled their eyes.

"Ignore the Kherian books for now," they said. "We should attempt to read something, but afterwards, you've got stories to tell, and I want them to hear them."

Lyra frowned. "Will you return the favour if I do?"

Nox paused, considering the question. "I guess so, but you first."

"After we read."

They huffed a breath. "After we read," they echoed,

cracking open a new tome. Demons lingered in their mind, but the story of undead monsters was for a child's nightmare, not Nox's life.

20

LYRA

After four hours of silent reading, Lyra was glad to finally abandon the Archives Hall.

It wasn't as fruitful of a venture as Lyra had hoped. Her knowledge of Attalin was at least better than before, but no obvious clue linked the Kherian mercenaries with the goddess. Instead, it was a dead end. Lyra knew not to fret too much. Investigations ran like this, but her exhaustion made it difficult to shake.

Lyra's body was on the brink of collapse, her mind constantly drifting to the plush duvet of her bed at the King's Mast. It had been crucial to attend the ball last night, and while she did not regret it, she still wished the timings had been better. Despite being cleared of yesterday's injuries, she still felt battered and bruised. A mental healing was needed as much as a physical one, and perusing through endless texts had not helped.

Still, she enjoyed Nox's company and, when their ventures in the Archives Hall ended, she had a story to tell. It was probably one of the least important things to do, but Lyra didn't mind wasting time with the werewolf.

One of Cerenia's many charming details was its endless desire for coin. Whether it came from open trade, behind-the-scenes deals, or happy flows of beer, there was always an opportunity to make and lose money in the capital city. On principle, Lyra rarely allowed herself to leave the city with less cash than she started. But tonight, it appeared she didn't need to.

"I'm going to guess that money isn't yours," Lyra drawled as she watched Nox hand over coins like candy to the tea room server.

The werewolf grinned. "Elias won't mind," they said, throwing the coin pouch in the air and catching it. "I barely even had to *try* when it came to picking his pockets."

A nicer side to the art of making and losing money in Cerenia was its tourist district. There, pubs and bars crowded one corner while the other side was filled with parks and tea rooms. Lyra had steered them to the latter, not particularly in the mood to deal with any drunkards just yet.

After the fruitless hours spent in the Archives Hall, the sun was beginning its descent into the horizon. With winter licking at Darcan's heels, Lyra knew that true dark would make its way over the land soon. She brushed the thought from her mind, though, enjoying instead the cosy interior of the tea room.

Glass windows allowed for natural light to seep in, but where the afternoon's fading light failed to brighten the room, a central hearth warmed everything. The black chimney contrasted starkly against the birch wood flooring, but Lyra enjoyed the difference. Circular tables matching the planks were set against the windows, plaid curtains shutting out the cold.

Lyra ordered black tea while Nox opted for a coffee. Neither drink was native to Darcan; instead, they originated from the southern continents of the world. Trade routes had been established between the democratic Ihath before Aurora's reign, and she had since secured one with the magocratic nation of Jaranna. Before such global movements, Darcan had rarely owned such delicacies and made tea from yarrow and nettle. Taking a sip from her cup, Lyra was glad for the change, even though she had never lived without it.

The tea room was quiet. After yesterday's upset, it was no surprise the tourists of Cerenia were hiding away. A large berth was also kept from Lyra and Nox, the other customers no doubt wary of the two armed warriors unwinding in these comfy confines.

Nox blew on their coffee. "This isn't really my crowd," they murmured, inspecting the mug. "I can tell because this coffee actually looks drinkable."

Lyra let out an amused breath. "I like knowing where the quiet places are," she replied. "It's good to balance the chaos and the order."

They raised a brow. "And that's why you joined the Tournament, eh? For order?"

"In a way."

"How boring," they said with a snort.

She knocked her boot into theirs. "Breaking in the heads of some nobles is *far* from boring."

"Is that what you got up to at the ball?"

Lyra shook her head. "More just small talk and listening in on their bland conversations. No one knew who I was, so I blended into the crowd. Breaking in heads will come later, I hope."

Nox sat up. "Be sure to get me an invite for *that*. But seriously, what was the point in going?"

"Castor, my sponsor, didn't give me much choice. He's like that, always has been."

From the first day Lyra had met him, she'd known he was a twisted, narcissistic man. She had been only twelve when they first met, and he was already nineteen. Their marriage had been set for six years later, but that hadn't meant she had avoided his torment.

"You have a history with him?"

An understatement, to say the least, but not something she was willing to explain. Only her closest companions knew about her past; it had taken months before she'd revealed it to them. Instead, Lyra canted her head. "You're awfully perceptive sometimes."

"I'm awfully perceptive *all* the time."

Lyra hid her smile behind her teacup, drinking her tea to the dregs. Her evening at the ball with Castor hadn't been as painful as her childhood visits. He spent the night trying to impress her with the excess of the nobility and manipulate her into adoring him. All those years ago, she had already been his, and so he cared little about making her life comfortable.

It was necessary to stay at his side for the next few days, all the better to undermine a man she already understood rather than a stranger.

"The Agonia Pits are a close favourite of the nobility," Lyra said, returning to the tale she was willing to tell. "They've been trying to legalise it for years now; I've always wanted to see the opposite."

Nox frowned. "I'd rather not lose my livelihood."

"I thought you were joking about being a pit champion."

They scowled. "Is it really that unbelievable?" Lyra didn't have an answer. "Not in Cerenia, of course. Same job, different arena. It's called Ironhavell in sunny Feynos."

She was slow to answer. "I can't say I've heard of it…"

Nox rolled their eyes. "No surprise there. You want to destroy Agonia? Well, you'll have to rid the kingdom of the rest of them, too."

"Pit fighting is a temporary solution to the permanent problem of life," she pressed. "Even then, it hardly *feels* like a solution when all it brings is misery and pain. No amount of coppers is worth that."

They snorted. "Spoken like the true reaper of Agonia's benefits."

Lyra's hand clenched into a fist. "I didn't *want* to fight in the Pits; it was forced upon me like so many others."

Only the smallest minority succeeded in the underground dwellings. Everyone else was a pawn or a prisoner. Lyra had spent many nights laying beside the girls who'd sell their bodies for a hot meal. She would listen to their stories, hush their whimpers as the world doled out every misery possible. To say she was the only one who had suffered in the cycle of Agonia was to be both ignorant and a liar.

"If Astrid hadn't helped me," Lyra continued. "I would still be there, trapped in its cycle of suffering."

Even spectators had miserable lives. Losing bets could get you on the wrong side of the anonymous owners, and their thugs would snuff you out if you failed to cough up what you owed. Before her punishments, Lyra had been keen to stay away from the monetary side of the Pits, instead spending her dwindling funds on watered-down beer and thin gruel.

"So you're going to end it?" Nox asked. "The cycle of suffering?"

Lyra blinked. "I might not have to," she started,

returning to the present. "Queen Aurora conducting the Tournament will go either one of two ways: Agonia will become worse, or Agonia will become better. If it doesn't become the latter, *I'll* ensure it will become nothing at all."

"Eloquent words," Nox mused. "Aside from potentially losing my own job, I like it."

Lyra smiled. "Thanks." She placed her teacup down. "So, after the Tournament, your plan is to return to Feynos?"

They nodded. "With enough money to sink a ship, I hope."

"Or you could stay here," she mused. "Help me make the fighting pits of Darcan a better place."

"Seems a bit too self-righteous to me," Nox said, finishing their coffee. "Maybe enlist Elias for something like that."

She rolled her eyes, but there was a smile on her lips. "Never mind."

The tea room server reappeared, and the two ordered more drinks. Nox paid again, courtesy of Elias' money, and they lapsed into a comfortable silence. Lyra's eyes drifted to the window, her chin resting in her hand as she watched the afternoon slip away. When their drinks arrived, the server lit the candle at the centre of the table, adding to the already atmospheric room.

"Do you think we'll see Elias and Avery tomorrow?" Lyra asked, finally breaking the silence.

"I will have no choice," Nox said. "I'm lodging with one of them, remember?"

"Avery, then?"

Nox shrugged. "I don't know the naiad, but I'm sure Elias will do his best to change that. You're the one that wants to help her, not me."

Lyra returned her gaze to the window. "Whoever Torr is, he will only be trouble. I'd rather not see another tangled up in something like that."

"And you have to be the rescuer?"

"Not necessarily," she admitted with a sigh. "But it doesn't hurt to try."

"You forget she already has a phoenix-blood on her side."

"Is that what Elias is? I never knew."

Lyra didn't know much about phoenix-bloods—no one in Darcan really did. Their existence during the Winthorpe dynasty did not exist, and all written work from the Dark Ages was almost impossible to find. She would ask Twylla, perhaps. The witch had an infinite knowledge of the world.

"Last of his kind in Darcan, apparently. Maybe one day I'll press for details."

Lyra's eyes lit up. "So long as I'm there, too."

Nox grinned. "Very well, after the interviews tomorrow, we can do it together."

"And then maybe get him to buy you some armour," she suggested. At Nox's frown, she tilted her head. "Come on! You can't possibly think it's not a *good* idea. Hells, we could get it now."

"Why would I need armour? Elias could probably make me some for free."

It was her turn to frown. "He could?"

They nodded. "Blacksmiths make armour, right?"

Her frown deepened. "Not all of them."

She thought of Elias again. A phoenix-blood would be a

perfect blacksmith with their prowess of heat and flame. His sword and armour were both magnificent pieces of craftsmanship, but did that necessarily mean he forged them himself? The immortal certainly must have had enough time to master both crafting weapons and armour, but Lyra didn't want to assume.

"Well, maybe this one can," Nox replied.

"He wouldn't be able to craft it in time for the Tournament, though."

Nox shrugged. "Like I'd need it. The point of fighting is to not get hit; wearing armour will eventually slow you down and *cause* you to get hit."

"All you're admitting to is your incompetency to cope with wearing a little bit of metal." Lyra drawled, giving the werewolf a teasing smile.

"Fine!" they snapped. "We can buy armour."

Lyra clapped her hands together. "Now or tomorrow?"

"Tomorrow," they decided. "Then we can bring Elias along and figure out if he *does* make armour."

She rolled her eyes. "Sure."

"I should get going, though. Elias might be waiting at the inn."

Lyra wanted to protest. Today had been nice, the much-needed calm after the storm of yesterday. Her body still ached from the exerted energy, and the phantom pains of injuries magicked away. For Nox to leave would mean the end of the comfort as it would draw her back to her thoughts and plans. As pathetic as it was, Lyra wanted a longer reprieve.

"Okay," she said instead. "I'll walk with you."

21

ELIAS

Elias scrubbed at his face, but the tears slipped down his cheeks anyway. An ache burned deep in his throat, the misery of his past breaking him into pieces. Elias had never told *anyone* about Kalla. She was a secret he felt ashamed to keep. Because it was all he had left of her, and he was too much of a coward to let it go.

He could not think about the Phoenix Wars without thinking of her. His encampment during the war had been mainly composed of blacksmiths like himself and many others whose skills related to craftsmanship for the war effort. Since he was young, he had made swords, but during the Phoenix Wars, he learnt how to craft armour, arrowheads, and anything required to win a war.

Back then, he had neither telepathy nor mindspeaking. Instead, with the help of his family, he had used sign language. All the phoenix-bloods in his village, along with many of the humans, knew it too, but no one at the encampment wanted to learn it. Elias was never able to talk about his opinions on the war honestly. He had started to hate it so much, but because he had still wanted their victory and couldn't risk desertion, he stayed.

Until a group of phoenix-bloods had returned to camp one night with a prisoner: Kalla.

It had been instantly apparent that she was a witch, but none of them had known anything of the clans, so all her limbs had been bound tightly to avoid retaliation. Even so, the commanders had decided she was too valuable to kill but too dangerous to be left alone without a guard. In came Elias.

Kalla was talkative and slippery at removing her gags, so they had needed someone she couldn't talk to. A mute soldier had seemed like the best idea anyone could think of, so he was dragged into guard duty outside a makeshift cell built for her. No one knew what her powers were, and none of them had expected her to be a Thoughtsinger.

She couldn't manipulate anyone like Avery. Instead, her skills lay best in telepathy. As soon as she had figured out Elias couldn't talk, she began mindspeaking with him, listening to his thoughts as responses. Kalla had quickly learnt just how little he cared about the war and how much he wished he could leave it all behind, and she used it as fuel to begin her own escape. Even now, Elias wasn't sure if she had lied to save her skin, but she told him of the plans his fellow phoenix-bloods had in mind with her as their prisoner, painting the story of a torturous life. It was the right nerve to hit, and soon enough, he joined her side.

They had fabricated her escape as a Dayburner attack. Elias had scorched the cell into burnt embers, and together, they left the encampment behind. He had thought he would immediately regret leaving everything he knew behind, but instead, it had been like a weight being taken off his chest. After a few days of travelling together, Elias had thought their misadventures had been done, but Kalla wanted to give him something back in return for helping her. At first, he had tried to refuse—despite everything, she was still a witch. She had read that cleanly from his thoughts, too, but she had been insistent on bestowing him with Thoughtsinger powers.

It had taken years and lots of travelling through Darcan.

They had avoided the east as much as possible, where the Phoenix Wars played out. In the end, though, they went to the Klyvning Swamps and there...

...we married the night I gained these powers, Elias said. *We only had eleven years together, but she was the brightest moment of my life. Even now.*

"What happened to her?" Avery's voice was quiet, barely a whisper against the yawning void of Elias' thoughts.

We had planned to stay and live in the witchlands, but her clan hated me. I was a perversion of everything they knew, and so I was exiled. We returned to Darcan and found the Phoenix Wars had worsened. My people were losing badly because an alliance between Darcanian and Kherian humans had formed. Together, they hunted down innocent phoenix-bloods and imprisoned them, while the armies were none the wiser. The clan was distracted by the warfare, thinking the women, elderly, and children were safe from the conflict when, in reality, they were facing much worse.

I made us stay in Darcan to search for my family. If they were still alive, I wanted to take them to either Oyend or Pedreikrari. I knew they might have hated me, but I just wanted them to be safe. We stayed in Darcan for three years, but I never found my family. Instead, the war was coming to an end.

Ironclaw's main base had been destroyed, effectively ending the conflict. Whatever was to come next, Kalla feared that I might not survive, and so we tried to flee Darcan. But at the port city, there was a blockade to halt all travel so that the ships could be raided for any escaping phoenix-bloods. They were using an enslaved immortal as a tracker who found us immediately. I was captured, but they let Kalla go free. That was the last time I ever saw her.

His words came out in a rush, his pent-up thoughts finally rushing free. More tears welled up in his eyes, and he scrunched them shut. Flashes of Kalla's face appeared behind his closed lids. Her copper brown hair and eyes like blue smoke, the warmth of her tanned skin and the freckles splashed upon her cheeks. The witch was almost as tall as him, the perfect height to press his lips against her forehead and promise her everything would be okay.

He opened his eyes, and the image was gone.

Avery watched him with wide eyes, her mouth open as if unsure whether to speak or not. She looked more ethereal here, even in her shock. Wearing her silks and her pointed ears proudly visible, it was like he was seeing a completely different person.

Elias couldn't bring himself to read her mind as his own thoughts were too present to ignore. He missed Kalla with every agonising breath but had never dared to admit it to a soul.

I don't know if she's dead or alive, or if she was captured, or if she ever had a happy life without me. I know nothing. Out of everything that happened, my one selfish desire is to know if my Kalla is happy.

Avery found her voice. "I'm sorry."

The words were foreign on the naiad's tongue, he knew, and it was that which silenced the war in his head. Sympathy wasn't a concept she was accustomed to, but reading Avery's mind, Elias found it ringing true. Not just for Kalla but for everything he had endured, even when she hadn't heard the last of it.

I've given you the truth, he said after a pause. *My people had the right to fight for freedom but were wrong in how they did it. Regardless, they never deserved to be erased from history and wiped from the world. So tell me, what happened after the war?*

She frowned, new questions bubbling in her mind. A lump formed in Elias' throat. Asking her what happened meant explaining what happened to him. Kalla was his heartbroken memory, but this other one was a tragedy wrapped in death. Did Avery deserve to know?

"I thought you would have been there to witness it," she said, voice small. "If you had been captured…"

She was avoiding the question, but her mind told him the truth. The phoenix-bloods were brutally murdered. The humans had switched tactics, giving up on war and beginning a genocide. Ironclaw's armies disappeared, and his people became defenceless, with only two choices left: run or die.

Elias had tried the former himself, and he'd ended up in chains. After everything, the phoenix-bloods had been killed by the mortals. It made no sense. The phoenix-bloods *won* the war. The final battle was their victory, and Elias sacrificed everything to ensure it.

There's still one problem.

Avery looked up and frowned, not expecting him to speak.

Why did no one come back?

"I-I don't think you understand," she hesitated. "They *died*, Elias. I thought you would—"

No, it's not that. He huffed a breath. *Do you know the abilities of a phoenix-blood?*

"Of course. Fire manipulation, fire immunity, heightened senses, and immortality."

You're missing one: resurrection.

A phoenix-blood trained in the arts of resurrection could survive death. It was more of a fight with fate than a skill one could learn. Not everyone who knew the ways of resurrection would return, and even then, there was still a price to pay—time. It took years to steep in the ashes of death to be rebuilt anew. But it still was a gift greater than any other phoenix-blood power: the chance for a second life.

So why had no phoenix-blood been granted it?

Throughout the entirety of the Phoenix Wars, thousands must have died. At least half of them would have known what it took to resurrect, and in the centuries that had passed, the price of time would have been paid.

Elias knew so because he had already spent it.

"Have you—?" Avery hesitated. "How?"

Ironclaw invaded the prison camp I was held in and turned it into the location of the Final Battle of the Phoenix Wars, he said. *A phoenix-blood renewed army destroyed the Mortal Coalition and freed us prisoners. I joined the fight, proud to battle alongside my people despite all those years I'd spent running. The Battle ended as a victory for the phoenix-bloods, but not for me.*

None of the prisoners had recognised me, but my comrades, who I'd abandoned, knew me immediately. I tried to explain, which only exposed my telepathy and mindspeaking. It branded me as both a deserter and a traitor. I didn't even bother to flee.

Elias shook his head, unable to say the words. Still, his point was made. The executioner's axe had met his neck, and everything had gone dark.

I resurrected two hundred years later to a world completely changed. I was the only one to come back. It's been fifty years since then, and still, I am alone. He looked

Avery in the eye. *You're the first person to know. It's the secret I've been unwilling to share.*

"That's not just a secret, Elias, that is your *entire* life you've kept inside. How—?" She couldn't finish her own sentence.

I shouldn't have come here, he said. *I shouldn't have said anything; I shouldn't have...*

He shoved his scarf back over his face, covering up the thing that exposed all of this in the first place. Elias had always hoped someone would recognise his lip piercing for its true meaning, but now that it had happened, he wished he could take that moment back. Too much connected to that metal ring, too much that he was terrified of facing.

"You cannot keep your life a secret," Avery murmured. "I've seen what happens if you do such a thing."

She looked up at Elias, and though she didn't say a single word, he felt drawn into her mind. She was allowing him to read her thoughts and steal a dark memory that lived abandoned in the recesses of her head.

It had been the fiftieth anniversary of Kavumir's destruction when Avery had gone to where the village once stood to mourn. Neither Bellama nor Caliadne had bothered to join her. The Phoenix Wars had since ended, but with the Dark Ages still in full swing, no one had stopped to rebuild. Avery would return to this abandoned place every decade, hoping to find it renewed, but it never came to pass.

On her return to the Forest, Avery had heard someone singing a Darcanian folk song of death and grief. The singing spread across the Forest, calling dozens of mortals into the ancient woodland. All were drawn to the music, and Avery raced past them, knowing exactly where they were headed.

Bellama's lake was covered in frost. The naiad herself was also decorated in flakes of snow as she continued singing. Tears that froze on her cheeks shone on her face, revealing that Bellama's water manipulation was forever gone, changed instead to ice manipulation. It was a secret she'd told no one, same with her Siren tongue.

Before then, Avery had not known if Bellama had gained her mind-controlling abilities. Caliadne's powers had appeared in full force at an age younger than when Avery's own manifested. It was the reason the youngest and eldest had their rivalry, and it distracted them from their middle sister's absent power.

When Bellama finally revealed her enchantments, it wasn't the Siren that had scared Avery but the ice and snow.

Avery had tried to stop Bellama from singing, but the younger sister threw shards of ice-like knives at her. Heavily wounded, Avery had fallen to the grass, only able to watch as Bellama had dived into her lake and froze over its surface. The singing had continued, and still, mortals had followed its compulsion. They had tried to enter the frozen lake, breaking bones on its hardened surface and spattering blood everywhere. Sometimes, small gaps would open up in the ice, allowing the compelled to drop through and seal them inside the frozen lake.

Avery had stayed in her lake to recover for twenty days, but Bellama had remained frozen in her lake for twenty-five years. Throughout that time, her singing never ceased. Avery and Caliadne would try to dissuade the compelled mortals, but it was futile.

After twenty-five years of singing, Bellama had returned, falling into her sisters' arms in tears as she mourned everything they had lost. The sisters huddled together, making wordless promises. None of them would forget what had happened, but there was also no chance of forgiveness.

"Bellama kept her powers a secret for fifty years," Avery said as the memory faded. "It destroyed her. A corruption, a weakness, an othering. She was ashamed and terrified, and those emotions exploded into the deaths of dozens." She watched Elias. "I don't think you're the kind of man to go on a murdering spree, but keeping your life locked inside for so long is going to destroy you, too."

Elias closed his eyes. Kalla drifted back into his thoughts—the only place she would ever be. He had thought in the fifty years since his resurrection, he might have been able to move on, but the grief had only burned on, growing harsher and brighter the more he thought of her. Elias barely grieved his own death because at least it had already passed. It was the unknown fates of his people and the love of his life that kept him frozen in place. If he knew the truth, could he finally let the past rest?

Elias had spent all this time trying to help others with their pasts, pretending as if it wasn't him who needed help. Lyra, Nox, and Avery all held tragedy in their lives, and not a single one let it destroy them, while Elias continued to allow himself to suffer. It was pathetic, but it was all he knew.

There's not many people in this world who can stop to understand the weight of this world, he said, opening his eyes. *Not like us immortals.*

Avery gave him a sad smile. "We were made to endure, just not alone."

Did he believe that? The truth was finally out, and Avery knew his past, whether he liked it or not. He would continue to help her. Torr still deserved to die for all he'd done as a duke's lapdog. Elias would help Lyra and Nox root out the Kherians, and he supposed Avery might tag along, too.

Afterwards, when the world had calmed down, he would

return to Vespis. The naiad would forget his past, and the mortals would never have to know. Elias could disappear again from the present and drop all the strays for good. He would stay alone, a coward and a fool until his last breath.

Even though every nerve in his body screamed to do otherwise.

Tomorrow, we will meet for the interviews, Elias forced himself to say. *We will meet with Lyra and Nox, the two mortals who saved your life yesterday. Do not undermine them because I think they will be imperative for our survival.* He stared into Avery's eyes. *When all of this is said and done, I want to remain good friends with you all. My time alone is complete. Our time together is just beginning.*

There was still a weight in his chest and an ache in his throat. His memories were still too fresh in his mind, his thoughts racing too fast. All he could focus on was his words, his promise.

Avery was silent, her doubts reverberating through her mind. Her true companions in life had only ever been her sisters and dryads; to accept the friendship of a phoenix-blood and two mortals was a task she was scared of. Elias almost wished he could take the words back, to not force this on her, too.

"Our time together is just beginning," Avery echoed.

22

A V E R Y

Long after Elias had left, long after the persistent daylight of the Forest, Avery could not escape the past. Hers and his, wrapped together and yet so far apart. It consumed her entire night, and as a new day lifted the sun, it was the first thought on her mind when she awoke.

Today were the interviews, and Torr would be waiting for her. Yet, with the promise she had made yesterday, Avery had three new companions who also expected her presence. She still didn't know what to think of it, especially with little memory of the werewolf. At least she could rely on trusting Elias, a concept she would never have imagined with other phoenix-bloods.

Although the trees of the Forest should have covered all sense of sunlight, the home of the dryads was blessed by Famara. As the goddess of light, she warped the logic of reality to her own will, doting on her nature spirits to keep them contented in eternal light. Only during the true midnight hours would Famara let her brother's darkness descend.

Avery checked her pocket watch. It was gifted to her by Bellama after she had found it in the pockets of a man she'd just disposed of. Her sister didn't care for the mortal sense of time and found the timepiece not striking enough to remain in her possession. However, Avery had found a need for it, so it became hers.

For the past ten minutes, Avery had been wandering around in circles. She hated to admit it, but the Forest was playing tricks on her.

Traipsing through the endless Forest always put her on edge, and it seemed to know it. As soon as she had left the copse, Avery was lost. Even with a destination in mind, she had been pushed further away from Cerenia and deeper into the realm she considered enemy territory. There was only silence, the usual murmurs of nymphs dead on the wind.

Noon had just passed, meaning Torr would be expecting her now. She guessed he would wait only a few minutes before storming into the Forest to find her at the lakes. Avery hadn't intended on that; instead, she wanted to meet him early at the edge of the Forest. But the Forest kept bending her away from her destination, something she wished it would do to Torr. He was a bigger nuisance than all the mortals Avery had dealt with combined, yet he roamed freely. She suspected his immortality had something to do with it, but she still found it unfair.

Her boots were silent against the wet grass, moisture heavy in the air. If she willed it, Avery could dry up humidity into the palm of her hand, a practice she'd once obsessed over to learn. She didn't bother; instead, she knocked past the low-hanging branches with an arm, knowing better than to cut the leaves with a blade.

She'd donned her mortal clothes again for the outing, bringing her daggers along. She was unlikely to need her weapons for the interview, but something in her blood told her to take them anyway. She left her hair unbound, letting the curls bounce around her shoulders in free falls.

Whenever she walked the Forest, Avery would feel

wholly alone. The dryads always kept their distance from her, but she knew they were everywhere, languishing and luxuriating in their immortality, never noticing any sense of threat in their home. It was a sentiment Avery had never followed; the instilled demand to look after her sisters and the years she had spent amongst mortals as a child had swayed her so. She shook her head at the thought; memories of old had no place in her mind right now.

Avery had hoped her aimless wanderings wouldn't last too long and that she would exit the Forest before Torr's arrival. But when she heard the rush of boots crushing pine needles underfoot, she found her shoulders slumping.

Torr sliced a leaf in two with his sword, feathering the pieces to the ground as he moved inches from her nose. She tilted her head up, fixing the expression of composure upon her serene face.

His breathing was heavy, eyes blazing. "Running away, little naiad?" he asked, snapping his sword into its sheath. "I don't think your sisters would fare well if you keep this up."

Avery crossed her arms. "The Forest took me on a detour; I always intended to meet you."

"And waste my time." His voice was a harsh burr. "Let's go. *Now.*"

She didn't reply, walking ahead to avoid his heavy gaze. Now, the branches moved out of the way, revealing the dirt roads that would take them into the capital city. She hated how easily the Forest could manipulate her travels, defiantly exposing the tricks it had been playing on her.

Before exiting, however, she turned to Torr, hands on her hips. "How did you survive the attack on the Palace?" she asked.

Since last speaking with Torr, that question had snagged on her mind. Despite the overwhelming ordeal of yesterday with Elias, Avery had not forgotten her desire to destroy Torr. Finding even the slightest chink in his armour was something she needed to do; whether to expose *what* he was or a weakness, she did not mind.

Unfortunately, he did. "I don't have to answer you," Torr spat.

She batted her eyelashes. "But isn't it fun to talk about your heroism and escapade?"

He shoved past her. "Not with wretches like you."

So much for that, she thought, following after him into the mortal lands.

***

Despite the damage caused two days before, Cerenia appeared almost unchanged. Scores of humans moved through the tight passages of the city, selling their wares or spending coppers. However, the scent of incense was inescapable as altars dedicated to the Twins, Famara, and Diaron were aglow with candles and offerings. In the wake of such a disaster, the Kingdom of Darcan had called upon their gods of peace and war for reconciliation. Banners of blue and red fluttered in the breeze; garlands of roses and cornflowers brightened the grey day. Avery murmured her own prayer to her mother, though she wasn't too optimistic it would be heard.

The Tournament fliers had all been changed, refreshed with news of its recommencement. Her eyes wandered the tangle of words, but Torr's fast gait left her unsure of its specific message.

As they ventured further, Avery realised the crowds were slimmer, allowing her freedom to move about without

Torr's manhandling. If he'd been directing her through, she would have missed the poster that had her halting in the mortal traffic.

At first, she only saw the word stamped at the top in bold, black letters: WANTED. Avery slowed, interest piquing as the image of a face drew her in. She recognised it immediately because she was supposed to be following him.

Avery's skin crawled as she devoured the rest of the poster. *Suspected to be connected to the Kherian attack on the Palace. Described as unassuming and mortal but is armed and dangerous.*

Whatever else the poster described was removed from Avery's sight as Torr tore down the paper. He crumpled it into a ball before stamping on it with his boot.

"What was that?" Avery demanded. " *You* were involved with the att—?"

"*Be silent,*" he hissed. "It's just a mortal who looks like me, but I don't want you drawing *attention.*"

"No one gets that worked up over a similarity," she pressed. "Especially not *you.* That's the first time you've even shown an ounce of emotion aside from hatred. You're scared. *You did this.*"

He backhanded her, sending Avery staggering back. If anyone around them cared, they didn't show it, giving the two immortals a wide berth. She glared at him, heat perfusing from her cheek as she cupped it.

"So I'm right," she said hoarsely, swallowing back tears. "You blew up the Palace?"

Avery knew the full story of the explosion, how Elias and the werewolf had become tangled up in it and a mention of the Corrupted One. She thought nothing of the latter, considering the culprits were men from another nation who apparently no longer believed in the Seven Deities. How could a kingdom do such a thing? Especially when she was living proof of their existence. These Kherians left a bitter taste on her tongue, so it made perfect sense to her that someone as slimy as Torr would be on their side.

But even then, why? He would only get paid if Avery competed in the Tournament, so why destroy it? Was there an ulterior motive? What was so much more pressing that she was just an afterthought?

"Even if that were true," he began, towering over her, "no one would believe you."

Avery squared her shoulders. "I am a Siren. I don't need anyone to believe me; they just need to be able to hear me." For effect, she dripped her power into her words, swirling her eyes into storms. "I can do anything I desire."

"Not without losing everything you hold dear," he crooned. "Your sisters will die at my hand, your prize money will be stolen by me, and all the rest who try to defend you will suffer endlessly. Even then, I will keep you leashed to me to make sure you can see all that you cannot save."

Rage coloured her vision. "You're bluffing," she huffed. "For all your words, I've never actually *seen* you do anything worthy of those threats."

"Because if you had, then someone you cared about would be dead, and I can't use corpses as leverage."

Heat thrummed in Avery's blood. So badly did she want to lash out against him, but to what end? She'd never seen him draw a blade, but Torr was a venerated assassin. According to Elias, the Haunted Shadow took jobs only from the richest and never once failed in his tasks. What could Avery, without her compulsions, do against that? Even if he *wasn't* a part of the Kherian attack, Avery knew she could not forget just how dangerous the man before her was.

Inhaling sharply, she allowed herself a moment to recollect, and then she exhaled, falling back into a dark calm. "Fine," she mustered. "I won't tell your secrets. Not even to my sisters."

He raised a brow, no doubt surprised she let it go so quickly. "Nor your friends?"

Avery scowled. "I have none of those. I thought you would have noticed that."

Torr grinned, vicious and sharp. "Good." He then grabbed her sleeve and pulled. "Then let's go."

Despite the harsh gait, she allowed herself to be carried along, her own feet barely able to catch up. Avery kept her gaze on the floor, refusing to let Torr see how her features changed. Grief and rage danced on her skin, threatening to crawl out into her hands and pull her daggers free. Torr was an immediate threat, no longer just to her, but to everyone. He was a terrorist, an enemy of the kingdom. He had to die.

And he had to die today.

23

NOX

On the morning of the interviews, Nox was abruptly awoken by Elias. It was an unappreciated thing, but with the phoenix-blood making so much noise in the cramped room, Nox had no choice but to remain awake. They stayed in bed, though, watching through slitted eyes as Elias oiled his armour and sharpened his sword. At some point, he'd taken some of Nox's knives and set them against his whetstone, the grinding noise grating to the ear.

Eventually, Nox rose from their bed. They went to change into their clothes from yesterday, but Elias handed them a satchel. Inside was a supple leather breastplate and fresh, clean clothes underneath. Nox frowned at Elias, but he only shrugged his shoulders.

It looked like you needed it, he said. *And don't worry, the breastplate can be resized, and the clothes are loose.*

Indeed, when Nox changed into those sturdy black trousers and a white shirt, they found the outfit completely suiting their tastes. The breastplate, however, was something Nox was wary of. Even when Elias offered to help them into it, they refused. It was only the sign-ups, after all. They could try out the armour later.

The arrows, on the other hand, well, Nox couldn't help but want to reject them. It had been years since they had ever *purchased* arrows for their needs. Instead, they would fix all their splintered arrows or create new ones from the broken pieces.

It was one of the many archery skills their truest childhood friend, Corrine, had taught them after running from home. Her fiancé would always gift her arrows from the village markets, but she'd always preferred using her father's teachings to craft her own. Nox had shared the sentiment, saving themself from spending their dwindling *feram* coins on something they could make tenfold better from scratch.

Who's Corrine?

Nox huffed. "None of your business." Though they knew Elias must have gleaned much of her story from their head already. "Let's get going, hm?"

Noon had already passed, and soon, Nox and Elias headed out for the Palace. Cerenia was quieter than the previous morning, and Nox wondered if that had anything to do with the day before yesterday's events or the change in weather. The Winter Solstice had been almost two weeks ago, and the new season had taken its hold on the day as grey clouds distorted the sun's usual rays. If it bothered Elias, he didn't mention it, so Nox, too, kept quiet, even as icy winds swept through their hair.

The first thing Nox noticed when they reached the Palace gates was the lack of Kherian corpses. The second thing was the coppery scent that remained on the washed stones. Their nose scrunched up, the memory of so many dead returning to Nox's mind.

You can smell it, too? Elias asked, just as Lyra Avenyard, the Undefeated Champion of the Agonia Pits, came into view.

Nox was still lost on the concept. How had they managed to not only *meet* this icon but save her life and befriend her? It was bad enough to gain an immortal companion from an unknown species to their side. But *her*? The name was just as well known in Ironhavell as the fact that the beer tasted like piss.

"How encouraging, she appears just as you ask that," Nox drawled, pushing their other thoughts away. They'd spent all day with her yesterday, so why was it suddenly so strange to be in her presence again?

Lyra raised her hand in greeting. To accommodate for the weather, she wore a fitted riding coat, wool-lined boots, and gloves. Even so, her cheeks were burnt red from the cold, her breath escaping her lips in clouds of white as she walked over to Nox and Elias.

"No wayward naiad then, I see?" she asked.

Nox shrugged. "I'm fine with it just being the three of us, anyway."

Lyra smiled, and Nox expected it to shift into a smirk. Instead, it seemed genuine kindness. With so many people around, wouldn't she want to hide that sort of weakness? Many stories of the Undefeated Champion were that of ferocity and arrogance—surely she'd want to keep up the act?

I think I'd prefer if she didn't keep up the act, Elias' voice met their ears. *You should hope for the same, too, don't you think?*

Nox didn't answer, knowing it was a conversation reserved only for them. If Lyra noticed, she didn't let on and instead led their trio to the Palace gates.

Nox recognised Captain Renner standing at his post, his face a blank page even as they headed straight towards him. He wore his hulking armour, but pinned beside the emblem of green and silver were two flowers. Renner raised a blond eyebrow. "I'm guessing you're here for the Tournament interviews, eh?" When the group nodded, he asked, "You know you can't team up, right?"

"We're... not teamed up?" Nox answered, wondering if they'd perfected being unconvincing.

Renner narrowed his eyes. "Well, you need to enter separately anyway." He opened the gate and nodded to Nox. "In you go, then."

Nox exchanged a look with Elias before shrugging. "Fine, let's go and get this over with."

"Head to the chapel; there are guards to lead your way. Before you enter, you will need to remove all your weapons. And don't even try to sneak any in; he'll know."

"He?" Lyra asked.

Nox didn't wait for a reply. Whatever ominous threat Renner was giving was no concern of theirs. They walked through the gate, which led through into the Palace grounds. Sure enough, guards in armour stood watch inside the grounds, forming a path to the left of them. When they first entered the Palace, Nox hadn't even realised there was a chapel on the grounds. It was farther out from the towered home of the Queen, taking them past the servants' living quarters and to the far west of the grounds.

The chapel was made of the same pearlescent marble as the Palace, traceries of silver light shining in the winter sun. Standing on each side of the double doors were two Queensguards and an empty box beside one of them. As Nox approached, they began the task of removing all their weapons. Their bow and quiver went in first before blade after blade clattered against the wood. Nox felt oddly bare without even a knife left to their person, but they yielded anyway.

The guardsmen watched on blankly. Once done, Nox

fixed the pair with a crooked grin.

"Are you sure that's everything?" one asked.

"Will something bad happen if it's not?" Nox asked instead, still grinning.

When the guardsman blanched, his partner cut in, "You wanna try answering that again?"

They sighed. "Unless you expect me to wrench out my claws, then no, it's not everything. I do hope you can make the exception."

The guardsman shifted uneasily. "Then I have no choice but to escort you; follow me."

He opened the chapel doors, and a flush of warmth curled around Nox. Unlike the coldness of the Palace antechamber, the chapel was coloured in hues of orange from the torches on every wall. Every inch of the chapel was decorated in roses and cornflowers, and atop the main altar was a bouquet of black and white flowers that Nox didn't know by name but knew were associated with Rasthena, goddess of life and death.

The pews were empty, but in front of the altar was a desk. It was like the ones used outside the Palace gates at the original Tournament, though only two men were sitting at the desk. One sifted through the stacks of paperwork as the other watched Nox and the guardsman enter.

"They say they have claws, sir," the guardsman said. "So I am here as a precaution."

Nox wanted to make a snide comment but kept quiet. The man watching them smiled blandly, the mirth not reaching his eyes. "Do you plan on using your claws as weapons?" he asked.

Nox narrowed their eyes. "No."

"You're dismissed, guardsman. We can take it from here."

"Yes, sir." A moment later, the chapel door closed, leaving Nox alone with the two men at the desk.

Nox guessed the one with the paperwork was an advisor, but the second one, the man asking all the questions, stood out. His clothes were different, and his loose robes did not match any other uniform of the Palace that Nox had seen. He had greying hair, streaks of black forcing themselves through the slicked haircut. Gold jewellery cuffed his left ear, sparking in the torchlight.

"What's your name?" the man asked, splaying his tanned hands across the table.

"Nox Parker."

His face twitched, but he nodded. "I am Cornelius Hattern, and I am what Her Majesty has appointed me as her Liemaster."

Nox raised an eyebrow. "Are you a telepath or something?"

Cornelius shook his head. "I wouldn't be surprised if my blood traces back to those of telepaths, but no, all I can do is know when someone is lying."

"You could have been useful two days ago," Nox said, crossing their arms. "Seems like you're a little late."

"I can admit you are right in that. However, given the unexpectedness of the attack and from who it came, my abilities were not realised to be needed. As you can see, those realisations have been met. Now, Bennet, do you have their application?"

Bennet, the advisor, nodded, handing a sheet of paper to Cornelius. Nox remained silent, letting the two men confer over the application in hushed voices.

Eventually, Cornelius looked back up. "I'm sure you've guessed what is about to happen."

"Sure, it's an interview that's more like an interrogation," Nox said. "You're going to ask questions, *more* questions."

He laughed anxiously. "Yes, indeed I am. Let's get started, shall we? Do you have any affiliations with Kheria or any organisation related to King Theron III?"

"No? Why would someone from Darcan want to affiliate with Kheria's king?"

Cornelius gave a humourless smile. "The attack on the Palace was not only Kherian mercenaries but also Darcanians under the assumption they were rooting for the nobility. This information was gleaned by captured Darcanians, but they did not know the true motive of the Kherians, who all committed suicide rather than be interrogated."

Nox's face scrunched up. A theory was developing in their mind, one that correlated to the cult stories they learnt at the Archives Hall.

No matter how little sense it made, the Kherians must have caused the attack in the name of Attalin and bolstered their numbers with Darcanian noble sympathisers. Neither concept gave Nox much reassurance.

"I shall continue," Cornelius said, clearing his throat. "Do you have plans to commit treason against the Queen of Darcan?"

"No."

"Do you—"

"Look," Nox interrupted. "Let's just forget all the questions. *I'm* the reason why the Palace wasn't truly shot to hells, so there is no way that I am the enemy. I recognised the Kherians at the Tournament and figured out what they were doing. They are bastards who would grab at any opportunity they can get to kill me, which, granted, is a similar view people *here* have, too, but frankly, they're better at hiding it. Kheria needed to be stopped, and so *I* stopped them. *I* ruined their bomb plot."

Bennet looked flustered as he barked, "You aren't here to make things up! Just because he is the Liemaster does not mean you can waste our time!"

"As much as I would love to agree with you," Cornelius drawled. "It appears they are indeed telling the truth."

The advisor gaped. "B-but if you stopped the Kherians, why did the bombs go off? And *how* did you know to ruin the plot?!"

Nox looked to the Liemaster. "Shall I answer him, or is this a waste of your time?"

"Explain to us both, in full."

The werewolf obliged, making sure to downplay Elias' role in the story as best as possible. It wouldn't look good to explain how he'd inadvertently made it all worse. Instead, Nox dodged that truth. Not lying, just not bothering to mention it. Besides, Cornelius and Bennet looked too shocked at the story to notice the loss of any missed details.

After concluding, the two men remained quiet for a moment longer, absorbing the information. Nox held back a grin, but they couldn't help the pride that tunnelled through them.

Finally, Cornelius cleared his throat. "I think that will be all, Parker." Bennet handed him a card and held it out for Nox to take. "You will need this to be let into the Palace for the Tournament."

Nox looked over the card. It was similar to the one they

had been given when they first entered the Palace for the original Tournament. However, this one was reversed in its colours. Gold ink scrawled out their name on black paper, a red wax seal embossed in the centre. Something told Nox that there was magic inlaid in the card—perhaps something to avoid forgery and false access to the Palace.

"The Tournament shall be taking place here. In two days, come here at noon."

Nox blinked. "What?"

"You heard me correctly. Here, the chapel, at noon. Thank you for your time, Parker, and good luck in the Tournament."

Nox didn't move. The Tournament was playing out *here*? The chapel? The chapel was a large building, but only for an event like a royal wedding. It had no competency to hold a fighting competition, and the Palace had already been breached. Did the Queen think holding the event here would give her the gods' blessing?

They were pointless questions, ones Nox would not be able to answer alone. With a shake of their head, Nox gave the men a mocking wave and left.

24

LYRA

Altogether, it took the three just under half an hour to enquire with the Liemaster. As Elias returned, the last of their group to complete the interrogation, a disorderly queue had formed at the Palace gates, growing longer still.

Still no Avery? he asked as soon as he reached Lyra and Nox. Lyra's expression softened at his genuine concern. During Elias' interrogation, Lyra and Nox had discussed the story of his meet-up with Avery at the Forest. From the explanation, not much had happened; only the naiad had agreed to meet them at the Palace. Also, Nox had mentioned Elias taking a quick trip to the Archives Hall yesterday morning. She'd pored over those tomes dozens of times before and knew not to enjoy what sort of information he may have gleaned. What concerned her most was that he sometimes looked at her more strangely than usual.

"Nope," Nox said. "Can we go now?"

She was half-certain the question was a joke, but from the ire that blazed in Elias' eyes, she wondered if his telepathy had found otherwise. Not wanting to make things worse, Lyra answered first.

"We'll stay. She could be running late."

Or she's already talked to the Liemaster and left. Torr might be more punctual than us.

"Even without being able to manipulate him," Lyra continued. "I'm sure Avery would have found a way to make sure we all still met up."

"And why would you know so much about her, eh?" Nox asked. "You've spoken to her like a total of twice. Why do you want to trust her? Or any of us, for that matter?"

"There's more to her than we know," she answered. "Besides, I've made friends with worse beginnings."

"Sure, whatever," Nox said. "If it doesn't get in the way of my victory in the Tournament."

"Well, in order to do that, let's figure everything out," Lyra said. "How did your interrogation go?" she asked Elias.

He shrugged. *The Liemaster could still tell if I lied or not. We did test it at first, but after that, I told the plain truth.*

Nox huffed. "Of course you would."

"He didn't really get a choice, did he?" Lyra asked. "None of us did."

After a moment of silence, Nox asked, "What about the Tournament's location?" Their voice dipped into a hiss, "The chapel? Seriously?"

"It's obviously not going to be in the chapel," Lyra said. "It'll be a meeting point for everyone participating."

Nox wasn't satisfied. "So where will the *actual* fight be?" Lyra didn't have an answer for the werewolf, so they turned to Elias. "Did you read his mind by any chance?"

No. He had mental barriers.

"Typical," they muttered.

"What about the audience?" Lyra asked aloud. "How are they supposed to attend? It would be chaos to bring everyone into the chapel."

There's not much we can do but make up useless theories. We'll just have to be patient and find out the answer in two days.

She rolled her eyes. "Typical."

"Oi." Nox turned to her. "That's my line."

Lyra gave them a broad grin. "It's my line now."

There was a sigh from Elias. *Shall we focus? We need to look for Avery.*

"Short naiads aren't easy to pick out of a crowd," Nox pointed out. "And why do we need her anyway? So long as I win the Tournament, I couldn't care less."

"And yet, that is something *I* can't let happen."

Recognition bolted through Lyra at that voice. She whirled around and found Avery standing behind them. Her hands were on her hips, and her chin lifted defiantly to meet their eyes.

"You made it," Lyra said.

The naiad fluffed a hand through her hair. "Of course I did." She looked at Nox, who didn't seem bothered by her presence. "Seems like you're the only one I need to bother defeating then."

Nox's gaze slid to hers, and their lips shifted into something feral. "And I assure you I will make it a challenge you cannot win."

Lyra felt inclined to stand between them, but someone beat her to it. A man, roughly her height, stepped into their path. He faced Lyra, his eyes sunken with hatred and dread.

Her gut twisted at the sight, recognising him immediately. *The Haunted Shadow.* He leered at her, Elias, and Nox. Goosebumps thundered across Lyra's skin. The assessment only took a second, yet it felt like a century had passed.

Torr scowled. "What did she say to you?"

Lyra was too shocked to answer; after everything she'd been told, she couldn't help but feel unimpressed. The first time she'd seen him, her focus had been on Avery. Now, well, the assassin seemed so *ordinary.* Creepy, yes, but nothing like the legends spun about his name. Killer for the highest bidder, bloodthirsty and rotten to the core. Was it all just a bluff?

Nothing. Hardly even a greeting, Elias answered Torr's question.

There was a moment of silence as they waited for Torr's reply. Lyra could hardly breathe—all her focus was on the assassin and his unforgiving face.

"Well?"

Lyra jolted in her surprise. Her eyes slid to Elias, unable to move her body as she tried to gauge his reaction. The phoenix-blood had spoken; she was sure of it. They had all heard it, so there was no need to repeat it.

Mindspeakers require a mind to talk to. He can't *hear me.* The disbelief in Elias' voice was as clear-cut as Lyra's own shock.

Avery elbowed Torr, no doubt sick of him standing in front of her. "*He* said, 'nothing,'" she answered, flicking a hand towards Elias. "You're just too mindless to understand it."

It was a concerning concept. Lyra had never heard of it before and doubted anyone other than the four present had either. She wondered what Twylla would think of it. The immortal Cometborn was the wisest person Lyra knew. If she didn't understand it, then maybe it was something to truly fear.

Torr scowled at Avery. "And here I thought you said you had no friends. Instead, you made us loiter around the Palace so you could *find* them. Pathetic." The naiad looked ready to object, but the assassin only rolled his eyes. "It's safe to say we're done here," he snapped.

Before any of them could react, he grabbed Avery by the collar and yanked. She scrambled, hands flying to her throat as the assassin tore her clean off the ground. Elias was already moving, chasing after as Torr dragged the naiad away. Lyra remained frozen, Elias' voice fading from her mind as the distance widened. Nox was also by her side, standing like fools as Avery and Elias disappeared down the street.

"I'm not following them," Nox said hoarsely. "This isn't our fight."

She was lost for words. "But… Elias… he needs—"

"Our help?" they supplied. "Look what playing lackey gets you: a mindless assassin dragging your ass everywhere."

"Elias wouldn't do that." Strength flooded Lyra's voice.

"So what? What can *we* possibly do? They've run off now; it's pointless to give chase."

A dozen theories and ideas filled Lyra's mind, but most of all, bloodshed sang in her bones. This was what she was built to do: *truly* fight. The Tournament was all smoke and mirrors, a brawl drenched in varnish, while the fight against the Kherians had been for survival. But this… this was justice—violence that craved a righteous end, one only they could provide.

"We won't need to chase." Her voice came out breathlessly. "We just need to meet them on the battlefield."

Lyra grabbed Nox's wrist, whose barks of protests had them trying to wrench free. She held firm, drowning out their words as the starry void flooded her veins and soaked her skin. Lyra closed her eyes and allowed the purple stars to consume them in one bite.

***

Any second longer in the void, and Lyra was sure Nox would yank themself out of her grip and end up being killed. The werewolf flailed about in the endless air as doorways of violet light hurtled past them in the midnight black.

Half of Lyra's concentration was on finding an escape and keeping Nox within her grasp. If they let go, any protection she could grant them would be cindered to dust.

You're a terrible passenger, Lyra thought to herself just as they punched out into the known world.

She landed on her feet at least, knees barking in protest at the sudden jump. Nox clattered to the ground, almost dragging her down if she hadn't let go of their arm. The werewolf scrambled to their feet, a clawed finger pointing accusingly at her.

"Next time you want to pull some shit like that, at least *warn* me first," Nox hissed. "You said you trusted me, but that doesn't go two ways. Not if you plan to kill me like that."

"Relax," Lyra replied. "You're not dead. And time is of the essence. Come on, I hope you can run across tiles."

Lyra hadn't known precisely where Torr, Avery, and Elias had taken off to, but she knew that the element of surprise was needed if she and Nox were to make an impact in a fight. So, instead of appearing down on the street level, potentially right in front of Torr, she had chosen the rooftops. Not only did it give them a better chance of finding the trio, but it would give Nox the best vantage point with their bow. Whether the werewolf had noticed the consideration, however, Lyra wasn't too sure.

"You know the city better than me," Nox said. "Lead the way."

Then they were off, skittering across the roof tiling as if both had been born for it. From this height, it was easy to follow the city's winding streets and, eventually, spotting the runaway trio.

They were in an alleyway that Lyra recognised as a shortcut between streets. It usually would have been a hubbub of activity, but its current occupants caused any civilian who entered to backtrack.

Elias held his sword aloft, the blade flashing in the winter sun as Avery stood at his side. Lyra was glad to see the naiad free, even if it did look like she was holding her arm in pain.

Torr stood ahead of them, his weapon not yet unsheathed. Even at this distance, Lyra could see the assassin's scowl.

"There," Nox said, sighting them, too. They looked at Lyra. "Now what?"

"Simple," she huffed, sitting on the tiles. "We watch and wait. This is only our advantage if we remain patient."

They rolled their shoulders, also taking a seat on the rooftop. "You just wanna hear what they're talking about, don't you?"

Lyra smiled. "What's wrong with being a little nosy sometimes? Elias would understand."

Nox snorted, and the two fell into silence. With the bloodrush of the void no longer screaming in her ears, Lyra could hear and see everything that played out. All she needed now was to analyse its ongoings to ensure a bountiful outcome.

"Leave us, phoenix-blood," Torr spat. "Give me back the naiad if you want to walk away from this alive."

Elias' hand was on Avery's shoulder, but he stared at Torr. Lyra hoped the pair were talking and wanted to be a part of the silent conversation that the assassin wouldn't ever be able to hear.

"He's not going anywhere," Avery supplied. "He... *we* want this sponsorship called off. I don't want to be any duke's slave. It's your turn to walk away; you're outnumbered. One immortal against two is still an uneven match."

Torr's teeth flashed. "Last chance, naiad. Don't make the wrong decision."

Defiance fuelled Avery's stare. "The only wrong decision I ever made was letting you leave the Forest alive. It's a mistake I won't ever allow again, not when it was *you* who caused the attack on the Palace. *You* who brought the Kherians to this city and burned the Queen's Residence to the ground."

Lyra's whole body turned cold. Beside her, all colour drained from Nox's face. Every thought in her mind disintegrated as her sword sang free from its sheath. "He has to die."

The clatter of an arrow against its bow came in response. "He has to die," Nox echoed.

"You stay here; the advantage is ours." And then Lyra became nothing but darkness tand purple light.

The travel was less than a split second, the perfect surprise attack. Her sword was aimed ready, the doorway sliding open for her to descend through. She didn't care about Avery wanting the killing blow. Lyra was ready for this fight, but not when it came straight to her first.

A hand punched through the void, seizing Lyra's shirt and wrenching her *out*. The darkness and purple stars faded away, forcing her back into the real world. She fell at the change of momentum, blood rushing to her head as she struggled to reassert herself and land safely. Instead, that same hand kept her aloft, holding her up by the throat.

It wasn't possible, couldn't be possible. The man with a mortal face, Torr, beheld her intently. His arm was unharmed; nothing was out of place. No magic instruments laced his body, yet he'd pulled her out of the void like a fish on a hook.

His grip on her throat tightened, her breaths coming out in strangled gasps. The desire to struggle was lost to her breath-starved mind—was she finished before the fight had even started?

"Your control is weak, Daughter of the Void." Torr canted his head. "Your mother never travelled to the void herself, did she? Stunted your powers before you were even born; how cruel."

She didn't know what anything he said meant, and she found it did not matter. It snapped a sense of clarity into her as his grip loosened enough for her to think more rationally. Her sword lay on the ground, abandoned as soon as she'd been captured, but her hands were free to play.

Lyra moved as fast as a hurtling comet, a knife sailing from her fingertips and a kick wrenching her out of his grasp. Torr barked in protest, dropping her and allowing her to duck and roll away. Snatching up her sword, she found Avery and Elias swarming to her side.

What was that? Elias' voice boomed.

"The void." Avery's voice was distant. "He *broke*

through the void."

"Forget about that," Lyra barked, but her throat ached at the words. "Is it true? He caused the attack?"

The naiad nodded. "Wanted posters are all over the city looking for him. Even the Liemaster told me all about the man who fits his description. I don't know *why* he did it, but I don't care. I just want him dead."

"Us, too."

"Us?" Avery echoed.

In answer, two arrows descended from the sky.

25

ELIAS

Arrows rained down upon the empty street like hellfire. Second after second, another was loosed. Elias lifted his head to see Nox laying destruction upon Torr.

The werewolf was deep in concentration, precise movements sending every arrow as directed. Elias thought of their memory and the mortal named Corinne. She was the one who'd brought this skill to light. Every shot was fuelled by Nox's air manipulation and werewolf strength, but the accuracy was defined by that mortal alone.

Cobblestones cracked where the arrows struck, sending up plumes of dust. Elias moved Lyra and Avery away from the attack zone, careful to avoid the endless strikes. Torr disappeared beneath the cloud of the broken road, his form obscuring as he descended into a crouch. Any ordinary mortal would be dead after the werewolf's first blows, but the assassin was unknown to them all. Whatever immortality flowed through his veins, Elias knew not to be disappointed if he walked out of the rain of arrows.

Be ready, he said to the women beside him.

They both nodded, but Elias could see they were shaken. Avery's arm no longer bled, a wound she'd given herself to escape Torr's grasp when they'd first entered the empty street. Lake water soaked her sleeve, and Elias's chest ached in shame. *He* could have healed her. Since the attack on the

Palace, he'd refilled his supply of healing solution. Avery's flask of lake water was precious, and yet she'd used it without hesitation. A stubborn naiad through and through, he reminded himself, one who would never accept another's help so easily.

Elias hoped he could one day snap her out of that.

He raised his greatsword, feeding flames directly onto the blade. The plume of dust was dissipating, and Elias pressed the advantage. He swiped the sword through the cloud, burning the debris to cinders as he brought Torr back into view.

The assassin was on the ground, broken arrowheads and splinters peppering his body. And yet, no blood leaked from his skin, no wounds flowered his frame. Perfectly whole and burning with rage.

"You three won't leave this place alive." Torr's voice was harsh, as if his throat had been lanced on coals. "Even if the werewolf tries to run, I will make all your deaths *mine*."

Not a second later, he was up on his feet, his sword clashing to meet Elias.' Sparks flew at the crash, but Elias met Torr's attacks with ease. Immortal grace furled their movements, making Elias hope neither Lyra nor Avery would try to intervene. His mind raced: how had Torr survived Nox's volley unharmed? The werewolf's accuracy was without fault—they'd all witnessed that. The assassin was made up of so many questions, and Elias wanted nothing more than to answer them all—just to allow Avery to stamp Torr's life out.

Sword to sword, Elias made no progress. Their strikes matched perfectly, *too* perfectly for his liking. It was a terrible idea, but Elias took one of his hands off his sword's hilt. Immediately, imbalance pitched him to the right, but his free hand became emblazoned in flame. Even as he fell, he threw that fresh blaze into Torr's face, a direct surprise hit. One to burn and consume all of his flesh.

The assassin did not even scream.

The fire cleared away, and Torr's face remained unchanged, only a horrid grin standing firm. He dropped his sword away, noting Elias' own halted movements. Torr raised his arms wide, taking a step back as if he were the performer of a show.

"Are you getting it now?" the assassin asked. "Is it all becoming clear?"

"You're immune." Avery's voice came behind them. "To phoenix flame."

Not just flames... Elias couldn't bear to finish his sentence.

Torr sheathed his sword and looked to the ground, where he plucked up a broken arrowhead. The hideous grin remained on his face as he dragged its jagged edge against his bare skin. The blade did not bite; it just slid smoothly across what should have immediately split open.

"Everything?" Lyra asked. "He's immune to *everything*?"

Elias turned just in time to see her fall to her knees.

Mindless, immortal, invulnerable. What else? Elias wanted to know the truth, but with death so close, he couldn't waste time looking for answers.

We have to run. Now. Elias let the words out in a shout, hoping that it would reach Nox's ears. The man before him would be none the wiser, and Elias had to take advantage of that. *Get out of here, all of you. I'll hold him off long enough to follow. Just GO!*

Lyra acted first, pushing herself back onto her feet and sword returning to its sheath. She went to grab Avery's wrist—to run or void, Elias didn't care, but the naiad slapped out of her grasp.

Listen to me, telepath. Avery's thoughts came in a rush. *This isn't your sacrifice to make. Our deal remains, but so does his.*

Avery, what are you—

"Torr, I want to reconsider," Avery interrupted his mindspeaking. "Let these reckless three go, and I will continue our agreement without protest. You've shown your hand, so I will present you mine. We have a Tournament to win, and no matter what these three try to do, I will take them down."

Despite her pallid face and bloodstained shirt, Avery stood fearless before Torr. Her eyes were hard, her back straight as if facing a thousand men. Even without her mind control, she was enchanting. Her words were poised, a sword fight she had mastered decades before she had ever picked up a blade.

"Take them down?" Torr demanded, throwing the arrowhead on the ground. "What's stopping me from doing that right now? You called me outnumbered but you four are *outmatched*. It would save you all the suffering if I killed them right now."

Torr's threat made Elias' heart thunder, but Avery didn't so much as blink. "But you will get to kill them," she insisted. "Once the Tournament is complete, you may have free rein over their bodies and souls; I couldn't care less."

I'm hoping that's a lie, Elias murmured to only her. She didn't react.

Torr narrowed his eyes at Avery. "You couldn't care less, and yet you fight so fiercely to keep them alive now. Why?"

"They're helping me win," she sighed, ruffling a hand

through her unkempt hair, scarcely showing the points of Avery's ears. "We had a deal for the Tournament to split the winnings. If you hadn't stuck your nose into it, then they would never have attacked you."

"Why not control them?"

Avery scowled. "I *can't*. The phoenix-blood is a telepath; he saw right through me before I even opened my mouth. I would have to endlessly make him forget and forget." She waved her hand. "It was just easier to manipulate him the mortal way."

"If any of this is a lie, naiad, I will cut out that silver tongue of yours."

"But then, how would I win the Tournament?" she asked airily, giving Torr a sweet smile of false innocence.

He ignored the remark. "Once the Tournament is over and your sponsor has no need of you, that's when *all* your deaths will become mine." Torr looked the three in the eye before his gaze lifted to the rooftops—no doubt at Nox. "You've all been death marked by the Haunted Shadow." His mouth formed a sneer. "Enjoy what is left of your pathetic lives."

The assassin turned and sauntered away. In his wake, Elias could hear Lyra's harsh breathing and racing thoughts in Avery's mind. His own head couldn't silence either, matching with the hammering of his heart.

"He's going to kill everyone," Lyra heaved. "Holy gods, he will destroy the entire kingdom."

"Us first, I think."

Elias didn't turn at Nox's voice; he'd sensed their presence from the rumbling thoughts in their mind. Instead, he bent down to pick up the broken arrows scattered on the ground. A moment later, Nox joined him, and the two refilled their quiver with the bloodless weapons.

"What do we do now?" Lyra asked once the pair had finished, standing once more.

"Isn't it obvious? Run like hells. We're *death marked*." Nox ran a hand through their hair. "No amount of money will save us from that—the Tournament is a waste of time."

"We can't just run," Avery said. Her gaze was still set on the road that Torr had walked down. Even without seeing her face, Elias could hear the breaking of her mind. Terror ran through her, and yet her body suggested nothing of it. "If we run now or later, he will still find us. We have two days of immunity—we can't waste them on running."

"If we stay, we'll *die*," Nox persisted. "Whatever he is, we cannot beat it. He may as well be a god. Have you ever tried killing a god?"

Torr's no god, Elias interjected, hoping to cut the argument off before it could begin. *And even then, gods still bleed.*

"Then *make* him bleed, Elias." The pleading in Nox's voice broke him. Even the swaggering werewolf had lost all hope. "Kill him before he kills us."

"And then what?" Lyra asked quietly.

Elias looked down at the pair of mortals and saw right through them both like glass. So young, mortality running thin through their blood like watered-down wine. They were right to be scared—frankly, he was too. He'd never faced an enemy like this, not even dreamed of it. Nox was right; they may as well have been fighting a god, not some unknown immortal.

"I have a plan," Avery declared, turning to face the three of them. Her mouth had formed a hard line, and her hands were clenched into fists. "We'll likely still need to go to the

Tournament to fulfil it."

Elias met her eye, the determination clear in her blue irises. *We'll figure it out,* he assured. *Together. We will fix this together. The four of us will survive this; I promise you that.*

26

NOX

Nox hated that they wanted to run. It made them a coward, lesser than a human, but when hadn't running been in their bones? Every new chapter in their life had started with fleeing. Maybe they would never stop—a coward throughout life and into death.

Even as a child, a *human*, Nox would sneak away. Scared to remain in a household of loveless touch. They had spent every night outside in the unknown. It had caused the werewolf bite; running from one life had thrust them into a new one. But at first, they hadn't been allowed to escape.

Captured and contained, terrified out of their wits. Freedom was all Nox had dreamed of in their childhood after the bite—not for the thrill of it, but for survival. Nox wasn't the child their parents had wanted them to be, but that wasn't something they could accept. Instead, it was something they needed to correct and perfect. Nothing good had come of that; nothing of the sort would. Staying in that household was killing Nox in the slowest way possible.

It was where their scars had come from. A muzzle with iron fitted between their teeth and tongue to silence the fire that refused to die. Whether it was the fire of the brave or the coward, Nox had always been uncertain. All that mattered was it existed and that it tethered them to life. Without it, Nox would never have ripped that muzzle out, rendering flesh into nothing but a jagged mess.

A scarred smile for the beast in borrowed skin.

Nox had always worn that title like a crown, but memories of thick and heavy nights just refitted the muzzle back into place. They needed to run, escape, be the coward, cover the flame, protect it.

It's what they had done as a child. Leaving behind blood and bodies of everything they had once known. At the time, it felt like there had been no other choice, and it had destroyed a part of their soul to complete it. Now, Nox would have done anything only to need to make that choice. Instead, there was no decision they could make. It was a done deal, *death marked.*

"I just wanted some gods-damned money," Nox huffed, forcing themself away from the past and future. Instead, they downed the rest of their beer.

With no better idea in mind, the so-called Death Marked had headed to the Broken Shield Inn, invading its bar for much-needed relief. The downstairs was a hearty tavern with over a dozen tables, a roaring fireplace, and a barkeep with more than enough kinds of alcohol to sate even the largest crowds.

However, it was quiet for the early afternoon hour, with only a few drunks dozing alone. Only their table had any commotion when all four crammed into a booth together. Even then, they had barely spoken a word, their cups clasped tightly in hand.

"I have a plan," Avery whispered. She hadn't drunk the weak beer Elias had bought her, only turning it nervously in her hands. "It might be a bad one, but… I think it might be the only one we have."

The bravado and strength she had possessed in the alleyway was gone. Self-doubt crept into her body with every fidgeting movement she made. Avery chewed her lip, and Nox wished they had more beer to drink to avoid watching the naiad descend into cowardice.

What is it?

Of the four, Elias seemed to be the only one who could think rationally. Lyra had lapsed into silence, her nails tapping endlessly against the wood of the table as she stared at nothing. Nox was still considering running out the door and escaping the country if they really had to.

Avery looked up at Elias, the slightest glaze of hopefulness in her eyes as she took the phoenix-blood in. "We need more allies," she said. "All this time, I had assumed they would be my enemy, but… we need to go to my sponsor for help."

Lyra's despondent silence immediately snapped. "Absolutely not," she hissed. There was a flush high on her cheeks, and her stare was downright furious. "We cannot rely on the nobility, least of all the one who *hired* Torr in the first place."

"But that's why we have to go to them. Torr is their employee and so am I. My sponsor will protect us. They have to if we remain useful, even after the Tournament ends." Avery looked at the table. "I hate being a noble's pet, but I'd rather trade a few years working for them than die at Torr's blade this week."

Was Nox willing to make that trade, too? A few years of servitude for their life? Or a risk to run and run, something their life had already been made up of since they were young. Would there even be a difference? What was better? A choice in how to survive wasn't usually that easily granted.

"One noble will turn into nine," Lyra said. "Nine corrupted aristocrats lauding over our lives for an unfair price." She shook her head. "If we turn to anyone, it should be the Queen."

"She has a *Liemaster*, Lyra," Nox pointed out. "We would have to admit everything. If that doesn't chuck us into the nearest jail cell, then it'll get her nobility in an interrogation chamber. The Tournament will be cut short, we'll have no allies, and oh, yeah, Torr will kill us."

Aside from the growing bruises lacing Lyra's throat and the half-healed wound on Avery's arm, they had all walked away from Torr unscathed—the assassin included, much to Nox's chagrin. They loosed every arrow they had brought, and not a single one had made a dent. Even looking at the collection of broken arrows reminded Nox of that failure— a failure that they could never correct.

"Invulnerable bastard," they muttered, waving a hand to call for another drink.

The barmaid swept past, claiming Nox's empty cup and replacing it with another. Of course, they'd already opened a tab in Elias' name. Even if death was coming for them all, Nox had no intentions of meeting it with monetary debt— or, frankly, meeting Lady Rasthena at all. The goddess of death should really learn to keep to herself.

"I don't think cursing the gods is going to help our situation," Lyra drawled, making Nox realise they'd said that aloud.

"So you agree that we should go to my sponsor?" Avery asked. She had been watching every movement Nox had made, practically on the edge of her seat in anticipation of their answer. It didn't make much sense to them, and it was unsettling to have her full attention.

Nox closed their eyes, wishing to shut out the world. Avery's question was simple, but its implications were far from it. Nox wanted to run, win, or abandon everyone, even though their mind was screaming not to. As ironic as it sounded, these Death Marked fellows were likely their only chance of a happy ending. Nox never believed they deserved a happy ending, but it never stopped them from desiring one. Still, there was one nagging reminder.

"Playing the nobles' game will be its own trouble…" they started slowly. "Truthfully, I don't want to rely on them, but… we're going to have to if we want to survive."

The rest of their sentence was lodged in their mind like a stone: *Because I'm not good enough to survive this alone.*

Elias' hand patted Nox on the shoulder. The action made them jolt, so unexpected to receive any sort of physical affection from another. Then Elias' voice followed after. *It's not about being good enough,* he said. *And if we all remain together, I hope you will never consider companionship a weakness again.*

The words must have been only between them, yet Nox's cheeks burned in embarrassment. Nothing in their mind could stay private from the telepath, and despite his reassuring words, Nox chafed beneath them.

"Okay," Lyra said, returning Nox to the conversation. "Finding your sponsor shouldn't be too difficult to complete. All the nobles attend the nightly balls at the Harrigott manor a few miles outside the city."

Nox blinked, surprised that Lyra was so quickly on board with Avery's plan. Was that why the naiad was watching them so intently? Did she know Elias and Lyra would inevitably agree to her plan, and she would only have to convince Nox? Then again, Avery was a *Siren*; if she really wanted her way, she didn't need to ask nicely.

Are we all going to attend the ball? When? Tonight?

Lyra shook her head. "Not all of us… We're too conspicuous that we'll likely get caught. If anything, it should just be me and Avery."

Nox sagged in their seat, taking a small sip of their drink. Were they disappointed to be left out? Maybe not so much the aspect of blending in with an aristocratic ball, but to not be needed at all? It was almost anticlimactic.

Apparently, Elias also disliked his position in the plan. *You'll need some sort of escape route, right? Nox and I won't attend the ball proper, but we should also come to the manor.*

"Hmm." Lyra steepled her hands together, lost in thought. "Provided everything goes smoothly, we won't need an escape. Castor's carriage will take us to and from Cerenia with my invitation." She shook her head. "And if we do need to flee, there's no chance all four of us will be able to outrun the nobles' purebred horses."

Nox sat up. "I can outrun purebred horses."

As a wolf, of course, but no one needed that specification. Transforming was a skill Nox had mastered years ago, and while it was impossible to avoid becoming a wolf under the full moon, they had learned to control it. More than once, Nox had used their wolf form to escape an unfortunate situation. Double the size of a normal wolf and just as durable, nothing could outrun them.

"That can work," Lyra said. "How many can you carry?"

"At a stretch, all three of you. Comfortably? Probably just you and Avery."

I can make my own escape, Elias said. *So long as I have a fast enough horse that can accommodate me.*

Lyra nodded. "I can arrange that. Though... we'll have to put this off until tomorrow night. I need time to get Avery and me presentable for the ball."

A full day to lose faith in this plan and one less day to run from Torr. Unease brought the group's mood even lower as Avery set her cup down and sank into her seat.

"Is there nothing we can do during the day?" she asked. "Or now? We're running out of time as it is…"

Lyra shook her head. "We'll be spending the day tomorrow preparing for the ball. All of you come to the King's Mast by noon at the latest, and we can organise everything."

"Organise what?"

Lyra didn't miss a beat. "Clothes, escape, which nobles we're going to control, all those sorts of things. Our aim is to be stealthy. If we tried to break into the ball right now, drunk and armed to the teeth, we would get arrested and disqualified from the Tournament."

The group fell into silence. No one else needed an explanation of the further consequences of that.

Nox lifted their cup in the air. "Onwards with the ball."

Hesitantly, the Death Marked rose their drinks and clinked them against Nox's. It was a pathetic toast, but possibly the last one the four of them would give. Only time would tell whether they would end up in a prison cell or at the end of an assassin's blade. Nox was ready to keep fighting; the coward inside had to die, or else none of them would survive.

27

LYRA

As the day came to a close, Avery departed for the Forest. She refused any chaperone, even claiming any 'mortal' presence would worsen her chances of actually reaching home. Lyra had given up trying to help out the naiad and trusted Avery to get back on her own.

Lyra had already started her necessary preparations for the next few days. So, with nothing else to do that night, she stayed with Nox and Elias at the Broken Shield Inn, keen to keep using Elias' open tab, even if Lyra thought its drinks were dire.

Still, it was amusing to watch Nox get drunk.

The werewolf knocked their shoulder into Lyra's, their face flushed red. "This was the best decision we ever made," they slurred. "Running straight into battle against an unkillable immortal is right next to that."

Lyra forced herself to laugh, the memory of the alleyway not yet an amusing one to her. She had lost her taste for alcohol now that the plan of attending the ball was in place. Although it had been Avery's idea to root out the secret sponsor, it was through Lyra's experience that they would succeed. She couldn't lose focus on that, or else they would not survive Torr.

You found us through the void, I assume?

Lyra turned her attention to Elias. It seemed he was just

as sober as she was. She had wondered what made him stay his hand, too. Was he afraid of being vulnerable in front of them? Not that she could blame him. So many secrets and stories must have been locked inside the phoenix-blood's mind, and a looser tongue and the slightest encouragement could bring it all out.

"Maybe," Lyra drawled. There was an easy smile on her lips as she considered teasing some of his backstory out.

Torr called you 'Daughter of the Void'; what does that mean?

Her smile dropped. "Let's talk about something else."

Either Elias didn't notice the change or didn't care as he pressed on. *How do you even* have *powers? Considering your* bloodline, *I wouldn't have expected anything, let alone whatever the void is.*

Lyra's heart lurched. Was he drunk and asking questions the sensible Elias would regret? Her face warmed, and she hoped that was the truth. It was common knowledge that human bloodlines were weak regarding powers, and purposely so. It was known best of all that this trend was caused by the nobility, whose bloodlines were the 'purest' in Darcan. If she were talking to anyone else, she would have assumed they were alluding to the former, but with a telepath…

I thought I heard something when you spoke to Castor.

Lyra was sitting comfortably beside Nox one moment, and the next, she had a dagger right beneath Elias' throat. A slight noise escaped the werewolf at the suddenness. Out of surprise or protest, Lyra wasn't too sure. Whether Elias even *cared* about the knife sitting against his jugular, his face did not say.

"Don't speak of things you don't understand," She

murmured. "I came here for a drink, not for talking of the past."

Nox grunted, seeming to agree with the sentiment as their grip on their cup tightened, but Elias wasn't so inclined. *I'm just curious,* he replied slowly.

Her face shifted into a sneer. "When are you not?"

Silence warred between her and Elias. Her grip on the blade did not lessen, and she had no intention of letting go until he made a point of backtracking. Instead, he stared into her eyes, a divot between his brows.

Nox broke the silence. "Let's stay on nice terms with one another, huh?" they asked, using a claw to slide Lyra's knife away. "A dead phoenix-blood won't help our situation."

But a runaway noble might.

Lyra's vision turned white. "That's it." She slammed the knife on the table and grabbed Elias by the collar. A heartbeat later, the void gripped them both. Darkness curled around her frame, and the pair of them disappeared.

***

There was one rule about the void Lyra tried to follow: don't warp when drinking. And although she had abandoned the beer a while ago, its effects became apparent through the erratic array of doorways smashing into one another. The blood rush ripped through Lyra's ears, howling like a banshee as she and Elias fell through the void.

There was satisfaction in seeing Elias' eyes scalded with fear. She had no intentions of letting him go, but the slight teasing of her fingers loosening deepened that anxiety on his face.

Before, he had been all cool-tempered and clearly aware of his advantage; now, even though she'd pared it back with this shock, Lyra couldn't deny this one revelation. *He knows, he knows, he knows.*

She tore her eyes away from him and thrust a hand out to collate purple stars into a doorway. Lyra's control felt lax, the stars straining away from her grasp. Violet dizzied her vision, and nausea roiled through her body.

Finally, the doorways lined up for her, and they re-entered the known world.

Lyra landed on her feet, but as she was the one who had dragged Elias in, she dropped him promptly on the ground. She smirked, watching him haul himself back to standing. She staggered across the room, wooden floorboards creaking underfoot as she found a wall to lean against.

Elias was no better. He was hunched over in a crouch, head between his knees as his breathing turned ragged. Sweat dripped from his forehead, peppering onto the ground. *I didn't realise the void was that hectic,* Elias said. *How can you stand it?*

Lyra shifted position against the wall, groaning. "It's not usually like that, but it can be difficult to secure the right location." Now that they were alone, she was less afraid of the truth he would spill. At least here, she could contain him.

He looked up and surveyed the room. *And you're sure we made it?*

"Of course. I would have said something by now if it was otherwise."

But this… Are you sure you booked a room at an inn?

Lyra snorted, but she could understand where Elias was coming from. A better word for the room was *apartment.* The top floor of the King's Mast had been converted into a single living space rather than divided into smaller rooms. According to the barmaids, a select few nobles liked to pretend they were 'slumming it up' with the rest of the rabble, so they stayed at public houses such as the King's Mast. However, the cramped quarters of the usual sorts were too low for the nobles, so the King's Mast's owner decided to cater precisely to the nobles' tastes.

A four-poster bed took precedence in the room, backed up against the furthest wall and centred. Lyra had left the duvet a mess that morning after realising she'd woken up late. Scattered on the carpeted floors were discarded garments, her ruined armour and spare knives. Lyra usually wasn't this messy, but thinking no one would *see* it, she'd left the room in chaos.

Adjoining the bedroom was also a private bathing room—one that was just as messy as this one, if not more, thanks to the gore and blood she'd so graciously deposited down the bathtub drain two days ago.

Look, Lyra—

She gave him no chance to finish his sentence. Lyra whirled on Elias, knife reappearing in her hand. His hands were up, panic rife in his eyes. Looking at his face, those exact words thundered through her head again: *he knows, he knows, he knows.* But now there was a question tagged to it.

"*How* do you know?" she demanded, jabbing the knife.

His eyes searched hers. *I want to help you, Lyra.* He spoke like he was calming a spooked horse. *I know it doesn't seem like it—*

"You're avoiding the question," she snarled. "*How* do you *know?!*"

Elias looked away, his throat bobbing as he swallowed. *Your mental barriers slipped when Castor kissed your hand.*

Castor. Always Castor. She thought facing him as his

sponsor would prove she was done with the past—that she had won. But even her mental barriers proved that was far from the case. She would always slip. Always because of him.

Elias continued. *I researched the rest in the Archives Hall but could hardly believe it even then. You've buried yourself well.*

"No," she gritted out. Once feverish with rage, her whole body had now gone icy cold. "I buried *her* well."

Lyra dropped the knife, huffing a breath as the blade clattered upon the floor. She turned away from Elias and heard him exhale as she sat on the bed's ottoman. Everything raged through her head, thoughts so long shoved away, screaming to be heard. Lyra covered her face with her hands, obscuring her vision in favour of the dark.

Celeste Whitehallow wasn't her. Even the Undefeated Champion felt more comforting than the name she was given at birth.

Nothing good came of mentioning it, though. No one wanted to know of the unfortunate, pretty, noble girl who objected to her life of privilege and ease. And even if they did, Lyra wanted nothing of pity, judgement, or anything. It was supposed to be a fact, something long lost in the past, but everyone who knew of it refused to forget it.

Lyra, this doesn't change anything. I won't pity you, judge you, or anything. I just wanted to tell you I knew the truth.

She opened her eyes, hands falling to her thighs. Elias was crouched in front of her, his immortal stare freezing her on the spot. Lyra blinked, and she became aware of the tears that prickled her eyes. She looked away.

"Were you in my head just now?" she asked, voice steadier than she'd anticipated. "You just spoke verbatim from my thoughts."

I might have. Sympathy resided in Elias' tone. *Mental barriers are easier to evade in moments of distress.*

She shook her head. "Well, you've definitely managed to distress me." The false humour tasted bitter on her tongue. "Why did you do this? Why did you goad me into threatening to kill you?!"

I knew you wouldn't slit my throat, he murmured. *And... well, I knew it was better first to have this conversation away from Nox. I thought raising your temper would make Nox slip away first, but well, it worked out in the end.*

Only a fool would consider a drunken race through the void and a knife to the throat a successful plan. Still, Lyra couldn't help the slightest whisper of a smile.

My curiosity will always get the better of me, he admitted. *In these past decades, I have become accustomed to always knowing the truth. Even so, I became used to your mind's silence, so when I heard it scream its rage against Castor... well, I couldn't leave it alone.*

She lost the smile, Castor's presence swarming her mind. "So, is this meant to be an apology?"

Yes, of course it is. I just thought... with the ball coming up, you should probably tell Avery and Nox, too. The context of your knowledge and experience will give this whole plan more confidence. I've started to trust your guidance because you know how to deal with the nobles, but I know there is much more you're holding back.

"You also realise I met you only two days ago, right?" Lyra canted her head. "There's people I've known for years who don't even know. Why should you have this knowledge where others don't?"

Because I'm a telepath, who finds out everything in the end? he asked; the upward inflexion made her mouth twist into that scowling smile again.

We need you, Lyra, he continued. *And as much as you don't want to admit it, we need Celeste, too.*

A lump formed in Lyra's throat. So much history resided in her mind, and she allowed another to unearth it. Her mental barriers slipped, and Lyra didn't need to watch Elias as he no doubt hunted through her family lineage.

Growing up, her father had done his best to keep a distance from her. After all, he had wanted a first-born son but instead had a daughter and a dead wife. Lyra didn't want the pity of a tragic upbringing, didn't want the disgust of realising she was a noble, a *runaway* noble who had faked her death. She had been granted a life of privilege and not a single day of hard work, yet she had objected to it? It was pathetic, really. Anyone else would think so.

She willingly brought herself into the underworld of pain and suffering, and it had cost her dearly. The scars on her body weren't all won in fair fights and dancing swordplay. Her home city had its own scores of gangs, and Lyra had found herself on the wrong side of their blade.

Trapped in the bowels of an abandoned house, her mentor's enemies—the Brass Brotherhood—crooned that she would die here. In a sense, she did. Lost to insanity and torture, the last scraps of Celeste Whitehallow had burned away, leaving only Lyra Avenyard to crawl into the light.

After that, she had had to escape: flee her home province and abandon every noble sensibility. Celeste Whitehallow was dead, and no one could ever think otherwise. So she had run to where no one would expect to find a poor noble girl: the Agonia Pits. That tale was an old one, replayed in the exaggerated exclamations of anyone who knew the rumours of the Undefeated Champion.

However, one secret from the Pits she had managed to keep was the void. Her powers hadn't even been brought to fruition until she had met Twylla. The witch had been a resident healer of the Agonia Pits, and all it had taken was her witch-blood presence to activate what had lain dormant in Lyra's veins.

Lyra had never known the origins of her powers and hardly understood the title Torr had so spitefully spat at her. The Daughter of the Void was supposed to be a matched set, her abilities curated and strengthened by her Mother of the Void. But Lyra's mother was dead, choosing to hide her powers and enter Lady Rasthena's halls rather than empower her infant child.

Twylla was the one who'd found the books on the ability, but even then, they were sparse. Lyra hadn't even known her powers were directly linked to her mother's own, that she had lost potential because of it. Torr had called her weak. Her maddening control of teleporting through the void was *weak*? What else could she have accomplished if otherwise?

Her powers weren't meant to exist; that was plain to see. And yet, it was more odds that Lyra took to defy. She was the dead noble bride, the cowering Undefeated Champion of the Agonia Pits, and the motherless Daughter of the Void. Everything made its own sense, even when it should have lacked just that.

Lyra opened her eyes, slamming down her mental barriers. Enough stories had been told for now.

28

A V E R Y

Avery's mind would not cease.

Nothing had changed. She was still competing in the Tournament, and Torr was still sniffing around her. And yet, *everything* had changed. He was untouchable; even with his human features, neither mind nor body could be threatened. Death was only his friend because he wished it so, slaughtering anyone who offended his path.

Which she, Lyra, Elias, and Nox had excelled in doing.

The walk to the Forest was quick. After leaving behind Cerenia, it came immediately to her senses. So when the trees materialised before her, she halted and asked the trees a question. "What is Torr?"

The whistling wind was her only answer, and her shoulders slumped. She had hoped one of the hidden nymphs would know of an immortal like Torr. He was undoubtedly centuries older than her, but so were many of the Forest's own. Could any of them recognise the impossibilities she had borne witness to? She hoped so, or else all her hopes and plans were for nought.

Ash trees drew back as the three lakes of Avery's home came into view. Bellama and Caliadne lay in the grass but sat up at her approach. Leaves rustled behind her, granting the closest semblance of privacy that the Forest could offer. Immediately, Avery saw the panic in her sisters' eyes, and she unsheathed the blades from her waist. Then, a familiar voice curdled in her ear.

"Don't bother, naiad; you know that won't get you very far."

Avery whirled on Torr, who leaned against a tree within its shadows. His hands were in his pockets, and his face in its usual scowl. Avery approached, wishing to cut him to ruin, but he just shook his head.

"Our earlier altercation has passed," Torr drawled. "Don't try to hurt me again, or I will kill one of your pesky sisters."

Bellama's sharp inhale was audible enough that another presence appeared at the sound. Nemesia of the ash trees suddenly materialised from bark and lichen, one moment a part of her tree, and the next, standing before them as flesh and blood.

The dryad's eyes were alight like fire. "Touch any of my daughters, Assassin of the Woods, and I will kill you myself," Nemesia hissed, an accusing finger raised.

Torr lifted his chin in challenge. "Daughter?" he asked. "I see no god. Wouldn't she consider this blasphemy?"

Nemesia's hard stare did not change. "You know blasphemy better than I ever would. Mother Famara sees and understands. These naiads may not be my own births, but they are my children. And you will die for harming them."

A branch snapped in response. Avery gaped as Torr *flinched*. He moved away from the tree he had leant against as the manipulated branch left a deep scar in its bark. Unharmed, Torr just shrugged.

Avery moved towards her sisters, who stood clustered behind Nemesia. Unlike the naiads, Nemesia was mainly nude, her long hair falling across her chest as ash leaves patterned her fair skin. She was the oldest nymph Avery knew, transcending even her dryad sisters. From the ire that fuelled those green, ancient eyes, Avery wondered if Nemesia knew the answers to Torr's many secrets.

"I've received that threat quite frequently today," he said. "I think you will find that you will fail. Do not forget the dryads' pact."

Nemesia didn't so much as blink. "Only the power of a god can kill you; I know that quite well. But do not act so arrogant—your bones will soon fade to dust."

Torr rolled his eyes. "Another ancient dryad lost in her old age. I didn't come here to hear you babble." He pointed a finger at Avery. "Win the Tournament, naiad, don't disappoint us. Or you will watch everyone you know and love *die.*"

He waited for no further response as he walked away, the trees falling silent at his departure. As soon as he was gone, Bellama fell to the ground, sobbing aloud. Her hands covered her face as her cries echoed. Caliadne was pale, her mouth agape and staring endlessly at where Torr once stood. Shock reverberated through the air, freezing Avery in place.

Nemesia's hand, feverishly hot against Avery's skin, grasped her wrist. "There is much to talk about, daughter— let's go somewhere quiet." Avery nodded, but no thoughts came to mind. There was a yawning void in her head, silent and raging with all the pitiful tormation she'd learnt today. Nemesia patted Avery's wrist. "We'll go to your lake. Bellama, Caliadne, if you want, you may follow."

The three sisters trudged after their dryad mother.

*****

Within the depths of Avery's lake was a small cave. It had only formed when the last of her sisters, Caliadne, and her lake had appeared. The cave connected to a larger chamber in the centre of the three lakes, which allowed the sisters to confer with one another when they wanted to be away from the surface.

The only way to enter was through one of the three lakes, so Avery formed an air bubble for Nemesia to float through as they hit the bottom of her lake. The entrance to her private chamber was crudely formed in the dirt, but the inner room was dry and free of water, a concept Avery most enjoyed as it allowed her to sleep peacefully on a normal bed that never got damp.

Nemesia walked past the bedchamber and into the central cave, where Caliadne and Bellama waited. The four could have swum through the same lake, but there was an unspoken agreement between the naiads never to enter one another's lake without reason.

The central cave was only furnished, thanks to Avery. Neither of her sisters' chambers held mortal trappings like a bed or dresser. But Avery thought it would be nice to place a matching set of armchairs and a low table into the vacant cave. Her sisters had initially protested, but now any disapproval was lost to the four immortals sinking into the soft pillows.

"You called him the Assassin of the Woods," Avery said. "You've known of him longer than he has disturbed our peace."

Nemesia nodded. "Centuries before even I was born, the dryads of the Forest protected him from harm and a pact was formed."

Avery's skin crawled. Torr was older than even Nemesia, the eldest of her ash tree sisters. Avery, in comparison, was only a child despite boasting two hundred and eighty-one years of life.

"Torr is invulnerable, though," she said. "What harm could he possibly need protection from?"

Nemesia shook her head. "All creatures of our world can be harmed by the deities above. The Forest of the Dryads is a haven created by the gods, and it protected him from their wrath. He was weakened, of course, but his pact with the dryads saved his life."

Killable only by the gods, that was what Nemesia had said. How could Avery bring that to life? She was the daughter of a god but did not possess that divine blood. Even if she somehow summoned a god, Torr would just scurry back into the Forest, his shield against even the strongest of beings.

Nemesia continued. "He was allowed to come and go through the Forest as easily as any dryad, and in return, he would not hurt us. The Assassin of the Woods became his name after he lured his targets into the Forest to kill them off. Still, a dryad will never die at his hand."

"But a naiad can," Bellama whispered. Icy tears traced her cheeks. "We've always been lesser than the dryads, but to the point that our lives are under that assassin's free control?"

It was an old tale Avery didn't enjoy hearing uttered. In the long centuries of the Forest of the Dryads' existence, its population had always been dominated by dryads of any kind of flora. Only the naiads ruined that pattern, but their presence was rare even then. Whenever a lake or pond started to form, dryads would wax and wane on the decision to kill the fledgling naiad. They enjoyed the aesthetics of water but not the nature spirit that came with it. Avery and her sisters had only survived infancy because Nemesia had claimed them as her children first.

"I cannot protect you, it's true." Nemesia looked at Avery, sadness ringing her green irises. "But that is why I sent you to the mortal lands all those years ago."

To Kavumir. The village was supposed to be the sisters' introduction to a second home of mortality. Instead, the phoenix fires of war had burned away that hope for the two of them. Only Avery persisted; stubbornness and arrogance for strength pressed her onwards. Not that it mattered. She was forced into the Tournament at Torr and her sponsor's hand, and she would use the latter to end the former.

"I need to contain Torr before he kills me and my friends."

Surprise opened Nemesia's mouth. "Friends?" she echoed, a wry smile formed.

Avery blinked. Her mind was racing so fast that she hadn't considered what else to call the three fools who had tried to save her life. *Twice.* It all came rushing back to her. In such a short period, they had connected with her more than the nymphs who clustered her home. Was that what it meant to be friends? She didn't dwell on that question.

Nemesia's fingers slipped beneath Avery's chin. "You have allies out there, in the mortal lands," the dryad said. "And you are looking for more, are you not?"

She forced a nod. The Death Marked would not be enough. Her sponsor was their only chance of survival. Unless...

"What if the dryads helped us?" Avery asked. "He *flinched* at your powers. If you and yours came to our aid..."

Nemesia shook her head. "The Assassin of the Woods will disregard the pact if any dryad tries to kill him. As you said, he is invulnerable. Even an army of dryads against him would still fall."

Avery's shoulders slumped. "Very well. I have another plan, but if it goes wrong…" She looked up at her two sisters. Bellama was still wiping tears off her face, and Caliadne was an impenetrable wall of silence. "You two need to hide."

Her last fear. The one she did not want even her fools of friends to know. The Forest of the Dryads might be a shield for Torr, but it was a cage for the remaining immortals who dwelled there. Avery had pushed the Death Marked into standing their ground because she had no other choice. She *couldn't* run from Torr, for she would always need to return home. Her final weakness belonged to her sisters as well.

"If Torr comes here with the true intention of slaying either of you, you must go dormant."

Bellama squeaked, mouth gaping. "But that—"

"It's been done before, and Nemesia can teach you. This is life or death, Bellama: you have to at least try."

Dormancy was a dryad art. The nature spirit would simply assimilate into her tree and become the bark itself. There, she would rest, her hours stretching to years until, eventually, she would awaken, possibly centuries later. It was a common practice, and it strengthened a dryad's ability to merge in the single mind of the Forest.

However, it was less used by the naiads. Water was more fickle than bark, after all. None of them had ever attempted it, as they had all agreed it wasn't something they *wanted* to do. Not since Bellama froze over her lake. The dormancy of water rang too close to that vision.

"Torr won't be able to hurt you if you are dormant," Avery continued. "Nemesia will help you return when it is safe. I swear I won't let you stay gone for longer than necessary. It would be cruel otherwise."

She gave neither sister a chance to reply as she rose from her armchair. "I have a ball to attend and a noble to manipulate. Get yourselves safe, and I will fix the rest."

With that, Avery hurried out of the cave, slipping past her bedchamber and swimming through her lake. She had no destination in mind, but she did have a plan to make.

29

ELIAS

Elias still wasn't sure if the best course of action had been to stay up and continue drinking, considering it would only end in his own inebriation. But after resolving things with Lyra, he supposed he didn't need to reserve himself. She had urged him and Nox to drink the night away at the King's Mast instead.

And so the next morning, Elias found himself in a regrettable state. A headache bloomed upon his temples before he'd even opened his eyes. Doing so made it worse, the stab of sunlight swallowing his vision whole. Blinking blearily, the world came back into clarity, even if it was too sharp to comprehend normally.

He was in his room at the Broken Shield Inn, at least. Sitting up, Elias realised he was alone. Nox's bed, still unmade from the previous morning, was empty. Their belongings were still there, save for the ones the werewolf had had on their person yesterday.

Elias swallowed uneasily, clenching his jaw at the sight. There was a dry lump in his throat that wouldn't be quenched even after a long gulp of water.

Nox hadn't disappeared; it wasn't right. Elias couldn't remember much of last night, only that the three of them had stayed at the King's Mast, drinking until the sun went down. His headache worsened at the thought; just how much alcohol *was* that?

Standing, he slowly began to dress. Despite the sharpness of his senses, he still felt muddled and dulled. As if too much movement would send him careening into the wall or onto the floor.

It was why Elias was surprised he managed to arrive at the King's Mast in one piece; better still, he even figured out where it was. It's not as if he could remember going through the *front door* before. Opening it, warmth flooded through, assuring Elias that Lyra had chosen a fancier inn than him for her own stay.

Elias' eyes scanned the tavern, and he was grateful to see Lyra sitting in one of the booths, nursing a steaming mug.

Her hair was unbound, trailing lazily across the table in endless platinum reams. If Lyra was facing any hangover, it did not show. She looked well-rested in her fresh set of clothes and sharp face.

Her eyes lifted at Elias' approach. She was alone, and yet the table was set for two. Elias raised a brow, but she only pushed the empty mug and teapot in his direction.

"Nox is still in bed," she murmured beneath the steam.

Both of his eyebrows raised at that. *In* your *bed?* He sat down opposite her.

Lyra waved her hand. "Don't get any ideas: Nox isn't my type."

I'm sure they would love to hear that.

"I doubt it would bother them, as I don't *have* a type."

Fair enough, Elias replied, and he finally picked up his steaming mug. Taking a sip, he realised it was coffee, not tea, so he finished the drink in one swallow. The scalding liquid didn't burn his throat, and he was forever grateful.

Lyra narrowed her eyes. "Immunity to flames is a

strange trick," she murmured.

One of many, he huffed. *I'm hoping you've ordered breakfast.*

"Brunch," she amended. "I ordered enough for three. It made sense that you'd come to find us here." Her voice went quiet. "We'll need all the strength possible for tonight."

Everything will work out. Elias tried to sound confident. Yet, there was a weariness in his tone. The subtle acceptance of defeat tasted as bitter as his coffee. With so much at stake, it was hard not to doubt what was ahead of them.

"Well, you two look cheerful."

Elias looked up at the sound of Nox's grating voice. Their mouth was set in a thin line, purple circles dancing beneath their eyes. Wearing last night's clothes, they looked positively rumpled and wrinkled. However, their loose hair looked brushed, and it seemed Elias wasn't the only one to notice.

"Did you use my hairbrush?" Lyra asked, frowning.

"And your perfume." Nox winked.

She rolled her eyes, but there was a smile on her face all the same. Nox shuffled into her side of the booth, and their hands claimed the teapot.

Please don't drink straight from the—Elias hadn't finished his sentence before the werewolf did just that. Opening the lid, Nox tipped the half-full teapot to their mouth, and dregs of coffee slipped down their neck. Elias huffed a breath, eyes lifting skyward.

With a smack of their lips, Nox set the teapot back onto the table with a clang. "Gods, I needed that," they announced.

"I could have asked for another mug," Lyra muttered,

sipping her own.

Nox ignored her. "I thought you ordered food." Just then, a barmaid came over. She held three platters of sausages, eggs, and toast. Setting them on the table, she disappeared only to return with smaller plates of cheeses, butter, and vegetables. Nox was already shoving food in their mouth before the barmaid had finished placing everything down, while Elias and Lyra waited, casting curious glances at one another and the werewolf.

"Will that be everything?" the barmaid asked.

"Just another coffee pot," Lyra said, picking up a slice of toast and a knife. She scowled at Nox. "With an extra mug."

The barmaid nodded and disappeared. Immediately, the three descended into silence to demolish the food. It had been an age since Elias had had breakfast made for him, especially something of this quality. His usual meals at home were basic loaves of bread and cold cuts of meat, and back in the war camps, it had been whatever game that had been hunted the night before, rationed out in dwindling quantities that had hardly felt worth it. Even the comparison between the Broken Shield and the King's Mast's food was noticeable. Had Elias really chosen that terrible of an inn to stay in? He almost thought about checking out, if only to check in here. Hells, considering the size of Lyra's rooms, the three of them could probably all fit in there anyway.

As he finished, Elias found his headache lessening, falling to the back of his skull. Another sip of his coffee, and he felt better than he had in a long time. In spite of everything hurtling straight towards them all, Elias felt content in this one moment alone. It was going to shatter soon, that he knew for certain. But for these next few seconds, Elias made sure to savour it.

Because he wasn't the only one whose thoughts had started to drift elsewhere, Nox's fingers endlessly tapped against their mug, sometimes clinking as their claws slipped in and out of their nail beds. Elias leaned back in his seat and slowly sifted through Nox's mind.

It was in chaos. A constant stream of complaints about the werewolf's headache was repeatedly interwoven with heavy footfalls of the same question. *How do I escape Torr?* Flashes of the assassin's face were rampant in Nox's mind, their fear licking up the edges of his frame. Elias was glad to see that his own, Lyra's and Avery's faces were also presented within Nox's anxieties. At least they had *some* semblance of concern for the three of them. And yet, there was one final question decisively taking up space in Nox's mind.

How can I still win the Tournament? Elias held back a groan, finally slipping out of the werewolf's head. *We're not prioritising* your *victory at the Tournament,* he said to both Nox and Lyra.

Nox's head whipped up. "Do you mind? Stay out of my private thoughts. Winning has nothing to do with you."

Lyra elbowed them. "You still want to win?" A grin broadened her face.

"Of course, I came here to get rich. I can't do that without at least *trying* to win."

Elias cut in. *We need to focus on the ball.*

"*Or* we could do both," Nox pressed. "Regardless of what happens, Torr and Avery's sponsor will expect her to attend the Tournament. Why not let me go all the way? It won't even be difficult. You two can drop out for all I care, but I'm winning."

Elias was ready to bite back, but Lyra was faster to reply.

"If you're so assured of yourself, then go for it."

He snapped his gaze away from Nox to her. *You're not serious.*

She crossed her arms. "Of course I am. It's not like there's any point in stopping them."

Elias looked between the two of them, mouth open. Nox was grinning like an idiot beside her, and a small smile grew on her face. He clenched his jaw, looking away from them both. Why were they being so difficult? Elias tried to think what Avery would say if she were here but feared she would also have sided with them. Even when staring death in the face, Elias had managed to befriend three people who still treasured the money and victory of a pointless competition.

A warm hand touched him, and he looked up to see Lyra reaching across the table. Her smugness was gone, but Elias did not expect her scheming to stop. "I understand what we need to prioritise," she said. "My original intentions to be here must also be shunted to the side. The Undefeated Champion of the Agonia Pits was supposed to come and destroy the Royal Tournament; now it's falling apart all on its own."

Elias listened intently. He hadn't heard Lyra's full motivations for attending the Royal Tournament before. Of course, he had Nox's memories to glean, but hearing the honesty firsthand was something he now considered a luxury from her.

"The Royal Tournament has become its own failure, but it won't end the illegal fighting pits," Lyra continued. "I might not be able to do it now, but I will tackle it another day."

"If we survive the Death Mark," Nox replied dryly.

When *we survive the Death Mark,* Elias corrected.

Lyra nodded. "You said it yourself: we're going to get through this, but we're going to take the world down with us, too. It's only right."

Was it? Elias considered the thought. He came here to stop an assassin, to end the cycle of corrupt nobles destroying lives—not to take the world with it. Everything and nothing had changed. He never wanted to win and had never meant to befriend three amazing fighters, but now he realised he could never have done this alone. He needed them, and they most definitely needed him. Strings of a plan began to weave in his mind, and Elias had no intention of letting go.

We've got a lot to figure out, he said before turning his gaze to Nox. *And you'll need a bit more training if you truly want to win this fight.*

Nox's brows raised. "You're agreeing?"

Elias nodded, and he realised he was grinning. *We have an assassin to kill, a noble to find, and a Tournament to win. We're going to need all the preparation we can get.*

"If that's the case, I have some friends for you to meet." Lyra's smile turned feline. "It's time for both to meet the Incarnatus."

***

Elias thought Lyra's bedroom was messy the first time he saw it. He hadn't realised then it could get *worse.*

The duvet was on the floor, as were half the pillows. Strewn across the vanity were cosmetics, clips and laces, and the occasional knife. Nox's bow and quiver were on the rug in the middle of the room. Lyra, who'd let Elias and Nox in, gingerly stepped over the fallen weaponry and grabbed the duvet.

"Seriously, Nox?" she asked, fluffing it and laying it flat

on the rumpled bed. "Do you understand how to leave a room how you found it?"

The werewolf was leaning against the wall, arms crossed. "I did leave it as I found it."

She stuck her tongue out but continued tidying up the bed. In the apartment, there was a small dining table with four chairs. Elias sat, rearranging the skewed flower pot and readjusting its wilting flowers. A petal fell in his wake, and with a single touch, he let it burst into flame.

I don't think I actually know what we're getting into, Elias said, breaking the silence. *Last I checked, the incarnatus were handmaidens of Lady Rasthena, not friends of an ex-pit champion.*

"How very perceptive, Elias," Lyra drawled. "The Incarnatus are my clan."

Another moment of silence passed before Nox said, "That clears up nothing."

She huffed, collapsing onto the bed. "Cerenia is basically split up between different... gangs." Her voice shuddered at the word. "I am the leader of one of those, and my Second and Third are coming here." Lyra smiled at Nox. "You actually know of one of them already."

The werewolf narrowed their eyes, but if they were going to say anything, it was interrupted by someone knocking on the door. Lyra sprang up from the bed, dashing forward. Hand hovering over the doorknob, she fixed Elias and Nox a fierce grin, clearly enjoying herself. She opened the door, and two women walked in.

Both were imposing in height. Shorter than Elias, but the one who entered first was the same height as Nox. She had brown skin and dark brown hair to match, braided away to keep her sight clear. Bands of bronze decorated the braids, stopping short at her chest. Leather armour covered her body, though glinting beneath the breastplate was dark chainmail. Sheathed at her thighs were axes and knives along her muscled arms.

The second woman looked disorientingly dissimilar. Almost at eye-level with Elias, her skin was paper-white, dazzled by hundreds of freckles. Blood-red hair flowed down to her waist, unbound and ruly with endless curls. She wore no armour and strangely seemed to be unarmed, too. Instead, she wore a grey floor-length dress, a black belt at her waist, and an array of charms and bottles attached to it. The trumpet sleeves of her dress revealed skinny wrists but emblazoned all over the flesh was black ink. Stars and whorls decorated her skin like rings and bracelets. But Elias stiffened at the true sight—a concentric sigil lay on the back of her right hand, and upon the palm of her left, there was its twin.

A Cometborn witch.

"Elias, Nox, meet Astrid Shernev and Twylla Cometborn. My Second and Third, respectively."

Elias couldn't stop his mouth from gaping. He knew of all the witch clans, seven in total—six possessed particular traits, as clearly distinguished in their clan name. Stormbringers manipulated the weather, Nightflayers: darkness and shadows, and the list went on. But the Cometborns held no boundaries; they existed outside the usual scope of witch-blood. A wicked force all on their own, practically an enemy to the rest of the six clans, and yet one stood right before him.

Sneaking a glance at Nox, he realised they, too, were gaping—not at the witch, but at Astrid. Then, he remembered what Lyra had said.

How do you know her? Elias asked Nox alone.

The werewolf's eyes were wide, their face not registering his words. "The First Champion of Agonia." Nox's voice was a whisper. "You *actually* became friends with the First Champion?"

"Only after I pummelled her a hundred times," Astrid replied. Her voice was harsh, but there was humour in her words, a lingering smile on her face. "How could I say no after that?"

Twylla squealed, running into Lyra's arms. Their embrace was tight, and Lyra's face was lost beneath the witch's blood-red curls. When they broke apart, she spoke rapidly. "I can't believe any of this is happening! Gods above, this is as exciting as it is *terrifying*." Her eyes were alight with a dazzling fire. She then turned to face Elias and Nox. "I've heard so much about you two; it's wonderful to meet you both."

Elias frowned. *You have?*

The intensity in Twylla's voice burned anew. "Of course, we've kept in close communication." Whatever that meant, she failed to divulge. "But you are the most interesting of all, telepathic mindspeaker. I really desperately wanted to meet you just to figure it out. And here you are."

Then her voice reached his ears. Elias hadn't bothered trying to break into her mind, and it was apparent this was the woman who had taught Lyra mental barriers. And yet, Twylla brought her thoughts to him with one straightforward statement.

It's nice to meet a half-witch.

30

NOX

Nox still wasn't sure they were processing anything right. The Undefeated Champion and the First Champion of Agonia stood next to each other in the same room as *Nox*. And the other woman beside them, what was her name? Something Cometborn? Weren't those witches?

Yes, Nox, Cometborns are witches.

They almost jumped out of their skin at the suddenness of Elias' voice in their head. In turn, he didn't look much better. His mouth had gone wide, shock coating his features like a second skin. Nox wondered which of the two women was the cause of that and if they should be worried.

Nothing's wrong, Elias answered their thoughts. Just... disconcerting.

Nox snorted, conjuring the attention of the three women huddled at the front door. Lyra canted her head, a smile on her face.

"Whispering over there, are we?" she asked.

"What else would we do?" they sniped. "You just revealed you have actual friends—you can't blame us for being surprised."

Astrid huffed a laugh, and Nox's whole body heated in pride. Lyra was also a Champion of Agonia, but Astrid was on another level. What Lyra achieved in one night, Astrid had completed day after day for months. She had destroyed every bastard who walked into Agonia's main arena, brutalising them with such quickness and ease that it had earned her a title no one else had been worthy enough to have invented for them.

Even so, Nox felt themself sizing her up. They were similar heights, and her build was just as hard as theirs, maybe even more so. Nox favoured their claws and archery, so their upper body was stronger than the rest. On the other hand, Astrid was perfectly formed from head to toe with muscle. Back in Ironhavell, Nox was unbeatable. Feynos' own fighting pits were no challenge to them. But did that mean they could take on Astrid? Every fibre in their being wanted to try, and Nox felt their claws itching to strike out.

"Let's move on to more pressing matters," Lyra said, clearing her throat. "Twylla and Astrid have come with some much-needed preparations for the ball. Without Avery here, though, there's only a few things we need to do."

Twylla clapped her hands together. "I will need something from you both," she said to Nox and Elias.

Nox's brows raised, and the witch busied herself with one of the many pouches on her belt. She produced a thin scroll of blank parchment and a pencil, twirling the latter between her fingers. "Who'd like to go first?" Twylla asked Elias and Nox.

"Uh…" Nox trailed off.

Lyra interrupted, holding her finger in the air. Her eyes were alight with mischief. "Nox can go first. It'll be simple."

Any attempt of protest was lost as Lyra moved over to the vanity and grabbed the hairbrush Nox had used only an hour before. She peeled off a strand of ash-black hair and handed it to Twylla. The witch tied the strand to the parchment, and Nox's stomach turned at the sight.

"This isn't going to kill me, right?"

Twylla's eyes flicked up to meet theirs. "Of course not. I'd use a blade to do that."

With the strand knotted in place, the witch began to murmur under her breath. Nox couldn't interpret the words, the syllables a tangle from another nation.

Looking at Elias for confirmation, he nodded. Klyvning tongue, the language of witches and enchantments.

As Twylla finished her murmurings, the hair sank into the parchment. Nox blinked, finding the strand seemingly wiped from existence. They tugged at their hair, concerned the spell might have taken the rest, too.

"Now, the fun part," Twylla said, pressing pencil to paper. Whatever message she scrawled out, she didn't show; she only snapped her fingers.

The parchment disappeared, and then, right before Nox, it reappeared, floating above their chest. Nothing was there only a second before, yet a spark of orange brought it right before their eyes. Nox snatched the falling parchment out of the air. Clutched between their fingers, Nox unrolled the note and read its message:

Hello, werewolf.

Nox looked back up, and Twylla stood in front of them. How she'd moved so fast without them noticing almost made them jump. She was all grins, but Twylla only held out the pencil.

"Now it's your turn."

They took the pencil, and Twylla returned to Lyra's side.

Nox could comprehend what had happened; a message from a witch had been passed onto them. What they couldn't understand was what 'their' turn would entail. Nox didn't have witch-blood, and a piece of paper with their hair inside wouldn't change that. Finishing the note, they looked up at Twylla with a raised brow.

"Now what?"

"Click your fingers." She was grinning, hands clasped together.

Why was this so exciting to her? Or was it just a prank to humiliate them? Nox hadn't thought of that, and now they were ready to tear the parchment to shreds.

Don't, Elias warned. This is Lyra. She wouldn't do that.

Actually, it's Twylla, Nox thought, knowing the telepath was listening. With a huffed breath, they snapped their fingers.

The parchment winked out of existence. Ash littered Nox's fingers, threads of smoke and flame cloying their senses.

Looking up, Twylla was already holding it. She unfurled the note and read it aloud, "'Hello to you, too.'" Twylla let out a laugh. "I was hoping for more excitement, but it's wonderful, right?"

What exactly is it? Elias asked.

Twylla put the note back into her belt pouch. "They're called paper blazes, and they're a very useful way to communicate."

"I've been in constant contact with Twylla through them," Lyra supplied. "And for the upcoming events, we will need it."

"All you need is to borrow a hairbrush," Nox muttered, staring at the smudge of ash still on their fingers.

"It's not just hair," Twylla said. "Anything that is a 'part' of someone can be used. Tears, eyelashes, flesh. The usual."

Nox shivered, glad that they had only lost a strand of hair. Even so, they weren't convinced. "You both seem so eager to help…"

"Of course!" Twylla exclaimed. "We won't come tonight to the ball for the sake of numbers, but we will attend the Tournament in the audience in case anything goes awry."

Nox threw their hands in the air. "Why? You just met us. Hells, I still only met these two a couple days ago."

"And yet a bond has already been forged," Twylla pressed. "One that will keep growing stronger." She shook her head. "I know itsounds outlandish, but we all have to help one another first before stopping Torr."

An ugly feeling grew in Nox's throat. Receiving help from others wasn't something Nox did. No matter the person, the dynamic always ended in betrayal or separation. Nox had never wanted to be the loner they were, but the world had deemed it their best trait, and they had long ago given up trying to twist that fate.

Sure, Nox didn't want to see any of their Death Marked fellows butchered by the invulnerable hand of Torr. But after all that ended, would any of them want to stay by their side? Nox doubted it.

No, dreaded it. All their fears were linked to that one sentiment: why would anyone want to help me? Short-term help was usually unavoidable, but the forming plan involving Twylla and Astrid told Nox enough that they were all expecting a war. One that Nox feared would end in tragedy.

Nox's hands clenched into fists as they closed their eyes. Silence drew out, waiting for their reply that refused to come out. Elias would know what they were thinking, but

Nox's mind would not quieten. Trust was like water; impossible to hold onto as it either saved your life or drowned you. Nox had never known a time when it hadn't eventually taken them under.

Their eyes snapped open. "Do whatever you like." Their voice was guttural. "Just don't let it get me killed in the process."

Before anyone could answer, Nox pushed themself off the wall and stormed out of the room, letting a phantom wind slam the door shut behind them.

***

A strange addition the city of Cerenia had that Avalward lacked was the public parks. Nox supposed it was due to the size difference. Avalward was a town with probably a fifth of the population, though that number swelled every night when Ironhavell opened its gates.

In the brisk air, Nox was alone in the park. A fountain spewed slushy water at its centre, the manicured lawn dusted in light frost. Stone benches dotted the place, *reminiscent of the Palace courtyard,* Nox thought. They lay down on one of them, stretching their legs out and propping an arm up to hide the sun's glare.

Hot blood rushed through their cheeks, threatening to burst through their skull. Had they gone too far? Was sticking close to these people a mistake? Or was it running away? Nox didn't bother to answer the questions. Nothing would come of it anyway. Death was coming for them all, and sitting around, worried they hadn't made enough friends in this life, was *not* going to be one of Nox's final concerns.

Something knocked into their outstretched foot. "Hey. Are you asleep? Dead?"

Nox had only heard the voice once, but they recognised it immediately. Sitting up, they blinked back the sunlight and found the First Champion of Agonia frowning at them. Her arms were crossed, and colour was high on her brown cheeks.

"What are you doing here?" Nox demanded.

She tilted her head. "I wanted to ask you the same thing…" her voice trailed off. "Nox, right?"

Hearing their name on her lips was another shot to their head. What was it with this woman? They'd never even see her fight in Agonia, but all the rumours, all the retellings of her battles, well—it was just *legendary.* She was the closest thing to an inspiration for Nox, simple as. Their cheeks burned at the thought, glad that Elias wasn't around to hear it.

"I came here to cool off," they said, the words felt mangled on their tongue. "I'm not one for discussions."

Astrid grunted in affirmation. "Same here. Action is more decisive than words."

They could hardly believe they were talking with Astrid in the first place, but having her *agree* with them? Now, that was impossible to comprehend.

"Lyra told me about you," Astrid continued. "You fought in another underground pit, didn't you?" she asked.

Nox nodded. "Ironhavell." Their voice was hoarse. "Feynos' finest."

"I'm guessing you went for the money?"

Nox immediately wanted to agree, but they held the words back. "I thought I needed to prove something." They looked up at Astrid and met her sun-warmed eyes. "Prove I was better than everything that assumed otherwise."

"And that's why you entered the Tournament?"

"I guess so," they huffed. "I know I'm better than these fools; the Tournament just acts as a way to show it. Besides, it's a better cash grab than all of Ironhavell."

Astrid's hummed laughter was ringed with a grin. "I can't blame you for that." Her eyes sobered, and she turned to face them. "Have you ever fought without that reasoning? There's always something to prove? Does it always have that price?"

Nox straightened. "Of course." The words came out as a push, but their next ones were softer. "Other than to survive, there wasn't another choice."

"Which is why you don't want Twylla and me to help." Nox immediately tried to protest, but Astrid cut them off. "I get it. You don't have a choice in this fight against Torr, but we do, so why on earth are we risking our asses?" A smile appeared on her face as she shook her head. "It's because we trust Lyra, and she trusts you."

"But... why? Won't it all come crashing down?"

"Everything comes to an end," Astrid replied. "Twylla is immortal and will live on for centuries without the Incarnatus, but we've all accepted that. Not because it's fate that we will age and she will not, but because none of us will regret the time we've spent together. Likewise, we won't regret this fight against Torr, and we sure as hells will not regret winning it."

"What if something happens that makes you regret it?" The unspoken question stood out in their mind: *what if I make you regret helping me?*

"Then I'll grieve for whatever is lost. But I won't let it stop me from trusting again. Our lives are too short to be alone." Her hand came up to rub their shoulder, and Nox wanted to lean into her touch. "The naiad arrived," she said. "If you still want to go through with this plan, now is the time to accept it."

Nox was quiet for a moment. The Death Marked were not alone; that wasn't a statement to fear. Astrid was no fool, not after all she endured during the Agonia. If she was willing to follow Lyra into the depths of hells to help, then Nox would not force her away.

They nodded. "No more running," Nox said hoarsely. "We stay together, and if we fall, we fall together."

Astrid grinned and patted them on the shoulder. "That's the spirit. Come on."

She rose from the bench, and Nox followed after. She stalked into the centre of the park's lawn, her boots leaving deep impressions on the grass. A moment later, her axes slid free from their sheaths. Her shoulders were squared, but a cunning smile lifted her face.

"Well?" she asked. "I know from the moment you saw me you thought about this."

Nox tried to protest, but Astrid's low laugh silenced it. "Fine," they bit out. "I am curious. In a sense, I'm Ironhavell's First *and* Undefeated Champion: *the Unhallowed One*."

She raised a brow. "You came up with that all by yourself?"

They scowled. "What are the rules?"

"Anything goes," she said with a shrug. "Just don't try to kill me, and I won't try to kill you."

Nox grinned, mocking a bow. "As you wish."

Astrid's smile turned feral just before she attacked. The twin axes flashed in the air as she closed the distance between them. Nox had no weapons on them, save for the one knife concealed beneath their shirt. They didn't bother grabbing it, though, not when their claws slid free. Curved to perfection, metal rang against them. The axe blades could not bite down on the claws; instead, they harmlessly slid off.

Nox twisted out of Astrid's closeness, knocking an axe out of her hand. Unbalanced, they flashed out to kick her down. Instead, with her hand now free, she grabbed Nox's foot and wrenched it to the right. Nox staggered until she let go and allowed them to fold up and roll. Coming back to their feet, Nox turned to see Astrid rearmed with both axes.

They didn't have time to react before she threw one. The blade tore open their shirt sleeve, nicking the inside of their forearm. Blood seeped down, but Nox barely registered the scratch. Instead, they looked for the fallen axe.

Settled in the grass, Nox threw it up in the air, catching it by the handle. "I've never fought with an axe before," they mused. "What's the difference between this and a knife? They're hardly different in size."

"Trust me," Astrid started, "axes are a *lot* better."

Nox threw their axe upwards again. "If that's the case, I may need to invest in a pair of my own."

She grinned. "I can teach you all I know."

"I like the sound of that."

The pair clashed once more. Axe blades grinding against one another as they both pressed their strengths against the blows. Nox's strength was purely upper body, and they found their feet slipping in the frosted grass. Astrid, on the other hand, held firm.

So Nox slipped out of the press of blades, ducking and rolling once more. Finally, they pulled out their knife, pairing it with the axe. The weight distribution was uneven, but Nox put the concern aside. In a sense, they had always been a dual wielder, just with claws, not blades. The difference was staggering, but they enjoyed the continued clash of metal against metal.

Again and again, Astrid and Nox met, but neither resisted. Sweat slicked Nox's palms, threatening to loosen their grip on the blades' handles. Astrid's breathing was ragged, and exertion bright on her face. But there was a maddening *light* in her eyes, and Nox marvelled at her enjoyment of the fruitless fight. Nox knew they wouldn't win, but neither would she, and the werewolf grinned alongside her.

"We should call a tie," Nox huffed.

"I thought we were only getting started," Astrid breathed, but she nodded. "I want my axe back first."

Nox turned the axe handle first for her to grab, but as she reached out, they sent a plume of cold air into Astrid's face. It was a harmless blow, but the shock was strong enough for Nox to steal the second axe from her hand. She gaped, and Nox started to twirl the twinned weapons in the air.

"So many tricks," she mused, arms lazily drawing into fists. "I can see why you have an even more absurd title than me."

The axes landed back in Nox's grasp. "Now you can see why I will win the Tournament, can't you?"

"I never doubted your word for a second." Her words surprised them. "But your action is ever so convincing."

Nox grinned. "Let's play, First Champion."

She matched the expression. "As you wish, Unhallowed One."

31

AVERY

Once she had finally arrived at their apparent main base of operations—Lyra's cluttered inn room—Avery had not decided yet if she would regret agreeing to this plan.

Spread out on the massive bed were four ball gowns. Two were suited to Lyra's height, while the others were shorter and slimmer. Avery eyed the latter nervously. Her taste for garments wasn't so... constrictive. The skirts were expansive and unwieldy, looking far too long to walk around competently. The sleeves were tighter than the usual shirts she wore in the mortal lands, and the undergarments she was apparently supposed to wear were even worse.

The fabric of the dresses was gorgeous, though. Avery ran her hand across the rich, silky material, shivering involuntarily at the sound. One dress reflected dark blue jewel tones, trimmed in silver thread, while the other was black with red embroidery. She couldn't keep her eyes off the sapphire dress, watching the colours gleam in the sun. The black dress wasn't so bad, but it absorbed all light and diminished its beauty.

"I think we've found a match!" a giddy voice called behind her, and Avery turned to regard the strange witch.

Twylla Cometborn was an unexpected creature. Avery could tell that her immortality had not yet been spent, and yet the witch boasted an air of experience and knowledge that should have suggested otherwise. However, her increasing foolishness was a trait Avery would not forget.

"Do I *have* to wear this… gown?" Avery asked. "I own many dresses at home that already fit me."

Avery, I've seen the dresses you're talking about, Elias said, somehow having a stake in this conversation. *And while they're lovely, they aren't… court-appropriate.*

Her face flushed red. "What do you mean by that?!"

Lyra was immediately beside Avery, making her jump. "The nobility are pretty strict on their fashion sense. Gowns like this are incomparable to any other dress when it comes to a ball. It's not about being revealing; it's about fitting the standard."

"And the standard is constrictive and voluminous?"

Lyra shrugged. "I've fought in a ballgown before. They aren't as constrictive as you think."

Avery regarded the sapphire dress once more. She hadn't even put it on yet, but her mind drifted to the possibility of needing to fight. Where would her daggers sit? How would she evade an attack? It shouldn't have been a necessary thought; at the ball, her sole weapon would be her tongue. No blade could be stronger than that.

"Okay," she said. "Let's try it on, then."

Twylla clapped her hands together. "Oh, this is so fun! I wish Astrid was here, though; she's a far better seamstress than I am…" She looked at Avery with a sad smile. "I was told you were short but my, you exceeded my expectations!"

Avery sat upright. "I think it's *you* that is the height outlier," she snapped. "You're practically Elias' height."

Twylla only grinned. "Well, this is normal for my kind.

Even Lyra would be considered below-average in the Witchlands."

The witch turned around and busied herself with an open suitcase, ending the conversation. Lyra picked up the dress and arrangement of undergarments and took it behind the dressing screen. Avery wasn't too pleased to learn she would need *help* putting her clothing on, but Lyra silenced her protests.

Once dressed, Lyra immediately started pointing out all the problems. "Too long on the skirt, even with heels. The waist could be taken in further, but it's not too noticeable. Bust is a little large, but again, not too noticeable." She prodded at the sleeves. "Can you lift your arms?"

Avery demonstrated and was pleasantly surprised her movement wasn't *that* restricted. She couldn't put her hands over her head, but there was still more give than she anticipated.

While walking out of the dressing screen, Avery couldn't help but hike the skirts up. It was decidedly far too long for her to navigate in. Not even the heeled shoes Lyra had shown her would save this dress. And so she was placed on an elevated box, where Lyra and Twylla began poking the hem of the dress with pins.

The door to the room opened, and Avery craned her neck to see both Nox and Astrid walk through the door. Both were sweaty and breathing hard, but there were mischievous grins on both their faces. Astrid dropped two axes onto the table Elias sat at, allowing Avery to see the sheen of blood on the blades.

She wasn't the only one to notice. "Oh, Astrid!" Twylla scolded, rising from the ground. "Come here, you fool, your face is bleeding." She glared at Nox. "And you, too. Gods, what were you two doing?!"

"Bonding in the only way two fighters know how," Lyra answered. "By beating each other up." She tilted her head to the side. "Who won?"

The response came in unison: "It was a tie."

Lyra shook her head, returning to Avery's dress. "Giving into a tie? You're losing your touch, Astrid."

"It wasn't so much a tie but a cutting of time," Nox explained. "There's plans to be made, right? Not just… putting on dresses." They looked Avery up and down with a frown. "Not that I don't *like* the dress, it's very… silky."

Her fists clenched, bunching up the fabric of her skirt as her cheeks burned red. She was used to compliments, especially backhanded ones from her sisters, but Nox's words unnerved her.

"I could probably wrangle you into one, too, if you want," Lyra cut in, pins between her teeth.

Immediately, Nox's expression turned flat. "I'd appreciate it if you did not do that."

Any reply was cut off by Twylla's fussing. She healed Astrid and Nox's scrapes with a smear of some ointment and the murmuring of a spell. Her eyes were aglow with magic afterwards, making the witch even giddier than she already was.

"It's such a beautiful dress, isn't it?" she asked no one in particular as she held up the hem. "The colours suit you, too, of course. Anything other than blue for a naiad would be odd."

Astrid pushed past Nox. "Twylla, you're doing this all wrong. I thought I taught you better than this."

Twylla sprang to her feet, abandoning the dress. "Oh, shush you!" the witch clamoured. "I'm doing my best."

Together, the three Incarnatus pinned the dress to a more manageable length for Avery. Then, behind the dressing screen again, she stripped it off and gave it to Astrid to sew. Apparently, today was meant to be a hemming lesson for Twylla, but the best seamstress of the three had decided to give up on that.

Tea was called from the inn's kitchens, and the group settled around the dining table to discuss the evening's proceedings. Avery's stomach burbled with anxiety, and she forwent the offered hot drinks.

"The ball begins at seven in the evening, but the carriage won't arrive until eight," Lyra explained. "It will come here intending that I am the sole occupant. Even so, the driver probably won't bat an eyelid at you, but in case, be ready."

Twylla took a sip of her tea. "We checked the public record of sponsors before we got here. Almost every single noble house has at least one sponsored fighter. However, it is Branigan, Eastbow, Greenford, Harrigott, and Winterbride who have the most."

Eastbow is safe, Elias said. *He was just an in-between for Torr. However, he is a knowledgeable man who is prone to listening to gossip. You could start with him and ask some questions about rumours.*

Lyra nodded. "Very well, it's a start. If he has nothing, we'll move onto Branigan, Greenford, or Winterbride. Harrigott will be the life of the party, so we'll have to leave him until last."

"Not surprising that Harrigott has many; he practically owns Ironhavell," Nox added.

All these names meant little to Avery. Although the noble houses had stayed the same since the Winthorpe dynasty began, decades after her own birth, she had never bothered to keep track of any of them. The Forest of the Dryads did not belong to one province, so Avery knew only the Queen's house.

"What about your sponsor?" Avery asked Lyra. "Which one is yours?"

The mortal's face turned grim. "Glasswood. I'm his only fighter. He won't be concerned with Torr or a Siren. His matters reside with managing his own province."

"Which nobles *don't* have sponsored fighters? If I'm not an official one, surely the blank one should be mine."

"Only Holloway hasn't participated," Twylla answered. "And it's pretty safe to say he would not go behind his sister-in-law's back."

Avery frowned, but a mindspoken voice answered her unvoiced question. *Rupert Holloway is married to Princess Anastasia, the Queen's sister.*

The conversation continued. Apparently, the focus on the nobles was no longer needed. "Elias, you have a choice of three horses," Lyra said. "Karina, Shade, or Essen. Shade and Essen are resting but should be fine for this evening. Whenever one of us is free, we can show you them in the stables."

He nodded. *Whichever is fastest will be my choice.*

Twylla spread a map onto the table. "In case you do need a quick escape, here are all the routes from the Harrigott manor back to Cerenia. It'll be wise to follow after Castor's carriage when heading there, but definitely familiarise yourself with these paths so you don't get lost if you have to get back alone."

"Finally," the witch turned to Avery. "We made a fake invite for you. It won't hold up to any amount of scrutiny, so just wave it at the guards and tell them it's genuine."

"So that's the plan?"

Lyra nodded. "A way in and a way out. With Avery's mind control, we'll have the whole evening to do as much as possible. Because we don't know exactly who we're looking for, there will be an element of improvisation."

Nox shrugged. "Doesn't sound too bad to me."

Avery fixed them with a glare. "Perhaps that's because you're not *doing* any improvising. You just have to sit in the dark with Elias and a horse."

You'll be fine, Elias said. *Lyra knows what she's doing. She has dealt with nobles before. She won't abandon you.*

"Finished." Astrid's voice cut through before Avery could reply.

Astrid rose from the table, holding up the newly hemmed dress. Although she had already worn it before, Avery's whole body thrummed with excitement as she beheld the gown. On the table were all its accessories, too, and she already wished to put it all on.

"This will work out," Avery said, still looking at the dress. "It has to."

32

LYRA

Evening swept through Cerenia faster than Lyra had expected. Everything had been laid out, and all she and Avery had left to do was wait for the carriage's arrival. Nox and Elias had already left for the stables, and Astrid had gone downstairs to look for the carriage, leaving Twylla to finish off the last details of Avery and Lyra's appearances.

Lyra's hair was pinned back in a chignon. It was the same simple style she had used for the last ball. With Twylla there, she could have gone for something more intricate, but Lyra didn't want Castor to question what company she had to fix her up. Although she had no intention of talking to him that evening, even the arrangement of hair could spark a rumour she did not want or need.

Avery's hair was another story. Her natural curls were impossible to ruin, so Twylla could not stop playing. The witch attempted many styles on Avery, much to her annoyance, before settling on a crown of braids with ringlets framing her face. The points of her ears were tucked into the hair, and a blue hairpiece ensured it all stayed put.

Although Twylla had brought new ballgowns for Lyra to choose from, she stuck with a dress she had originally packed. It was emerald green, trimmed in silver thread. The colour combination was a favourite of hers, matching well with her eyes and hair, but they were also the royal colours of Darcan.

There was rarely a reason for Lyra to dress in such finery, but it had never stopped her from purchasing many gowns. She tried to keep up with Cerenia's fashion trends without spending too much. It was a necessary expense in such circumstances, but she still always overindulged.

The long-sleeved dress concealed her scarred, muscular arms, and a fine pair of gloves hid her calloused hands. Her shoes were flat-soled, but the floor-length dress made it appear she was wearing heels. It gave the illusion she was a smaller woman, even with her rigid posture.

As Lyra's second attendance at the masquerade, she was provided with a new mask and matching accessories. Her first gown had been dark red with a ruby-encrusted eye mask, but today, Castor had decided to give her a silk half-mask. It covered only the left side of her face, the fabric perfectly matched her gown, and its sculpt was fitted to only her.

As a rogue guest, Avery had no commissioned accessories. Instead, her mask was plain and unfitted. Astrid had found it by chance in one of Lyra's many chests of drawers. Covering the upper half of her face, Avery's scowl was plain to see. Lyra almost wished they had a full face mask for the naiad. Even in her finery, there was a chance she'd be recognised. Her mind control would only go so far; they needed to rely on blending in as much as the Siren tongue.

"Oh, you two both look so beautiful," Twylla said, clasping her hands together. "No one will suspect you are out of place."

Just then, a spark of orange appeared before the witch's face. Lyra didn't wait for Twylla to read the paper blaze. It was Astrid's signal that the carriage had arrived. She rose from the bed, rearranging her shawl and looked to Avery.

"Come, the ball awaits." She gave the naiad a lopsided grin.

Outside, the freezing air of the night cut through Lyra's dress like a knife. She recognised the carriage outside the King's Mast, but its driver was new. The door was already open, and Lyra helped herself in. Behind her, she gave Avery a hand and stepped inside.

Astrid was at the steps, holding the door. "Good luck," she said. "Find that sponsor and make them yours."

Lyra smiled. She could never forget just how much she depended on her friends. Her survival in this world had been because of Astrid and Twylla, and having their confidence was something she would never let go of.

"Let us know if anything happens here," Lyra said. "And get some rest."

Astrid gave a mocking bow. "As you wish, my lady."

She closed the door, and Lyra shut the curtains. A moment later, a whip cracked, and the carriage lurched forward. Lyra had to grab Avery to stop her from toppling over. It was clearly the first time the naiad had been in a carriage then.

Avery straightened her dress and patted her curls. Her face was aflame with embarrassment. "You couldn't have warned me?"

"Look, before we get to the manor, I have something to tell you. Elias has probably already hinted at it, but there's a reason why I know the nobles so well. All of the Death Marked may as well know, so let me tell you now."

Avery was frowning, but Lyra still forced herself to explain. Celeste Whitehallow could not be a secret in this circumstance. Not anymore. Although Lyra had a sneaking suspicion the naiad would not understand half of what she was about to say, she at least had the entire carriage ride to do it.

***

Lyra had been right. It wasn't judgement she received from Avery but questions and confusion. She answered as much as possible, but the main history had been explained. She was of noble blood, and these courtiers they were about to mingle with were supposedly her people.

The carriage began to slow, and Lyra glanced out the window. They were riding up the carriageway, joining a queue of many others who had just arrived. Their turn would be after these guests had been admitted and, if nobility, introduced to the ball. Lyra explained this to Avery, who was shaking in her seat.

When the carriage came to a halt, Avery caught herself this time. Immediately, the door opened, and a servant of Harrigott's extended a hand. Lyra took it, stepping down and back into the frosted winds of the night.

They were at the front entrance of the manor where torchlight burned from the many braziers on the wall. Dozens of guards and servants lined the stairway, a plush carpet set upon it. Linking arms with Avery, they strode up the stairs to the open double doors into the house. A guard stepped in front of them, barring their path.

Lyra procured hers and Avery's invitations from her silk bag and handed them to the guard. Immediately, the naiad had the man in her grasp. "They're the same, aren't they? All in order."

The guard barely glanced at the invites, already nodding to Avery's words. "All in order." He gave the invitations back and moved out of their way. "Enjoy your evening, ladies."

Servants led the way from the manor's antechamber into the ballroom. Neither of them was a peer, so they were given no introductions to the crowd. Lyra had been told about this before her previous attendance at the ball, explaining why she could enter anonymously into a noble's ball.

The ballroom itself was a large room aglow with candlelight. Its wooden floors shone with fresh polish and were perfect for dancing. The walls were creamy white, dominated by half a dozen large windows with wine-red curtains open to see the expansive night sky. Above, the hand-painted ceiling gave a scene of gods and mythic creatures in a dance. Bolted between the open palms of Heresa—goddess of loyalty, celebration and hospitality—a crystal chandelier was ablaze with white candles, dripping wax into their little saucers.

Guards lined the walls between the windows—torches burning above their heads. A grandiose fireplace crackled and spat opposite the only doors in the ballroom. Despite the room's immense size, it was crowded with over four dozen courtiers. It was a sea of silk and colour that Lyra knew too well.

Chatter and idyllic laughter filled her ears, glasses clinking, plates of food and metal utensils scraping against one another. Lyra swept her gaze over the crowd. Last time, it had taken her almost all evening to find every noble. The masks didn't help much, but now she had a better idea of searching them out. Many would be linked with their husband or wife, and Lyra knew Eastbow never went anywhere without his dearest.

Already, she saw his eldest child of six, Edmund, walk by. She wouldn't have been surprised if Eastbow's entire brood was in attendance, even though the youngest was only fifteen.

Lyra held onto Avery, hoping to lead her further into the crowd and perhaps closer to another Eastbow, when a different voice reached her ears. "My dear, I did not know you had a friend in your company. Who does *she* belong to, then?"

She turned and found Castor standing before her and Avery. His own clothes for the night perfectly matched Lyra's colourings—emerald green and silver, with a half mask that covered only the right side of his face. She was a mirror to him, and she hated it.

Her plan to avoid him hadn't worked out too well, but there was another reason she explained the story of Celeste to Avery.

"Him?" the naiad asked. "Wouldn't he have been too old for a mortal girl?"

Lyra clenched Avery's arm tightly. "No," she said through gritted teeth. "It is quite normal to betroth the young."

Castor stared at them both with raised brows. "My dear, what is she—?"

"Go find a corner to sit in and stay there for the entire night." Avery's voice was soaked in power. "If someone asks what you're doing, just say you regret ever hurting a girl of the name Celeste."

Lyra couldn't protest as the command took effect. Avery had already explained that a mask would not disrupt her powers. All she needed was a target's ears; even in the chattering ballroom, she had not gone unheard.

Castor's body slumped, and the visible side of his face went slack. Without another word, he trudged over to the room's far corner. With his head facing the wall, he sat down and went still.

It took a long moment before Lyra could think of a way to react. Was it something Castor deserved? Yes. But was it necessary? "That was a bit much," Lyra finally said. "If anyone was watching…"

"Then I'll make them forget," Avery said primly. "He would have bothered us the entire night if I hadn't given him a long-term demand. You've said it yourself: he's not a man to give up easily. Who knows what he would have done if we had let him do what he liked."

Lyra continued to stare at the back of his head. Before the Tournament, it had been nine years since she had last spoken to him. Even then, he had not changed. If anything, he was *nicer* because he thought she was someone else. Still, he reminded her of everything she wanted buried, and she despised him for it.

Lyra had been seventeen when she had run away from all she had known as a noble, but the beginning of the end had started when she was fourteen. One curious evening, she had found a letter hidden behind the only painting of Larissa Whitehallow in the entire summer manor of Neulith. Unstamped and open, Celeste had found its contents to be an old memory from when she was even younger.

Nine years old, to be exact. Her signature on the letter was barely legible, but it was there.

Mr Castor Aldred Glasswood, aged sixteen, formally asks to betroth Miss Celeste Adelina Whitehallow, aged nine. Once signed, Miss Celeste Whitehallow and Mr Castor Glasswood shall bind together once Miss Whitehallow is of age, sealing contracts in the name of the Order of the Seven Deities.

Signed, Castor A. Glasswood & Celeste A. Whitehallow

Her lady's maid, Agnes, had found her cradling the letter, crumpled and speckled in tears. Celeste had been too scared to tear the paper again, and a bitter part of her reminded her that it wouldn't change anything. For five years, she had been betrothed. What was it now that she knew? No one had ever discussed marriage or anything to her, even at fourteen. She thought it was because they still saw her as too immature, a child through and through. But it wasn't that; no, her fate had already been sealed. There was simply nothing left to discuss.

Horrified, Celeste hadn't wanted to be Castor's bride. In the years before this discovery, she had met with him dozens of times, and she already hated him. He was controlling and narcissistic, a cruel teenager who would not be a good husband to her.

Celeste had always been uneasy about the idea of marriage but understood it was her 'duty' as a noblewoman. However, she thought she would decide which eligible bachelor she would marry and wouldn't have to decide until she was older.

Celeste was immature and childish, but she wasn't stupid. Everything in her gut screamed to flee, to run away from this one thing she did not want. But she knew that would be a swift death or a prolonged misery. Neither of those options were the ones she wanted. The girl wanted to cradle her own life and death in her hands—she did not want to be passed around.

Agnes had been Larissa's maid before her passing. The mother of Celeste had only one request on her deathbed: 'Keep her safe, but keep her happy first and foremost.' Larissa was an intelligent woman. She knew there was a stark difference between the two.

And so, Celeste had met Brenner. He was a bastard, the regretted child of an unmarried noblewoman who had passed him off as a stableboy. His mother had raised him at a distance on her manor, but soon rumours came to his feet, and the boy knew then it was wise to flee. Brenner had done everything Celeste was too cowardly to do alone. She didn't care, though; he was a starting point to the end, and that was all that mattered.

Lyra blinked out of the past. Castor could not hurt her anymore. Her mentor, the Incarnatus, and now the Death Marked, would steady her. She wasn't alone, and she didn't have to be.

"I think I see Eastbow," she said, forcing herself to take in the crowds again. "Come, we have a sponsor to find."

33

NOX

Nox hated horses. Sometimes, they questioned if horses shared the sentiment.

Their arms were wrapped around Elias' waist, fingers clasped so tightly that Nox thought their claws would come free. A burning ache ran through their thighs from tensing up against the horse's flank. Every shift in the animal's rhythm sent Nox's heart stuttering, sure that they were all about to be upended.

The horse they had commandeered from Astrid was a beast called Essen. He was the largest of the three Incarnatus steeds and the swiftest for long distances. Elias had them follow after Lyra and Avery's carriage at what he called 'a slow pace.' In reality, Nox could not stop their teeth from clacking together at every jolting movement.

We don't need to follow them directly to the manor, Elias said. Even with the whistling wind tearing away all sound, the mindspeaker's powers allowed uninterrupted communication. *We can use Twylla's map to figure out these travel routes.*

So long as I can get off this horse, Nox thought bitterly.

Even though they knew Elias heard their thoughts, the phoenix-blood showed no signs of acknowledging it. Nox lost track of time as Elias rode them through the endless dark. With their superior sight, Nox kept watch of the roads and houses they cantered past. This was apparently a popular area for noble estates. According to Lyra, the sprawling homes stayed empty almost all seasons of the year and were only occupied by their owners when the nobles deigned to visit Cerenia.

This far from the capital city, the dirt roads that snaked across the Wychar grasslands reminded Nox of home—not Feynos, but their birthplace, Canwal. The western province was bitterly cold as the Eternal Mountains clung to its border. Nox always remembered every night as a wintry one. Their rundown home could not keep warmth, even with a fire in the pathetic hearth. Nox's parents were rarely home anyway: their father at the local tavern and their mother at her sister's warmer house.

Such absent parenting meant that Nox had a lot of freedom. Too much, arguably. Even though they had been a sickly infant—one that the entire village had come together to save—as soon as they had reached age five, Nox had been forgotten. During the day, they would attend school and play with the other children, but at night, to entertain themself, Nox would sneak out of their house and adventure along the dirt roads and through neighbouring fields.

It was because of these nightly runaways that a werewolf had bitten Nox. Only six years old, Nox had crawled back to the village where one of the many widows had helped nurse them back to health. Not realising what had caused the bite, any chance of curing the oncoming lycanthropy was lost as Nox was returned to their parents.

In the coming days, Nox had become a werewolf, which had also awoken a dormant magic gene in their bloodline. Gifted with lycanthropy and air manipulation, Nox's parents had become terrified of their only child. Wanting to conceal their existence, Nox lost almost all their freedom. Only on full moons did Nox forcibly transform into a wolf and escape the confines of their parents' home.

By the age of twelve, the situation had worsened, as Nox's parents had hired a man to 'cure' their child's lycanthropy. Nox would fight back, mainly verbally, as they were physically restrained until the man put them into an iron muzzle. They still fought back until the man ripped out the muzzle, slicing Nox's cheeks open and forming their scarred smile. Covered in blood, the muzzle was returned to silence them.

The abuse continued until the next full moon, when Nox had transformed, escaping the restraints and killing both their parents. Returning to human form, they had stayed in the house for three days in shock, unable to process what had happened.

When the man had returned for a visit and saw the bodies, he had tried to kill Nox. They had defended themself, hands transforming into claws and gutting their abuser. Gaining this sense of control over their lycanthropy had also broken their shock, and Nox had fled the house.

With nowhere to go, they had left Canwal and started stealing from farms and villages to survive. Nox had tried to teach themself to control their powers but to no avail. Every full moon, they would forcibly transform and awake, covered in blood with fractured memories of the night before.

Suddenly, Elias pulled at the reins, and the horse came to a stop. Nox lurched in the saddle, almost falling off as momentum took its course. They let go of Elias and ungracefully slid out of the seat, leather and metal scraping against them before landing on solid ground.

Elias followed suit, though his dismount was much more

coordinated. The horse grunted, a cloud of white escaping his nostrils. Elias opened one of the saddlebags and threw a blanket over the animal as the cold set in.

"Are we done then?" Nox asked, realising they hadn't been paying attention to the roads.

Looking around, Nox could see the glowing lights of a manor house. Carriages emerged from its expansive driveway, a fountain gushing water at its centre—the Harrigott manor, then. Elias had ridden them to a far corner, behind a fence and just off the property. No light reached this far out, but neither Nox nor Elias needed it.

For now, Elias said. *Your mind is somewhere else. We don't need to rush. We have the whole evening ahead of us.*

Nox turned away from him, heat rushing to their cheeks. Of course, the telepath would have heard all of Nox's past rushing out. It probably had distracted him as much as it had them. Nox scratched their face, nails scraping against the jagged lines of their scars.

"Sure." Their voice was hoarse. "I don't mind."

You can talk about your past if you want, Elias said, not skipping a beat. *I could probably tell you some truths, too.*

Nox turned around. "Now, *that* I'm intrigued to hear."

Despite the cold, Elias only wore his scarf around his neck, allowing Nox to see him grin. *Of course, you would. Sit down. It's a long story.*

"I bet. How old are you again?"

You have a choice: two hundred and nine or four hundred and nine.

***

Nox rubbed their face. "Gods, no wonder you're the least

worried about dying. You've already done it before."

Thanks.

"And seriously? Your piercing means you're married? Does mine have any unintentional meanings?" They pointed at the stud below their lip.

If you were a phoenix-blood or your partner was, then I suppose it could be taken as married, Elias said. But you're not, and there are not many people around who would know to look for it anyway.

Nox's shoulders slumped. "Yeah, I suppose you're right about that."

In Tenneria, werewolves had faced their bout of attempted genocide, but they had still managed to survive. For Elias, however, it had become an irrefutable reality. The immortals who could resurrect just didn't. All except one.

"Do you think about returning to Padaven? The homeland of your people?"

Nox's grasp on geography wasn't too strong. Having only lived in hovels, their education had not been blessed with learning about the world's continents. However, Elias was kind enough to explain where the phoenix-bloods originated from. Padaven was a nation in Oyend, the southern continent of Korallian, and its population was predominantly phoenix-blood.

Elias shook his head. Padaven is not my homeland. My blood may belong to Padaven, and my people once lived there, but I cannot go there. Falbikuth means exiled. It is a title worn by all of us who live in Darcan. I might be the only Falbikuth of Darcan left, but I am still one.

Nox remembered the word. Elias had said it when they went to the Broken Shield Inn for the first time. It had meant nothing to them then, but Nox could see why Elias had not explained.

"So you're going to stay in the kingdom that destroyed your people?"

Elias sighed. It wasn't the kingdom that did it. It was an ugly amalgamation of human hatred and a desire to find someone to blame. The Falbikuth wanted freedom and equality, but we went about it poorly. Although our actions did not deserve genocide, it was not the actions of these mortals who caused it. The closest thing I can have as revenge is knowing I outlived those who saw fit to kill me. It's not much, but I don't care.

Could Nox believe the same? It was a perplexing thought, and they lay down in the grass to ponder it. Frost crunched beneath their head as they stared up at the sky. Both moons were visible in the night.

The True Moon faded from its first quarter beside the Broken Moon's almost constant waxing crescent. The tale of the Broken Moon was simple: a god had destroyed more than three-quarters of the moon, leaving it as a permanent crescent. Its only possible phases were waxing crescent or new. Nox was glad for the strange moon because their wolf transformations only occurred under the True Moon's gaze.

They exhaled as shivers ran up their skin. "Gods, it's bloody freezing out here," Nox said, their voice a cloud of white.

Good thing I have another way we can pass the time. Come on.

Nox sat up, the moons forgotten as they watched Elias slip his gloves off. Barehanded, fresh plumes of fire appeared in Elias' palm. He stood, parading the flame in front of Nox. It lit up his face in the darkened night, casting shadows across his grinning face.

Control the flame, he said.

"Come again?"

I already told you that to win the Tournament, you need to strengthen your air manipulation. Elias gestured to the fireball. Start with this. Snuff it out, enlarge it, contain it. Anything.

Nox regarded the flame. They had thought Elias' comment on training had been unimportant, a throwaway. Even staring at his palm, Nox still didn't think this was something to be taken seriously. Since they were both supposed to stay hidden out here, enlarging a flame would only announce their presence to the manor's guards.

Nox flicked a hand, sailing the cold breeze to claim the flame. Instead, the fireball redirected itself, avoiding the gust.

"Seriously?"

I wasn't going to make this easy for you, Elias replied, keeping the fire alight. You already have great skill, but you lack the drive to let the power surge. It's why you could only make a ceiling of air when the debris fell on us, why you couldn't hold it up for so long. Your usage is quick and subtle, an admirable display. But we're playing on a grander stage now. You need to let it explode.

"Is now really the best time to do it?" they asked.

Now is the only time we have left. The Tournament is tomorrow, and our Death Mark immunity is almost up. I know the location is not the best, but this is our only chance.

Nox stood up, giving a quick stretch. "Okay, I'm convinced. But if this goes to hell and we get caught, you're taking full blame."

So long as you can snuff out the flames, we won't get

caught.

No pressure, then. Nox huffed a breath, flexing their fingers to take measure of the airflow. It was a bitterly cold night, the wind high and sharp against their skin. They held out a hand and cut the oxygen out of Elias' palm.

It should have doused the fire completely, but Nox somehow missed. Elias hadn't moved, and yet one moment, it was in his hand, and the next, the fireball had slicked up his wrist and continued to burn on his shoulder.

You can control the air without using your hands, Elias explained. It's a helpful way to control an attack, for sure, but it's giving you away.

Nox shoved their hands into their pockets, fists clenching the material to keep them contained. They already knew that, of course, but it was as Elias said. Nox's strength was in the subtle and the quick. Hand movements weren't needed for such things, but they always unconsciously needed that physical extension of power for more significant attacks.

The ball of flame returned to Elias' open palm. Any other person and their skin would have burnt. Even when it had travelled up his arm, not quite touching his clothing, the fire should have still singed his hair when it landed on his shoulder. The phoenix-blood would always remain unharmed so that Nox could do just about anything.

Spurring the air, the wind gusted in their ears as it tunnelled towards the flame. Not to blow it out like their first attempt but to feed its fire. The ball grew but stayed comfortable in Elias' control. Warmth rose to Nox's face, sweat beading on their brow as they beckoned more air. Explode, Elias had said. Explode.

Its heat grew, turning from orange to a yellowish white. The flame flickered against the breeze, remaining small. It must have been Elias keeping it contained, but the oxygen and heat were all Nox's doing.

An idea bloomed, and Nox whipped their hand out of their pocket. Elias watched the empty gesture that they made, a flick of nothing. The flame enshrouded his arm again, still burning bright in the night. Then, a whoosh of air claimed the ball a second later.

Nox's eyes immediately adjusted to the darkness, and they saw Elias smiling and nodding in approval.

Misdirection, he mused. Anything else?

He held out both hands, and two new blazes appeared. They were larger than the previous ball, glowing red in each palm: a new challenge but a welcome one. Hands back in their pockets, Nox sent the wind whistling once more.

34

AVERY

With so many people inside, the heat of the ballroom was unbearable. Even with the windows open, it did little to alleviate the warmth. Avery was glad to have the little fan Lyra had given her; its fabric matched the dark blue of her dress. She swatted the air with it, conjuring only the slightest waft of cool air. Her mask clung to her face, the sweat and silk chafing against her skin. This was an enjoyable setting? For whom?

Definitely not for the noble she had left frozen in the corner. She didn't pity Castor and had given him a lesser punishment than any random nymph would receive if they crossed her. According to Lyra's stories, Castor Glasswood tormented her life for eight years. The least Avery could do was shut him up for one evening.

"Over there," Lyra murmured. "That's Eastbow and his wife. Control just him; I'll keep the lady entertained."

Arms linked, Lyra and Avery prowled over to the Duke of Vespis.

He wore a velvet suit in bottle green with a gold chain of a pocket watch on the waistcoat. He was a bearded man with thick, light brown hair. His mask covered his eyes and nose, coloured with gold and black. Even so, Avery could spy inquisitive blue eyes and skin covered in freckles.

Despite being in deep conversation with his wife, Lyra interrupted in a way that apparently wasn't inappropriate for a duke. Eastbow crowed his greetings to both Lyra and Avery, who bowed their heads in false deference. Lyra spun an exciting tale for the wife while Avery had Eastbow's full focus.

She took a breath. "I must ask," Avery began, forcing Siren sweetness into her words. "What do you know of the sponsorship of a woman named Avery Nash?" She kept the question hushed so that only Eastbow could hear, but the power of the Siren worked no matter the volume.

His eyes glazed over. "Avery Nash?" he echoed. "Now that's a funny one… it isn't an official sponsorship. Only we nobles know. One of our own organised it and refuses to reveal their identity, not until after the Tournament. Supposedly after Nash wins." Eastbow shook his head. "Foolish little plan, exciting though. My bet is she belongs to Victoria. She is all those things: foolish, little, but exciting."

Avery glanced at Lyra. The mortal nodded, apparently recognising the name. It was a better start than Avery had hoped, though it could still mean nothing.

She dropped the mind control and allowed Lyra to engage in some pointless conversation—enough chatter to make their presence unsuspicious, but all such mindless rambling that Avery didn't even pretend to pay attention to. Instead, her head swivelled through the hall, hoping to find this Victoria.

The Eastbows bid Lyra good night, and immediately, she grabbed Avery's arm and dragged her on.

"Victoria Greenford the Duchess of Raevell is who he's talking about," Lyra whispered. "Her house is weak, but she is bloodthirsty. She's been trying to build connections to strengthen her position for years. Acquiring you and Torr isn't too bad of an idea for someone as desperate as her."

"She's one with a lot of fighters already, isn't she?" Avery asked. "As a cover?"

"Most likely." Lyra's gaze swept over the crowd, hunting for their new target. "And keeping herself anonymous would give her more power than if she admitted it."

Avery nodded along, but really, she barely understood. The politics and spectacle of the aristocracy were all just a game of pointlessness. These nobles created problems for themselves and everyone around them, and for what? Was this dance of deception and suffering really worth its so-called rewards?

Lyra's spinning search stopped with a shake of her head. "I can't see her. Let's get some drinks before we start looking out of place."

Avery wanted to argue, but without knowing what Greenford looked like, it wasn't like she could continue the search alone. Lyra led her to a long table crowded with glasses and bottles. A servant appeared at their side and started preparing the drinks. Avery was handed a frosted glass filled with some amber liquid. Nymphs didn't require a diet of food and drink, and while they could easily imbibe, Avery always found it pointless.

She gave the drink a sniff and grimaced. Sour. What was it with mortals and their taste for harsh drinks? She pretended to sip it to keep up those so-called appearances Lyra wouldn't stop talking about.

Just then, Lyra grabbed her arm again. "I know where she is. Come on."

Avery was whisked away before she could stop fake drinking. Her bewilderment upset her glass as she tripped after Lyra and almost covered them in amber. "What are you—"

"I heard Jeanette Branigan—the Dux of Sarlos' second

sister— mention Victoria," Lyra whispered. "Said she's by the fireplace talking to her mother-in-law. Viridiana Ambrose is not a widow to get on the wrong side of so play this carefully."

"Who? What?"

"At the drinks table, I overheard it. Did you really think I brought us over there just for refreshments? I'm wearing a mask I can't properly drink in."

Avery couldn't argue with that, so she focused on where they were heading. Few courtiers stood beside the fireplace, the ballroom's heat too overwhelming for many of those in attendance, aside from two women, one with greying hair and the other with a pregnant belly.

"Victoria's the younger one. Get rid of Viridiana," Lyra whispered as they interrupted the conversation between the two noblewomen. "Good evening, my ladies; how wonderful it is to meet you both!"

She continued her babble while Avery sized up Victoria. She appeared in her late twenties and was just as short as Avery. Victoria's black hair was arranged in a hairnet that Lyra had called a crispinette.

Pearls decorated the netting, offsetting the shine of her ebony braids set inside. A short veil trailed behind her.

Her mask was made of a white fabric that did not cling to her and covered only the lower half of her face. With her large belly, her gown was loose-fitting and long-sleeved in a steel grey satin. She didn't look particularly bloodthirsty to Avery, but she couldn't stop to ask Lyra.

Instead, she took stock of the older woman. Her face was wrinkled, and surprisingly, she wore no mask. Avery cleared her throat. "My lady, would you mind if you left us to talk with your daughter-in-law alone?" She only posed it as a question to avoid any suspicion from Victoria, but she hated the deferential tone she used.

Still, the command took its effect. "Yes, yes," Viridiana muttered. "I have other guests to talk with…" She drifted away like a ghost.

With their distraction gone, Avery didn't bother with formalities as she descended on Victoria Greenford. "Answer all questions we ask you," she commanded. "Are you Avery Nash's secret sponsor?"

The duchess froze up. "Y-yes, she is mine. I hired the Haunted Shadow to find the Siren naiad of the Forest."

Elation rose through Avery; this was the fool to whom Torr and she belonged. Still, she gave Lyra a sidelong glance. "She doesn't seem very threatening."

Lyra shrugged. "She was wilder before her marriage. She was 'ill' for almost a year, with many presuming she was concealing a pregnancy. Now, with a husband from a much stronger house, she is more demure."

Avery stared at the duchess's belly. "And much more pregnant."

Lyra cleared her throat. "Let's keep focused." She fixed her eyes on Victoria. "Why keep it a secret?"

"Mind control is practically cheating; any sponsorship would be refused, and she would be disqualified. It would reflect poorly on the sponsor. That and… I did not want to make myself known to the nymph."

Which had spectacularly backfired. It was pitiful how this woman thought she could outsmart what could not be controlled. Only Torr could evade her Siren's tongue, not someone as weak as this mortal.

"Why risk the rumours to the nobles?" Lyra asked.

"To stop any of them from trying to sponsor her themselves. The rumour became its own kind of armband and made my fellows play into the theatrics."

Her forced sponsorship was a mere spectacle to these pompous men and women. Hers, Lyra's, Elias,' and Nox's lives were on the line because she did not want to be a noble's toy. Avery grimaced but said nothing on the matter.

"Tell me more about the sponsorship," Avery demanded. "Why bring Torr into this? Why go through all of this just to win a competition?"

"I organised everything, conferred with the assassin, and sent him off to Eastbow's, but the Siren was not our first choice."

Avery's heart thumped. Our? Who else was involved?

"I could not afford to hire the Haunted Shadow, not without someone noticing. Not that it was my plan in the first place, not my plan at all, but it is now."

"*Who* are you talking about?"

Victoria looked up, face frail. "My uncle-in-law, Benedict Ambrose."

The name meant nothing to Avery, of course, but Lyra's face lost its colour. Her lips pursed together, and the mortal stared at nothing. Avery wished to understand, but Lyra's mind was elsewhere.

"Who is Ambrose?" Avery asked Victoria.

"Duke of Hyvera, a powerhouse in his own right. Ambrose was a failing house until his father took over. Benedict furthered its strength and is one of the richest men in the kingdom. He is... obsessed with royal blood. His great-great-aunt was the first Queen of the Winthorpe dynasty, and he ensures no one forgets it."

Lyra rubbed her temples. "Couldn't be simple..." she muttered, returning to reality. "No, this is fine. We have double the noble power than we were expecting. Ambrose is a far stronger house than Greenford. Regardless of what Victoria says, Benedict is definitely the leader of this. We need *him* to make this work."

Avery nodded. "Point him out." She turned to Victoria. "Stay here and tell anyone who approaches you that you need to be left alone."

Abandoning the duchess, Lyra and Avery wove through the crowds of courtiers. Everyone's masked faces were a blur, unrecognisable in this sea of expense. Avery couldn't deny that finding one person within this mess would be difficult, but hadn't Lyra already mastered this task? What was taking so long?

"He's not here," came the answer. "The bastard's gone and left."

"Left?" Avery repeated. "Just like that?"

"His wife is still here, along with all their children. This isn't a coincidence. He must have seen us and fled."

Panic gripped Avery. "What do we do now?"

Lyra turned her gaze to an unassuming servant. "We drag him back."

She stormed towards her target. The man wore the same slacks as all the servants, but Avery noticed his handkerchief's orange, yellow, and green colours. Did that denote him as Ambrose's own?

"You." Lyra pointed at the servant. "Tell me where your master has gone."

The servant gaped. "I'm afraid I can't—"

"Answer her questions," Avery interrupted.

"I don't know. He did not tell me where he went in case I was mentally manipulated."

Avery gaped, a sound like a squeak exiting her throat. She snapped her mouth shut, face burning at such an outward reaction. Still, her mind was reeling. Victoria Greenford was an easily captured fool, but this Benedict Ambrose knew precisely who he was dealing with..

Lyra hissed a curse. "Can you find someone who *does* know where he is and begin an honest and uncontrolled conversation with us?"

Avery shifted uncomfortably. Honest and uncontrolled. Not how this was meant to go. Instead of forcing the nobles to help them, they would have to beg. It should have always been a possibility, but Avery had been so convinced the mortals wouldn't be able to deflect her powers. Even now, she was speculating ways to turn this back into a controlled conversation.

The servant nodded, looking away from them both. Sweat poured off the man's head, shame and embarrassment colouring his face red.

Despite the worsening revelations, Lyra was unperturbed. Her face had returned to a cool calmness; her eyes narrowed at the servant. The plan Lyra had apparently made went unshared with Avery.

"Find this someone and relay this message: we want to discuss matters about his assassin and fighter," Lyra proclaimed. "He doesn't have to attend in person, but it is a matter of life and death. Tell him his *invulnerable* assassin has gone rogue and is planning on killing his fighter before she can claim victory."

Avery wasn't too sure about slipping in a lie, especially if she could not have Ambrose under her control. How were they going to convince him without his personal attendance?

Victoria's power would only go so far. Just what exactly were they agreeing to?

The servant, still lost to Avery's commands, did as bidden. He walked away, heading into the cold night. Avery wondered if she should follow after them and confront whoever else was involved in the complicated line to avoid her control.

"Don't bother," Lyra said, cutting through Avery's thoughts. "Ambrose has obviously planned this ahead; if we try to hunt him down, he will just get away, and we'll lose our chance of gaining his help."

Such ridiculous theatrics to avoid a Siren made Avery thrum with annoyance. This was supposed to be *her* night of playing puppeteer, but still, she remained under Ambrose's bidding.

"What we do need is Elias," Lyra continued. "If we can't control Ambrose, we can at least get a read of his mind. Ambrose's greed will agree to help us so long as we give him a handsome enough offer. It's as you said: we can sell a few years to save us from Torr now. Elias' telepathy will assure that it's an honest exchange."

Avery nodded. It was the best possible option they had. Ambrose knew all about her mind control but was clueless about Elias' telepathy. Avery would let the whole group converse without her if it meant Ambrose came out of hiding.

"So what do you propose?"

"We'll still need Victoria and somewhere better to talk…" Lyra looked around. "Come on."

They headed back to Victoria, who stood idly on her own. Other courtiers gave her nervous glances, but anyone who attempted to talk to her had been thoroughly scared off.

Avery dropped the demand, and Victoria shook herself back into herself. She remained herself for all of two seconds before Avery dropped another command: to follow every demand Lyra made.

"Get us a room," Lyra said to Victoria. "Talk to Harrigott or a servant; it doesn't matter, but we need somewhere to talk *now*."

Victoria nodded and detached herself from the fireplace. She slipped through the crowds, hunting out her targets. Avery had never used her powers like that before, allowing another person to take control of it. She was slightly surprised it had worked but glad nonetheless.

Lyra rustled through her clutch, pulling out a strip of paper and a pencil—a paper blaze for Twylla, Avery recognised. She had already given up a strand of hair to make the connection, but she hadn't yet needed to use the writing materials in her possession.

"We'll keep Victoria to ourselves," Lyra said as she scribbled a message. "Elias and Nox can scamper around the estate to find Ambrose. It's not as if they've had anything better to do in the cold."

She was about to snap her fingers when shouts and jeers were heard from outside the ballroom. Curious courtiers opened the doors, and everyone turned to watch the commotion as a familiar voice yelled through the open door.

"AVERY! HELP!"

A flash of movement could be seen as Nox and Elias were suddenly dragged down the corridor by an entourage of guards. Even after disappearing from view, Nox still shouted her name, causing many guests to look around the ballroom for the person in question. Avery's face burned in embarrassment.

Lyra crumbled the written paper blaze into a ball. "Hells' sake. What on earth were they doing?" She looked at Avery. "Come on, you've got an audience to manipulate."

35

ELIAS

It had been a mistake, and it most definitely was his fault.

When practising with Nox, Elias had purposely shut out the werewolf's thoughts to keep him unaware of their subsequent movements. It had felt strange to be misled so obviously without his telepathy, but it was a fun interaction. However, even without Nox's mind, Elias understood them well, making it easy to goad them into pushing their limits.

Suffocating the flames became easy for Nox, but forcing the fire into extreme blazes was not so much. Elias had used his powers to evade much of the manipulated air, working Nox hard to achieve the feat. It had consumed them both, and when Nox had finally succeeded, exploding the sky with a volley of fires, the two had celebrated with raucous shouts.

And then the guards had found them.

Even without Nox's whooping, the fiery blaze had been sighted from the manor's doorstep. Neither Nox nor Elias had cut the flames off in time to go unnoticed, and with his telepathy also absent, they had both been caught.

Nox had wanted to kill the men and run, but Elias had a non-violent approach. They were already here on precarious terms, so trying to ally with a noble while butchering their guards seemed a poor choice. Instead, the two surrendered themselves and were led inside the manor house. They were going to be detained and interrogated in the mansion's underground cellar, but thanks to Nox's shouting, Avery would be able to control the guards and rescue them. Sure, Elias and Nox had utterly messed up, but it was only a temporary setback.

Or so he had thought.

A servant halted their group with a hand. They were still in the antechamber of the manor house, just metres away from the ballroom's ongoings. Elias could still hear the chattering whispers of the courtiers, though the door had since been slammed shut.

Elias turned his attention back to the servant and immediately read the mortal's mind. He belonged to the duke, Benedict Ambrose, and he had already spoken with Avery and Lyra.

"These two are under the Duke of Hyvera's supervision," the servant announced to the guards holding Elias and Nox. "If you may unhand them and give them to me, that would be most appreciated."

A moment later, Lyra and Avery appeared. Everything unravelled in his mind as he found the information the two had learnt from the evening's festivities and the job he and Nox were supposed to do. Instead, their capture had ruined all their plans, and the four of them were trapped inside the manor.

Already, Elias could see the stormy grey of Avery's eyes, manipulation ready to claim everyone in the corridor if she opened her mouth. Then, she stopped short at the servant, and her power dropped.

"You again," she murmured.

The servant nodded. "I see you have brought your friends along for the arrangement. My master will be ready to receive your discussion in the room the Duchess of Raevell has kindly arranged."

The titles of Victoria and Benedict held their power as the guards holding Nox and Elias released them. All four of them stood dumbfounded, watching the servant.

He held out a hand. "If I may, I'll lead on."

Although their group never entered the ballroom proper, Elias could still hear the reactions of the guests who sighted him and Nox. The servant led them through the house, avoiding the bustling party in exchange for hushed, labyrinthine corridors.

More or less alone, there was a chance for the group to speak to one another. Lyra's voice was barely a hiss, but it still echoed in the quiet hallway. "What happened?" she asked, concern on her half-masked face. "Are you two hurt?"

Nox gave her an unconvincing smile. "Well… let's say… things didn't go exactly to plan." Their eyes lifted to Elias. "Care to explain?"

Elias sighed. *My phoenix fire gave our position away.*

Lyra's look of concern turned to suspicion. "And why were you waving around fire?"

Practising for the Tournament.

"And you two were so wrapped up in that that you *forgot* you were supposed to be *hiding*!?"

Lyra's question came out as a shout, harsh enough that the group came to a halt. Even the servant looked perplexed, but now both Avery and Lyra were sporting angry faces.

It was an accident, Elias said hurriedly. *We messed up, I know, but we can still win this. Trust me.*

Lyra's skirts were bunched up in her fists as she met Elias' stare. Her rage was something he had already contended with, and now, he sorely wished he never would again. Time drew out far too long. Even when the servant coughed for attention, Lyra didn't budge.

Then, she released her skirts and huffed. "My horse better be fine." She glared at the servant. "I don't care who sorts it, but you *will* make sure the horse these two idiots rode in returns to our hands after this meeting."

The servant bowed his head before beginning to walk again. Elias let out a breath, met Lyra's eye one last time, and mindspoke one more 'thank you.' She didn't reply and followed after the servant.

Having already been inside Eastbow's home, Elias recognised the same expensive taste of another noble. Oil paintings of Harrigott family members, landscapes of another province, and allusions to gods and myths covered almost every wall.

The servant led them to the back of the house and rapped on a closed door. A moment later, a masked woman opened the door. She allowed them inside, but the servant did not follow; instead, he smiled blandly.

"My master will be in touch. Blank envelopes will be delivered with his responses. Once read, you must burn them."

He bowed his head at the masked woman, Victoria Greenford, and dismissed himself. The door closed behind him, and they awkwardly entered the drawing room.

Only a few candles had been lit, giving the room a dim glow. Even so, Elias could see wallpaper in paisley green and wooden floors with a large decorative rug. In front of the unlit fireplace was an arrangement of matching armchairs and sofas. Greenford settled alone on a couch, her skirts spread out as she held her stomach.

Opposite her, the rest of them sat. It was a unified front against a single duchess, but with the servant and his master lurking nearby, it felt like they were standing on ice.

"I suppose it is time we all acquaint ourselves," Greenford said. Removing her mask revealed the lower half of her face. In response, both Lyra and Avery took theirs off, too. Greenford's mouth opened in surprise. "The Undefeated Champion of the Agonia," she mused. "I thought Castor had snuck you in…" She glanced at Avery. "But for you to work alongside your old opponent, how strange indeed."

Even without telepathy, Elias saw the discomfort plain on Lyra's face. If she was that easily recognised as the pit fighter, would she also be recognised as a dead Whitehallow?

No one replied, but Greenford seemed more than content hearing herself talk. "The mind control has run its course, and I am clear-headed once more," she announced. "However, even in its haze, I knew I wanted to help you, no matter how barbaric your methods were, to start the conversation."

Elias took this as the opportunity to root out the truth; strangely enough, he found it. Victoria Greenford knew her position as Torr's employer was a precarious one. He wasn't a manipulatable man; not even a mind-controlling naiad could bewitch him. And it wasn't even *her* money that had bought him. Greenford had much to lose and nothing to hold over Ambrose or Torr.

The Death Marked, however, were a willing prize in her palm. She recalled each of them in the Tournament and the stories of how they had fought the Kherians in the wake of the gunpowder explosion. They weren't famous assassins but had the skills and powers to rival one. Best of all, they were desperate for her help, and she could arrange the terms.

A knock on the door altered that thought—there was Benedict Ambrose, too.

Elias rose from his seat just as an envelope slipped beneath the door. He could hear the thoughts of the deliverer and how that servant's instruction was to stay and eavesdrop. In fact, a *long* line of servants loitered in the hallways of the Harrigott manor, a precaution when dealing with a Siren that also hindered a telepath.

He took the letter and opened it. Elias scanned it first and then read it aloud for the gathered group.

Well met, fighters. It appears you have been marked by the Haunted Shadow's blade and wish I stop him. I know all your names and faces, so I can see the value in keeping you four alive. Victoria no doubt believes the same. We will be willing to help you as long as Elias Hearth, Lyra Avenyard, and Nox Parker agree to some terms.

Become officially sponsored fighters in exchange for our protection. You will be required to fight until a minimum of the quarter-finals, and our deal will be met. The money from your victories will be given to Victoria and me as payment.

Avery Nash's deal will remain the same: an unofficial sponsor with the Haunted Shadow as her chaperone. So long as you become Champion of the Tournament, you will still receive a prize cut, but the majority shall be returned to me.

If you agree to these terms, I will be willing to explain how I will protect you.

Elias scanned it one last time, committing it to memory. It was a skill of the Thoughtsingers, and he had the barest attainment of it. Once he trusted himself to recall it fully, he set the letter and envelope on fire. Ashes rained to the floor, but he made no move to clean it.

"Benedict, in his usual infinite wisdom, is correct," Greenford said after a moment of silence. "I will sponsor both Elias Hearth and Nox Parker while Benedict will arrange to take Lyra Avenyard off Castor's hands."

A shadow of a smile appeared on Lyra's face, though it did not reach her eyes. "He won't like that."

Greenford shared the same expression. "He won't have a choice." Then she sobered. "My only question is this: *why* do you want our help?"

No one answered. In a way, Elias was surprised the duchess even asked. He had assumed that Greenford wouldn't care that four commoners would plead for her help. Ambrose hadn't seemed concerned with the why and wanted to claim more souls to control.

The Haunted Shadow is an assassin impervious to mind powers, Elias began. *I cannot speak to him with my abilities; he is mindless. I'm sure you already know that.*

Greenford nodded.

It isn't his only shield. His body is physically invulnerable. Nothing can hurt him. Not a blade, not a flame, nothing.

Elias made sure to let his mindspeaking be heard by the eavesdropping servant outside. Ambrose seemed a confident man, but Elias could only guess that was because he was an ignorant one. Everyone involved in this fight had to understand the threat, down to the last detail.

Torr was involved in the Kherian attack, Elias continued. *He admitted it to us. Not only is he planning to kill us four, but he has also tried to decimate the kingdom. After your employment with him is complete, he will be a danger to everyone.*

Greenford inhaled gravely, watching Elias closely. Looking through her memories, he saw she had been taught from a young age how to spy lies and embellishments of the truth, and she hunted his eyes for any of that. Elias regarded her in kind. The truth was far more horrifying than any lie he could conjure, and as they stared at one another, Greenford recognised it.

"I believe you," she said. "I wish I didn't, but I do. You cannot defeat him yourselves, but you believe we can." She smiled. "You are right to think so."

Elias met her mind and found her words askew. Greenford had *no idea* how Benedict was planning to resolve this. The Haunted Shadow had been a nightmare for decades, but now, knowing that he was physically invulnerable as well as mentally terrified her to no end. He wasn't something that could be defeated, and that was why Greenford wanted him gone. She favoured the Death Marked for their strengths but also their very fatal weaknesses.

"I'm attending the Tournament to *win*," Nox blurted out. "It will most likely come down to Avery and me in the finals—will you disregard the deal if *I* win instead?"

Their hands were fists in their lap, and their jaw clenched. Elias could hear their mind seething. No matter how much it destroyed them, Nox wanted to win more than anything, but they would allow Avery to win if it meant they all survived. It lightened Elias' heart to know the werewolf could perform such a selfless act.

Greenford frowned. "Avery has mind control," she said flatly. "There is no possible way you will win."

"So you're allowing her to cheat."

Greenford crossed her arms. "Victory is victory no matter how dirty your hands become. Avery Nash *will* win the Tournament, no matter how hard you try." She flicked a hand. "However, if it makes you feel better, I'm sure Benedict will keep up his side of the deal if you impossibly win."

Nox grunted in affirmation, but inside, they wanted to rip off the duchess's head for doubting them so thoroughly. They already had ideas on defeating Avery, yet Nox had been written off.

Elias returned his focus to Greenford's mind. Although she didn't know what Benedict was planning, she still trusted him. His confidence in the letter convinced her, and her terrors and doubts revolving around Torr slowly slinked away. It should have instilled Elias with that selfsame confidence., but another nagging voice reached his mind.

I don't trust any of this, Lyra said coldly, forcing Elias' telepathy to pick her up. *Not without Benedict here. She's safe, though?*

Greenford is safe, he responded only to her. *She only wants to help, mainly because she wants to use us afterwards.*

A smile twitched on Lyra's lips. *Well, that's hardly surprising. What of Ambrose's servants? Did you get anything from them?*

One is eavesdropping outside as we speak... he trailed off, stretching out his powers to glean any more minds on the other side of the door. *He's just dispatched a runner to relay our conversation. None of them know where Ambrose is—I think over ten servants are running this line of communication.*

And the one who does know is too far away. Lyra shook

her head. *We're agreeing to the plan, then? Playing as sponsored fighters?*

We have to.

She didn't reply mentally, but Lyra cleared her throat. "Alright," she said. "I think it's safe to say we all agree to your terms. We will fight in the Tournament in the name of Ambrose and Greenford."

Even though it wasn't even Greenford's idea, she grinned widely. It was a victory in her eyes, a battle she had won. Elias couldn't believe it; Greenford was a puppet for Benedict, and her delusions blinded her from that truth.

A second later, there was another knock at the door and a letter swept under. As Elias approached, he found that the servants had relayed two letters: one for if they accepted and one for if they rejected the terms. It was not that the servant knew the contents of the letters; they only had to deliver the correctly marked one, depending on the group's decision.

The sheer organisation of this communication unsettled Elias.

How long had Ambrose been anticipating Avery's attempt to mind control him? And, if it were so important, why did he not protect Greenford from the same attack? Of course, she was only a pawn to Ambrose, but she still possessed much sensitive information.

Elias shook the thought from his mind and opened the new letter.

It pleases me that we have come to an agreement. The official sponsorships are being penned and purchased. Upon your departure, a servant of mine will provide you with a corresponding armband that you must wear during the Tournament's proceedings.

Your protection is also protection for the kingdom. I am in possession of an immobilising cage that can be unleashed on an unwitting target. Once the Tournament has concluded and the Haunted Shadow's chaperone duties are complete, my soldiers will interrupt his departure and trap him in the cage. Regardless of any invulnerability, the assassin will physically not be able to escape. It is a tried and tested device and shall work against him.

You will not need to concern yourselves with the preparation or logistics of the cage. Keep your focus on victory, and we shall see the terrorist caught for his crimes against the kingdom.

After such, we may discuss your further employment.

Again, Elias burned the letter. Even though both letters had been unsigned and written in two different scripts, Ambrose still felt their physical existence was too great a risk. Greenford's presence also ensured the letters were destroyed, though Elias doubted the duchess realised that.

"I believe that is all the discussion we need," Greenford claimed. "Unless anyone has any questions?"

Much to Elias' surprise, all eyes turned to him. His mind raced, trying to think if there *was* anything to ask. Would he even get a straight answer? Unlikely from Ambrose, and Greenford didn't know enough to tell him anything new. Slowly, he shook his head, dropping his gaze to the floor.

Nothing.

Immediately, Greenford stood. "On that note, I have a ball to attend." She returned her mask to her face and swept towards the door. "You'll be expected to stay here until Benedict's servants give you leave. After that, Castor's carriage will take you back to Cerenia. Your stay at the party is over."

36

LYRA

After Victoria's departure, someone locked them inside the drawing room. Of course, Lyra could have avoided them all individually if they wanted, but she found no point. Her mind was working overtime, endless theories repeating.

The nobles could not be trusted. Their plan could not be trusted. Lyra needed an escape plan.

She and Twylla had already had their suspicions about how the Tournament location would work. The chapel was a meeting point, and a transportation method would be used. If their hunch was correct, then it was a method Lyra or Twylla could manipulate. Most preferably, it would be Twylla, considering Lyra would need to focus on winning her matches and keeping Ambrose and Greenford off her back. If they ever found out about her escape plans, they might call the deal off, regardless of whether it was legitimate or not.

Out of everyone in the drawing room, she chose Elias to tell her plans. Avery and Nox would want to focus on their victories, and she had already voiced her doubts about the nobles to Elias. He would understand her distrust despite not using his telepathy on her.

I've never heard of an immobilising device like that, she told him. Her mental barriers were still up, but she allowed the imaginary door in her mind to stay open, as if she were calling across the street to relay the news to a neighbour. *And I don't think Twylla knows of it, either.*

We can ask her when we get back, he said. *A fresh location can also give us a better perspective.*

Lyra nodded and then broke the silence of the group. "Are we all taking the carriage back then? Who'll take Essen? *If* Ambrose's men actually retrieved him."

Guilty expressions flashed across both Nox's and Elias' faces, but Avery answered first. "I see no point in going back to the city with you," she said. "I'll make my own way back to the Forest. My skin feels dry. I've been away too long." She traced a hand over her dress. "If we survive tomorrow, I'll return the clothes."

The door to the drawing room clicked open, and a servant led them out. Following that, they were taken from the manor house to the driveway. Courtiers watched their group curiously, and Lyra was glad she had already placed her mask back on. Without it, Victoria had immediately recognised her, and Lyra did not want to repeat that.

Outside, Castor's carriage awaited them, and to Lyra's relief, a saddled Essen. The horse looked completely unharmed, but she couldn't help but pat him down and whisper apologies for being temporarily abandoned. She still thought Nox and Elias were complete idiots for exposing their location and losing Essen, but it wasn't something that could be changed now. A new plan was made, and even though Lyra didn't like it, at least she wouldn't be facing it alone.

I'll ride Essen back to the King's Mast, Elias said. *You two can take the carriage.*

The farewell was an awkward one. Lyra would see Elias again in less than an hour, but with Avery, their next meeting might be their very last one. The nymph fiddled with the mask, crumpling its fabric with her fidgeting.

"I'll see you all tomorrow," Avery said hoarsely. "We will succeed. We have to."

She waited for no reply before slipping away from the group. Her departure was slow, traipsing off in a dress she still wasn't used to. Lyra wished she could help, but she knew Avery would want nothing of the sort.

The carriage driver stepped down from his seat and opened the door. Immediately, Nox jumped up inside, barely giving Elias a goodbye. Lyra hesitated, eyeing the phoenix-blood as he saddled up on Essen.

"Don't lose my horse again," she said sternly. "And get back swiftly."

Elias nodded. *Safe travels.*

Inside the carriage, Nox was sprawled across one bench, hands cupping the back of their head. Lyra took the opposite bench just as the driver snapped the reins.

"Enjoying yourself?" she asked as the carriage jostled into the night.

"This could be our last night alive," Nox declared. "And I am riding in some asshole noble's carriage without his notice." The werewolf gave a feral grin. "'Course I'm enjoying myself."

***

As her fourth journey following this route, Lyra knew how long it would take them to reach the King's Mast. So when the carriage lurched to a sudden halt, she assumed the worst.

She drew back the curtains warily, sneaking a glance at the outside world. Lyra expected all kinds of foes to halt their way: highwaymen, guardsmen, Torr, even Castor himself, refreshed and seething. Instead, they were on the desolate roadway leading into Cerenia and had just stopped short of the city.

With no threats abound, Lyra opened the door just as the driver was heading his way towards her.

"What's happening?" she asked, voice sharp.

The driver shook his head. "City's packed. Can't get in like this. You're gonna have to go in on foot."

She frowned, but Nox took the man's words as an order and slipped out of the carriage. They held out a hand for her, and she stepped down. The driver snapped the door shut and hopped back up into his seat. He sent the horses racing back into the night and away from Cerenia with no farewell. Dust trailed after him, and Lyra watched dumbfounded.

"Not a normal occurrence then?" Nox asked.

Lyra blinked, reasserting herself. "Well, the city is known to be busy, of course, but I thought with the Kherian attack, no one would risk being out at night." She cocked her head towards Cerenia. "With the Tournament tomorrow, though, I can't say this is a coincidence."

"Want to figure it out?" they asked, a brow raised and a crooked smile on their face.

Lyra returned the smile. "I don't see why not."

It didn't take long to reach the city proper, and immediately Lyra was overwhelmed. Streams of people were indeed about, heading all in the same direction and further into the city. During the daytime, this quantity of citizens wandering about was regular, but with night racing across the skies, it was excessive.

Nox removed their cloak and swept it onto Lyra's

shoulders. "You're going to stick out," they explained. "This is a night of commoners, not partygoers."

Lyra wrapped the cloak tighter around her body, concealing her dress as best as possible. Her mask was already shoved inside her clutch, which she also hid beneath the heavy material of the cloak. She pulled up the hood, too, appreciative of Nox's foresight and effort.

Keeping close to one another, they pushed into the crowd of people. Chatter filled the air, drowning any chance for Nox or Lyra to speak. Sweat began to develop on her gloved palms as the heat of so many bodies packed together reached her.

Lyra's stomach churned. A nighttime gathering like this was usually met with merriment, but this swarming crowd was full of dejection. Whatever they were going to find, Lyra could tell it wouldn't be much good.

There was a tug on her sleeve, and Lyra looked up to find a paper face in front of her. Nox was showing her a wanted poster, no doubt snatched up from a wall, and while it took a moment to focus, Lyra recognised the image as Torr. Her brows rose, but she didn't say anything, and neither did Nox, who just shoved the poster into their pocket.

As they walked, Lyra started to piece things together. They weren't just heading towards the city centre but the absolute middle of Cerenia: the Palace. And as they neared, whispers of dissent started to fill the air, and Lyra's ears yearned to hear all.

"What's the point of this Tournament if we can't go see it?"

"Kherian bastards are gonna try and blow the Queen up again no matter if we're there or not."

"War is going to be declared; I just know it."

"The noble pricks did this. Hoarding the fights so only they watch 'em."

Lyra almost wished they had waited for Elias and his telepathy to figure out the full extent of the whispers. She could picture enough theories in her head but not enough to walk away from the crowd.

Fortunately for them, at the Palace gates, no one was whispering.

A man was standing on a crate, yelling at the already riotous group of people huddled around him. Soldiers of the Common Guard pushed forward to drag the man down, but even more commoners pushed them *back*. In the corner of Lyra's eye, she saw Nox grinning at the sight.

The man was repeating the same thing over and over, an unofficial herald for the people. "This was to be kept quiet from the public, the true participants of the Royal Tournament! Only the Queen's nobility can attend the matches! Everyone else is barred! The very ones who were accused of destroying the Palace are now reaping its benefits! The attack was at the helm of Kheria! But the war won't be with them! It'll be against the nobles!"

A cheer ricocheted through the crowd, and Lyra stumbled at its tumultuous movements. It was obvious to them a riot was about to break out, a pressure point worth hitting, coming closer and closer. Torches lit the air, and smoky skies disfigured the faces of everyone around Lyra. But she didn't need to see their expressions to know their feelings. Even this late into the night, the people's anger did not seem ready to be sated.

She grabbed Nox's arm. "We need to go!" she yelled over the din.

Their eyes met hers, temporarily full of panic and shock. Nox nodded, and she tightened her grip on their arm. Lyra didn't want to use the void, not in such a crowded place with so many eyes, but escaping this cram would be impossible without potentially being trampled in the process. She squeezed her eyes close and let the void take them away.

They started to fall, Lyra's hood rising up and away from her face as she opened her eyes. Stray hairs tickled her face, but she concentrated on keeping hold of Nox. Gritting her teeth, she watched as a purple doorway started to form, racing towards their feet.

Boots collided with wood as Nox and Lyra landed upright in her rented rooms at the King's Mast. A clatter of teacups came in response, and they both turned to see Twylla and Astrid sitting at the table, staring up at them, a steaming teapot at their side.

She ignored their stares, releasing Nox to sit on the ottoman, a hand going to her side. Lyra was breathing hard, skin flushed from the energy exerted and the sudden warmth of the room. She scrubbed a hand across her face, plastering her hair onto her sweaty skin.

"Hello!" Twylla chimed, taking a sip of her drink. "I take the ball was eventful?"

Nox frowned. "Is this normal to you?"

Astrid shrugged. "Sort of," she admitted. "You should have seen Lyra when she didn't know how to control it. How many trees have you fallen out of?"

Lyra shook her head, but a grin started to form on her face. "Five."

"Hm," Twylla mused. "I thought it was seven."

Nox huffed a laugh but sobered up quickly. "Catch your breath for a minute," they told Lyra. "I'll go find Elias."

She nodded. "Stay out of the crowd."

They didn't reply and instead headed out of the room. However, both Twylla and Astrid caught the words..

"What crowd?" Twylla asked. "What's happening?"

"There's a protest outside the Palace starting," Lyra began, still breathless. "It's about the Tournament because they're... *shit.*" She stood up and stared at her friends. "This changes everything."

"What does?" Astrid demanded, also standing up and grabbing Lyra's shoulders.

It was a habit for Lyra to start pacing back and forth, losing track of her words when something important happened, and so Astrid had since learnt to keep her stuck in place. She noted that mutely, but her mind continued to race.

"Only the nobility are allowed to attend the Tournament's recommencement," she forced out, making herself stare into Astrid's eyes. "Neither of you can come. All our plans... we can't do it."

***

Nox did not return for another thirty minutes, giving Astrid enough of an excuse to go out to find their missing friends but also to glean even more information. It left Lyra and Twylla alone, a rare opportunity to privately discuss the doomed escape plan.

All of them knew the chapel was only a meeting point for the fighters and that the actual location of the Tournament remained under wraps. But without Twylla and Astrid being able to follow after them as spectators, it truly felt like they were alone.

"I don't have the strength to do it," Lyra whispered. "We've practised before, and I have never been successful. How am I supposed to—?"

"You won't be alone," Twylla soothed. "Your companions are all quite crafty; besides, you'll have my charms. And remember, this is only for if things go wrong. You, of all people, should try to stay positive."

Lyra grimaced. "Not when the nobles are involved."

The door slammed open before the witch could reply as Astrid, Nox, and Elias swept into the room. Lyra's shoulders sagged, relief running through her to see everyone safe. They all settled at the table as Astrid launched into explaining all that she learnt.

The decision to only allow the nobility to spectate the recommencement had been made the day of the original Tournament. Still, it had been intended never to be released to the public. Instead, the people would be told that the spectator stands were already at total capacity and that everyone would be barred from entering. The servants of nobles leaked the information, but their true names were kept concealed to protect their identities.

"It's too late for either of us to sign up to fight," Astrid muttered. "And there are too many unknown variables to allow us to sneak in without being caught. There's probably already dozens of countermeasures in place to stop that sort of thing in the first place." She glanced at Twylla. "Including the magical kind."

What about Torr? Elias suddenly asked. *He's not a fighter. Last time, he was in the spectator stands. There isn't a chance Greenford or Ambrose would let him into their theatre box.*

"They probably made some other arrangements," Lyra said bitterly. "Paid off the right guard, convinced them Torr is just another worker. Considering all the effort both of them have gone through to acquire Avery, it is doubtful they would just leave Torr out. Regardless of what we do, he will be there, while Twylla and Astrid will not."

The finality of her words sent the room into silence. Lyra knew the evening had gone too smoothly, that something would lurk in the shadows to ruin it all. Lyra was never usually so pessimistic, but the sneaky dealing of Benedict Ambrose had made her lose her positivity. He was hiding something, and without knowing how to flee the Tournament, they were all trapped.

"You don't need us," Twylla said. "We were only ever insurance. The nobles have given their word that they will protect you; you cannot disregard that. I know it seems like you are the beggars of the deal, but they are also expecting victory from you. There is power in that—strength. They cannot abandon you."

Lyra nodded, but her mind was elsewhere. She would need to practise tonight and neglect her sleep to ensure that power and strength were ready. The others didn't need to know. Only Twylla could help her with this.

Nox huffed a breath. "So that's all settled. Let's hope nothing else happens."

Lyra elbowed them. "Don't tempt fate."

"I think we should get drunk again," they said in response.

Lyra was glad to hear the chorus of disagreement, even when her own head was full of dread and fear. *I have to void us, or we are all dead.*

37

A V E R Y

Fresh sunlight dappled the copse of ash trees, which swayed upon a mild breeze. The weather of the Forest of the Dryads never changed; its immortals didn't need the convention of seasons to keep them alive. Instead, winters would threaten their livelihood, so the Forest remained in perpetual spring, detouring to summer only if Mother Famara wished it. Not that it mattered to Avery; she'd done what the god had ensured never to occur within the Forest.

She made it rain.

Lake water shimmered through the air, fat droplets defying gravity as Avery willed it before letting it drop to the grass. Again, the water sank and fell, her endless rainstorm.

She sat at the edge of her lake, its level lower thanks to the continual stream of manipulation bringing it into the sky. Only her lake water could perform this well under Avery's touch. Even her sisters' lakes held a looser control, but Avery desired the strength it brought her. She changed the weather in a world without rain.

Avery was staring so intensely into her own storm that she barely noticed Nemesia step out from the cluster of ash trees. She stood tall, unwavering against the flood of blue. When their eyes locked, the lake collapsed. It retreated into the ground, refilling the coin-shaped hole.

The Tournament was today, and Avery's body ached in

anticipation. Her sisters were gone. When she returned from the ball, Nemesia explained both her sisters had successfully gone dormant in their lakes. They had shed their bodies in exchange for water, and neither would return until Avery said so. She was glad they were safe but found it strange to be so alone.

Avery jutted her chin out at Nemesia, waiting for her to speak. "The Forest whispers," the dryad began, "the assassin is on his way."

Avery nodded. She was already dressed for battle. New blades shone on her armour, gifts from Elias. She'd cleaned the blood and gore from her leather breastplate before wiping it down with oil. Her daggers were honed to razor sharpness. She'd even braided her hair up, though Avery had required the assistance of Nemesia and her dryad sisters to complete it.

Avery stood, and Nemesia held out her arms. An age ago, it would have been awkward to embrace the dryad. Despite her place as Avery's mother, there wasn't any true touch or connection between them, just soft assurances and reminders that she would never be alone.

"You will survive this," the dryad assured, pulling from the embrace. Nemesia's fingers lifted Avery's chin. "For you are full of vengeance and desire, and you are the strongest of us all."

Avery's heart thudded in her chest, blood roaring through her ears. "I'll make you proud," she murmured.

Nemesia tucked an errant strand of hair behind the naiad's pointed ear, uncaring that Avery was trying to conceal them. "You already have."

Behind them, there was the rustling of leaves. Avery looked deeply into Nemesia's eyes, remembering the sharp green of her irises before turning away.

Immediately, Torr stood a hair's breadth from her. She tipped her head up, meeting those eyes of malice. He was in disguise, pitifully so. A black wide-brimmed hat shaded his eyes, and a scarf was around his throat, ready to be pulled up at any moment. With the wanted posters of his face all over Cerenia, she wasn't surprised at the attempt but knew anyone could see right through it.

They exchanged no words before he clamped a hand on her wrist and dragged her out of the thicket. Her protests were lost beneath the swishing of foliage. The assassin's pace was unmatched, faster than any of the previous times he'd dragged Avery anywhere. All her focus unravelled, barely able to hold a hand to her face and avoid the occasional attack of a branch. Her face burned as she knew the Forest was laughing at her.

Their walk to the Palace was uneventful. The city of Cerenia had gone quiet for the day. Only the participants could enter the Tournament, so the civilians of the capital were sequestered in their homes, dissent threatening to slip out of the cracks. Guards lined the street, patrolling the city to squash any more protests. Although Avery hadn't been there to witness it, Twylla had explained the tale through a paper blaze. Other warriors walked the streets, and a dizzying stream headed to the Palace. According to Twylla's latest note, Elias, Lyra, and Nox would already be inside the grounds.

An orderly line was outside the Palace gates, and Avery made to join it when Torr grabbed her arm and forced her to face him. "Don't lose, naiad, and I might spare you."

It was likely a lie, but she pretended to buy it. "And my friends?" She blinked up prettily at him.

His grip tightened, and a slight noise escaped her. "Don't push it." Torr released her, and Avery started to run.

***

Having arrived late, Avery found Lyra waiting for her outside the chapel. The mortal stood beside the door, where a continual stream of participants, Palace employees, and guards filtered in and out. Avery could hardly understand why. The frosted wind of the mortal lands was inescapable outside, burning her fingertips red and wracking shivers across her skin.

Avery followed Lyra inside, and immediately, that all changed.

The chapel was already packed with warriors, bringing the room's temperature to sweltering heights. Avery started removing her furs, heat scorching beneath the clothes as she felt sweat develop on her skin. How could these people stand the constant flux of warmth and cold? Winter was horrible.

Lyra kept a hand wrapped around Avery's wrist in the cram of bodies, navigating the pair in the unwavering crowd. Leather scraped across her face, the occasional sheathed blade threatening to smack her in the head. Avery tilted her head upwards, but she could see nothing but the end of Lyra's platinum braid.

But then, two figures came into view.

Elias saw her first, and the elation was clear on his face as they beheld one another. Avery's heart thudded at the sight, and a genuine grin lifted her cheeks. Nox, arms crossed and unsmiling, raised their brows. A moment later, they gave a small wave.

"And so," the werewolf announced as Lyra and Avery halted, "the Death Marked reunite for their final stand."

Before she could reply, a man barged past Avery, almost pulling her off her feet as he strode further into the chapel.

The four of them tightened their small circle, with Elias holding her so she would not fall.

All the pews had been taken, and no one had dared stand ahead of the altar, leaving the area clear of warriors. Aside from that, the chapel was the same as the last time she'd been there. Warm, cheery light flowing down on the sea of red and blue flowers and pearlescent etched walls. Carvings of the Seven Deities decorated every inch of the building, but Avery's eyes could not focus on the details.

"Well, now that you're here," Nox said. "I can finally declare what I've been thinking the entire time we've been here: this feels like a trap."

Lyra raised a brow. "A trap? In the Palace? Why would the people who already watched us almost die want to trap us? The first time proved well enough we're tougher than that."

Avery shifted her balance. "I think I agree with Nox; any moment now, I'm going to be trampled."

It won't come to that, Elias tried to assure her. *I won't let you get trampled.*

Before she could reply, a heavy thudding filled the chapel, silencing everyone. The noise came from Captain Renner, who stood at the altar, a heavy staff in his hand. He pounded the staff onto the ground again, sending reverberations through Avery's bones. Once satisfied with the quiet, Renner began to speak.

"Welcome all," he boomed, his voice bouncing off the cavernous walls. "Today, we shall be deciding who of you will be the victor of the Royal Tournament! Many of you have already tried for this title and dare to return to claim it, for which we thank you greatly. The proceedings of the Tournament shall run as they originally did so, with a reiteration of the rules for any newcomers. But first, the one thing that must be on all of your minds: the location." Renner's voice was full of self-satisfaction, clearly enjoying his position of authority and knowledge. "We shall be taking a detour through the catacombs of the Palace, where everything will become clear. Follow me!"

Avery tried to hide her panic as the crowd surged forward, carrying her along. She could only spy Elias, head and shoulders above the average person, as he looked fretfully around. But she, Lyra and Nox had all been swallowed up by the crowd, leaving the naiad alone as they marched forward. Avery's gut twisted as she considered Renner's words: *the catacombs.*

Renner had called it a detour. Would they only travel through the catacombs and battle on open ground? Or was the Tournament going to take place further below the Palace? Avery hoped for the former, but both options seemed undesirable to her. Anything to do with the catacombs meant only one route of escape and a scary chance of being crushed beneath rubble. So what the hells sort of plan was this? Avery could imagine her companions processing the same theories, which did not ease her worry.

The air smelt of dust and bones the moment she entered the catacombs. A hidden doorway had slid back adjacent to the altar, the panel carved with icons of Attalin and Diaron, the two gods most linked with misery and destruction. Avery shivered as the daylight faded, replaced instead with smoky torches. Her eyes watered as the hammering in her heart worsened. She'd never felt so alone in such a thick mass of people, making it difficult to breathe.

The crowd marched on for what felt like hours. Avery lost track of time the moment she was in the catacombs proper. It was an endless underground tunnel of white walls and dusty floors. As the descent began to flatten, the appearance of bleached bones cropped up, too. Skulls were embedded in the walls, empty eye sockets staring into Avery and sending shivers down her spine. She tried to focus on the path ahead, but in her peripheral vision, she saw the endless glare of the dead.

Then, all of a sudden, the passageway opened wide into a room of impossible heights. It reminded Avery of a cave, though most obviously artificial and infinitely larger. A stairway brought the crowd down into the cavern. The brightly lit structure was embedded with shimmering crystals that blazed blue light. The ceiling was over fifty feet above the dugout floor, making Avery wonder how far below ground they were.

Standing at the top of the stairway gave her a full view of the cavern. In the middle of the chamber was a circular marble structure. It spanned the entire cave and was hollow in the centre. Avery held back a gasp when she realised just what it was—a warp gate. Once active, the empty circle would fill up with magic and take whoever entered to the corresponding warp gate.

Avery's eyes were wide. *This* was the plan? To use a power that the Kingdom of Darcan abhorred? She couldn't help but wonder how long this plan had been in the works; warp gates were usually ancient structures, fallen apart from disuse and time. This one looked newly built, and the marble was clean of decorative carvings.

The large space before the warp gate was enough room for all the participants to stand together, albeit tightly. Avery squirmed against the bodies of the surrounding warriors, the tang of mortal blood ever present in her nose. She craned her neck upwards, trying her best to locate Elias in the crowd, but she was too short to see far enough and immediately gave up. In time, when she was free to move, she would find him.

Nervous chatter had continued throughout the journey in the catacombs, and as they all came to a halt before the warp gate, it began to intensify. A moment later, a resounding crack met Avery's ears, no doubt Renner and his staff again. She hated that she couldn't see him, only the endless armoured bodies of strangers.

"This is a warp gate," Renner yelled, his voice echoing in the cavernous hall. "It will take us all to the true location of the Tournament. There is no need to panic, but of course, if you are too scared to enter the gate, you can always just leave and save us all the trouble of your cowardice."

Avery was surprised to find no one moved. Renner grunted. "Let's begin, shall we?"

A whooshing noise filled the air, and the light of the warp gate activating suddenly blinded Avery. She covered her eyes, cursing the newfound brightness as Renner started yelling again. While she didn't catch his words, the crowd surged again, a fervent energy crackling in the people around her. Avery blinked rapidly, letting the group carry her as she found no time to brace herself before being swallowed by cerulean light.

38

LYRA

The transition from the catacombs and exiting the warp gate was a startling one. After so long in crowded spaces, Lyra had become used to the overheating of warm bodies, but as soon as she exited the warp gate, the heat was stolen from her. She exhaled sharply, a cloud of white escaping her lips as goosebumps appeared on her skin. It was even colder here than in Cerenia, and as Lyra took in her surroundings, she found the place very unlike the capital city in all qualities.

The air smelt cleaner, and the skies were clear of smog. Lyra's boots crunched under frosted grass, the plains stretching endlessly for miles with nothing interrupting it. A thick crowd stood in the grass, growing smaller as they headed towards something. With a little help from the void, Lyra had been able to stick with Nox in the catacombs and beyond. Together, they had trailed behind the group of participants and were among the last few to exit the warp gate.

Dark shadows cast over the plains. Turning, Lyra's heart jumped to her throat as she faced snow-capped mountains—the first time she'd ever seen them up close. The warp gate was embedded into the rock, an ancient crevice of magic that belonged to the Eternal Mountains as much as Darcan.

The gate fluctuated, sending a shuddering echo through

the ground, making Lyra's bones shake. With one last look back, she saw the light of the gate die, closing them off from Cerenia indefinitely.

"Well, there goes any chance for an escape route," Nox said, frowning.

Lyra didn't so much as blink. From the moment the Tournament had been re-announced with the meeting point of the chapel, she and Twylla had theorised that the warp gate within the catacombs would be used. It was a new installation to the Palace that was more rumour than fact. To confirm its existence meant that Lyra's sleepless night had paid off. If all went wrong today, it was between her and this warp gate for them to return home.

Lyra bumped their shoulder. "Don't worry about it," she said. "Everything will work out. It has to."

Nox raised a brow but didn't reply. Lyra scanned the grassland before her. The crowd of participants had dispersed, and waiting for them was an outdoor coliseum. The wooden structure tiered upwards like a cake, and already many people were seated in the ringed grandstands. The nobility were the only ones allowed to watch the new Tournament, a precautionary measure courtesy of the Queen.

Lyra scowled at the thought. Weren't they the ones accused of causing the original's destruction? And Torr, who had truly been at its helm, *was* on a duke's payroll. It was all just another gross display of this kingdom's corruption, rotting like an untreated wound. Lyra wondered if the Queen would oversee it, aware of the mess she presided over.

Her eyes lit up at the sight of Elias and Avery huddled together, forcing away her unpleasant thoughts.

"Come on," Lyra breathed, dragging Nox along. "Our

parents are waiting for us."

The werewolf's face paled considerably. "Gods above, do *not* start calling them that."

She grinned, eyes lifting to see the coliseum. Inside, it did its best to replicate the Palace courtyards: twenty chalk rings, wooden benches divided in half for the winners and losers, and high above, the opera boxes for the nobility. But as the cold winter wind from the mountains lashed across her skin, it reminded Lyra how truly far from home she was.

Canwal was one of the most western provinces of Darcan, bordering the Eternal Mountains that separated the mortal lands from the Klyvning Swamps. Lyra had never travelled this closely to the impenetrable mountains before; she especially had never expected to do so in winter.

She and Nox reached Elias and Avery. "Everyone has their armbands?" she asked in greeting. In response, Nox and Elias showed her their green and black cloth bands while she presented her yellow and orange one. Lyra smiled. "Let us all meet at the quarter-finals."

Nox started to move to the coliseum, but Lyra grabbed them first, pulling them into a hug. The werewolf froze in her arms, but she only tightened her grasp. Her voice was low enough for them to hear: "I hope you win."

They huffed a laugh against her shoulder. "You know it." Breaking the embrace, Nox met her eye. "I'll see you on the other side."

She let them go, and the werewolf headed alone into the coliseum. Lyra turned to Elias and Avery, who seemed locked in private conversation. Catching Elias' eye, she gave the phoenix-blood a quick wave goodbye before also heading in.

Staying alone in the Tournament was to keep them

innocent of colluding with one another. Avery hadn't wanted any of them to separate, but when Lyra had reminded her of the threat of disqualification for working together looming over them, the naiad had eventually agreed to the plan.

Inside the coliseum, Lyra quickly claimed a seat on one of the many participant benches. Already, she could feel Castor's glare on her. Lyra refused to glance upwards at Castor and, instead, let her eyes roam the inner circle of the coliseum.

Once everyone had filtered inside, the front doors slammed shut. A second later, the sound of Captain Renner's staff hitting against wood made her look up. She almost rolled her eyes—just how many times would that man use the staff like that? It was giving her a headache.

Erected above the coliseum was a wooden tower. Renner and an advisor stood inside it, overseeing the entirety of the space. Lyra watched curiously. Had the Queen truly not shown up? She had only appeared once during the first Tournament but had, at the very least, introduced the games. This time, her absence felt like a hidden message— this place wasn't as safe as claimed. The Death Marked were still trapped; the void was their only possible escape route.

Within the bag she had concealed beneath her cloak were five charmed necklaces. They were suffused with Cometborn magic, fashioned to strengthen Lyra's powers. She wouldn't need them unless Ambrose and Greenford trapped them here, but Lyra couldn't help but pat the bag, reassuring herself the necklaces were still there.

She had already shown them to Elias. He was the only one who knew about her plans with the void and would be the only one able to help.

Unfurling the scroll, the advisor began his welcoming

speech; it was almost the same as the original Tournament, making Lyra not bother to concentrate fully. She knew the rules, and none had been changed, nor were any more added. All that had changed was the Tournament's scope.

The number of participants had been drastically depleted in the wake of the Kherian attack. Instead of splitting the Tournament into multiple days, the fights could all fit into one. It would take numerous hours, but before Diaron's darkness took over the sky, a Champion would be named.

"With that all said and done." Renner's voice brought Lyra out of her reverie. "Let the Royal Tournament recommence!"

Names started to be called instantly. The words had flown so fast through the ice-whipped air that Lyra had almost misheard them. She strained to listen out for her friends' names but realised she didn't need to when hers was one of the first called.

"Lyra Avenyard."

Lyra jolted at her name and hurried down the steps. She pushed all dread out of her mind, focusing on the present. All her doubts and escape plans were for if the nobles betrayed them, not if Lyra failed in the Tournament. She had to win these fights, or else the deal was off. Victory was her route to freedom, as it always had been.

The Royal Tournament was the Agonia Pits' mirror, and on this day, she hoped to shatter it.

39

NOX

Nox knew from the moment they entered the coliseum they had been made into a target.

At the top of the encircled benches, Nox created a large berth between them and the next person. Even then, they had someone's attention. One man sat alone, his chosen seat facing the one Nox had selected for themself.

Nox had always been used to this. How could they not? Try as everyone might, people in this world didn't like what looked, acted, or *seemed* different. And Nox ticked all those boxes. Whether it was the scars, the fact they were a werewolf, or just their general *existence*, at least one person had a problem with it. It had happened at the first Tournament, so it was no surprise that it would happen in the second one.

Before parting ways, Elias had offered Nox a scarf similar to his own to cover their scars. He had meant no insult, rather more of a precaution. They hadn't taken it, though—not this time, at least. Nox knew in time, they would have no choice but to hide what burdened them. But not now, not against the fools who seriously thought they had the slightest chance of defeating Nox Parker.

Nox had always been assured of their skills, but with an invulnerable assassin on their tail, a part of them wondered how the full moon could have helped them today.

Their strength would have been unmatched with a full moon cresting the skies. Werewolves could half-transform at any point during the lunar cycle; claws and fangs came quickly to Nox at forming, but only the most disciplined of their kind could change into wolf form whenever they wished. During the full moon, they had no choice but to transform, sometimes losing themself in mind and soul on the worst nights.

Nox had become better at controlling it, and it was preferable to willingly transform rather than the moon's fullness forcing it upon their bones. A long time ago, they had known nothing of this and barely understood it, even after years of forcible transformations. Nox's wolf pack had changed that, the mother pitying their ignorance but sensing their hidden strength.

Nox had only been fifteen when they joined the wolf pack at Corrine's insistence. The pack was a found family of werewolves. Everyone inadvertently held a position of sibling, parent, or partner, all without being related. The mother of the pack was the reason Nox had succeeded in life. And yet, she was the one who had sent them away. After five years of living with so many others, the pack still deemed them too far detached. Nox didn't belong.

Packless, with no allies, they had become a wanderer once more. Even Ironhavell wasn't much of a cherished memory—just a means of surviving.

The Tournament had changed that. For whatever reason, Lyra, Elias, and Avery were now a part of Nox's life. In any other context, they would have been affronted at that. They had befriended the last of an immortal species, a Siren naiad, and the Undefeated Champion of Agonia while also gaining an unkillable enemy. And yet, Nox wondered if those three could become their new pack, or something close to that—people who would stay, no matter what.

It was a sentiment rarely given out to someone like Nox.

They shook their head, wanting to rid themself of such thoughts. With the Tournament victory so close, Nox could not afford to lose focus. Sure, they were Death Marked and would eventually fight the said Siren naiad, but none of that mattered. Nox *was* going to win. Tooth and claw, blood and bone, the winnings would be theirs, no matter the price.

And yet one competitor thought himself perfect for ending that plan. Not because he was in any sense a true threat in combat, but because he decided he was *born* to get rid of someone like Nox. As the first set of matches slipped past, Nox's threat drew closer to them, and only then did Nox smell it.

Silver. Powdered silver lined this man's pockets; silver rings glinted on his knuckles, and silver chains looped his neck. Nox inhaled sharply, the metal's scent clogging up their nostrils. He wasn't just any man. He was a wolfhunter.

Malachi Kailiver stalked after Nox as they took their position in a chalk ring. His name was one of the first to be called out, just like them, but Malachi did not falter as he planted himself in front of the werewolf. Their eyes locked, and the man had the gall to grin.

Despite everything, Nox's stomach churned. This was just any ordinary fight, they reminded themself. Nothing changed just because he was a wolfhunter. Any weapon could harm Nox; silver just hurt a *lot* more. They gritted their teeth, clenching their hands into fists in an attempt to sate the dread that dredged through their gut.

The last time Nox had faced wolf hunters was when more than half of their pack had been wiped out. It was an illegal practice because it was *murder*, but that stopped none of them. When prejudice forms, it only festers.

"Match rules?" the referee asked.

Malachi opened his mouth, but Nox was faster. "No weapons, no powers."

The wolfhunter considered that, and then a lazy smile formed. "Silver ain't a weapon, son," he told the referee, displaying his many accessories. "And werewolfism counts as a power, wouldn't cha say?"

Nox scowled. "No weapons, powers allowed," they amended. The referee looked to Malachi for his opinion, and he shrugged.

"Whatever makes the dog happy, it'll be put down soon enough."

"Weapons aren't allowed in this match, but powers *are*," the referee yelled over the sound of Nox growling. "On my count… start!"

One thing Elias had been most excited to train Nox with was their air manipulation. And funnily enough, it was the last thing they had wanted. Nox hadn't been entirely sure where the power had come from. Before the werewolf bite, it had lain dormant within their body. As most Darcanian humans go, magic was weak in bloodlines, and Nox had been no exception. But the bite had awoken the power to its full strength. The problem was that, initially, they had no clue how to use it.

Years of practice had changed that, of course. But Nox hated using it, hated the idea of the rest of the world knowing about it. Being a werewolf had its problems, but one with actual *powers*? Forget it.

No one knew about the air manipulation; not even all the members of their old wolf pack knew. Once Nox had left, even fewer people knew. Elias had been the first person in two years to learn of it, and they'd only used it because there was no other choice. The two of them would have been dead otherwise.

After suppressing it for so long, it surprised them how much their perception of their power had changed from last night.

Manipulating air left Nox feeling dizzy and giddy. Hells, even a little *happy*. They'd first taught themself its power just to control it and keep it at bay. But with someone who had had centuries to understand power and manipulation, Nox didn't want to stop practising.

And now? Well, now it was precisely what they needed to win.

Malachi's hand had already been halfway down his jacket pocket before the referee called the start of the match. It was where the powdered silver was—Nox could smell it beneath the layers of wool and steel. Malachi pulled out his hand, fingers dusted in metallic shimmer, aiming straight for their eyes. Nox didn't move and instead silenced his lungs.

He jerked. The dust fell harmlessly to his feet as his mouth opened and closed like a fish, straining to fill his body with air. Nox watched blankly, their hands at their sides, no longer needing to use their arms as an extension of their manipulation. It was just like suffocating Elias' flames. All they had done was single out the space Malachi stood in and stole its air. If he made one step forward, he would breathe again. A part of Nox wanted to tell him just that to keep the match interesting.

When Malachi started to turn purple, they decided to drop it anyway. Killing an opponent was against the rules, and he wouldn't be able to surrender if he couldn't breathe. At least it had destroyed his cocky swagger, his arrogance and that stupid grin. Malachi began coughing violently, gulping for air while hacking up spittle and snot. Nox snorted, rubbing their hands together as a fresh gust formed at their fingertips.

Malachi was more resilient than he looked, or maybe he was faking it; Nox couldn't tell. But the wolfhunter dug into his jacket pocket again, throwing the powdered dust with a flimsy swing. Nox managed to dodge most of it, but flecks still found their way onto their face.

The gust died immediately as a growled scream escaped Nox's lips. They clawed at the particles stuck to their skin, burrowing deeply to create as much pain as possible. Nox's fingers burned, too, as they wiped at the silver, making them switch to using their sleeve. Even then, the powder would seep between the fabric, causing an itch beneath their clothes. Giving up, Nox sent a blast of air at their face, clearing up the majority of silver in one swoop. When the pain faded, they found tears staining their cheeks, blood mixing with it from where they had scratched at their face.

Malachi was now standing with a hideous smile as he looked at his handiwork—torture, pain, misery. Nox growled. It was just *cruel.*

He ran forward, his arrogance carrying him to a deluded victory as he sent out a punch stamped in silver rings towards Nox's chest. The werewolf dodged easily, still wiping at the tears and blood on their face, before kicking Malachi in the back. He dropped like a stone face first into the upturned dirt and came up spitting grass from his mouth.

"How typical, the dog plays dirty," he huffed, raising his fists.

"How typical," Nox mocked, "the human plays the victim."

As Malachi pounced, Nox sent up a solid wall of air. He smacked straight into it, the sound of bones crunching audible to the ear as blood spurted out of his nostrils. They dropped the wall and lashed out with a kick, catching him off guard as he staggered backwards. Nox spied the silver dust on the ground, and an idea formed in their head. While Malachi held onto his nose, anger teeming in his eyes, Nox sent a whisper of wind to carry the powder upwards. It caught immediately, whipping straight towards Malachi's face, blinding him with his weapon.

He barked out in alarm, covering his eyes as tears streamed down his cheeks. Nox unsheathed their claws, sending an echo of cries in the amphitheatre as they sent one downward slash upon the wolfhunter's chest, splitting open his shirt like a knife through paper. Finally, Nox clapped their hands together, sending a *whoom* of cold air across the entire arena. Malachi lost his connection with the ground as he was pulled upwards and kicked out of the ring without Nox touching him.

The referee called the match, but there was only blood rushing in Nox's ears as they beheld Malachi. A feral smile tipped the werewolf's mouth, and their claws slowly sank back into their nailbeds.

"Victory is mine," they whispered, letting the words carry on a breeze so only the wolfhunter could hear its truths. "You are nothing but a waste of breath, and one day, I'll cut you off for good."

Nox walked away from the ring, already waiting for the next success.

40

ELIAS

In both Tournaments, Elias noticed how almost no one would try expressing any strength of the supernatural. The Darcanian bloodlines were so thinned from magic that it shouldn't have been surprising for him to see. Only healing powers subverted the trend, keeping the Queen stocked with many healers of a high calibre in the Palace.

Still, he had watched every match closely, listening to the callout of rules and seeing if anyone reacted at the forbidding of powers. No one had stood out; so many competitors consisted of mortal blood, short-lived and weak. He sometimes pitied the failings of humankind. And yet, buried within the mortality, an ebbing of power lifted through the winter wind.

It made enough sense to him that people hid their powers to avoid discrimination. Lyra had said that was her plan for their match before it began. Since her reputation from the Pits, she had also wanted to avoid revealing to the world she suddenly had powers.

Lyra had still never explained her powers, despite everyone's deep-rooted curiosity. Neither he, Avery, nor Nox had seen anything like it, and they wanted to know as much as possible. But Lyra's silence on the matter meant he had no explanation as to *how* she had the powers, which was the biggest headache of it all.

The nobility were the original breeders of non-human

hatred. They prided themselves on not being 'tainted' with magical blood, which would otherwise disrupt their so-called human 'purity.' So how on earth had it fallen into Lyra's bloodline? Too many theories ran through Elias' head; was she not actually a Whitehallow? Was the prejudice just a massive lie for the nobility to hoard magic? Of course, he would never dare ask, but he still tested her mental barriers to try and find answers.

After Nox's brutal display of claws and teeth, Elias saw it first, the hidden wielder and her subtleties. She looked to be in her early-forties, but he sensed an air of wisdom beyond her apparent age. She had brown hair pulled into a braided crown and blue eyes. Armed with only a dagger, Elias hadn't expected her to go far in the Tournament. Until the ground had shifted beneath her feet, and the scent of witch-blood hit him like a stone.

"Delphia Ryer wins the match!" the referee cried as her opponent staggered out of the ring, his hands covering his eyes.

She hadn't touched him to conclude the match. All that happened was the twist of her foot, and suddenly he was blind. Elias knew witch-blood quite well, as Twylla had since figured out, but this one was different. It was diluted in a sense, humanness coating her frame like it was a part of her. And appearance-wise, she looked almost *too* old for a witch. Their slower ageing meant they spent most of their centuries of life looking less than twenty-five. So unless this witch was even older than *him,* something else was going on.

Delphia walked away from the fighting ring, settling on the winners' bench close enough for Elias to sneak into her thoughts. He expected some resistance; most witches excelled in mental barriers since they lived among Thoughtsingers, but her mind was completely open, free for him to find the truth.

She was an Earthcarver, which came as no surprise. Delphia manipulated the earth to send dirt into her opponent's eyes to catch them unaware and lose. But he was intrigued to find she wasn't a true Klyvning witch; hells, she had never been to the Swamps. Her Stormbringer mother had fled from the witchlands and fallen in love with a Darcanian mortal, giving the world the first true half-witch Elias had met.

And she wasn't in her early forties at all; Delphia was double that. While that wasn't old by his or Avery's standards, in comparison to everyone else participating, she was probably the third oldest in their ranks and looked nothing like it. Sitting back in his seat, Elias decided he would want to fight her next if he could have the chance.

Incidentally, he was not the only one to desire their shared battle. Delphia used her earth manipulation to turn the tide by distracting her opponent or kicking them off their feet; the witch used whatever sly move possible to keep her powers undetected. But Elias had done the exact opposite, blazing his flames in his matches. Despite the marvelling display, he was still far from showing the true extent of his powers. And Delphia knew it. She was too smart to think otherwise, and it was goading her into the perfect trap.

She wanted to beat him badly. Her victories were done through insignificant shifts of the earth, but against Elias? An earthquake was coming.

Her name had been called first, and as if sheepishly, Elias stepped into Delphia's ring. Her thoughts were unignorable; already, a plan had formed in her head. It was the perfect victory; Delphia thought she knew everything that Elias would pull; she had decided how to catch him unaware. But it would all be for nothing—no one expected a telepath, no, a *Thoughtsinger*, to be right under their nose.

"Match rules?" the referee asked.

"No weapons," Delphia said, jutting her chin out. "Powers only."

Elias knew it was coming, but he hesitated in his reply, feigning surprise. A moment passed as if he was considering the suggestion before nodding. Delphia rewarded him with a grin, stepping backwards to discard her dagger into the grass outside the ring. Elias followed suit, unsheathing his greatsword and the various knives Lyra had gifted him.

He would have preferred to keep them in a safe place instead of the frosted dirt—he also didn't trust Delphia not to harm them with her powers. Collateral damage was one thing; destroying his prized weapon was another. But if he had left the blades on the winners' bench before the match had been called, it would have been obvious that he had somehow known the match rules. Elias could not allow her to suspect anything was awry, or he could be disqualified, ruining his end of the deal. Despite everything, the true reason for being here was for the nobles so they could capture Torr.

"On my mark!" the referee yelled. "3... 2... 1... Begin!"

Elias had become better practised at directing his flames with his sword, but he still sent a fantastical display of his powers across the palms of his hands. Delphia gave him a quick smirk, and from her thoughts, he knew she saw him as only an inexperienced mortal. Sure, she sensed immortal blood in his veins, but Delphia only took him for a half-blood like herself, not a fully-fledged phoenix-blood. Then again, no one would consider such an idea nowadays. Why would they? The phoenix-bloods were long gone. Not even Elias could find them.

He sent out an arc of fire in Delphia's direction, who stood her ground. During the Tournament, she had shown nothing more than the slightest manipulation of dust and thin dirt. Still, with someone acting so brazenly right before her, she now decided she could afford to reveal her biggest secret to the mortals.

With the shift of her foot and the flick of her wrist, a chunk of earth uprooted itself from the ground, sailing straight towards Elias' flames and taking the brunt of its impact. He watched the mud soften to liquid, melting in brown drips as the fire guttered out.

However, the chunk of earth kept coming, and he had to duck and roll to avoid being hit. Coming up from his knees, Elias sent another wave of flame to the left, feigning an attack for Delphia to defend herself from. She took the bait, stamping the floor with her foot to send a wall of hardened dirt to protect her flank. With her right side exposed, Elias dashed forward, swinging a kick to take Delphia off her feet.

She landed hard on her back, the dirt wall collapsing beside her. Crumbling to pieces, she shot her hands out to send the decimated chunks at Elias. He raised his arms, crossing his forearms over each other before separating, a blaze of fire erupting from his skin at the movement. It flared out, the momentum halting the flying earth and melting it back to the ground.

Elias looked down to find Delphia gone. Turning, he had no time to avoid the stream of dust that hit his eyes. He held back the instinct to rub his eyes despite the stinging of his sudden blindness taking over. He heard another volley of rocks detach from the ground, no doubt aimed at him again.

Still blind, he went to his knees, slamming open palms into the dirt to send up a careening wall of pure flame between himself and the attack. It worked, mostly, as broken pieces of earth scattered onto him. Elias let the wall die and lit up two of his fingers. The idea was a pretty stupid one, but Delphia was still controlling the dust on his face, making sure his streaming tears did nothing to alleviate his blindness.

He heard her thoughts: *What is he doing?* just as he stuck his fiery fingers directly into his eyes, swiping flames across the waterline and beneath the lid. Aside from the sensation of poking his own eyes, he felt nothing worse, the fire eating away at the dust immediately. Elias blinked twice, wiping his face of tears as his sight returned. A moment later, the fire on his fingers winked out.

Delphia looked horrified, as did everyone watching. Her thoughts raced, the disbelief of what she just witnessed playing repeatedly in her mind. *Can't be a normal fire user; they have no immunity to flames. What the hells is he?*

Elias knew not to answer and, instead, clenched his hands into fists to send punches of fire in quick succession towards her. Delphia gaped, dodging the first volley before sending a wave of flying rocks to cover her. An idea was forming in her mind, one that would act as a winning move on her part, which was exactly what Elias couldn't let happen.

She raised her foot to slam it to the ground, and her fists clenched as all her strength went into the blow. Elias leapt towards her, his hand outstretched and drenched in flames to clasp around her raised ankle. Delphia's scream ripped through the air, the searing of flesh rippling beneath his closed palm. She collapsed to the dirt beside him, lashing out with her uninjured foot to kick Elias square in the face. He grunted, blood spurting out of his nose, but kept his grip on her ankle.

Delphia flailed about, trying to free herself from his burning hand. He didn't mindspeak it to her, but all that ran through Elias' mind was one word: *surrender, surrender, surrender.*

Instead, she attempted her foiled plan, planting both palms onto the ground and twisting her fingers through the grass. A crack met Elias' ears, and he looked down to find the earth he laid on was cut into a square. Panic made him let go of her ankle, knowing what was to happen next.

Less than a second after he rolled out of the cut-out, the portion of earth flew upwards. The intention to sail him into the air and out of the ring was only *just* avoided. The square of dirt lost momentum, gravity restarting as it came crashing down. Screams and cries echoed in the air, out of fear, thankfully, and not injury.

Elias rose, rubbing his hands together to create a fresh wave of flame. He needed to end it *now.* Delphia was injured and would not receive care until the match's conclusion, so he had pulled off such a move. The agony rippling on Delphia's face reminded him of Keera, his first-ever opponent for the Tournament. Elias had spent his lifetime harming others, but watching this unnecessarily prolonged torment made his gut twist.

I'm sorry, he murmured to Delphia, a look of surprise appearing on her face just as he struck.

The plume of fire hit her square in the chest, sending her rolling over in the dirt. With her burnt ankle, she had no chance of standing again, not when Elias sent out another attack, hitting in the same place. She wore a breastplate, and the smell of burnt leather filled the air. Again and again, he pushed Delphia further back and, eventually, out of the ring.

Silence descended in the crowd; the echoes of the surrounding matches the only suggestion of life. Elias' breath came out in harsh gasps, a thundering roar sounding through his ears as the flames in his veins subsided. Delphia's body was smoking and unmoving, the leather breastplate resembling black tar. A moment passed before she eased herself into a sitting position, her shoulders shaking as she forced air into her lungs. Even a half-witch was difficult to kill, but Elias still felt relief wash over his body as she met his eyes.

"Elias Hearth wins the match!" the referee called. Thunderous applause ricocheted through the audience, something he almost hadn't expected. He thought these mortal-blooded warriors would despise the spectacle of an all-out supernatural battle, not scream and holler at the display of utmost calamity. With his scarf in place, Elias allowed himself to smile, wondering if the Queen's effort to rectify her kingdom's quarrel with magic-blooded beings was paying off.

Two healers ran forward, hands splayed wide to clasp Delphia's injured ankle while the other peeled off her ruined armour. She ignored them, staring darkly into Elias' eyes as her fingers tightened in the grass. Even from the distance between them, he heard her demanding thoughts.

What are you?

Again, he didn't bother to reply, turning away to take in the applause of the coliseum. Despite the blood that slipped down his face, Elias felt his grin widen as he raised his fist in the air, allowing this semblance of victory before everything came crashing down again.

41

AVERY

Avery's matches had been easy. In her first, the fool had asked her, like the chivalrous mortal he was, what terms she wanted. She'd asked for weapons only to keep the participants and the audience unaware but had also suggested he'd let her win the match.

As far as Avery knew, there were no rules about using one's powers before the match began.

The mortal did a decent display of bladed attacks, but the compulsion stuck throughout until, eventually, he did just as she asked. He faltered in his steps, far too close to the ring's edge, and Avery pushed him out with the hilt of her dagger. She'd barely even broken a sweat.

She kept up the tradition for every match. When the referees caught on, she called the words her good luck charm they needn't think about. Avery rarely used her compulsion in such small nudges. Usually, everything had to be full-blown, stormy grey *power.* But with these men, her irises hardly changed shade. Avery saw it as a good thing to end the matches so simply. She needed her energy, her strength. Against Torr, her compulsion meant nothing anyway. She could expend it as much as she pleased. But with so much at stake, she knew not to tire herself out even after the Tournament's conclusion. None of her companions trusted the nobles, so she would have to be ready to engage with any mortals if necessary. So long as she could keep herself upright and not breathless, everything would go smoothly.

She spent most of her time on the winners' bench, scanning the spectator stands of the coliseum. Only, they weren't the cramped benches of the originals, but just rows and rows of theatre boxes. Each was decked out in different colours—a garish display finished off with matching banners. Thanks to the gaudy colours of Lyra's armband, Avery could single out Ambrose's cosy confines for the Tournament. Still, the man kept himself quite concealed within—not that she could do anything to him at this distance. The wind would snatch away her words. No amount of her power could change that. Whenever Ambrose reared his head, though, Avery always made sure to catch his eye.

His hair was a similar shade to his banner—ridiculously orange—and paired with a receding hairline. Spectacles sat on his nose, and he peered through the glass, twiddling a moustache. The man had been intimidating without a face, but seeing it now, she wondered if all the nobles were as feeble-looking. Unmasked, Victoria Greenford had been anything but frightening. When it came down to it, it was the potential of their wealth and power that conjured so much fear, not the mortals themselves. No wonder they adored attending masquerades.

After Elias' fiery display against the earth user, the quarter-finals officially began. Once fewer than forty fighters were left in the Tournament, each round had an ordained ten-minute break in between. Food and drink were passed out, and even those on the losers' benches got a pick of the spread. When offered, Avery only took a glass of water, the liquid ice-cold against her teeth. These long days away from her lake had waned her alertness. Nymphs weren't in desperate need of sleep, but with her constant dallying in the mortal lands, it was all Avery craved. The glass of water helped somewhat, as did the continual gales of winter wind.

Before the destruction of Kavumir, Avery had left the Forest more often than this, though for less violent deeds. While her sisters had still been at school, Avery spent four years travelling the entirety of Darcan. She had found the Forest of the Dryads boring in comparison to the open world of the kingdom. She might have been content within the Forest's confines if she had never been given access to the mortal lands. It had given her a taste of freedom.

She found mortals intriguing but weak. Still entrenched in their numerous wars, Avery found the violence strange. Nymphs were voracious creatures themselves, but it was never with true malice, not in the way the mortals dealt out violence. In one instance, she had helped a lost family find their way to the village she had just left. In thanks, they had given her a few coins. Avery understood currency, but she had never owned any money herself.

After that, she had gone about trying to acquire more. It had landed her in trouble with a gang of highwaymen who wanted to rob her blind. At the time, Avery had been no Siren, but that was the first day the power had manifested. She told them to back off, and for some reason, two of them did. It had terrified Avery as much as the unaffected mortals, but they had still pressed on and stolen much of her money.

Avery had privately asked Nemesia about this mind control ability, but the dryad hadn't been too sure herself. She had sent out questions to the rest of the Forest, hoping to glean an answer from the nature spirits older than her. Eventually, Nemesia had received it. Avery wasn't just a naiad; she was a Siren, and there was a significant chance that Bellama and Caliadne would be as well.

Neither Avery nor Nemesia had told the sisters, hoping to let the ability manifest naturally in them both. Avery would only use her new powers outside the Forest, mostly as protection from mortals who tried to hurt her again. It was weak then, unable to manipulate everyone her words touched and could not wholly save her. So, Avery had gone to a weaponsmith, acquiring her first-ever set of blades.

Those daggers and knives were now over two hundred and fifty years old, and their age showed. Avery had changed her weapons many times over the centuries as the craftsmanship of mortals never lasted long enough for her. Only her current pair had withstood time and still shone like the first day she had held them six decades ago.

Cheering and whooping filled the coliseum, breaking Avery out of the past. The new round was about to begin, but first, the prize money was brought out of hiding and put on a pedestal. Despite Avery wishing to win that bag, she still considered it an utterly pointless display. No one still in the running had forgotten what they were fighting for, and placing the bag of coins in such an obvious view, Avery wondered if it was superficial, with nothing of worth inside.

The names started to be called, and Avery listened intently. Out of the Death Marked, only Elias was named. She watched the phoenix-blood stride into an empty ring, curious how the match would play out. He was no longer required to win. Ambrose's terms had been met. The nobles would get their money and glory, and Torr would be captured. Still, Avery hated the idea of willingly losing. Especially for someone as powerful as Elias, it felt almost a waste.

His opponent, named Senan Sayle, was a burly man of the same height as the phoenix-blood. Appearing to be in his late thirties, the mortal was scarred and rumoured to be a dishonourably discharged soldier. Avery had heard the whispers during her time on the winners' bench, but in comparison to Elias, Senan was no threat.

"Match rules?" the referee asked.

Elias only shrugged. A complacent gesture Avery found unusual. Senan, on the other hand, eyed Elias' sword. "No weapons. No powers. Fists."

The phoenix-blood sighed before unbuckling his sheathed sword and laying it outside the ring. Avery knew his body was laced with knives and daggers, mainly given to him by Nox and Lyra, but he made no effort to remove them. Not that he would use them to cheat... would he?

"On my count. Start!"

Senan lashed out with a kick, but Elias grabbed the man's foot with a crushing grip. With a shove, Elias sent him staggering back.

Avery awaited his next play, but then, the phoenix-blood turned around. Senan rushed forward just as Elias stepped out of the ring.

His opponent went toppling out of the ring with him, but Elias sidestepped Senan's fall. Instead, Elias bent down, picked up his sword, buckled it to his waist, and gave the referee a nod.

I end this match with a surrender, he announced to the arena. He slid the armband off, denoting Greenford as his sponsor, and set the fabric ablaze. *I fail as your champion.*

Even with his scarf up to his nose, Avery recognised the glare Elias had aimed at Victoria Greenford. When his head cocked to the side, she knew he was giving Ambrose the same look. Two mortal nobles who thought they could manipulate an immortal of his strength; it was amusing to watch his dramatics, and Avery huffed a laugh.

Elias could have defeated Senan, but he had walked into that ring knowing he would not bother. Ambrose's game had finished, and so he had cut the ties. Ash ran down from Elias' hands, swept up by the winter wind as he walked to the losers' bench.

First of the Death Marked to fall, but not the last. Because there could only be one winner, and Avery would break every rule to see it be her.

42

LYRA

Lyra's last fight was upon her, and after watching Elias' own surrender, she had an act to emulate—a quick and decisive end, one to spur confusion and scorn a noble. She was grinning as she descended the steps, already imagining Ambrose's scowling face—and possibly Castor's, too. Lyra never intended to be a victor, especially not with a leash around her throat.

However, when her opponent entered the ring, she couldn't stop her legs from shaking.

Even after nine years, she didn't need to hear his name called to recognise his face. His nose was still misshapen, and his ears thickened from repeated blows. He gave a crooked grin, revealing missing teeth. His hair was still close-cropped, and his alert eyes still swallowed her whole. Eamon Quine, the Unbroken Ox of Agonia, swaggered up and gave her a mocking bow.

"Lovely Lyra," he said in greeting. "How sweet of you to fight with me once more."

Another complementary title gilded in spite. Before Lyra had become Champion, it had been her nickname in the Agonia Pits—Lovely Lyra, for she was only good at looking pretty. It had helped fuel the rumours surrounding her parentage, as many thought she looked awfully like the Winterbrides. The rumours were true in a sense—her mother's maiden name was Winterbride—but no one ever recognised her as the dead Celeste Whitehallow.

Even when blood and bruises swelled her face, the name would be crowed at her, Lovely Lyra, until the end. It was somehow more insulting than the hidden title of 'the coward,' and Eamon knew it.

He had been a fan favourite during the Pits' prime. When Astrid had been its only Champion, Eamon had been believed to be her successor. He was older and stronger, but his arrogance and slow mind had never let him steal her title. Even so, Astrid had admitted to Lyra long after that Eamon was among the few pit fighters she had feared. If they had stayed any longer, he most likely would have taken the crown.

That was until Lyra had claimed it first.

Eamon had been one of the other fighters who enjoyed brutalising her during the punishment. Astrid would be her final fight, and Eamon would take first or second. However, on the fateful day when Lyra had won, Eamon had been absent. She had escaped the Pits before he could stop her, but she had never beaten him in a fight.

It seemed he recalled the memories, too. "Had I fought you that day, you would never have taken the title of Champion," he said. "In hindsight, we all saw it; Astrid was training you; she purposely lost to you." Eamon shook his head. "Undefeated? More like undeserved."

Lyra stood her ground, but inside, her heart was pumping madly. This wasn't even supposed to be a fight but a quick surrender to focus on the actual problem. And yet, she *couldn't*. Eamon would hurl his insults if she walked away, blind to his arrogance again. She had to fight. No. She had to win.

In one smooth motion, she unsheathed her sword, throwing its scabbard to the ground. "My terms are simple,"

Lyra said, voice husky. "Weapons allowed."

Eamon gave her an easy smile. "I was expecting that," he admitted. "No longer in Agonia, you can hide behind pretty blades and hardy shields."

Shoving both hands in his pockets, Eamon retrieved a pair of knuckledusters. They were made of steel and studded in spikes for each finger, reaching out like claws. Dried blood flecked their tips, previous victories patterned across their scratched surface. Lyra swallowed uneasily. She would have the upper hand in reach, but Eamon was well-trained in swooping in close.

"Match rules," the referee declared. "Weapons allowed and powers not. On my mark… start!"

Eamon moved like a harsh breeze; one moment, he stood on the opposite side of the ring, and the next, he was throwing a punch. Lyra barely dodged in time, the claws of his knuckledusters slicing through loose strands of hair as they grazed her cheek. She hissed a breath, the scratch leaking blood immediately. Lyra hadn't even raised her sword before Eamon struck again, and she ducked low to avoid his next attack. Low to the ground, she swiped her blade at his ankles, but he merely hopped over the slashing sword.

"Slow," he chastised.

Lyra's grip on the blade tightened. He was playing with her. In their bouts at the Pits, she would have already endured half a dozen fists. With his claws, though, one punch to the gut would easily send her to the healers. He wanted to drag this out, and for once, Lyra was willing to play into his whims.

He struck again, but Lyra was already waiting. She deflected the claws with the flat of her sword and, with the momentum of her back heel, pushed him back. His approach had been to dive in light and easy, and it was only because of that that she could repel him. Eamon flew back quickly, toes dancing on the grass. It wasn't much of a victorious play, but it was a start.

Lyra attacked next, diving into his easy step in a whirl of steel. Eamon's armour was almost nonexistent in comparison to her arrangement of mail and iron. She had exchanged her leather armour from the first Tournament for the tough metal in expectation of a confrontation with Torr and the nobles. It would hinder her speed, but she had a werewolf who could outrun anything if they needed it. The barking of a curse was all Lyra needed to know that she had struck her target, so she dropped back to assess the damage.

A long streak of blood was slashed across his chest. Shallow, thanks to Lyra's precision, but a red reminder of her strength. If she had pushed harder, it could have been a lethal blow, but that could have also left her exposed. She needed to be quick and light, wearing him down while keeping herself afloat. Hesitate too long, and he would capture her with those claws.

It dragged her into the past, watching him dance from toe to toe. His fighting style had not changed. Only its lethality had. Lyra couldn't tally how many times they had fought; the six-months of fights were an endless blur. The Unbreakable Ox rarely lost a battle; as his title claimed, he had never broken a bone. Lyra recalled her own broken knuckles when trying to strike him down, the popping of her joints when he dislocated a limb. The rushing of blood in her ears was drowned out by that snapping sound over and over again.

It disoriented her and deafened her to the battle at play. When Eamon lunged, his knuckledusters were outstretched to rake the claws down her face. Lyra tipped back, more on instinct than awareness, missing the blades' deep bite but still taking their edge. The blades cut down from her forehead to her lip, and blood distorted her vision immediately as it poured down. Scratches lay across her eyelids, featherlight and unbloodied. It was a lucky blow, even as her world turned red.

She spat a wad of blood out of her mouth, wiping her face with the back of her sleeve. Eamon had backstepped, limbs loose as he marvelled at his handiwork. Another display of his arrogance: he could have ended the fight with a kick out of the ring, but that wasn't the victory he wanted. Eamon wanted her close to death, or close enough that she would scream out a surrender. It was what he was used to nine years ago, but she would not give it to him today.

The past tried to bury her, Lyra's mind drawn too close to those awful memories. But she could never forget them because it was a lesson. Astrid had been her teacher, and in a way, so had Eamon. Lyra's resilience kept her aloft, and her experiences in defeat honed her to seek victory.

And yet. That wasn't what she was here for. Lyra watched Eamon, blinking blood from her eyes before latching her gaze to her armband. Eamon wasn't her target; the Pits weren't her master, and the Undefeated Champion wasn't an abhorred title. Ambrose, Greenford, Torr. Those were her focus. This wasn't a victory at all. It was a means to an end.

"No one wins," she rasped, blood slick against her teeth. "We both fall."

Eamon didn't hear Lyra but saw her throw her sword to the ground. His easy smile faded, confusion as much as unease replacing his swaggering. One dash through the void could end this faster than a blink, but Lyra still could not reveal that power. Nor did she want to depend on it.

She was as mortal as Eamon and the nobles; she had to prove her humanness was not a hindrance.

Crouching low, Lyra spurred into a sprint. Eamon raised his arms, expecting to block a blow. Instead, it gave her easy access to his waist. Her hands wrapped around his torso, her momentum shoving them both back. Eamon was standing too close to the edge of the ring, and they both fell. He grunted, back hitting the ground and decisively outside the chalk circle. She landed ungracefully on top of him, also removed from the space, holding a knife beneath his throat.

"You lose," Lyra declared. "And I surrender."

She rose from the fallen state, sheathing the blade. The referee announced Eamon's defeat but couldn't make himself finish his sentence. The guardsman had been close enough to Lyra, yet he still refused to believe it.

Lyra grabbed the referee by the collar. "I said I surrender. No one wins. This match is defunct."

She let go of him and tore off the armband on her sleeve. Elias was waiting for her on the losers' bench, and she kept her head high as she stormed towards him. Yet, a voice followed after her.

"COWARD! UNDESERVED IN VICTORY! UNDEFEATED IN RUNNING. COWARD!" Eamon shouted, a chant to the masses.

Lyra froze as he continued to pummel her with his words. Her fists were clenched at her sides, and still, blood trickled down her face. He was a sore loser, of course, but he was also angry at her for accepting defeat. Lyra could hear it in his voice, and when she turned around to watch him, she saw it in his face.

Eamon's cheeks were ruddy red in shame, and spittle covered his lip as he yelled. Mud and dirt stained his clothes, the one line of blood shiny in the winter light. His hands were still encased in those claws, with fists clenched to begin a fresh fight with her.

"The Tournament is beneath me," Lyra said, silencing his shouts. "And so are its victories."

"Then, why fight?" Eamon bellowed. "Why win? Why *surrender*?"

"I fight for another cause," she said. "And I won because you deserved to lose. My surrender… I don't need this win as desperately as you do. Back then, I needed the win, and I eventually took it. You couldn't do the same today. I wish you luck in your future, so long as you don't spit on mine."

This time, Eamon had no retort, and she took it as her excuse to walk away. She left her armband trodden in the mud as she stalked towards Elias. A healer followed after her, a bowl of water and washcloth in hand. As Lyra sat beside Elias, the cooling touch of the healer's magic swept away the claw marks on her face.

The healer left the bowl for Lyra and nodded. "Congratulations on your victory," he said before walking away.

Lyra couldn't help but smile—an unexpected commendation but a welcome one. She took the washcloth and swiped at the dried blood left on her skin.

Was that meant to be a victory? Elias murmured, taking the cloth from Lyra to help.

She frowned at his mothering but didn't stop him. "It was to me," she replied. "No noble, pit fighter, or assassin can dictate my life."

43

ELIAS

The terms had been met: all of the Death Marked had reached the quarter-finals, and now only two remained in the running. Lyra sat beside Elias, knee bouncing up and down as she glared at the theatre boxes. Even without his telepathy, Elias knew they were both of the same mind.

Was Ambrose going to hold up his end of the deal?

No one in the Ambrose theatre box or his many guards and servants seemed focused on capturing an assassin. Even though Ambrose had said it would be conducted *after* Avery's victory, surely some preparation would be needed. All four of them had been watching Ambrose's retinue, and nothing of the sort had occurred.

Elias rose from the bench. *Come. Let's take a walk.*

Despite Lyra's frown, she followed dutifully after him. There wasn't much room to promenade in the enclosed space of the coliseum, but Elias led them just fine. The walk wasn't to stretch their legs or to sightsee. Rather, Elias hoped to get close enough to reach the congregated minds in the theatre boxes.

Lyra caught on as they stood beneath Ambrose's seating. "Any luck?" she murmured.

Elias shook his head. *Too high up. I can't hear anything properly.*

Distance was a tricky weakness to his telepathy. When searching for the Forest, he had been able to stretch it wide to get a snatch of any minds. But Elias needed an unobstructed connection to listen into Ambrose's mind. Without it, all he could hear was the stray, senseless murmur, like someone's shout being snatched up by the wind.

"What's the plan instead, then?" she asked. "Because we have to do something. While Avery and Nox fight, we have to ensure we win."

Elias nodded, glad to have her by his side. Her history with the nobles had and would continue to define their survival as a quartet. And now, her powers would assure it, too.

Let's get out of here.

Sneaking out of the coliseum proved an easy challenge. Lyra struck up a conversation with one of the guards standing beside the doors while Elias slipped out. The doors had been slammed shut when everyone had first arrived, but with the considerable number of workers entering and leaving the coliseum, the doors had been left open. What Elias lacked in stealth, Lyra made up in charm. Her distraction allowed him to exit unnoticed, and soon enough, she followed.

They hurried away from the workers, keeping to the side where Ambrose's theatre box stood. Elias looked up at the exterior of the coliseum. The trap of beams that held the wooden structure looked perfect for handholds, much to his relief.

He pointed at a section of the wooden planks. *Void us up there.*

Lyra practically jumped out of her skin. "Are you kidding?" she hissed. "*This* is your plan?"

It seemed relatively simple to Elias. Using the void to launch them up the coliseum's exterior would get them close enough to Ambrose, just on the other side. So long as they were the same height, wooden planks wouldn't obstruct his telepathy. The mind that Elias had failed to meet last night would finally be his, and the truth would be theirs.

We're already here, he said plainly. *What else is there to risk?*

Lyra crossed her arms, looking away from him. "It's not the nobles or the guards I'm worried about, though. It's... *him*."

Torr. The man who could break the void. Elias lowered his head, ashamed to have forgotten that fear. Still, this path had already begun, and they couldn't afford to backtrack now.

We just need to stay out of sight, Elias said. *Torr will have no reason to suspect us, and as I can't communicate with him, we'll go unheard, too.*

Lyra chewed on the inside of her cheek, still unable to look Elias in the eye. He understood, of course; despite his assurances, so much could still go wrong, but that had to be the cost. Whatever the cause, they all needed to risk everything they had to survive this day.

She huffed a breath. "Okay, let's get this over and done with."

She didn't wait for his response and instead grabbed his arm, pulling them through the void.

The short distance meant they had no time to fall through the starry place Elias was still unused to. Instead, it was more like a jump across a flowing stream, leaping over violet traceries and landing on solid ground.

Or, in their case, creaking beams.

Elias' hands grasped the wood, nails biting into the planks. Lyra was beside him, her free hand also holding on. The narrow beams at their feet made manoeuvring difficult, and with the icy wind whistling through his hair, Elias forced himself not to look down.

Lyra met Elias' stare. *Are we close enough now?* she asked mentally.

Elias focused on his telepathy, and the sounds of internal monologues and memories washed over him in total clarity. He recognised none of the minds, only that they were other preening nobles, but he gave Lyra a nod.

Then, he started to sidestep to the left, Lyra following after. Shuffling across made the structure creak and groan, the beams not appreciating their sudden weight.

He halted after a particularly loud groan from the wooden frame. *If this whole thing falls apart, you'll be able to save us, right?*

She squeezed his arm. *Why do you think I'm holding on?*

He grinned. *Was just checking.*

Elias had misjudged where to void up to, so they continued shuffling across the beams, gravity threatening to take its course. The minds he could hear weren't affiliated with Ambrose, yet Elias wished he could pause and investigate them all. So many secrets lay in the heads of these mortals, and they were all within his grasp. He'd always been teased for being nosy—unashamedly so—but this was different. It was a hunger for secrets that weren't his. Kalla had called it a good trait, a necessary one for a Thoughtsinger. A witch's strength could not rise unless she *desired* it.

But Elias was only half-witch, after all. He could not read

everyone's thoughts as seamlessly as Kalla could.

He shook the witch from his head and dove into a new mind—a Branigan's. Another shuffle onwards, and he found it: an Ambrose guard regretting his overindulgence in whiskey last night. Elias ignored that and flitted to the next; there were over ten people within the theatre box, and most were Ambrose's servants. In the middle sat Benedict Ambrose, and Elias felt no shame as he tore into his head.

Benedict Ambrose was forty-nine and married to Eleanore Ambrose, a noblewoman from Hyranda. He had two daughters and two sons, one of whom was a bastard who had since been dispatched. His youngest daughter, Gwendoline, was married to Harrigott's youngest to keep the girls out of trouble, and his eldest, Edana, was beloved in the courts. However, his trueborn son, his *heir*, struggled to ensure his legacy.

A legacy that Benedict planned to bestow a crown on.

In his years of nobility, he had only ever seen the past two rulers of the kingdom as decisively weak. Zachariah II had died due to the stress of the crown, and Aurora was planning on forsaking the royal bloodline for her own selfishness. Benedict had more royal blood and far more experience than either of the Queen's so-called 'children.' They did not deserve to rule; he did.

Aurora needed a new successor, and with Benedict's many ideas and goals for the betterment of Darcan, it could only be him. He would not usurp Aurora yet because he first needed to test his method.

The Royal Tournament was his invention, made for him to bring the Haunted Shadow into the Queen's halls. The assassin would be victorious in the competition, dispatching the false heirs, and when Benedict was ready, he would take out Aurora, too. It had failed; for that, Benedict could only blame his foolish niece-in-law. He hadn't been able to pull the strings at risk of discovery and had given it to Victoria, not realising she would mess it all up.

It was the saving grace of Eastbow—how ridiculous a thought—that had allowed the Haunted Shadow to claim a Siren for the Tournament. Benedict hadn't believed the myths and was sceptical that any of this would work, but that was the Tournament's purpose, after all. If the Siren could win a competition through manipulation, she could give Benedict the throne.

Even with the Kherian attack on the Palace—something even he had known nothing about—everything had still been going smoothly—until last night's upset at the ball. He thanked his intuition for fleeing the manor when he had and cursed Victoria for getting so quickly caught by the two women. Still, he had been safe and granted a second chance of victory.

Avery Nash would win the Tournament, and the Death Marked would die.

Elias almost fell off the coliseum as he flew out of Benedict's mind. Lyra had to steady him, forcing her strength into keeping him aloft. His heart raced at an unignorable pace, not because of his barely avoided fall but the truth. It invaded his mind like a parasite, and he wished it were false.

Benedict didn't need the Death Marked, not after the Tournament. He didn't even need Avery, the Siren who should have secured his ascension. No, she was now the Haunted Shadow's target, and Benedict wasn't afraid to lose her. Benedict had assumed the nymphs were a docile lot, easy to control, but this naiad had proved otherwise. So he would cut her free and claim another. After all, the Haunted Shadow had said there were *three* Sirens.

The Haunted Shadow was far greater an asset than the Death Marked. Benedict could not scorn the assassin, and to get what he needed, he wouldn't have to. The trap was a lie. Victoria had no involvement in this plan, but the Haunted Shadow did. His prey would be expecting his capture, only to find their own. Stuck out in the middle of nowhere, the Death Marked could not flee. The Tournament had been a half-success, but it was only the first step in his ascension. King Benedict Ambrose would still find his throne.

Elias retreated, sucking in a deep breath. *We need to leave. All four of us. Now.*

"Wh—" Lyra spluttered before responding mentally. *What are you talking about? We can't just leave.*

He tightened his grip on her arm, fingers threatening to bruise her. *Please, trust me,* he pleaded. *We have to leave, or we're all going to die.*

Lyra's eyes widened, and she nodded, but before darkness could fill his vision, a voice interrupted. "Huh, so the assassin *was* right."

Elias shifted, careful to stay upright on the beams, but he still turned to where the voice had spoken. On the grass, surrounded by a pair of guards, was a man. He had olive skin and black hair, crude light creasing his eyes. He didn't look very important, but he started to get concerned from the tightening of Lyra's grip on Elias' arm.

Who is he? he asked.

"Leonidas." Her voice came out in a breath as she stared at the man. "Ambrose's son."

We need to go. We can just leave them behind.

Lyra shook her head. "I can't afford to let them see the void; no one can know."

Then how do you suppose we—

Elias couldn't finish his sentence. Not when an arrow embedded itself just inches above his head.

Leonidas was wielding a crossbow, but when he acquired the weapon, Elias missed it. The heir handed the crossbow to a guard, who started to reload it. "That," Leonidas began, "was a warning shot. Get down here if you don't want to see the real deal."

Lyra paled, but Elias knew what to do. Immediately, his palm warmed with flames as he pulled the arrow shaft out of the wooden planks. It caught on fire, and he threw the arrow in Leonidas' direction. As it flew, smoke belched outwards. A grey haze rose over them all: the perfect smokescreen.

Elias grabbed Lyra by the shoulders. *Void, now.*

Purple stars bloomed.

One second, he was on the planks, the next on the grass. Lyra let go of his arm, and he heard the singing of her longsword releasing from its sheath. "Get inside," she barked. "Grab Avery and Nox. I'll deal with the noble."

Elias wanted to argue, but time was of the essence. A rousing shout came from the coliseum, and he rushed towards the closed gates. Elias heaved them open, hinges creaking as he tripped inside. He was too late. The final match had started.

Avery and Nox were trying to kill one another.

44

NOX

Avery stood with only a blade raised, a cruel smile on her face. At this distance, Nox couldn't see her irises, but from the slacked jaw of her opponent, they knew storms were rife within her eye.

"Accept your defeat," the naiad called. "Walk out of this ring."

Her subtlety of this charade was over. Submission and compulsion were hers, and so was this match. Avery's opponent stepped out of the ring, and the crowd went wild.

Nox's whole body trembled in anticipation. The semi-finals were complete. Only two fighters remained—them and her. The werewolf and the naiad. The victor and the vanquished.

Nox couldn't stop grinning.

"Avery Nash and Nox Parker!" the leading referee of the coliseum cried. "Please enter the ring for the final battle!"

Neither had been given any time to relax before this last match—the audience wouldn't allow it. Contagious energy filled the coliseum, the losers and nobles hungry for the conclusion—the champion.

Nox rose, rolling their neck to allow the joints to crack. Old blood still rimmed their nails, claws not yet set free. The referee stood in the middle of the amphitheatre, but at Nox's approach, they found the fighting ring had been extended. Instead of the usual circular ones, this mimicked the shape of a coliseum. With so much more moving space, Nox would struggle more with pushing Avery out of the boundary with air. The werewolf didn't let that faze them, though. Whatever the cause, this victory would be theirs.

Avery stood on one side of the new ring, her mouth forming a glower. Nox stepped into the ring, taking their place opposite to the naiad.

"Rules?" the referee asked.

Nox cocked their head. "Let's go all out; it is the finale, after all." They grinned, raising their arms. "Powers and weapons galore."

A moment of silence descended in the coliseum. All eyes were on Avery, but the naiad hardly seemed to notice. Instead, her gaze swept across the spectator stands, both the nobles and the original participants, before turning back to Nox.

"I accept."

The crowd went wild, and Nox frowned. Did they prefer Avery over Nox? Why did everyone think she was so much *better?* Nox didn't hate the naiad, but times like this made them want to strangle her just for the sake of it.

"Weapons *and* powers are allowed in this match!" the referee bleated. "Let the victor of the Royal Tournament be decided!" He stepped out of the ring. "Begin!"

Avery might have been an immortal Siren, but she was also short and old, which meant Nox was infinitely faster.

Something Elias had accidentally taught them about the naiad was her eyes. Her irises would betray the fact when she was about to control anyone. Avery's eyes were swarming grey; they had been since she'd entered the ring. It was why Nox had to speak first and lay out the rules. Giving her anything more than affirmation could doom

Nox before the match even began.

And now? Well, the werewolf just needed to make sure she stayed quiet.

Avery opened her mouth, and Nox shut her up. A flick of air locked into place around her head, emptying the space of oxygen. The naiad lurched, falling to her knees and back into breathing space. Nox scowled but didn't set up another box of emptiness. Avery was too busy coughing to speak, and besides, they still weren't allowed to kill opponents.

The naiad sat up, and Nox pounced. Steel clashed against claws as Avery parried against their attack. Her daggers arced over her head, Nox's claws sliding off the blades. She shifted, slashing one dagger towards them. Nox dodged, but the tip of the blade nicked their cheek. They rolled, coming up to their feet just as Avery did, too. Blood hardly welled from the scratch, but Nox was aware of every trickle it sent down their face.

Avery was breathing hard, but when her mouth curved again to speak, Nox cut it off. Her eyes blazed, and yet she didn't try to inhale.

Instead, she did something a lot worse.

The naiad sheathed a blade, and with her spare hand, she brought frost and snow. It flew up from the grass, melting to dew as it collected in her palm. The pool wasn't much, and Avery's face began to redden. Nox dropped the air block, and she fell back to her knees, winded from the fresh gasp. Her manipulated water dissipated, settling back into the grass.

Nox wasn't sure why she was trying to conjure up a sphere of water, but it definitely concerned them. If she were going to use it to attack, she would have thrown what little amount she had formed as soon as possible. Nox discarded the information and pounced again, and this time, Avery was too slow to counter. Nox's claws sank deep into her forearm, tearing cloth and flesh clean off. The crowd gasped, and the naiad also let out a strangled cry. A twinge went through Nox's gut. Guilt? At a time like this?

Avery met their eyes, and they were startled to find them clear blue. Her injury must have snapped her out of her ability to control. "You're a bastard," she breathed. "Now…"

Nox refused to let her finish.

They kicked her in the stomach, and she fell to the grass. Nox hadn't even processed if Avery *was* about to use her powers. They just didn't want to risk it. Any sense of control spoken from her mouth would mean the end of the match. They'd come so far, beaten so many people. If they were about to run straight into a death mark, Nox sure as hells wanted to prove themself as a victor first.

Rage coloured the naiad's face as she cradled her arm. Nox canted their head. Avery was still on the ground and seemed to have no inclination to move. Could they just pick her up and drop her out of the ring? It almost seemed too easy.

They flicked a breeze into her face, and as she swatted it away, Nox made their move. Unfortunately, Avery didn't stay put. A knife appeared from her fingers, one they recognised to be *theirs*. Nox had traded different blades with Lyra, and it seemed she had given hers away.

"Traitor," the werewolf hissed as the knife embedded into their leg.

Nox closed the air around Avery, suffocating her for the last time. The naiad barely noticed, though, her face unchanged from its rage. Goosebumps traced up Nox's arms, the only warmth they could feel being the blood slipping down their thigh. Avery's hand moved, and so did the water around her knees. Only then did Nox realise she was closer to the ground on purpose.

Her manipulated pool of water came close, not to the werewolf, but to Avery. It slipped over her head, forming an orb. She inhaled gravely, and all the blood drained from Nox's face. Naiads could breathe underwater and talk, too. And Nox could do nothing to stop it. They dashed forward to grab her by the neck. Avery began to speak, but her words were drowned out by the swinging of hinges and a mindspoken voice.

AVERY! NOX! AMBROSE IS GOING TO LET TORR KILL US. WE HAVE TO LEAVE.

Nox halted to a stop, almost teetering over from the sudden loss of momentum. Elias stood at the open gates of the coliseum, gasping for breath. Avery was frozen, too; her orb of water sluiced back to the grass as the airless box dissipated.

She and Nox shared a glance. A simple request from the phoenix-blood—an easy one to complete, too. But was that really it? Flee? Elias and Lyra had taken it into their own hands to discover the liar, and now Nox and Avery had one final moment to make their own choice. Torr might be invulnerable and will not die today, but the same could not be said for his allies.

Avery staggered to her feet, and the two of them stared up at the theatre boxes, at Ambrose himself. His face flushed underneath their glares, the entire coliseum looking up to him, too. Avery and Nox were meant to be fighting, but silence filled the space as the pair stood stock still.

The naiad huffed a breath. "Give me a breeze, why don't you?"

Nox had only a moment to react before Avery threw her dagger into the spectator stands.

45

A V E R Y

Her dagger found its home—Ambrose's skull.

The throw would have been impossible without Nox's air manipulation, and the cold wind continued to whistle through Avery's ears even after she released the blade. She watched Ambrose's forehead cave in, and the duke staggered to the ground. As soon as he disappeared from sight, Avery grabbed Nox's arm.

"Let's go."

Nox nodded. "But first," they started before disappearing from her side.

Avery whipped around to see the werewolf running towards the prize money display. A whoosh of cold air tipped the bag from its stand and into Nox's waiting arms. As they ran back to Avery, they grabbed her uninjured arm and dragged her across the grass.

She stumbled after them, a ridiculous smile lifting the werewolf's cheeks despite the sound of the coliseum screaming. She cringed at the noise, panic reaching her as the guards started to move. Accusatory fingers pointed down at them, the remaining nobles shouting and spitting unintelligible words. None of it mattered; Ambrose had betrayed them. Torr would still come after them, but at least her sponsor was dead.

Nox led her towards the coliseum's exit, even when dozens of soldiers clustered around it. Elias was lost in that crowd, and Avery's heart jolted at the thought. Had he been caught? As she and Nox came close, the werewolf sent out a wave of cold air, knocking most men off their feet. The effort was fruitless as more soldiers blocked the way.

Just then, the losers' benches began to creak.

Hundreds of warriors, all the ones Avery and Nox had defeated, were coming straight towards them. Avery tugged on Nox's arm, the werewolf not yet noticing the coming storm. They turned, eyes widening as they swore.

"We need Lyra," Nox said.

"No." Avery's eyes turned grey. "We don't." She looked at Nox. "Project my voice. I need everyone to hear."

The compulsion took effect in the werewolf, and the wind started to whistle through her ears. She shivered at the breeze, afraid it would steal her words rather than increase their sound. Avery exhaled a breath and met the eyes of her would-be killers to give one simple command.

"STOP."

The word forced itself over the entire coliseum, the shout becoming a warcry against the world. Blood filled Avery's throat, an immediate pounding greeting her head at the strength of her own powers. She spat out a glob of red, but the pain refused to cease. Everyone around her had frozen. Avery was the only one still in motion. She turned to Nox, but even the werewolf was stuck; their breeze, dead and gone. With the crowd at the gates paralysed, she spied Elias amongst them, another statue of her making.

"And here I thought you couldn't make another grave mistake."

Avery's blood turned to ice. Everyone in the coliseum was frozen, but one other—Torr.

He was in the spectator stands, now half-empty from where the warriors had made their descent. Slowly, Torr made his way down. His sword was in hand, catching the winter light.

Avery wiped the blood off her face and forced herself to meet his eye. The assassin moved with ease between the frozen warriors, his gaze never leaving hers. She wanted to scream, but any word from her mouth would shatter the compulsion. Having used it on so many people, she couldn't layer demands like she could with a sole victim.

Even so, Avery shifted into a fighting stance. The world may be frozen, but they still had their eyes. Everyone would bear witness to the assassin who could not be killed and realise he was the true threat to them all.

Torr was still at a distance but no longer lost within the crowd of frozen men. Taking the opportunity, Avery threw a knife at the assassin and aimed again for the head. Torr didn't even try to dodge, letting the blade's edge knock into his forehead. A long sigh emptied his lungs as the knife fell, and he grabbed it by the hilt. It should have gone cleanly through his flesh and been wedged into brain matter. Instead, he tossed it into the air and gave Avery a hard stare.

"Want to waste any more blades? I see you've already lost one." Torr's head tilted up to the theatre boxes behind her. "I'm not surprised your telepath figured out the truth, but I didn't think you'd do something as stupid as *that...*"

Avery clenched her jaw, resisting the urge to snipe back. He sighed again, realising her efforts of silence.

"I'm going to kill you, Averaline, along with your friends. What were their names?" Torr looked at the werewolf at her side. "Nox Parker, that's that one, and the phoenix-blood,

Elias Hearth. Poor hiding place, telepath. You should have stayed with Lyra Avenyard in the void while you could."

Avery wasn't sure whether to be relieved or not that Torr couldn't single out Lyra. If she was in the void, then she was out of her mind control's range and unfrozen somewhere else. The mortal was their only chance of escape. Torr hadn't attacked yet, but even with Ambrose dead, she knew he would not let them flee without a fight.

"Release the mortals, naiad," Torr said. "I've never thought you could hold your tongue for so long." She set her mouth into a thin line, but it didn't stop him from pressing on. "Come *on*, Nash. If you don't speak, I'll cut out the tongues of everyone here, starting with the werewolf."

A noise came from Nox, and Avery looked at them. Their eyes were wide—the only way they could react was with that slight sound of panic. She whipped her glance back to Torr but held her breath.

He glared at her for a long moment. "Fine, I'll play my hand first." His words came out like a rattle, a dark grin lifting his cheeks.

"Three out of four is better than nothing. Now I can pay my dues." Then he paused, considering the frozen men and women.

"Though I don't think I want there to be an audience." He shrugged. "I guess I can deal with them, too."

And then Torr began to change.

He rolled his shoulders, joints popping audibly enough that it sounded like branches snapping as he grew larger than any man. His skin turned stone-grey, decaying into rotted flesh in an instant. Shadows streaked across his limbs, and his veins pulsed like black diamonds. He flexed his fingers, and claws that shone like jewels appeared, long and curving even farther than Avery's blades.

Two horns, made of the same onyx as his claws, shot through his forehead. Torr's eyes were black, with no irises or whites left to be seen. Cracks echoed across his skin, the change burning away the edges of his clothes. His left arm seemed distorted, a scar of bright green racing up the flesh and disappearing behind his shoulder.

Avery fell to her knees, her heart pounding to a frantic beat. She couldn't believe her eyes. He was a monster, now shedding his human flesh. It was the deepest horrors of nightmares, an unkillable creature. He turned to the gathering of petrified warriors and joined the crowd.

Those closest to him started to burn.

"No!" Avery cried, and the compulsion shut off.

Everyone started to move, the eerie silence of the coliseum replaced with the screams of fresh death. But even that soon began to fade as darkness reached Avery's eyes. Blood rushed through her head like a hurricane of agony, her heart racing until she swore it would stop.

She had no chance for fear when the rest of her body collapsed to the ground, and everything winked out.

46

NOX

Fear froze Nox to the ground, but so did one other thing: realisation. Torr wasn't just a monster; he was a trueborn creature of corruption, bloodshed, and deceit.

He was a demon.

The textbook Nox had read just two days ago in the Archives Hall came rushing back. *The Corrupted One met with the damned souls and started to cultivate physical bodies for these tortured beings. Akin to godly forms, these new bodies for the dead were to be invincible, allowing them to wreak as much havoc as they pleased.*

Drawings from children's books depicted what the demons supposedly looked like, and Nox had always thought it must have been an exaggeration. No creature could look like evil, so obviously *monstrous*, with onyx horns, teeth, claws, and decaying flesh.

Until Nox was looking at one, possibly the *last* ever one. Torr, the Haunted Shadow. Immortal assassin, invulnerable demon. There was no denying it; this was the final revelation and the ultimate delivery of death.

Flames cloaked in inky darkness danced upon Torr's blade, cindering the grass to ash as the participants of the Tournament started to flee. The fire flickered and stopped like a taper burnt to its end, but the demon continued his torment.

His sword cut through flesh like wheat in a field. Anyone who tried to fight back met his invulnerable resistance. Nox was frozen as if Avery's compulsion still affected them; all they could do was watch as blood soaked Torr's blade.

The demon moved like water, fluid as a dancer lost in the music of the violin. Centuries of bloodshed had refined him to its perfection. Mindless as he was, Torr held the precision of a prodigy of death.

A hand landed on Nox's shoulder, and they jumped out of their trance. They looked up and found Elias meeting their gaze. *Grab Avery and get out of here.*

They frowned, switching their gaze to where the naiad stood beside them. Only Avery *wasn't* standing; her unconscious body was sprawled out on the floor, loose strands of hair spilling across the grass like weeds.

"No," Nox forced out, turning back to Elias. "I'm not leaving you to fight *him* on your own." They didn't need to be telepaths to figure out what the phoenix-blood meant. If Elias had planned for all three of them to flee, he would have thrown Avery—and maybe even Nox, too—over his shoulder and legged it out of the coliseum. Instead, his sword was clenched between both hands, smoke already curling from the hilt.

I can't leave these people to die, he said. Elias' face was a storm of hatred aimed at Torr.

"*We* won't leave these people to die," Nox amended, pulling a knife free from their belt. "But… listen, if we *all* run, then Torr will follow us. Realistically that will minimise the casualties."

Elias looked down at Avery, his sword dipping ever so slightly. *It doesn't feel right to run away.*

A lump formed in Nox's throat. After everything they

had learnt of Elias, they understood how desperately he wanted to escape the burden of being branded a coward. Nox knew it well themself, despised it from the first moment it had greeted them. Even now, they wanted to fight, wanted to rage against this demon and all his burning hate. Avery had seized her revenge, but what of theirs? Torr had death-marked them all, and Nox wanted nothing more than to return the favour right now. But all of them would have to flee if they were to survive this.

"We have to." Their words were barely audible. "Together."

A mighty roar ripped through the stadium, and they both looked up, and Torr met their stares. He was still in the thick of battle, blades and arrows clashing against his skin.

"Will you play hero?" Torr yelled. His voice was grating, as if coals scorched the back of his throat. "Or run like cowards?"

The guardsmen were still in the spectator stands, bows creaking to imitate Nox's own attempt to kill the demon with arrows. Torr wasn't fazed, his sword dragging through the mud as he strode towards them.

"I can deal with the rabble later," he continued. "But you, I will kill you three now."

The demon pounced.

Elias met his blade. Their swords clashed in a sparking display. Neither could move, bearing down on one another as the grass shifted beneath their feet.

Get out of here! Elias shouted. *Lyra will open the warp gate!*

"I don't think so," Nox growled.

In the same motion, Nox threw the prize money bag to

the ground and a knife at Torr. It bounced off one of his curving horns, causing the demon's fighting stance to teeter. That subtle impact against his head shifted the weight of gravity into Elias' favour, and Torr went tumbling to the ground.

Fire blazed inside the coliseum, eating up the grass as Elias slashed and slashed with his sword. Nox's eyes stung, the thick smoke blurring the world into obscurity. The blackening ground came close, and they moved to pick up Avery's unconscious body. Lighter than expected, they shifted to putting her over their shoulder and grabbed the money bag, too.

"Elias!" Nox shouted, but the cry disappeared under the roar of flames.

Phoenix fire was everywhere, spilling across the arena like oil. If they weren't careful, the entire coliseum would go up in flames. Torr wouldn't become the killer of the Tournament, but Elias and his suffocating powers.

It was irrational for him to continue the blaze; they all knew it would do nothing against Torr, but if Nox were in that position, wouldn't they do the same thing? And wouldn't Elias be the one to pull them out of that crazed state?

Awkwardly, Nox dropped Avery again. Her head lolled, but they could see the steady rise and fall of her chest. The bag of money was deposited on her lap, coins clinking every time she breathed. Looking back up, Nox flexed both their hands.

It was just as they and Elias practised. They could make phoenix fire stronger but also take it away. Wind whistled through their open palms as they stole the oxygen from the air. It hit Nox like a wave, planting them in the grass. But it wasn't enough, and the fire continued to overpower the coliseum, smoke rising into the cold sky. If Nox was to drop the air now, they feared they wouldn't be able to grapple it again, so instead, they forced themself to move.

Every step was a struggle, their own manipulation pushing them back. But the oxygen needed for the flames started coming to them, heat licking their bare palms. They hissed against the pain, forcing each step until...

Nox clapped their hands together and sucked all the air out of the coliseum.

The entire population of the arena collapsed, save for Nox and Torr. It lasted only a few moments, long enough for Nox to be sure all evidence of smoke and flame was gone before they restored everyone's breath. A collective gasp rolled through the coliseum, and Nox found themself joining in. Aches ran up their arms, a slight wobble running through their legs that threatened to topple them over. But they stayed upright and met Torr's eye.

Despite the circle of blackened grass surrounding him, the demon was unharmed. His clothes had been burned away, revealing every inch of that cracked, rotted skin that shone in black finality. His sword was misshapen, no doubt the heat of Elias' fire having melted and warped it into an unusable state.

A tremor went through Nox's arms as they held them out, a mockery of the time Torr had the same thing just days ago. "Impressed?" they shouted, unsure if they were addressing the demon or everyone present. "Or scared?"

Nox...

They looked down at Elias. He was still on the ground, exertion flushing his entire face red. Beside him was his sword, slightly bent from the flames he'd pushed through its metal. Just how far had he gone to melt his *own* weapon?

Even his breastplate was warped, his gauntlets ashen and scarf smouldering.

"We're running," they said. "*No—*"

Nox had no time to finish their sentence before an arrow embedded into their back.

The impact toppled them into the grass, face-planting in a way they found highly uncharacteristic. If it weren't for the display of air manipulation, Nox would have stopped themself from falling, but their limbs still shook at every small effort, and the pain of an arrowhead ripping through their back muscles did not help. Stars bloomed in their vision; all breath stolen from their lungs as they forced themself into a crouch. Darkness sat in the corners of their eyes, threatening to take them down cleanly.

Distantly, they realised they were talking, an unintelligible chatter of words that strung together. "Snaptheshaftsnaptheshaftsnaptheshaft."

Instead, something metallic slipped onto their tongue. Nox bucked, trying to spit it out, until they realised Elias was pouring something into their mouth.

It's a healing potion! he shouted. *I didn't remove the arrowhead; I can't give you too much of the stuff, so there won't be enough magic to heal it fully.*

They swallowed, a burning taste of cinnamon and blood running down Nox's throat. "Did you at least snap the shaft?"

Of course, I did.

"So, who is trying to kill us *now?* And why have they stopped?"

The people of the Tournament tried to kill you *for suffocating them,* Elias answered. *And they've stopped because... well, because Avery is awake.*

Nox fought the urge to roll their eyes. "I still don't understand how you can fear that na—"

Water spattered onto their face, cutting their sentence short as they discovered it was raining. It took them another moment to realise the droplets weren't coming from the sky.

Avery stood in the middle of a rainstorm, both arms raised. Blood slipped down one sleeve, but she hardly seemed fazed as she clenched both fists. The rain fell like ice upon Torr, the hissing of demonic steam and cold water audible to the ear. Her hair was pasted to her cheeks, the wet tangles loosening the pitiful plait she had twisted her hair into. Even from just her side profile, Nox could see the rage and determination contorted on her face.

"What the fu—"

You two are still injured, Elias interrupted. *Take Avery and get out of here! Lyra has a healing tincture on her. She'll open the warp gate.*

"Lyra? How?"

The phoenix-blood didn't answer; instead, he rose to meet the naiad in the rainstorm. Nox staggered to their feet, anticipating resistance from their aching body. But aside from a burning sensation between their shoulder blade, they felt normal, as if they hadn't just suffocated an entire population of people nor taken an arrow to the back.

Elias cut the rainstorm short with the raise of his sword. Torr took the blow with an arm, the blade glancing off what should have been a clean amputation. Then Avery was dashing towards Nox, almost slipping in the new squelch of mud under her feet.

"Elias told me you needed help," she said breathlessly. "What is it?"

They frowned before realising it just as she did. "He lied."

Avery had no time to react before Nox grabbed her wrist and dragged her towards the coliseum gates. Her protests died as they deposited the prize money bag in her arms. Then, in one quick swing, Nox lifted her off her feet, sweeping her onto their shoulder. Immediately, they picked up in speed, and Avery bounced hard against their muscular back.

Nox focused on sprinting to the warp gate. If they derailed their thoughts from running, it would send them swinging back to the coliseum and Elias. The phoenix-blood's pitiful battle would only end in his death. Could he not see that? Nox thought that if the three of them could not fight Torr, they would at least escape together. But now, Elias sidelined them *both* for no reason, and Nox had leaned into it.

All they had wanted to do was win, get the money, and destroy Torr. They'd done almost all of that—the last task an impossibility for them all, especially now with the demon status revealed—and yet, all that they could think of was Elias fighting his last breaths for them all.

A pulse of purple light brought Nox back to the present. The warp gate was just before them, dormant as before, the empty hole revealing nothing but hollowed-out rock. Lyra stood alone with her back to them, looking up at the warp gate.

Nox halted, skidding in the mud before swinging Avery out of their grasp. She teetered, almost falling over. Once she had righted herself, Nox whisked the prize money from her hands and hugged it against their chest.

She scowled. "Thanks."

They gave her a razor-sharp smile. "No worries." Nox looked up from her face and started to frown. "Now, this doesn't really look like a working warp gate to me... Lyra?"

Lyra had a hand on the circle's edge, her fingers smoothing over the many intricate carvings. "Is that what Elias told you?" she asked, finally turning to face them both. Blood covered her top lip, the trickle blooming from her nostrils. "Where is he?"

Nox and Avery exchanged a glance, neither eager to answer. "He's just following," Nox said vaguely. "What's happening here?"

Lyra bent down and opened up a bag. Rustling through the contents, she held up a necklace. "Can either of you sense the magic in this?" she asked.

Nox shook their head, and so did Avery, causing Lyra's shoulders to slump. Even so, she put the necklace on and faced the warp gate again. "In a few minutes, one of you needs to replace this one with another." She gestured to the open bag. "Keep going until I finish."

Nox bent down and picked up a spare necklace from the bag. There were five in total. "How long does one last? What's it for?"

"It's Cometborn work," Avery answered. "Power enhancing charms. You plan to power the warp gate using the *void*?"

She cleared her throat. "I have no other choice but to try."

"Is that it?" Nox asked. "What do you mean, *try*?"

Lyra squared her shoulders. "Like this."

Giving none of them time to respond, she turned to place her outstretched fingers onto the curve of the warp gate. The air started to hum with power as her palms flattened against the stone.

Then, Lyra's veins started to darken. Nox rushed to her side and found her eyes were full of violet stars.

47

ELIAS

Elias recalled the first time he had clashed swords with Torr. A true swordsman, the demon had never relented against any of his blows, no matter the amount of strength or fire fed into the attacks. Now, it paled in comparison.

Torr's clenched fists were covered in fissures, rotting flesh erupting demonic ash and smoke. Elias had destroyed the demon's weapon, melting it into an unusable mess, but Torr had just claimed a new one from the dead, continuing his assault against Elias as if nothing had changed. Even so, his hilt's leather grip was wearing thin, the loosened shavings curling up and fluttering away on the cold breeze. Torr bore down on Elias, taking the upper hand despite their height and weight difference.

The ground beneath Torr's feet was cracked, and his boots shot through with claws like black diamonds. They grappled with the grass for purchase, and Elias struggled beneath the demon's strength.

He knew this was a losing battle from the start, but he couldn't walk away now. He had to save these people from Torr's torment, even if it meant the end of his own life... until he realised that no one inside the stadium wanted him alive.

That final realisation came almost too late as he threw a blaze of fire at the singular arrow that shot through that air.

The shaft and fletching burned up immediately, wood and feather cindering to ash at his fiery touch. With those elements missing, the arrowhead lost all momentum, thudding to the grass just feet before him.

It allowed only a pause from Torr as the demon was also greeted with raining arrows. The two locked eyes, both their swords lowering just as the true onslaught began. Elias took the opportunity to run, evading Torr, whose blade sang through the air once more. Whether to cut *him* down or the arrows, Elias was clueless. He sent a cover of flames over his head, hoping it would slow the arrowheads once more.

The coliseum ring neared until he stood on the opposite side of the losers' bench. Above his head, Elias could hear the jeers and screams of the nobility in their theatre boxes.

Sparing a glance, he saw the Noblesguard waving their arms and shouting. He couldn't tell if they were trying to help the Queensguard battling in the centre of the coliseum or figuring out a way to flee with their charges. Too far from Elias' telepathy range, he forced himself not to care.

But he couldn't stop looking up at the empty theatre box, the one where Ambrose's dead body lay. If Lyra were here, he would suggest they void up there, if only to retrieve Avery's dagger and check if the duke was actually dead.

An arrow sinking into the wood beside Elias' head brought him back into the present. Just why exactly was *he* being shot at? Nox had been targeted for their masterful display of air manipulation, but Elias hadn't harmed a single civilian. Torr was the threat here, one he had been actively fighting until the arrows came his way.

"Don't kill the fire user! I want him tried and accused like the rest for killing my father!"

The shout rang out above Elias' head in a voice he wished he didn't recognise. Leonidas Ambrose was in a theatre box, not his own, leaning over the railing and pointing accusingly at Elias and the archers in the stands. He knew that Lyra wouldn't kill the heir, but Elias was pretty sure 'taking care of him' would involve shutting Leonidas up for a bit longer than this.

His demands were also ignored by the guardsmen as a new volley of arrows came to Elias. All Leonidas' shouts had done was announce his location to everyone, including Torr.

The demon had returned to the warriors of the coliseum and continued culling them like cattle. Knives flew from his fingers like shooting stars, meeting the throats of half the archers who still fruitlessly shot at Torr. Still, no blows affected him, but the more he fought in his demonic form, the more his clothes burned away.

Even at this distance, Elias could clearly see the bright, ghoulish green scar. It was ropy and thick, running from the fingertip and down his back to the base of his spine. Either the smoke played tricks on Elias' eyes, or the scar was *glowing*. Was it actually an injury? On a demon? Elias could hardly believe it, but he knew it was the closest thing Torr had to a weakness, one he desperately needed to exploit.

Watching the demon, Elias almost missed the stream of dirt that flew at him. Throwing both arms up, he sent a wave of flame to burn it away, but not before a knife sailed past, slicing open Elias' cheek. He hissed, and the fire guttered out, revealing Delphia Ryer standing before him.

"What the *hells* is that thing?!" the half-witch screamed, pointing behind her. Her brown hair was a mess, coming loose from its braid, the errant strands sticking to the dirt and blood on her face. "What have you brought here?"

The demon has nothing to do with me! Elias shouted back, eyes wide. *He's trying to kill me and my friends!*

Her mouth twisted. "The friends who killed the duke,

and you allowed to get away?"

He clenched his jaw. *Did you not hear me? That* thing *is a demon. I let my friends run, hoping he would follow us* away *from the coliseum. I don't want to see any of these people die.*

Delphia's face suddenly paled. "A demon? An *actual* demon?"

Yes! Did you not see the horns?!

She answered the question with a glare. "So if *you* leave the coliseum, the demon will follow you and save everyone here."

Not so simple, he sniped. *I can't let him follow me yet, not without endangering my friends.*

"Two people's lives are worth more than hundreds?"

Three, he corrected. *I can't let any of those three die. They are the best chance to destroy the demon.*

Before she could have the chance to respond, Elias knocked her to the ground. Torr's sword sailed through the air, sticking into the grass and shaking at the impact. Delphia's eyes blazed with shock, even as Elias helped her back up, her gaze snapped between the sword and the slow-approaching Torr. Unarmed, the demon flexed his hands, allowing each claw to catch the winter light. Curved sharper than any scythe, Elias could already see all the blood that drenched those glass knives.

You need to run, he told Delphia, who only shook her head.

"I can contain him," she huffed.

Before he could protest, Delphia slammed her foot. The ground began to shake, a crack splitting open the grass that tunnelled towards Torr. It opened between his legs, sending the demon stumbling as Delphia raised both her hands. Two large chunks of earth broke from the ground, and they flew straight towards Torr to crush him in between. Elias winced as the dirt towers consumed Torr, slamming together in perfect finality. Delphia let out a ragged breath and looked at Elias.

"Contained."

Despite the truth of her words, it was only short-lived. Black diamond claws punched through the dense earth of the stacks, only one hand at first pulling free of the roots and dirt before a second followed. Then, as the entire structure started to crumble, Torr strode out and back onto flat ground, unharmed as always.

And this time, Elias didn't have the chance to warn Delphia to run.

The demon pounced, claws extended as they slid through the leather cuirass the witch wore. She gasped, the sound already choked with blood as she collapsed to the ground. Torr pulled his claws free, still crouched over her prone body as droplets of her blood spattered onto her paling face.

No!

Elias ran forward to hit Torr, knock him over, or blaze him with fire; it didn't matter. Just *something* to stop his movements as he raised his arm again to strike. But again, Elias just was not fast enough. Torr dragged a singular claw along the witch's throat, opening a red line like a smile across Delphia's skin. All the light died in her eyes, a soft exhale cementing the fresh death into Elias' bones. He halted and stared into those empty irises, wishing it could all be an act.

Torr rose from his crouch, turning slowly to meet Elias' gaze. The demon cocked his head to the side. Since Avery and Nox had fled, Torr had become eerily silent, as if spending time in this form rendered him incapable of speech or anything other than murder and violence—mindless to a fault.

We will kill you, Elias vowed, despite knowing the demon could not hear it. *We will find a way to destroy you, not send you back to the hells, but* obliterate *your entire being. You don't deserve to live after all the suffering you have caused.*

His own mental declaration left him breathless, the words sinking into his skin like a scar. Elias straightened, raising his sword just as Torr pounced once more.

Both the demon's arms were outstretched, claws shining to cut him into ruin. Elias' sword trembled in his hands, Delphia's death so fresh in his mind he couldn't concentrate. His vow felt oddly pathetic now, his lack of resolve exposed through the shaking in his body. His inaction had cost the witch's life, and now his cowardice had almost cost him his own.

As Torr's claws came crashing down, Elias' sword only drove one hand away. The demon's left hand slashed, biting into Elias' ruined armour. The warped cuirass and melted mail were useless against the glittering claws that sunk through the gambeson and into vulnerable flesh.

Elias groaned, black stars filling his vision. The claws sliced down his abdomen, opening a well of four clawed lines. Hot blood erupted from the wounds, and Elias staggered away, clamping a hand over his stomach as he fell to his knees.

He sent up a wave of flames, obscuring himself from sight as he pulled himself to his feet. He couldn't stay here, not anymore. Elias turned towards the coliseum gates and forced his feet to move.

The gate was open, revealing the landscape that opened up to the mountain range. It was the tiniest blot in the sea of grey rock, but Elias was sure he could see the warp gate.

Could see it changing colour.

Thank the gods, he breathed.

Then, with his arms cradling his injured stomach, Elias sheathed his sword and ran like hells. He refused to look behind him at the massacre and destruction he had allowed to happen. None of it would matter in the end—all the death and misery—not when Torr would follow him. He would follow Elias and his friends to the end of the world—until only one of them was left alive, and he sorely hoped it wouldn't be that demon.

48

LYRA

Magic swirled through the grasslands as blood slipped down Lyra's face. She felt it drip into her mouth, the coppery taste making her stomach churn like a thousand seas.

Power reverberated through the air, the hairs on her arms standing on end as wisps of black and purple flitted from her fingertips. There was a constant roar in her ears, the void and all its stars screaming to be released from her veins. The darkness seeped into the warp gate, filling the carvings with amethyst light and blooming like ink dropped in water.

Lyra's breathing was harsh, sweat forming on her brow. Her mouth moved in an uninterpretable mutter, echoes of encouragement and affirmations that Twylla would also whisper. It felt like the only tether to this power as her body began to sag.

The warp gate was not even half-full with power. The purple light fluttered, Lyra's strength fading. In horror, she realised the gate was actually *draining*. Lyra planted her other hand on the rock, and both palms dispensed the void into the gate. Even so, her entire body shook, the slow crawl barely reigniting.

"Change the necklace," she ground out. "*Please.*"

She felt the changeover as leather cords slipped over her head. The new pulse of magic was invigorating but hardly monumental. Lyra's head burned.

Vaguely, she felt a hand on her shoulder, honeyed words pushing past the screaming in her ears. "Keep pushing," Avery demanded. "Do not stop."

Lyra's back had straightened, the compulsion forcing false strength into her bones. Could she really do this? Or was Lyra dooming all of them to die?

She'd never successfully done this before. Twylla used to test her into making the void a tangible thing. In all of the witch's books on the void, it was one of the main strengths. Not only could its users enter the void, but the void could enter *them*. They could bring it into reality, a pocket of emptiness to be used as a weapon.

Lyra had tried this very thing a total of three times. The first time, they had left Cerenia for two months in search of an abandoned warp gate to play at such a scale. They hadn't thought to bring power-enhancing charms back then, so the results were wholly pathetic. And while the charms had proved helpful, for the second and third visits, they had not yielded success.

If she failed today, they would all die at Torr's hand.

The assassin saw right through her and *knew* she was weak, stunted. The Daughter of the Void was nothing without her mother, but what did that mean to Lyra? Larissa Whitehallow was dead, and so was Celeste Whitehallow. The dyad had been ruined since birth, and Lyra had broken it even further. She didn't deserve this power, even this fleeting version of it. So why did she bother calling on it now? Why did she think *she* could save everyone?

They were questions Lyra didn't bother to try to answer. Another necklace was placed on her, even though the second one had not been removed. Could the charms stack up in magic? Lyra doubted it, or else Twylla would have suggested it. Avery's continual demands forced her to focus on the gate, pushing more power inside. She also made her thoughts surround Cerenia, visualising the warp gate beneath the Palace. Once back in Wychar, they would be far away enough from Torr to truly escape. Even if there was one last concern in her mind, she refused to give it weight. Not until it came into play.

"Elias is coming!" Though she knew it was a shout, Nox's voice sounded so far away from Lyra. The roaring screams of the void stole it from her ears just as the icy breeze tore through her lungs.

Then, the screaming stopped: the void gate was complete.

Lyra's legs buckled, but she slid awkwardly to the ground with her hands still glued to the mountainside. Even though the gate shone with complete amethyst light, Lyra knew that if she took both her palms away, all her efforts would dissipate. Despite the pain running through her body like a permanent ache, she marvelled at her own beautiful creation.

Stars danced inside the gate, forming miniature gateways that split off even more haphazardly than the true version. Darkness curled around the arched entrance, filling the cracks with violet flecks.

Lyra grinned, her heart hammering in her chest as she watched the dazzling array. "I did it."

"Elias isn't the only one coming."

At Avery's tone, Lyra snapped her head back to the grassland. Elias was within clear sight, but another figure slowly moved behind him. She couldn't recognise the form, its shape too enshrouded in what looked like shadows and smoke. Arching above its head, were two curved horns and glossy claws curled from its hands.

"What is that?" she asked breathlessly.

The naiad jutted out her chin. "Torr's true form. His demon form."

Lyra would have preferred a punch to the gut. Torr was a *demon*, true and real. The stories of exorcism and saviour gods turned to dirt in her mind. This damned soul had an unkillable form, and he would use it to destroy them all.

She whipped her head to Nox and Avery. "And you left Elias to fight it alone?"

Avery's face went red, an excuse no doubt about to pour from her lips when another answered first. *I told them to run.* Elias' words thundered through her head. *If you need to blame anyone for that foolishness, then that person is me.*

Lyra looked up at the phoenix-blood, and her body went cold. His scarf was gone, revealing a slash across his face. The strike looked shallow enough, but blood still seeped into his mouth. But the wound on his stomach made Lyra want to look away.

Four serrated claw marks gouged out chunks of flesh, leaving it in a ribbony, bloody mess. His clothes and armour contained most of it, but his dash across the grass had jostled the injury enough to leave a fresh splatter of blood on the ground. He was clinging to the blood-soaked ruin of his armour, breathing heavily.

Are you all alright? he asked. No one could reply as they all stared at him. Elias ignored the eyes as he pulled out a glass bottle. He swallowed its contents, and colour began to leach back into his face. *It might not be enough.*

Lyra wished to argue, already seeing the tincture work its magic. Tendrils of flesh either dropped off his body or resealed itself against the red ruin of his stomach. The bleeding slowed, and the yellowing of fresh bruises faded.

"So let's go!" Nox cut in. "We have a working warp gate and a demon on its way to kill us!"

Lyra nodded. "All of you go first," she said. "I'll follow after you." The lie tasted bitter on her tongue. "It'll take you back to the gate in Cerenia."

Nox clapped Elias on the shoulder. "You should go first, considering you're the liability of the group right now."

The phoenix-blood scowled but moved towards the void gate's edge. Elias hesitated, halting so that his exhaled breaths dissipated into the amethyst light.

How sure of this are you? he asked.

Lyra didn't meet his eyes. "We don't have room to be unsure."

His jaw clenched, but then he nodded. With one last look at everyone, his eyes met Avery's last. *See you soon.*

The last thing Lyra saw of the phoenix-blood was him shaking his head just before stepping through the void gate. A whoosh of energy thundered through the archway, and Lyra shuddered against its power. A fresh nosebleed began, clotting up the dried blood on her face. She didn't attempt to wipe it away, instead keeping her hands locked on the rock.

"Avery," she said beneath the blood. "You're next. Control whoever you must to get to the King's Mast so Twylla can heal Elias."

"We'll wait for you," the naiad said.

Lyra was glad the telepath was gone; otherwise, he would have heard that one word that slipped past her barriers: *don't.*

Instead, she only shook her head. "I don't want to slow you down. It'll be easier to sneak out of the Palace in pairs."

But the naiad did not move. "You're hiding something." Her eyes were narrowed.

Lyra huffed a breath. "I have no idea what you're talking about. Will you just hurry up? Torr's about to reach us."

To confirm it, she gave Torr a backward glance. He'd kept a slow pace as if the burning of his demonic form stopped him from rushing forward. What had happened to everyone inside the coliseum? No one had said anything, but she doubted that could have fared any better than Elias.

Lyra turned back to Avery and nodded at the gate. "Come on."

"Why not send Nox first?"

They both looked at the werewolf, who'd been uncharacteristically quiet since Avery started arguing. Nox gave a shrug matched with an easy grin.

"Because," they started. "You're not the only one who can tell when Lyra is lying."

Before either of them could react, Nox moved. They grabbed Avery by the waist and, in one quick movement, threw her into the waiting gate. The immortal staggered. Panic or shock—Lyra couldn't guess—widened Avery's eyes before she disappeared underneath the purple light.

Lyra spun on her foot to face Nox, but they only pulled her aching fingers off the rock. Power sucked out of the gate in one swoop. The circle shuttered off, all the light fading from within its centre and on the carvings. Lyra fell to the ground as if she'd been punched in the gut, losing all bodily control.

"What have you done?" she demanded, though her voice had no strength.

"It wasn't too difficult to figure it out," Nox said. "In

order to keep the gate functioning, you would have to stay here with *him*. There's no way in hells that I'm allowing something as ridiculous as that to happen."

"But now we're *both* stuck," Lyra pressed. "What happened to just wanting the money?"

Shadows filled the werewolf's eyes. "I couldn't leave you, and I know you wouldn't leave me either."

She didn't know how to answer, only because she found it to be the truth.

Nox crouched beside her as Lyra shifted awkwardly, leaning against the now-dormant void gate. Torr stood in the grass, one step away from the rocky plains of the Eternal Mountains. He met their gazes, and despite everything, she canted her head, letting defiance rage freely through her eyes.

"What shall we do now?" Nox asked.

Stars still flickered behind Lyra's eyes, an idea forming fresh in her mind. It was just as terrible as the rest, but a demon was bearing down on them, and she wanted nothing more than to survive.

She linked her arm with Nox's. "I want you to trust me." Darkness filled her veins once more. "Hopefully, we will get out of this alive."

The werewolf grinned. "Until the end, Lyra Avenyard."

Just as Torr's sword came striking down, the two fell into the void's dark. The last thing Lyra saw was the demon's hand punching through, readying to do as he'd done days before and destroy her one power. But his hands came up empty. There were no stars to grasp—no way in or out.

Lyra and Nox dropped into infinite black.

Acknowledgements

To Mum and Dad. *The Royal Tournament* would not have been possible without your support.

To my sister, Meg, for being the necessary critic of the family. While not all your insightful suggestions made it into the final draft, I still appreciated every single one.

I'm extremely grateful to Hayley and Kaz for not only putting up with my nonsense all these years but also encouraging it.

I would like to extend my sincere thanks to everyone from Trowbridge Writing Club 2, especially those who could make time to read earlier drafts.

Many thanks to Beth, Angel, and Cai for being along for the journey and having a profound belief in my work.

Special thanks to Liza for starting this. This has always been for you; I hope I made you proud.

About the Author

G. E. McConaghy is a lover of fantasy and action, especially when combined. Her debut novel, "*The Royal Tournament,*" is the first book of the epic fantasy series "*The Death Marked,*" which follows a fated group of four and their unlikely role in a war of myth and legend. She has a BA with Honours in Creative Writing from Bath Spa University and lives in Wiltshire, England. She works alongside her feline assistant, Fizz, who likes to type on the keyboard, too. When she isn't writing, she enjoys playing video games with her friends.